PRAISE FOR JOY CALLAWAY

"The Star of Camp Greene is a comp[...] other things off in order to keep turn[...] [...]ously re- searched and full of heart, it illuminates a stateside training camp during WWI and is full of secrets, hope, jealousy, friendship, danger, and love. Readers will be eager to visit Callaway's backlist if they aren't already a fan."

— CAMILLE DI MAIO, BESTSELLING
AUTHOR OF *COME FLY WITH ME*

"In *The Star of Camp Greene*, beloved historical fiction author Joy Callaway takes up the topic of a lesser known yet highly significant and fascinating locale of the stateside war efforts of World War I. With as- siduous research and beautiful language, Callaway writes with obvious love for her subjects and delivers a tale of both tragedy and triumph. Readers will be swept into leading lady Calla Connolly's world from the very first page."

— ALLISON PATAKI, *NEW YORK TIMES* BESTSELLING
AUTHOR OF *FINDING MARGARET FULLER*

"From the city, the wartime bravado, the music and Calla Connolly, it all melded together and stole my heart. Calla's strength of character grabbed my attention and glued me to my seat as I kept turning the pages until I reach the most satisfying end. This novel is a triumph!"

—VANESSA MILLER, AWARD-WINNING AUTHOR OF
THE AMERICAN QUEEN, FOR *THE STAR OF CAMP GREENE*

"Joy Callaway never fails to bring the past to life in brilliant color. This book has it all: the lush mystery of the mountains, the dauntless resolve of a woman at work, and the breathtaking art of building something that will last for generations. I absolutely loved it."

—AMY JO BURNS, AUTHOR OF *MERCURY*,
FOR *WHAT THE MOUNTAINS REMEMBER*

"A stunning portrayal of the building of the Grove Park Inn that reveals not only its grandeur, but also the struggles of the laborers tasked with its construction, Joy Callaway brings the famed Vagabonds to life with immaculate research and rich details in this intriguing, elegantly written historical fiction that readers are going to love!"

—MADELINE MARTIN, NEW YORK TIMES BESTSELLING
AUTHOR OF THE KEEPER OF HIDDEN BOOKS,
FOR WHAT THE MOUNTAINS REMEMBER

"Callaway is back with another insightful rendering of a place and time in history, bringing her trademark attention to detail, warmth, and heart to a story centered around one of the nation's most beautiful and fabled hotels, the Grove Park Inn in Asheville, NC. Readers will root for Belle as she uncovers more than she expected, and discovers herself along the way."

—MARYBETH MAYHEW WHALEN, AUTHOR OF
TEN NOVELS AND COFOUNDER OF THE BOOK TIDE,
FOR WHAT THE MOUNTAINS REMEMBER

"For anyone who has ever had to find their voice in a crowd shouting to be the same as everyone else, Sadie Fremd will be your hero. With lush gardens so generously described that one feels as if they can pick the flowers, All the Pretty Places is immersive, engaging, and full of wonder."

—PATTI CALLAHAN HENRY, NEW YORK TIMES
BESTSELLING AUTHOR OF SURVIVING SAVANNAH

"Joy Callaway's All the Pretty Places is a fascinating, heartwarming story that brings to light a time and place where only the wealthy had access to the beauty and restorative power of gardens. Callaway draws us into Sadie's world with gorgeous prose (you can practically feel the rich, damp soil and smell the sweet lilacs) that transports readers to the lush landscapes that Sadie will go to any lengths to protect."

—ADELE MYERS, AUTHOR OF THE TOBACCO WIVES

"Masterfully written with elegant prose and exquisite detail, Joy Callaway crafts a story as sumptuous and colorful as the Gilded Age gardens she transports readers to. All The Pretty Places is the story of a young woman fighting for personal and professional integrity and freedom, as well as a searing social commentary on poverty, privilege, and class discrepancy. I found myself cheering for Sadie with each page and tearing up at the emotional and nuanced ending."

—Yvette Manessis Corporon, international bestselling
author of *Where the Wandering Ends*

"*All the Pretty Places* is a verdant, gorgeous novel, filled with lush scenery, fascinating characters, and engaging drama. Callaway skillfully transports her readers into the Gilded Age gardens of the late-twentieth century, where the yearnings of the heart come into conflict with the economic realities of the time. I was instantly swept away and stayed enraptured by the story to its very last page."

—Lauren Edmondson, author of
Wedding of the Season

"If you yearn for a more gracious era, when natural beauty was a human birthright, you'll adore Joy Callaway's *All the Pretty Places*. Sadie's struggle to be taken seriously in an age when women are considered as ornamental as roses and her desire to freely pursue both her talents and her heart create a warm and engaging novel. And the fact that the story is based on Callaway's real-life ancestors only makes *All the Pretty Places* an even more satisfying read!"

—Kim Wright, author of *Last Ride to Graceland*

"Callaway's dialogue captures the cadences and concerns of the American upper crust, and the society drama is sure to please fans of such aristocratic historicals as *The House of Mirth* and *The Gilded Age*."

—Publishers Weekly for *The Grand Design*

"A treat for historical fiction fans."

—Booklist for *The Grand Design*

"The story is a thoroughly enjoyable read with the characters, including The Greenbrier, coming vividly to life."

—Historical Novel Society for *The Grand Design*

"A beautifully written historical romance novel. Joy Callaway has impeccably researched the life of Dorothy Draper from her days as 'Greenbrier' debutante to her return as the hotel's decorator. Five Stars!"

—CARLETON VARNEY, PRESIDENT OF
DOROTHY DRAPER & COMPANY, INC.,
FOR *THE GRAND DESIGN*

"*The Grand Design* is a spellbinding tale of a woman's quest to escape the confines of upper-crust society and make her own way in the world. With vivid characters, illuminating prose, and perfect pacing, this novel is as captivating and confident as the heroine at its center."

—KRISTY WOODSON HARVEY, *NEW YORK TIMES*
BESTSELLING AUTHOR OF *THE WEDDING VEIL*

"Joy Callaway's *The Grand Design* is a sumptuous look at the complicated life of famous interior designer Dorothy Draper."

—AIMIE K. RUNYAN, BESTSELLING AUTHOR
OF *THE SCHOOL FOR GERMAN BRIDES*

THE STAR OF
CAMP GREENE

ALSO BY JOY CALLAWAY

What the Mountains Remember

All the Pretty Places: A Novel of the Gilded Age

The Grand Design: A Novel of Dorothy Draper

The Fifth Avenue Artists Society

Secret Sisters

THE
STAR OF
CAMP
GREENE

A NOVEL OF WWI

JOY CALLAWAY

HARPER MUSE

Published by Harper Muse, an imprint of HarperCollins Focus LLC.

This book is a work of fiction. The characters, incidents, and dialogue are drawn from the author's imagination and are not to be construed as real. Any resemblance to actual events or persons, living or dead, is entirely coincidental.

Library of Congress Cataloging-in-Publication Data

Names: Callaway, Joy, author.
Title: The star of Camp Greene: a novel of WWI / Joy Callaway.
Description: Nashville : Harper Muse, 2025. | Summary: "Sometimes true heroism is found in dreams deferred"—Provided by publisher.
Identifiers: LCCN 2024045758 (print) | LCCN 2024045759 (ebook) | ISBN 9781400244331 (paperback) | ISBN 9781400244348 (epub) | ISBN 9781400244355
Subjects: LCSH: Women entertainers—Fiction. | World War, 1914-1918—United States—Fiction. | Influenza Epidemic, 1918-1919–United States—Fiction. | Camp Greene (N.C.)—Fiction. | LCGFT: Historical fiction. | Novels.
Classification: LCC PS3603.A4455 S73 2025 (print) | LCC PS3603.A4455 (ebook) | DDC 813/.6—dc23/eng/20241129
LC record available at https://lccn.loc.gov/2024045758
LC ebook record available at https://lccn.loc.gov/2024045759

Printed in the United States of America

25 26 27 28 29 LBC 5 4 3 2 1

For Momma Sandra Wilkerson—I love you so much.

CHAPTER 1

MAY 3, 1918
CAMP GREENE ARMY TRAINING CAMP
CHARLOTTE, NORTH CAROLINA

I first realized I was a star when I was twelve. It was a moment just like this one, where the reverberation of my voice hung glittering in the air, nearly as bright as the spotlights, until the applause swallowed it up in a deafening swell that made my heart all but stop. Adoration is an addiction. Everybody warns about the perils of drink, but nobody thinks to tell a young girl that once she's become the darling of her town, she'll want to become the darling of her country and then her world. And once she's done all that and realized that life off the stage can turn nightmarish in a blink, she'll crave regular roaring applause or risk absolute despondency.

The shouting was riotous tonight. It was my kind of crowd despite my having a persistent headache and a throat that felt much like the strep infections I got frequently in girlhood. I ignored them both. They were only nuisances. Colds came up now and then, determined to ruin all the fun, but I wouldn't allow it. I couldn't allow it. I'd never canceled a show. Not once in my thirty-two years. At first I persevered through any sort of discomfort for the audience's love, but now, recently, I kept on for myself. Onstage, my thoughts were fixed on the music and the laughter and the moment. There were no questions, no grief, no shadows. Those all met me at the curtain, but for the glorious time in the spotlight, I was the girl I used to be.

1

"'Pack Up Your Troubles'!" someone hollered from the back of the theatre. I grinned and mopped my forehead with my palm, pushing my black curls—neatly set by yours truly and long ruined by my tumbling across the stage—back against the brim of my little pixie cap.

"Now, I think we should give poor Mr. Keeghan here a break for a minute or two, don't you suppose?" I shouted. "He's been playing for an hour straight." I could hear the fatigue in my piano man, Stuart Keeghan, in the way he'd lazily trilled the notes on "When Johnny Comes Marching Home," and he'd barely been able to keep up with the pace of my cartwheels and flips before that. I stole a glance at him, and he nodded wholeheartedly. His face was flushed with exertion. I supposed at times I forgot that he was my parents' age and not mine, that it was only me and him keeping this show afloat instead of the full crew we had in New York.

The crowd booed, and I stepped to the front of the stage and gave them the same disapproving glance I'd made when I'd played a teacher managing unruly pupils in the musical *Roses in the Garden*. They'd used a likeness of me making that expression on the cover of the *Saturday Evening Post*, wearing a sultry sequined gown that was most certainly not my plain teacher costume. The magazine had been so popular, the art had been transformed to posters.

The boys recognized the expression immediately, and the noise changed direction to cheering. I smiled and tipped my head at the audience. I didn't know how many were there—you never could really tell because of the light.

"How about a joke or two?" I said, my voice seeming to barely project as it did in other theatres. My head throbbed, and at once, although I was standing absolutely still, my body felt like it was spinning in circles. The heat, that had only moments before bathed my costume from pantaloons to outer skirts in sweat, was now absent and the fabric felt as though it had been plunged in ice water.

I forced my attention to the light, hoping its constant would steady me, only to realize it was held fast by someone up in the rafters who was not entirely sturdy themselves. I went on anyway.

"Any of you fellas planning to propose marriage to your sweetheart soon?" I yelled. My throat smarted and I swallowed to soothe it. Some whooped and a few called out, "Only to you, Calla!" I laughed and curtsied, pitching my outer skirts away from my pantaloons a bit so the crowd could see the American flag design on the underside of the simple white. Lydia Bambridge always created the most interesting costumes for my acts, so that both my show and my dress caused a spectacle. There was a roar of applause at the sight of the Stars and Stripes and several "will you marry mes" cut through the noise.

"When you do get around to asking that lucky girl for her hand, do remember what I'm about to tell you," I started, leaning close to the crowd like I was telling a secret. "See, back in New York, a very patriotic friend of mine was considering marriage to a fine man. He was handsome, smart, kind—and he called her all the loveliest names: *sweetheart, sugar, darling.*" I paused and nearly stumbled as my body swelled with heat and vertigo. I was suddenly unable to recall the last thing I'd said.

"Well, what's wrong with *darling?*" someone shouted, reminding me that I was in the middle of a joke. I grinned and walked slowly back toward the piano, bracing myself on the case of the opened baby grand when I reached it. Perhaps it was only my blood sugar plunging. I hadn't had much to eat—a grapefruit at breakfast, a slice of buttered toast at lunch.

"Nothing at all is wrong with *darling,*" I said. I cleared my throat to stop the sting. "But when he proposed, he made a terrible mistake. Rather than her name, rather than *angel* or *dear*, he called my friend the worst thing you can call proud American stock like us. He called her *hunny.*"

I waited for the boisterous smack of laughter, and I suppose there *was* laughter, but it sounded far away. A light smell of lavender incense met my senses, and at once my mind whirled with confusion. Perhaps I'd forgotten where I was. It wouldn't be the first time. The stage was an elusive place. Only one person I knew burned lavender incense during shows and that was Andrew Gerald, the music conductor on *The Bye and Bye Show* at the Palace Theatre in London. Perhaps the laughter was dull because I was telling patriotic American yarns to the British.

"If the piano man is rested, I'd love to hear 'I Have It All.'" The voice was distant, from somewhere in the back perhaps, but the request mirrored *The Bye and Bye Show* as well. It was always the second to last number.

"Yes, absolutely," I heard myself say, though I couldn't truly make sense of anything at the moment. It was unnerving.

I stepped forward and looked to my right, expecting my fiancé and costar on the show, Caspar Wells, to appear from the curtain, but he didn't. Of course he didn't. My Caspar was dead. He'd been killed on the Somme, forced to jump out of his kite balloon after the cable snapped and the balloon threatened to cross enemy lines. But then again, if I was back at the Palace Theatre, smelling Andrew's incense and singing "I Have It All," perhaps he was still alive. At once I felt light. Perhaps I had imagined the news of his death, all of it a nightmare—the quivering man who'd delivered the news to my Liverpool flat; Caspar's final letter that came later, speaking of the horrors of war, the desperation to hear me sing him a song to enliven his heart, and the promise that if the war continued, he and I would go around putting on little shows for the men about to go to the front. Mr. Keeghan plunked the first few notes, but Caspar didn't materialize to sing his part.

"Caspar?" I shouted, plastering a smile on my face to hide my fear that my hope wasn't hope at all. Mr. Keeghan repeated the introduction, and just as I was about to resign myself to singing Caspar's part, right as tears flooded my eyes, he appeared on the far end of the stage. He was wearing olive drab, an American army uniform, rather than his usual tuxedo. I found the change perplexing, but perhaps he was planning on a surprise finale later, a plea for my people, his comrades, to enter the war on their side.

"*I have a mansion in Rome,*" he sang, his familiar baritone washing over me. "*But I call a palace home. I've got piles of diamonds, a fancy yacht, but it's not a lot if I haven't got you.*"

I couldn't take my gaze from his face, the straight nose that rounded at the tip, the eyes that pitched downward at the outer corners. I wanted desperately to arrest his stare from the audience, to see the love, the desire soften the sun that beamed from his face on the stage to stars that shimmered for me alone.

"*I'd like your palace, your mansion in Rome,*" I sang. My voice was weak and my headache pulsed with renewed fervor in my temples. "*Your diamonds and your yacht too. I'll have it all . . . except for you.*"

The crowd roared in laughter, and I smiled, waved, and stepped toward him. Usually Caspar did something humorous at this point. He'd toss paste diamonds at my feet or take my hand and pretend to beg, but he didn't so much as turn my direction. My skin flushed hot and cold, but I ignored the warning. Surely it was just relief at seeing him and realizing my reality was only a nightmare after all.

"*I can give you a king-sized bed, goose down for your head,*" Caspar responded.

I reached for his arm and he allowed it, but didn't clasp my hand like he usually did.

"*I'll take the first two, so long as they're absent you,*" I sang. "*You're—*"

"I apologize for the interruption, but I must." A voice boomed over the song, silencing us and the crowd. Caspar jerked away from my clutch, and as the spotlight swung away from our faces, over the canvas tent ceiling and three hundred men in olive drab fatigues, to land on a young officer at the entrance, I realized my error. My brain felt bruised as the headache persisted. Confusion and grief grasped hold of my heart. I wasn't in London. I was at an army training camp in North Carolina, Camp Greene. I recalled it now: the army band playing at the train station upon my arrival that morning, the Red Cross ladies handing me flowers and warm donuts, the crowds lining the streets to greet me, and the shock of the camp being a true camp—nearly all of the forty thousand soldiers were staying in tents. At Camp Sherman in Ohio and Camp Lee in Virginia there were barracks.

"The gents in charge will have no choice but to assign you to the Broadway division after that performance," I said to the man I'd thought was Caspar. I laughed. Laughter always righted things—at least in the moment.

"Aw, thanks, Miss Connolly," he said. He had an accent, from somewhere in New England. "I wish there was such a thing. I'll be a rifleman. Not sure I'm as suited to war as the others seem to be." Face-to-face, he didn't look as close to Caspar as I'd assumed. The nose was similar, but the eyes were different, and he was at least a few inches shorter than Caspar had been.

"Calla, please. All of my friends call me Calla and—"

"I need everyone's attention," the officer shouted again, his height and the velocity of his tone silencing the voices that had doubtless begun to speculate about the reason for his interruption. "I've just received word that we lost a few men on the front in Flanders. If you have any familiar attachments to men already over there, you can go to the administrative building to review the telegram listing the names of the fallen and request leave if necessary."

Several men pushed through the crush of their comrades toward the back of the tent, their faces drawn and pale. I felt the echo of shocking grief as I watched them depart. Some would find themselves subject to the same horrible feeling that came with knowing they'd never see their loved one again. Caspar had been such a vibrant presence—magnetic and steady and magical all in one. He told me he was coming back to me, and I believed him. So much so that I hadn't even cried when we'd kissed goodbye.

I watched more men weave through the crowd and out the door to check the telegram. Being shocked by death in wartime was an interesting phenomenon. No one really believed that anyone they knew would die in this war, even though they knew that thousands would.

"Miss Harkins has made herself available to book rail tickets," the officer said, and then his eyes met mine. In the wake of the soldiers' departure, the tent was nearly silent. "Miss Connolly, if you'd be so inclined, hurry along with the rest of the show. The men need rest."

I wanted to say something in reply, some sort of retort to let the officer know that merriment was as vital to well-being as rest—I would know—but the men's faces silenced me. All of the emotions were there, as plainly as Caspar had described them in his letters: fear, anger, regret, terror. My body ached—my head to the point it felt as though it could combust—and I had begun to sweat so much that moisture washed my face. Even so, I would not abandon these men to their melancholy as Caspar had been abandoned.

"I suppose we could all simply retire," the man I'd mistaken for Caspar said.

"And end the evening with sorrow? Absolutely not."

I'd come home to New York, to Broadway and my parents' Bronx townhome after Caspar's death. I couldn't bear to live in Liverpool without him, but his final letter was always with me, and his desperation for a song, for hope, in his final days haunted me day and night. The only respite from thinking of it was the stage, so I'd immediately accepted Lee Shubert's request for me to star in his new show, *Fancy Free*, ignoring the whispers that I wasn't grieving properly. When America entered the war a year later, I understood the reason for my return home and my heart that wouldn't heal: I was meant to enliven the troops, to give them cheer in their darkest hours, to put on the little shows at the front that Caspar had hoped we'd do together.

I'd been so confident in my calling that I'd declined two new starring roles and wrote a letter directly to General Pershing instead, requesting clearance to go to the front and put on a tour modeled after the private shows I occasionally took to the Gilded Age set on Fifth Avenue—just me and Mr. Keeghan. I told General Pershing the show would travel easily and I'd finance it myself, but I'd been denied on the grounds that I could muddle the focus of the men. After much persistence, however, General Pershing suggested I invest my efforts in the stateside army camps instead, insinuating that if I proved myself valuable and able to stay out of the necessary mechanics of war, he may reconsider his stance. I looked at the despondent men in front of me. If I couldn't cheer these men, an ocean away from the action, how would I prove to Pershing that I deserved a place at the front where brightening spirits actually mattered?

"What's your name?" I asked the man still standing beside me.

"Guy. Guy Werths," he said.

"Well then, Guy. Suppose you're the guy to help me make these men smile again?"

"Gee, I haven't heard that one." He laughed.

I turned too quickly toward Mr. Keeghan, who had almost nodded off at the piano bench, and nearly fell. Dizziness consumed me.

"'Over There,'" I said, barely able to make out the words, but somehow both Mr. Keeghan and Guy heard me. Mr. Keeghan struck the opening notes with a fervor I was shocked he possessed in his current state.

"Let us remember what we are fighting for. You are courageous, loyal, and brave." I forced my voice over the piano notes and then starting singing with Guy. My throat protested with each breath.

By the first *"Over there, over there,"* everyone in the tent was singing again and smiles were restored, but I couldn't utter another note. Every word exhausted me, my throat was swollen, and my breath was shallow. I signaled to Guy to keep the song going while I danced. At the end, feeling a bit more stable, I launched myself into a cartwheel, but my arms collapsed beneath me and I fell on the stage.

I tried to get up but failed. I couldn't move. My breath was coming in short, shallow gasps. Mr. Keeghan stopped playing. Guy stopped singing. I fell back against the rough wood, vaguely registering that in doing so, I hit my head. Men were shouting, but the noise sounded distant. Then someone picked me up.

I tried to force open my eyes as I was carried through the tent. I tried to latch on to the smell of the room—stale sweat—or focus on Guy's face as he hefted me through the throng in hopes to regain some of the lucidity I'd lost, but I was tired, so tired.

"This is silly. I'm all right. I just need a cracker," I said in a whispery voice that sounded nothing like my own. My eyes were heavy, but I refused to allow them to close. Guy didn't answer, but paused in what I gathered must have been a sort of makeshift lobby. Posters with my likeness and name papered the walls.

"I'm tired," I thought I said, though I couldn't be sure if the words actually sounded. Guy was talking to someone, and I couldn't keep my eyes open. Then there was a table beneath me and rain on my face, and just as quickly the sound of a door shutting and silence.

"If you can hear me, it's me, Guy. We're on our way to the hospital. I'll stay with you."

Though I knew I should claw my way to consciousness, it was impossible, so I let myself go. Somewhere an angelic voice was singing Mother's favorite song, "Too-Ra-Loo-Ra-Loo-Ral."

CHAPTER 2

My nightclothes were itchy. I yanked at a sleeve, surprised it felt more like cotton than silk, and turned on my side. I'd have to have Mother order new nightgowns from Wannamaker's, I thought as I drifted back to sleep. Perhaps the discomfort was only that this one was old.

Mother was humming "Too-Ra-Loo-Ra-Loo-Ral," though the notes were barely on pitch. The dissonance rattled me to consciousness.

"Mother, please stop. You sound like a rooster with laryngitis. It's the middle of the night," I mused without opening my eyes.

The song—I suppose that's what it was, even in its sad state— stopped, but then a door opened and shut and I heard whispering, a voice I didn't recognize.

"I told you I'm tired," I attempted again, but then there was the rattling of a cart across a wood floor. That was the last straw. I opened my eyes and tried to heave myself upward against the pillows but was startled to find that I could not. I had no strength, nor did I know where I was. In front of me resided a cold potbelly stove in desperate need of cleaning, a stark white wall, and a shabby little table with a glass pitcher of water and a discarded mercury thermometer.

"Miss Connolly?" A meek, unfamiliar voice came from behind the metal spindles that made up the headboard.

"Where am I?" I asked. Just then, I could smell it. The stench of illness permeated the air. It was on my breath too. I turned over, a gesture that took much effort, and came face-to-face with a little nurse no more than five feet tall standing beside a metal cart laden with a veritable buffet. Croissants and pancakes and Danishes—everything my former manager and longtime Broadway star, Lenor Felicity, used to forbid me to eat since she'd introduced me to vaudeville and Broadway at age twelve.

"Why, you're here at Camp Greene," the nurse said with an extraordinary amount of cheer. "You're in the officers' convalescence quarters at the base hospital. There's nowhere else to put the ladies and you're . . . well, you're Calla Connolly. We couldn't exactly throw you in with the soldiers."

At once I recalled stepping on the stage of the makeshift Liberty Theatre under the canvas. I recalled the way my head pulsed and my body ached. I remembered the way my throat felt as though it had been skinned. It still felt much the same. But I couldn't recall collapsing or being admitted to the hospital. The last thing I remembered was shouting hello to the crowd and motioning to Mr. Keeghan to start the show.

"We're terribly relieved that you're coming back to us," she said. She stepped toward me, then reconsidered. Her entire body, including half of her face, was covered in starched white linen. "It was a perilous night, Miss Connolly, but we knew you would pull through. You just had to. Kirsten said that she knew you'd make it. She kept watching you to make sure you weren't turning blue, but you didn't and your fever broke."

"Blue, you say? Did you suppose I could transform into a blueberry? Or perhaps you supposed I was one of those people with blue-pigmented skin like the Blue Fugates of Kentucky? That's not how it works, miss. The Kentucky blues are born with the hue." I tried to smile but coughed instead. Congestion rattled my chest. My voice sounded gravelly and foreign, and my neck right below my jaw felt horribly swollen.

"No, no," she said, clearly not at all inclined to display any sort of mirth at my jokes. Perhaps what I'd said hadn't actually been funny. I couldn't tell. My mind felt slow, like I was stuck in that state of acute drowsiness right before slumber. "Not that. It's . . . well . . .

turning blue is a sign of . . . well, it's a sign that you're going to die of this Spanish flu, ma'am," she said, lowering her voice to a whisper. Though I could see only the top half of her face, I knew her skin had paled. In the absence of color, the dark circles beneath her eyes were startling. "It's going around like wildfire, claiming lives in a matter of a few hours sometimes. We're trying to contain the infected in the hospitals, but it's nearly impossible. It comes on so quickly."

"Oh, I'm sure I didn't have anything like that," I said. My tongue felt thick around my words. "Just a little cold."

"With all respect, Miss Connolly, those stricken with a cold don't hallucinate. Though you were battling a fiery fever, you were quite irate when you were conscious, arguing with Kirsten and me, calling us Lenor and asking over and over why we would try to ruin you when we'd brought you to Broadway in the first place. Then occasionally you would ask us where the rest of your money was."

I let my eyes close. I was cold too.

"The Lenor you were speaking of . . . is it Lenor Felicity? The two of you are practically mother and daughter. That's what the papers say." The nurse's voice sounded distant. "Never mind me," she amended quickly. "It's none of my business."

"I'm not surprised that Lenor was haunting me. She has for years," I said, my tone barely above a whisper. The moment the sentiment crossed my lips, I knew I shouldn't have said it. I'd never spoken openly about my troubles with Lenor save the once, and I learned to regret it after.

I could feel the nurse looking at me and forced my lids open just a hair to meet her startled gaze.

"Please excuse me. I don't know quite what I'm saying. Everything is a bit jumbled, it seems," I forced out. "I owe an awful lot to Lenor. She's like family."

I could say both of those things honestly. Many families—my lovely parents not included—were vile to each other. Family was really why Lenor was as awful as she was, why she clung to fame like it was the last life preserver on a sinking ship, why she'd thought it her right to introduce me to Broadway only to steal my earnings and my roles and, after I fired her, falsely smear my name. Lenor mistook admiration for love because she'd never known the real thing.

"I know. When you're fighting such an illness, the mind can dream up any number of strange scenarios," she said. "I had a feeling the two of you were close like everyone said. She missed you terribly when you were in England, didn't she?"

I closed my eyes again and kept quiet. If I spoke, I'd say something else I shouldn't. It was difficult to bite my tongue at the moment. After our falling-out, Lenor had convinced the director she was having an affair with to spread a rumor around Broadway that I'd made an untoward advance at him. The following week she'd had her lackey, Mr. Crispel, descend on my front stoop with information about a London West End producer looking for a lead for his new show. I knew Lenor was only trying to send me away before the absurdity of the accusations wore off, but my family needed the money urgently, so I'd telegrammed the producer, who'd hired me on the spot.

"My mother would miss me too if I was all the way across the sea," the nurse went on. "It was obvious that Lenor was quite sad. She only took on those small roles while you were away."

I wanted to say that I had a lovely mother who *had* missed me terribly, and that Lenor's small roles had nothing to do with me — unless you believed the old saying that you reap what you sow. Come to think of it, perhaps that was why Lenor had extended an olive branch when I'd returned to New York and convinced Mr. Shubert to cast me in his show, though he swore to me it hadn't taken much convincing. By the time I returned from England, Lenor's director beau had been caught seducing not one but two actresses, negating his claim that I had been the one to make an advance at him. Despite the quelled rumor and Lenor's peace offering, she hadn't been able to reverse her original reaping with my return. She spent the year I was starring in *Fancy Free* doing the short opening number for B. F. Keith's vaudeville circuit. She would never admit it, but her star was dimming.

"Then again, it could have been worth it to leave her," she said. "Was London what you dreamed it would be?"

I wasn't entirely sure why she kept talking to me when I wasn't responding, but perhaps this was part of my recovery. Perhaps conversation assisted the brain in coming back to itself.

"Yes. It was marvelous," I said. I swallowed and my throat smarted. "Being there changed my life. Before, I had one focus: success. But then I arrived at the Palace Theatre where I starred alongside my dear—" I couldn't say his name. My eyes welled and I let the tears fall. *And in the light of his love, fame wasn't all that mattered anymore.* I sobbed at the thought.

"Now, now, Miss Connolly. I'm sorry to have pressed you so. You must not allow yourself to get upset in such a fragile state. You're over the worst of it, we think, but we can never be too cautious. There's pneumonia to consider," she said, her voice soothing and low. "Though I know losing Caspar Wells must have crushed you. The departure of such talent was felt the world over."

"I'll never hear his voice again," I whispered, swallowing the urge to keep sobbing. I recalled the way Caspar's fingers stroked my hair in bed each night, the timbre of his voice singing lullabies in my ear, the mischievous glint to his eye when he performed with me in *The Bye and Bye Show.* My mind stopped on the last memory. "Did I . . . did I call for him on the stage last night? Mistake another man for him?"

"Yes, that's what they said, but you were quite unwell," the nurse said. She approached me now, pulling at the fabric across her nose and mouth as she did. She peeled the blankets back from my feet and nodded approvingly at something, then drew the fabric back over me.

"I'll have to apologize to that poor soldier," I said. I coughed again.

"Don't you dare," she said, smiling. "That soldier is my fiancé, Guy, and I have no doubt last night was the best night in all of his twenty-two years. One of my fellow nurses was at the show and she told me that when you launched into 'I Have It All,' you seemed to be looking around for Caspar. She said she heard Guy's friend Crowley encourage him to step onto the stage and offer his voice." She paused. "He'll have to be monitored quite acutely for flu, but he'll be speaking of the time he sang Caspar Wells's part with Calla Connolly for the rest of his life."

"I'm sorry I put him at risk," I said, emotion welling in my swollen throat. It seemed lucidity came and went with this illness. My mind felt cloudy again and a ripple of chill washed over my body. "I knew I wasn't well, I suppose, but I thought it was only a sniffle."

"The flu is everywhere," she said. Her face, which a moment ago had been bright with happiness, was now drawn and serious. "It tends to come in waves, and we've reached the crest of one now, it seems. One of the men in Guy's tent fell ill last week and, unfortunately, perished." She reached for the thermometer beside my bed and motioned for me to open my mouth. I complied and she fell silent, focusing on the way the mercury rose up the glass tube. After a few minutes, she took the thermometer back to her cart and withdrew a notebook and pencil from a shelf below the pastries.

"One hundred and two degrees. Still a high fever, but much lower than yesterday's 106," she mumbled, scribbling as she spoke. "Today is Saturday, May 4."

"May 4?" I startled, jerking upright despite the heaviness of my body. "I've forgotten myself. I've got to be at Camp Sevier by seven o'clock. Have someone fetch Mr. Keeghan, wherever he is, and tell him to ready for our departure."

"Miss Connolly, you can't . . . ," the nurse attempted, but I ignored her. I looked around for a clock but found none.

"What's the time, miss? I'll need to dress and get to the train station." My brain lurched with vertigo, but I forced my legs to move closer to the edge of the bed anyway. The nurse hastened to my bedside and blocked my way up.

"You're battling a severe flu. You'll not be going anywhere, I'm afraid," the nurse said almost apologetically, and her face reddened.

"And your piano man, Mr. Keeghan, was sent home to New York with the instruction that he's to be monitored for flu. I'm sorry. I don't mean to mother you, but performing tonight is not possible. You could risk falling ill again and perishing this time, not to mention infecting others."

"You don't understand," I said, slumping back against the mattress. "I must perform." I could feel the grief, the familiar memories that flipped through my mind pressing in on every side despite my illness. The stage was the only thing that prevented sorrow from swallowing me whole. When I was performing, I was full of purpose, uplifting the soldiers, leaning toward Caspar's dream. "I must impress upon General Pershing that I can be counted on. Otherwise he'll not reconsider my request to go to the front. If I don't, all of the men will fight—and some will die—in despair, without a song in their hearts, without a recent memory of cheer to enliven them. Caspar told me so."

"The front?" she whispered as if in disbelief. "I'll go right now and wire Camp Sevier to let them know of your condition," she said to me. "Even General Pershing would have to rest if he were to contract the flu."

"I suppose you're right," I said. My teeth chattered. I couldn't perform in this state, even if I wanted to. My best course would be to get well quickly.

The nurse nodded resolutely and reached for a small glass of milk hiding behind the croissant, then dug around in her apron pocket and pulled out a tiny jar of what appeared to be cinnamon. She sprinkled the cinnamon in the milk and swirled it around a few times before snatching the plate of pastries.

Behind her, the wall seemed to billow and move. I stared at it, thinking that perhaps my flu was worsening, before I realized that the wall wasn't a wall at all but rather a sheet fitted neatly to the ceiling and the floor. I wondered if there was someone behind that sheet and how they fared.

"I'll go send the telegram right away on my break as long as you promise to take this cinnamon to soothe your fever and eat at least two of the pastries," the nurse said, interrupting my inspection of the makeshift wall. She deposited the plate in my lap and then handed me the milk. The cold made me shiver and I hunched down into the covers. "And here, take this aspirin for your aches." I held out my free hand for the small pill and swallowed it down with the milk. The drink tasted like Mother's French toast. I hadn't had it since before we moved to New York City, since Father worked in the buggy factory in Columbus.

"Thank you. I'll return in half an hour," the nurse said. Then she took two envelopes from her pocket and set them next to me on the bed. "A few letters your piano man left for you before he departed for New York. He was given them at your last stop and forgot they were in his briefcase."

"Thank you," I said.

"I'm Goldie, by the way. Goldie McGann."

"I appreciate your help, Goldie," I said. A light moan sounded from beyond the sheet partition.

"Is someone next door? Beyond that sheet just there?" I whispered.

"Yes," Goldie said, her eyes grave. "He's very ill and he's dearly loved." She grasped the handle of the cart and pushed it out of my room, leaving me with my pastries.

Absent Goldie fluttering about, I noticed there was a small window past the foot of the simple iron bed. It boasted a view of a pine wood and a rain so drenching and mighty that it poured in sheets over the lip of the roof.

I lifted the croissant to my mouth and took a small bite. I had no appetite, and my throat smarted so badly that I couldn't eat more. I set the croissant down on the plate and opened the first envelope, noticing the British two-pence stamp immediately.

Dear Miss Connolly,
I do hope you'll receive this correspondence. I'm Basil Omar.
I served alongside Caspar Wells from the time of our training
until he perished.

I swallowed hard and put down the letter, unsure if I could go on. If whatever Basil planned to say was something devastating about the nature of Caspar's demise, I couldn't bear it. I knew of Basil. Caspar had often written of the young boy he'd taken under his wing, saying that Basil's friendship and interest in the theatre had been a welcome distraction, a balm to his nerves—until they were ordered to the trenches and the boy fell apart, and Caspar with him. I recalled the despairing letters he'd written from the trenches, saying that Basil had begged for singing lessons to keep his emotion at bay as the shells shattered and the enemy drew closer. Caspar had obliged, though he mentioned, between recounting his own heartbreaking fears, that the boy wasn't naturally inclined to song.

I picked the letter back up and forced myself to keep reading. Caspar would want me to.

> *I was recently injured in battle. As if by a miracle, I suffered a broken leg and concussion and have been temporarily discharged from service. It came at just the right time. Fear without ceasing is a torture.*

I ran my hand over his handwriting and tears filled my eyes.

> *In any case, I was saved and here I am. During my time in hospital, I've been reading the papers and saw a mention of your valiant tour in America and thought to take a chance and write.*
>
> *Caspar and I were in the trenches together for weeks at a time, and we'd sing together, pretending we were on the stage at the Palace Theatre instead of about to meet the grim reaper. Just before we encountered the Huns and Caspar died, he promised to include me in the act the two of you were planning on performing at the front if he could convince the army to allow it, so that I might have a bit of luck on the London stage when the fighting ends. I admit I thought the possibility of the act all but abandoned with his death, but when I saw*

*the piece about your American tour, I was heartened to real-
ize that General Pershing must have given you his blessing
and that you would arrive here at some point soon, to carry
out the dream you and Caspar created together. I pray I'm
right about your intentions. It would honor Caspar much,
and there are countless men like me, men who are losing hope
and desperate for cheer.*

I shut my eyes and envisioned myself in front of these men, their
faces brightening—if only for a moment—with my music. My
voice couldn't end a war or spare their lives, but it might give them
the strength to continue on to tomorrow. General Pershing would
come to see things as I did. I was sure of it. It was only a matter of
time until I was somewhere in France.

*I also wonder if you would consider honoring Caspar's prom-
ise to me if you come? To include me in your act? It would
provide so much joy in the midst of this terrible war to perform
alongside you, and I have no doubt it would give me a considerable leg up professionally. I am descended from a long
line of army men, and my uncle, a childhood comrade of Sir
Douglas Haig's, who is commanding a troop on the German
front, continues to insist I was born to fight. I was not. I was
born for the stage. I know I will be forced to reenlist when I am
well, but if you come here, at least I will be able to do what I
love before I face the fight again.*

*When you come, I could also return to you something I
have of yours that I took from Caspar's jacket that he left in
the trench that day, along with his tag. I thought of mailing
it with this letter, but you are indecent in the likeness, and I
know it would be devastating to you if it fell into the wrong
hands.*

I knew exactly which photograph he was speaking of. I was
nearly nude, wearing only a flimsy chemise and undergarments

of cotton lawn and Brussels lace, a combination I still wore often. I hadn't thought of the photograph since I gave it to Caspar upon our engagement. I suppose I hadn't realized he'd taken it with him or that it wasn't among our things when I moved. The likeness had been captured for a producer and fledgling fashion-designer friend of Lenor's who'd convinced me to pose for his new lingerie line. I'd only been twenty and had accepted because I was between shows and Father was between mills and we needed the money. I'd almost instantly regretted the arrangement. When news broke that he'd gambled his funds away before the line could launch, I was greatly relieved and the photograph was never used. Years later, he mailed the likeness to me in London and I'd given it to Caspar. Now this boy had it in his grasp. I hoped he hadn't shown it to his peers, but if he had, I couldn't do a thing about it.

At least Basil was a Brit and not an American. It didn't really matter if it wound up in Sir Douglas Haig's hands. It wouldn't pass across General Pershing's desk, and that's all I cared about. Though General Pershing was no prude, he couldn't well endorse a floozy for the army's entertainment. I was no such thing, but I wasn't an idiot either. I'd never thought the photograph particularly scandalous, but in the wrong hands, an innocent modeling job would be made out to be suggestive, a major smudge on my character. Lenor's lie about me had eventually fizzled, but something as tangible as a photograph would not.

I kept reading.

> *I pray you'll consider my plea, Miss Connolly, and come to us quickly. I shouldn't ask you to cut your tour of the States short, but I suppose I am. I cannot face the front again without hope of a future after this war. I am a shell of the man I once was. Please come without delay. I beg you. Send me a wire to Duchess of Westminster's Hospital and tell me of your plans.*
>
> *Caspar's friend,*
> *Basil Omar*

I stared at the name and a darkness fell over my spirit. I wasn't in charge of my goings about as Basil assumed, and the resolve I'd clung to moments earlier, the confidence that I would gain General Pershing's approval, was suddenly shrouded in uncertainty. I folded the letter, put it back in the envelope, and set it on my bedside table.

Every moment I was here I was away from the front. I couldn't convince General Pershing I deserved clearance or help Basil launch his way to the stage or cheer the men as they marched into battle if I was in this hospital, battling this terrible flu. As if my body was set to remind me that I wasn't over it yet, the pain in my throat began to throb and the swirling in my head returned. I took another bite of the croissant anyway.

"I need you to hear me." The low murmur came from the room next to mine—or rather, from beyond the sheet. I stopped chewing and listened. The voice was familiar, though I couldn't quite place where I'd heard it, nor could I make out any words very clearly. "I know you need rest, but this is a matter of certain death for a great number of men if it can't be resolved with Pershing." The sentiment struck me. The urgency of the words and the tone converged, and I recalled a memory I'd forgotten from the night before: a young officer who'd interrupted the show to break the news of the losses at Flanders. The voice was the same.

I had always been a tremendous eavesdropper. It was the only way to figure the true character of those in the spotlight—to listen in when they were not washed in the glitter of the stage. It was why I didn't trust any of them anymore. It was also a marvelous way to pass the time. When I was a child I'd be sent to the back of the stage after my act was over while the adults finished the show. To entertain myself, I'd press my ear against the wall or under the door and listen to stars and producers argue about the production or egos or lovers.

I remained absolutely still in my bed. There was a long silence, and I wondered if perhaps the officer had left the ill man's bedside.

"I beg you, General. I know I should have come yesterday the moment I got the letter, but I didn't know how ill you were and I was occupied with duties. Please hear me. I can't figure it out on my own." His voice broke on the last word and I hung on the end of it, willing him to continue speaking. "General Dickman wrote in his letter that General Pershing has heard rumors that the Germans will attempt to take Paris again in the next month or two to take advantage of the progress they made at Flanders. The French and British are tiring, and they'll need mighty reinforcements from our troops if Ludendorff orders the operation." The officer paused. "Dickman said Pershing has asked us to put together a regiment under the Sixth Brigade that will be assigned to stronghold the Allies' footing at the Surmelin Valley—the pathway to Paris. It's where the Allied troops are the most fatigued. The regiment would be ordered to stay at the defense of the line no matter what—even if the French and British retreat. If it comes to it, the stand would be vital and could turn the tide of the war but would mean great sacrifice for the men assigned to the regiment." I could hear him take a deep breath. "We're being asked to identify soldiers suited to such a perilous task—men of great skill and competence, but also prone to trouble or whose moral judgment we find lacking." He stopped.

The words made my skin prickle with horror and my breathing shallow. I thought of the faces that had greeted me in front of the Liberty Theatre upon my arrival. I wondered how many of them would be assigned to this terrible but worthy mission. How could they possibly decide who to call?

"How?" His voice returned, echoing mine. "Surely we can't choose these men, to play God this way. Of course there are men who charge in front first in all battles, but they're supported by numbers, matched by the other Allied troops, and they know their role ahead of time. In this case, the particulars can't be shared with the soldiers. If the others are forced to draw back, leaving them alone to fight for the valley, they'll serve as the buffer the Allies need, but many will die. General, I need to know what to do, how to tell Pershing that we can't help with this assignment."

Silence followed and I wondered about the state of the general. Was he able to nod, to shake his head, to utter whispers I couldn't hear?

There was a loud clatter.

"General! Nurse! Nurse!"

A rush of footsteps pounded down the hall beyond my door, and in the next moment, there was screeching of furniture, the general's name being called, the pleading with God, the sobbing. It was clear the man was gone.

"Damn that Calla Connolly." The officer's voice ricocheted beyond the sheet and off my walls, startling me. "You ordered me to manage her visit here, General, but you didn't know what you'd asked. I was so busy I couldn't come speak with you. You were supposed to help me figure out how to deal with Pershing's request. I can't believe you're gone. You were our . . . my leader, my example. What will we do without you?" His tone softened and he sniffed. "If she hadn't been here, we would have had time. We would have settled on a way to move forward. And I could have said a proper goodbye."

I could hear his anger spark again, the roar return to his words.

"But because of her visit, because I was occupied with the particulars of her ridiculous show while you slipped away, I'll have to find a way to go on without you. I might be forced to choose these men. Many will die. It's . . . it's her fault." The last word was equal parts sob and shout.

I froze, my soul shriveling in my chest despite the persistent aches. I was here to save lives, to cheer men. If I'd somehow doomed a regiment of men to death, I'd never get over it. I'd offer my own life instead.

I pushed myself out of bed, ignoring the vertigo and confusion that riddled my brain. My legs protested when they hit the cold wood and they ached, but my heart pounded out of my chest, urging me on. I couldn't remain tucked in bed, not when I'd inadvertently caused such catastrophe.

"Three thousand men could be in peril," he said.

"Forgive me!" The words burst from my mouth in a sob. My legs faltered and I snatched at the sheet to steady myself, but it fell to the floor as I did. The general lay still and blue in a bed that matched mine while the officer towered over us, his body rigid with anger and despair. His eyes fixed on mine, brown and gold, ferocious, above a cotton mask like Goldie's, his hands balled in fists at his sides. A nurse I'd never seen hastened toward me and attempted to lift me up, but I refused. I curled into my knees and cried instead— for the perished man in the bed beside me, for the men I didn't know who would perish because of me, for Caspar, who had perished without me. I heard the officer swear.

"Dry your tears and face what you've done." His voice sneered over my sniffing. "Your presence has put thousands of lives in jeopardy."

CHAPTER 3

Something no one seems to consider is how much illness interferes with mental faculties. Though I'd had a fever morning through late afternoon, it had officially broken as of dinner and my senses were sharpening—along with my temper. I glanced over at the empty bed across the room. The sheet wall hadn't been restored, and the extra space won me an unfortunate view of a small mirror above a worm-eaten chest of drawers. Even from this distance, I looked a fright—pale, weak, tired. I recalled my earlier hysterics with a sense of confusion and anger. I'd been sure that my presence had warranted the officer's accusation that I alone had endangered thousands of soldiers' lives. In my feverish, bewildered state, I'd convinced myself that I was no better than a murderer, that General Pershing was right to refuse my request to go to the front, that I'd only be a distraction, an interference, that I could put lives at risk. But now I thought of the officer who, though he had been in shock and grief, had at least been in his right mind. He'd watched me fall to the ground. He'd heard me accept responsibility for the problem, knowing full well I'd had nothing to do with it. In addition to my show, there had also been the news of the men lost at Flanders that night, the coordination of travel for those grieving, that took him away from the general's bedside. I ached for the men who had lost their lives in this war, for the men who would lose their lives in the months—possibly years—to come, but their deaths were not my fault.

I glanced around the room, wondering where they'd put my belongings. Caspar's last letter was tucked in my lingerie bag in the top of my largest Louis Vuitton trunk. At once alarm tightened my chest. I needed to hold the letter, to read Caspar's words I'd memorized about the state of the men on the front and the need for a show to cheer their spirits. I needed a reminder that my pursuit of the front wasn't for my own selfish ambition or praise but was entirely selfless, a service to the men risking their lives for mine and a tribute to the love of my life. But then I recalled I had such a letter in my grasp. Basil's correspondence sat beside me on the bedside table, its contents an echo of Caspar's sentiments.

I relaxed and sat back against the pillows. A woman after praise would have taken the bids to remain on Broadway. I'd had offers I'd turned down. Two starring roles, in fact. In *Keep Her Smiling* and *Head over Heels*. A woman after praise wouldn't have been able to pass them by—and the glory that came with them.

Despite reassuring myself of the truth, despite Basil's letter, doubt still unsettled me. I needed Caspar's words because it had been his experience, his death, that had set me on this course and dictated my intentions, forever changing the reason I used my voice.

I plucked the small bell from my bedside table and rang it for the nurse. Perhaps my belongings had been taken to my room at the Selwyn Hotel. Mary Pickford had told me that I absolutely had to stay there, that when she and Charlie Chaplin came to Charlotte to raise support for bonds, her agent had arranged for them to stay at the hotel overnight and that it was nearly as luxurious as the New York Ritz-Carlton. I looked down at the threadbare quilt across my legs, thought of the vegetable soup adorned with three pieces of vegetables I'd had for lunch, and was homesick for goose down and a fine steak.

"Did you ring, Miss Connolly?" Goldie appeared in the door behind me. Her eyes were damp and red, and she sniffed as she walked to the end of my bed, withdrew the quilt from my legs, took a quick look, and covered them up again. "Still no sign of blue."

"Yes," I said, but speaking launched me into a terrible coughing fit. The noise sounded dry, a rattling rather than the productive rumble of healing, and Goldie's eyes went wide.

"Are you feeling unwell? Are you able to breathe?" Goldie asked, lunging quickly for the pitcher of water at my bedside. She handed me the glass as I continued to cough. I took a sip, concentrating on the feel of the water soothing my throat, then nodded.

"You've been upset," I said. "I should ask you the same questions."

"We all are," she whispered, busying herself with rearranging the pitcher and the bell and the thermometer, doubtless in an effort to distract her brain from the urge to fall apart. "General Alexander was beloved. He was about as decorated as a man his age could be, in charge of the Third Division's Sixth Brigade, and the whole camp too, yet he never spoke of his own victories. He never forgot a name—no one's. He was a champion of all people, and his compassion never ceased to amaze us." She sniffed. "He was well two days ago, shimmying on his belly with the men in the practice trenches out there." Goldie nodded toward the windows. "Generals don't usually do things like that. They just strategize and oversee, but not General Alexander. He believed his presence would make the men feel better, and it did." All I could see were woods, but I suppose there were trenches dug somewhere beyond them, constructed to help equip the soldiers in such warfare before they encountered it overseas. "He took ill during dinner in the mess hall. He was conversing with a small group of soldiers who'd expressed fear about the war. His fever spiked far too quickly, and the pneumonia set in within hours."

"I'm sorry for your loss." The sentiment seemed insufficient. It always did.

"Thank you," she said. "Now, what can I do for you? You rang."

"Oh." I coughed, but this time the terrible stinging and itching didn't emerge. "I was just wondering if you could check sometime on the whereabouts of my belongings."

"They're at the YWCA Hostess House in camp—the lodging facility for the wives and fiancées and mothers of the soldiers who come to visit," she said. "Colonel Erickson, commander of one of General Alexander's regiments, the man you became acquainted with this morning, ordered the soldiers to see to the retrieval of your things the moment you fell ill."

I groaned. "I'm surprised he didn't toss my trunks into the brush pile and burn them. He made it plain that my existence was as loathsome as a tick or a mosquito."

"I doubt he truly believes that," Goldie said, her eyes soft. "Being in medicine so long has taught me that people tend to lash out when they're hurt or grieving or ill, and it's not always directed in the right place."

I made a noise to indicate I doubted he was simply directing his pain in my direction and Goldie laughed, a light tinkling noise like wind chimes. Mother had had a host of chimes back in Ohio before we moved to New York and always said they gave off the most appealing sound. Lenor told me I should never laugh sincerely, that my true laugh was a cackle, suited for the role of a witch but nothing more. So I'd trained myself to chuckle daintily, especially around men. I was sure men liked listening to Goldie laugh. It sounded sincere and delicate.

"In any case, Colonel Erickson's always been a little prickly anyway. Don't pay him any mind." She lowered her voice. "Perhaps it's because General Pershing has kept him home—he's from Charlotte—rather than sending him overseas. He was asked to command a regiment that trained here last year, but when it deployed in November, he was left behind and reassigned to General Alexander's brigade." Her eyes met mine, and I could tell she was considering whether she should say more. "It's rumored he was a standout at West Point and was recognized for his service after tours in Panama and Mexico, but he withdrew from the army only a year after he was commissioned captain and went to France to study architecture. In fact, I heard he was in France when the war broke out. They say he joined the French army as a volunteer before the United States decided to become involved. I suppose the army could see that sort of thing as being overzealous."

"Or perhaps he saw the injustice perpetuated by the Central Powers and wanted to do something to help peace along," I said.

I couldn't believe I was standing up for Colonel Erickson. Then again, it wasn't truly him I was standing up for; it was the men who pressed valiantly toward what was right regardless of opposition.

Goldie shrugged. I thought of what Goldie had just said, that General Pershing himself had ordered Colonel Erickson to his post here. I wondered what sort of relationship he had with the general, if there was any way his unfavorable opinion of my efforts could circulate back to the front.

"I'd like to have a word with Colonel Erickson when he's able. Would you be so kind as to arrange it? I don't like to leave any situation on the wrong foot," I said.

Goldie hesitated.

"You're ill, Miss Connolly. With General Alexander's death, Colonel Erickson will be commander ad interim over his brigade and the camp in his stead. Further exposure would not be wise."

"I understand," I said, though the image of Colonel Erickson drafting a telegram smearing my name intruded and the urgency to set things right persisted.

Just then there was a knock on the door, and another nurse came in with a cart of dinner. It was nearly as paltry as lunch—a bowl of brown beans and corn bread—accompanied by two letters. I only knew about corn bread because of my stay at Camp Lee. Southerners had a strange appetite for sandy textures—first, for breakfast, the godforsaken grits that tasted much like an ocean shore, and then corn bread, a dense loaf that could have reasonably been crafted from the breakfast scraps.

This nurse, an older woman around Mother's age, set the tray in my lap.

"Eat it all, miss. There's been some who find themselves relapsing into illness without proper nutrition," she said. "And the receptionist at the main hospital just sent those letters over to your attention."

I smiled and nodded. At least a substantial amount of broth accompanied the beans. The corn bread would be much improved by the flavor.

She left, and in her absence, I noticed Goldie standing by the window. She kept staring at the same spot toward the setting sun, then sniffing and looking down at her hands.

"I'm sorry you're so troubled by the loss of General Alexander. Is there anything I can do?" I asked. I took a bite of the beans and nearly choked. The salt from the bacon extinguished any other flavor.

"It's not only him. It's my fiancé too—the one who sang with you last night. He brings me a wildflower every morning and leaves it at reception before he starts his drills. He's never missed a day in three months, but he didn't bring one today," she said. She lifted her fingers to the back of her head, where her blonde hair was coming loose of its pins beneath her cap. She tucked the strands in as best she could, sighed, and turned to face me.

"There's a chance he overslept and has been occupied since," I said.

"Or he's been stricken with flu and admitted to the general hospital. I wouldn't know right away since I'm here in the officer's quarters," she said. The tone of her voice was strained, and she could barely keep eye contact without her eyes tearing.

"If I infected him, Goldie, I'm sorry. Like I said, I didn't know what I had, but I knew I was sick, regardless. It was irresponsible of me to continue on." My throat felt tight.

"I don't know if you were close enough to him to put him in harm's way," she said. "I wasn't there, of course. Even if he is infected, it's likely not your fault. I already told you that. There are plenty of others. I checked the soldiers' hospital on my break, and they had no record of him, but . . . there's another possibility too." Goldie's gaze met mine. She lifted her hand and held her naked fingers in front of her face before lowering them. "He's been quite an admirer of yours for some time, Miss Connolly. He hoped to be a musician before he found himself in soldier's garb and . . . well, perhaps he's fallen in love with you instead." She covered her mouth with her hand—though it was unnecessary as the cotton mask was already doing the job—and began to sob.

"Goldie—" I started, but she waved her hand at me.

"He has a little photo of you from the papers—they all do, really—and they tack them on the bunks in the tents. Before, you were just a picture, but now he's shared a stage with you."

"I am thirty-two years old, Goldie," I said as loudly as I could muster without throwing myself into a coughing fit. "At least ten years Guy's senior. And besides, you and I are friends now, aren't we? You've saved my life. I don't have the time for men anyway. They are terribly needy."

Goldie smiled and seemed to relax. It was true that I'd never steal a man away from anyone—I didn't believe anyone could be stolen unless they wanted to be, in any case—but the part about not having time for men was a complete and utter fabrication. I adored men—which was why Lenor had likely decided on them to fabricate a scenario that would bring about my downfall. I adored the way they flirted with me and the way they kissed. I relished the way their bodies enveloped mine in the dark and the way they swore they loved me.

"I suppose you're right," she said. She sat down on a rickety ladder-back chair in the corner of the room and slumped her chin into her hands while her elbows rested on her knees as though she'd been carrying this fear all day long and the sudden relief of it stole her vivacity. "I know you lost your love. Do you suppose you'll ever try again?" Goldie's voice was meek, and she hazarded a glance at me as though wondering if she should take the question back.

"I don't know," I said. "Caspar loved me, and I was crazy for him." There had been other men after Caspar, and yet I could barely recall their faces. But Caspar's memory still arrested me, still stirred the deep longing I'd felt both in his presence and his absence.

"My parents don't like Guy," Goldie said. "He's a Yankee, and they're afraid he'll take me away to Rhode Island and I'll never return."

"My mother disliked Caspar at first for the same reason. He was a Brit and begged me to set up house with him immediately after his proposal even though we weren't yet married." I laughed and then coughed.

"Did you do it?" Goldie asked, her eyes wide.

"No," I said. "But I did stay in England after our show was over. We rented neighboring flats in his hometown of Liverpool. Mother and Father hoped I'd come home, but there was no way I was going to leave him." I tipped my head back against the pillows and closed my eyes. It was true that I'd refused to live with him openly before we were married. I knew what doing such a thing could mean to my career. But we'd never slept apart in the six months we were engaged. I replayed it all the time—the first night in his flat. I could still hear the sharp *click* of the hinge latching. The smell of lacquer from the newly finished wood floors. He'd turned to me in the dark of his foyer and took me in his arms. We were still wearing our stage clothes from the final night of *The Bye and Bye Show*. He'd kissed my mouth and then my neck while my hands discovered his body. Before, there had been only stolen kisses and whispered promises; now there was nothing but the two of us. I could still feel his hands shaking as they touched my skin and feel the weight of him, the feel of us together. I bit my lip, hearing his voice in my ear, *"I'll love you till the end of time, Calla."* I'd said it back, swearing I'd live my life loving him.

I opened my eyes. I had to get back on my tour, back on the stage. I had to prove myself to General Pershing and obtain clearance to the front. Otherwise I was doing less than loving Caspar. Otherwise our memories would strangle me.

"When do you suppose I'll be ready to return to performing?" I asked Goldie, who had resumed her survey of the window.

"I regret to say that it'll be at least seven days. Before that you'll risk infecting others," she said.

"Seven days? But I'm the only performer visiting the camps, you know, and I'm supposed to go to Camp Gordon in Atlanta tomorrow and then Camp Hancock in Augusta, Camp Wheeler in Macon, then over to Camp Montgomery in Montgomery."

"I'm afraid you'll miss most of them," Goldie said. "Should I telegram the others to let them know you'll be delayed?"

"I suppose we must," I said. Emotion balled in my throat. I thought of the men who had been looking forward to merriment being told I'd not be coming and of the idle hours I'd spend trapped in an infirmary with my ghosts. "However, I need to be prepared to resume touring as soon as I'm well. Would you mind asking about a date to reschedule when you send the telegrams?"

A sharp knock on the door interrupted me, and Goldie called for whoever it was to come in. Colonel Erickson entered the room and Goldie stood quickly, nearly toppling the chair.

"Miss Connolly, Nurse McGann," he said politely, though his tone was sharp. He withdrew the wide-brimmed campaign hat boasting a colonel's black-and-gold cords, pressed it to his chest, and tipped his head at Goldie. I noticed he didn't bother to look at me when he greeted me and hadn't even applied pomade to his hair. The mop of chestnut brown was damp with sweat and angled every which way. Enlisted or not, celebrity or civilian, men typically tried to make themselves presentable to me. Clearly this Colonel Erickson didn't care in the slightest that Calla Connolly thought he resembled a caveman, both in manner and appearance. I glared at him, at the cotton mask covering his nose and mouth. It was quite unfair that he had the advantage of cloth to disguise his clear disdain, while mine was laid bare. I could hardly help it. He had made me feel like the worst sort of person while I was terribly ill, and I wouldn't accept his accusations this time.

"I'm sorry to interrupt," he went on, addressing Goldie. "I've just come from drills in the trenches and the rifle field and thought I'd stop in before I went to the artillery range. I don't want the men to think they'll have a regular desk sort for a commander when they're so used to Alexander."

I couldn't bear the sight of his face, so I looked at his feet. I'd always thought feet funny things. When I was young and nervous, auditioning for my first starring roles, I'd survey the producer's shoes and imagine I was performing for a room full of them. Imagination helped divert my anxiety then. Perhaps now it could distract my mind from the insatiable urge to strike him. Colonel Erickson wore boring, regular-issue field boots instead of high brown officers' boots, possibly in an attempt to fit in with the rest of the soldiers, but it wouldn't work. He was much over six feet tall and his posture, which suggested he'd been strapped to a washboard as an infant, indicated that he was the strictest sort of person—not at all like the average soldier who would be keen to do just about anything else than run drills in simulated trenches.

"To what do we owe the pleasure, Colonel?" I asked finally. The silence was uncomfortable.

His eyes met mine for the first time since he entered the room. He looked terrible. Worse than Goldie. The whites of his eyes appeared nearly the color of ripe beets and his lids were swollen to slits. It was unusual that a man wander around in public displaying such clear emotion, but then again, everyone had to have at least one redeeming quality. Perhaps this was his. There was a chance Goldie was right and I'd simply been his scapegoat in a moment of deep grief. Perhaps he was coming to apologize.

"Nurse McGann," he said, turning away from me to focus on Goldie. "I'm sorry for this inconvenience, but I require a private audience with Miss Connolly. It won't take long."

"Whatever for?" I asked, but he ignored me.

"Yes, sir." Goldie smiled at me. "I'll return shortly to get you ready for sleep, Miss Connolly." When she passed Colonel Erickson, she stopped. "I . . . I want to express my sincere condolences. We all adored General Alexander."

"He was quite a man," Colonel Erickson said, his voice low. Then he cleared his throat. "As I said, I won't be here long."

I listened to Goldie's light footsteps pad across the hardwood floor. I heard the heavy wood door click shut, but Colonel Erickson didn't move. My heartbeat quickened. I hoped he'd come to apologize, but if he was here to blame me for interference, of murder yet again, I'd tell him I was guilty of no such thing. The very idea of it was maddening. I'd had nothing to do with General Pershing's orders or General Alexander dying before he could help Colonel Erickson figure out how to handle them.

"Now then," he said finally. He walked to the other side of the room, snatched the ladderback chair Goldie had occupied minutes before, and set it at the foot of my bed. He folded himself onto it, the result looking much like a china doll compelled to fit on doll-house furniture. His eyes met mine, but he said nothing.

I sighed and the gesture induced a coughing fit. When I settled, I forced a smile. "Colonel, I know why you're here."

"You—" he started, but I waved my hand at him.

"Men and women alike have followed me into changing rooms, into bathrooms, into alleyways to ask me to sing them a favorite song—one I failed to sing onstage—but I regret to tell you, Colonel, I can barely speak without heaving, much less singing, so your request will have to wait."

His eyes narrowed and I laughed, not bothering to transform the noise into something Lenor would approve of. I paid for my merriment, coughing so hard I truly lost my breath and tears sprang to my eyes.

In a gentlemanly gesture I could hardly believe, Colonel Erickson stood and crossed to my bedside table, plucked the water pitcher from its stand, and poured me a glass. He handed it to me, then deposited the pitcher back on the table.

"I don't know any of your songs," he said simply. He stood in front of my bedside table, surveying the offerings: the water, the handkerchiefs, the thermometer, and a clear bottle I hadn't noticed before. "Has Nurse given you doses of this Tanlac?" He picked up the bottle and turned it over in his hands. Then his eyes met mine, and I could see he'd calmed.

"Not that I know of. She's given me aspirin and a cinnamon tincture of sorts, but I don't recall anything else," I said. "Why?"

"It's awful, for one," he said. "Like moonshine and the worst combination of woodland foraging." He set it back down. "And the manufacturer has just been accused of quackery. They gave this to me in regular doses when I fell ill with flu last month. Major Sheaff—the physician in charge of the hospital here—told me they were doing away with the use of it."

"You contracted this terrible flu too?" I asked, surveying him. It was difficult to envision certain men ill. Short men, slight men, fat men, old men were built in a manner that allowed the mind to entertain the idea that they could become sickly, but men like Colonel Erickson, men who were tall and as solid as stone, seemed nearly invincible.

"Yes. I was one of the first in camp, actually, which is why I feel fairly safe visiting here now. My sister is a spooler over at the Chadwick-Hoskins Mill just down the road and there was an outbreak there. I made the mistake of bringing her a sandwich on my day off," he said. I'd always wanted a sibling. On Broadway there had been multiple acts with twins, and I'd always envied the way they leaned on each other.

"Did she fall ill as well?" I asked.

He shook his head. "No, thank God." He folded himself back onto the chair. "I fared all right. Much like you seem to be doing, but this flu is highly unpredictable." He glanced at the empty bed situated perpendicular to mine across the room. It was then that I realized he'd been avoiding the sight of it. He sniffed and I pretended to study the faded fleur-de-lis detail on the potbelly stove, but when minutes passed without a word, I stole a glance at him and realized he was crying. Not sobbing, but his eyes were wet, cast down at his hands now clasped in his lap. A lump welled in my throat at the sight of him and I pinched my lids closed to stop the tearing. Even in my feverish state that morning, I'd sensed the desperation in his voice.

"I'm sorry that you felt my presence such an imposition," I whispered. "I'm sorry that you lost a man you respected, that you feel out of sorts in his absence. And I'm sorry that you're mourning him now. But I must say, Colonel, I cannot accept the accusations you hurled at me this morning. My being here does not jeopardize thousands of lives."

"I know," he said. He palmed his eyes, wiping the moisture away. "That's why I'm here. I came to apologize." He paused. "I was desperate for Alexander's guidance this morning. I knew he didn't have much time, and that if he died without telling me what to do, it was likely I'd have to decide the fates of many men on my own. His death means that I'm assigned to his role—at least for a while." It wasn't the same, and yet I felt the weight of his words acutely in the way I'd shoved my life aside to carry out Caspar's final wishes.

"But I do have to admit that I can't quite understand why you came," he said. The moment the words were out of his mouth, my body ignited with fury. My cheeks burned. He must have seen the flush on my face because he held up his hand. "I don't mean any offense by it. It's just that the army as a whole seems determined to make the boys merry, but war is anything but. It's one thing to bolster strength, to encourage confidence and might, but it's another to distract them with singing and dancing as though they're training for the circus instead of a fight for their lives. It feels like a lie."

I breathed and tried to remain calm. It wouldn't do for me to lose my temper. I recalled Goldie saying that he'd served in the war with the French before he'd returned home. He was speaking like a man who'd experienced great horrors, like a man who hadn't been afforded a moment's peace as he marched and hid and fought as Caspar had, like a man who had left the trenches despairing and buried his spirit there.

"If a man's brain is subject to continual tension, his body will not perform and his good sense will falter. General Pershing said something of that sentiment himself. Terror is only alleviated by joy. Those allowed moments to remember who they are outside of this war will find the strength to face their darkest hour. A variety show hardly has the power to sweep scores of soldiers into such a state of amnesia that they've forgotten why they're here."

I leaned back against the pillows, exhausted.

Colonel Erickson nodded. "You're right. They're aware of the perils of war, but they're men," he said softly. "Men know they can die but don't truly believe in their own mortality, especially when they're doing something valiant."

"Is that how you once felt?" I asked. I knew full well he understood his fragility. It was clear in the way he allowed his emotion.

He stood then, not answering the question, and turned the brim of his hat around in his hands. He'd come to apologize and he'd done it. I had no reason to believe that his opinion of me had suddenly changed in the last few minutes, and now there was nothing left to say.

"Please extend my thanks to the entire camp for the kindness everyone showed me when I fell ill," I said.

"You're fortunate you got sick here, at this camp. Our medical staff is the best in the country," he said, meeting my gaze for a moment.

"Thanks to them, you'll be relieved to know that I'll be out of here and on my way in a week, I'm told. Off to train the next group of soldiers for the circus. Perhaps I'll wire one of the Ringling brothers and beg them to send an elephant down by rail." I realized as soon as I said it that making light of his concern about my tour wasn't likely going to end our conversation on the best note. Then again, it was unlikely I'd ever see him again.

He chuckled and shook his head. I stared at him, taken aback by his reaction, wondering if perhaps he was coming down with another wave of flu.

"Unfortunately you'll be staying longer than a week—likely until peace," he said.

"What?" Surely I'd heard him incorrectly.

Colonel Erickson sighed. "It is not what either of us wants, but you can't leave. Not after what you overheard this morning. I came to see Alexander when I knew the nurses had a break to speak to him in private. No one told me there was anyone on this side of the room—there has never been anyone here. I assumed they'd put you in the room near Major Sheaff's office."

I couldn't breathe.

"What you heard was classified, a matter of great national secrecy, I'm afraid."

The echo of Caspar's loss, the desperation to hold on to him, to help men like him and Basil flooded through me, overpowering my ability to control myself. They couldn't hold me here like a prisoner. I would never get to the front. I would have to live with the regret, with the way I let Caspar and the other men down for the rest of my life.

"No." I choked out the word and began to sob. "No!" I shouted, pitching forward so swiftly in my bed that the quilt flew away from me, exposing my wrinkled nightgown. "You can't force me to stay here. I don't know anything. I heard nothing at all except that there's a regiment that could be in grave danger. It's hardly news. Everyone is in grave danger. It's a war." I uttered the words in a screeching cry and had no idea if he'd comprehended all of them. "And it's your fault that I heard it in the first place. If you hadn't blamed me for you not getting to General Alexander in time, I never would have gotten out of bed. I never would have paid any attention to what you were saying." He stood over me, the earlier gentleness in his eyes replaced by a hard glare. He started to say something, but I reached for Basil's letter and held it toward him. "You have to let me go. I want to cheer the men," I said, my voice a whimper.

Colonel Erickson extracted the letter from the envelope and looked it over, his face clouding as he read Basil's words, his brows rising toward the end of it, likely at the mention of my photograph. In my desperation to make him understand, I'd forgotten that part. My cheeks burned. Then he folded it back up and handed it to me.

"I posed as a lingerie model for a fashion designer when I was younger. The photograph was never published, but sitting for it was a poor choice nonetheless. My family needed the money," I explained, though he hadn't asked. I doubted he could think less of me than he already did, but I couldn't have him speculating to his peers. "Please give me your word you'll keep the knowledge of the likeness to yourself."

"My mother was French and sold lingerie and dresses at a department store. I'm hardly scandalized, but you're right to assume others would clutch their pearls," he said. "You have my word."

The room fell silent. He stared out the window. I was relieved, but he'd said nothing about letting me go.

"Is that all you wish to say? You read his letter. Did it not break your heart? Please don't force me to stay here."

"I'm sorry for this boy's plight and sympathize with the horrors he's seen, but this decision was not my own, and now that I realize you assume you can simply move about the camps and in combat zones as you please—"

"Of course I don't think that. This boy, Basil, believes I can go about at will because of my fame and because I'm a woman, but I know I can't do a thing without clearance," I hissed, but my tone didn't deter him.

"I wired General Dickman, the commander of the Third Division who's in DC for a time, and he wired central command, General Pershing himself, to inquire of protocol," he went on as if he hadn't heard me. "The instruction was to keep you at camp in order to monitor you and ensure that you don't speak about what you heard." He took a breath. "You won't be allowed any external privileges unless chaperoned by me. Any letters or telegrams will be read and censored by one of the lieutenants here before they're sent. That's camp policy," he said. "General Pershing realizes this might seem severe, but what you overheard was too delicate." Colonel Erickson's voice was even, nearly monotone. He kept stealing glances at the empty bed as he spoke. "Only the two of us know this information here at Camp Greene. If it's made public, you'll be charged with treason and will have to live with the realization that you've single-handedly crushed soldiers' resolve." He paused.

"You'll need a plausible story as to why you're staying here—both for your family and contacts outside, as well as for the soldiers and staff here in camp. You'll tell everyone—Nurse Goldie included—that you have received exceptional care here at Camp Greene and feel you owe your life to the soldiers and nurses and physicians who have helped you recover, so you've decided to show your appreciation by entertaining the camp for several months. You can use the annex of the YMCA building for your rehearsals. It has a piano."

"I won't say anything," I said through my tears. "And my mother will never believe that story. She knows how desperate I am to make this tour a success, to prove to General Pershing that I should be allowed to go to the front. Please let me go. As Basil mentioned, my fiancé, Caspar, died in France, and in his last letter he said he would give anything to hear me sing to him. Caspar had planned to convince Sir Douglas Haig to send for me so that we could perform at the front together, cheer the troops together. He can't go now, so it's up to me."

I watched Colonel Erickson's face blanch and thought there was a chance he'd come to see my side.

"The army won't allow you to leave," he said, the candor returning to his eyes. "Though I can tell you that perhaps your fiancé's wish will still be granted after all, by Lenor Felicity—at least on this side of the pond. Pershing mentioned he was planning to ask her to step into the tour in your stead. He's promised the troops entertainment, I suppose." He squinted out the window.

My stomach lurched with nausea. I'd run into Lenor on the closing day of *Fancy Free* the day before I'd set off on tour. She was standing on the sidewalk outside the Booth Theatre waiting on Charlie Chaplin, who was wrapping up a performance next door. She commented that she'd seen the papers broadcasting news of my arrival in the camps, calling me "America's Sweetheart" and celebrating my generosity toward the troops. Everybody knew I was doing it to honor Caspar—I'd said that much in interviews—but instead of mentioning my tribute to him, Lenor spoke of how advantageous the tour would be for my career. I knew by the set of her jaw and the glint in her eye that she was jealous I'd come up with the idea. I'd tried to remind her that I wasn't doing it to bolster my popularity. I'd told her it had been Caspar's dream and mine to someday perform for the despairing men at the front and that I hoped this was the first step, but she hadn't heard me. Instead, she'd praised my ingenuity. I knew without doubt Lenor would agree to take my place. What if she was permitted clearance to the front while I was forced to languish in this camp? Perhaps somehow my Caspar would hear her voice instead of mine and think I'd failed him.

"This is your fault. Yours." I collapsed onto the bed, turned over, and sobbed. At once Colonel Erickson's hand was on my back, gently patting my aching bones like you would a moderately adored pet.

"I know it's a disappointment, but there's no need to upset yourself like this. Your singing won't be the reason the Huns still their guns. Men are going to fight and die regardless. You'll have an opportunity to cheer them another day."

I didn't lift my head, but he removed his touch as I shrugged it off. I heard his footsteps leave my room, and as the door clicked shut, I pressed my face to my pillow and screamed as loudly as I could.

CHAPTER 4

I was supposed to be released from the hospital at 12:03 a.m. on the dot—exactly seven days from my arrival to the second. The army was precise like that. I felt that surely they were mistaken, that I'd really been in captivity for at least two decades. I'd been so bored, so down in the dumps, that the whole course of it felt like one never-ending night. My bitterness over General Pershing's decision and Colonel Erickson's callousness at my ruined ambitions, mingled with intermittent fear over the secret I'd overheard but didn't quite understand, had been left to fester, resulting in a notepad full of new songs—none of which I'd ever sing. They'd positively wreck spirits. I snatched the bound paper from my bedside and flipped it open, surveying the cheery titles—"What Does It Matter?," "We're All Going Down," "The Men Doomed to Doom Men," "Why Should I Dream?"—and then shut it. I'd have to throw it in a fire somewhere later.

Outside, the night was entirely black. I couldn't see any moonlight or starlight. I recalled Goldie saying that the *Farmers' Almanac*—the metric by which the whole city of Charlotte based their predictions on the weather, apparently—said it was to be an exceptionally wet spring and that we'd likely have clouds for the next few weeks. I didn't enjoy dreariness, especially when I was already dreary.

I glanced down at my "going-home costume"—at least that's what Goldie kept calling it—a drab muslin patient's gown with a white sash of similar material. I'd asked for my trunks but was refused. Goldie said the physicians weren't entirely sure if the virus could be spread through fabric and that wearing my costumes in the hospital might exclude the dresses from wear when I was home. She kept referring to my being released as "going home," though she knew full well I wasn't going home at all but simply being transferred down neighboring Tuckaseegee Road to the camp proper and the YWCA Hostess House.

Goldie thought of my transfer as a joyful occasion. I'd had to tell her I was staying on my own grateful accord. The grateful part wasn't a lie. I knew the staff here at Camp Greene had saved my life. Even so, mustering the enthusiasm to tell Goldie I'd decided to stay had been difficult. I'd practiced feigning excitement by writing a letter to my parents first, telling them I was staying at Camp Greene indefinitely because I wanted to thank the soldiers and staff—but also because I'd fallen desperately in love with an officer. I needed something believable, and they'd watched me go off course when I'd fallen in love before. Still, writing that I'd fallen in love with someone had nearly made me retch. I'd cried for an hour afterward, feeling like I'd betrayed Caspar's memory, even though my heart wholly belonged to him.

By the time I broke the news to Goldie, I was wildly convincing because I'd told myself I was only playing a part, that this Calla Connolly who was thrilled to remain at Camp Greene was one of my characters. Goldie had responded to my news by jumping up and down and gushing about the fact that there was a sizable bedroom available at the new Hostess House—apparently the first one had burned down. I didn't find that fact to be a good omen, but it didn't seem to faze Goldie, and when she'd burst into my room with the news that she'd spoken to the Hostess House mother, a woman named Francis Kern, and that the bedroom was mine, complete with a hand-carved armoire they'd salvaged from the fire and quilts made by the Hostess House guests, I'd pretended she'd just said the room was a well-appointed guest suite at the Ritz Paris and smiled and clapped with her.

"Your auto transport is here, Miss Calla," Goldie whispered, gingerly stepping into my room as though I were still sharing it with another patient. She didn't have her mask on today, and I was struck by how lovely she was. She resembled a fair-haired Evelyn Nesbit. "I apologize that they were a bit delayed. The driver nodded off waiting for the call."

"It's not a problem," I said. I'd told Goldie to call me Calla, that we were friends, but she told me she couldn't and that "Miss Calla" was the absolute best she could do. I slid my legs off the bed that I'd made the way Mother had always instructed me as a child— *"Tight and tuck the sheets, tight and tuck the quilt."* If there were ever any lumps in the bed, I'd have to start over again. It had been more difficult than I'd thought to stand long enough to do up the bed, and by the time I'd finished, I'd been thoroughly out of breath.

"Would you like to walk arm in arm with me or would you prefer a chair?" Goldie asked, yawning. I noticed she was grinning ear to ear and held her hand behind her back.

"As long as I can lean on you, I'm sure I'll be fine," I said. "What's happened since I saw you this evening? You look radiant, as though you've swallowed the sun."

Goldie blushed, the pink sweeping her pale skin.

"You know I've been terribly worried about Guy." She took her hand from her back, revealing a daisy. A decent amount of dirt was still attached to the roots, but she lifted it to her face anyway. I'd been worried about Guy too. She hadn't seen him since the night he sang with me, and though she'd checked around the hospital to make sure he hadn't been brought in, I suppose I worried that he'd contracted the flu and perished before he could seek treatment. "He's well and perfectly healthy and still in love with me," she said, only taking her gaze from the petals for a second to glance at me.

"Did he say where he's been all this time?" I asked.

"Oh yes," she said. She pursed her lips and shook her head. "He was ordered to the confinement barracks for a week the night of your show."

I felt my eyebrows rise and she laughed.

"He didn't do anything wrong—at least, not really. He was so inspired by his time onstage that he went directly to see his friend

Sidney Duncan, to see if he'd happened to sneak his fiddle into camp—they're from the same little town in Rhode Island—Jamestown—and played together all the time back home. Guy can't say enough about Sidney's playing. Anyway, it turns out Sidney had the fiddle and they got to singing and then they were discovered by Major Gordon."

"They were placed in corrections for a week for singing?" I asked. "I understand there's lights out and all, but it was a Saturday and the men had leave."

"No. Guy was placed in confinement because Sidney is Black."

I stared for a moment, and I suppose my mouth must have gone slack, because she looked down and went on.

"There's a rule in camp . . . well, also in town, that white people can't go inside Black people's dwellings and they can't come into ours," she said quietly. "I don't know the reason for it, really, but that's how it's always been around here. Sidney and Guy grew up together—a lot of the men did—and they don't understand these rules, so they break them." Goldie paused.

I'd witnessed racism in the city—in my hometown of Columbus too. Some did horrendous things in order to blame somebody else for their shortcomings and problems. Still, there were no laws in place that got in the way of camaraderie and understanding in the North like there were here.

"Some of the officers like Colonel Erickson look the other way when they see the men interacting. They know most are New Englanders and unfamiliar with the laws. But some officers don't." She shook her head. "The trouble is, it's Guy's third time in confinement—the first couple of times were for missing articles of his uniform and arguing with his drill sergeant—and regardless of why he's there, I know that the army keeps an account. He's been assigned a rifleman now. He won't be charging across the field from the trenches, but that can always change." Her eyes filled.

I thought of the orders from General Pershing that I'd overheard Colonel Erickson lament to General Alexander the day of his passing. The regiment assigned to the dangerous mission would consist of men of strength and skill, but men prone to trouble or of questionable moral character. Someone who'd disregarded the rules and been sent to confinement three times would surely be a contender for the latter category. My skin prickled. I thought of Guy's voice. He belonged on Broadway. He couldn't be struck down on the battlefield as Caspar had been, his talent lost to the world forever.

"Perhaps I can convince Colonel Erickson that I need Guy to round out my act," I said. If I could somehow prove Guy was valuable to me, surely the officers would see past his disciplinary marks. "I'll need accompaniment for my show, solo performers too. No one will want to see the same set day after day, and from what I recall, Guy and I got on swimmingly onstage."

"Day after day? The *Trench and Camp* said you were only performing on Saturdays, sometimes during the dances at Lakewood Park, and sometimes just for the soldiers here," she said. "Regardless, I know Guy would be over the moon."

The news shocked me. I suppose I should have read the camp's newspaper. I was used to putting on shows nightly. That sort of frequency was perfect for me. Mother always said I'd been born with a mind that never slowed. It had been a fortunate attribute in my early years on Broadway. In my time away from the theatre, I used to dream up ways to make productions more memorable, my roles go deeper, but now, off the stage, my thoughts often imagined horrors—Caspar's demise, Caspar calling out to me—and the future that could have been. These past years I'd learned to rely on the stage for peace. It was the only place my mind was forced to take an intermission from grief. It was the only place I felt truly alive and Caspar's spirit smiling. The stage had been his heaven too.

"That's terribly disappointing," I said, hoping my voice didn't give away the swell of emotion I felt. "I'll still need to rehearse daily, though. Guy could join me. But that'll only occupy an hour or two. What am I going to do the rest of the week?" Out the window, I heard the sharp clang of the welcome bell.

"That's the driver, I suppose," Goldie said. "At least he had the forethought to avoid the auto's horn. It would have woken the entire hospital." She hastened to my side, and I stood. My legs felt like great boulders. I couldn't lift them to step, but instead shuffled toward the door.

"We'll find some worthy activities to occupy your time the rest of the week. I've been asked to assist you in your recuperation so that you'll be fully well to perform as you wished. We'll figure this out together," Goldie whispered. "We all know how much you're sacrificing to be here."

We entered the dark hallway, and I was at once glad for the dim. My eyes blurred at the implication of her last sentence, reminding me once again that I'd failed Caspar and I would fail Basil too. I sniffed, breathing in the stale stench of illness, like an unwashed mouth, at once aware that my room had likely smelled the same until I'd begged for a toothbrush and a tube of Zodenta Tooth Soap. I'd been given Colgate Dental Cream instead, and the peppermint taste was so strong I'd nearly needed a rinse. Even so, a brushing regime would likely do wonders for the overall aroma Goldie was subject to daily.

It took us quite some time to get to the front door, though the officers' quarters were no larger than a small house. Goldie reached around me, turned the knob, and cool, fresh air and the sound of crickets engulfed me. I breathed deeply, inhaling the light scent of pine from the trees just beyond us, amazed the crackling in my lungs had been reduced to a small squeak.

"Ladies," an older gentleman wearing dungarees and a linen shirt said to us. He stood next to an old Ford auto adorned with several dents and rust that crowned the wheels. "I'm Timothy, your driver." He opened the door and yawned. Goldie stepped in the cab first and I followed, clutching Timothy's hand hard as I hoisted my body onto the seat. "It's mighty nice meeting you, Miss Connolly. My wife's loved your music for years. There's a place in town . . . well, it's not a nice place for people like you or my wife, but it's a tobacco shop called Johnny Clements. There's a Victrola in there and they have a few of your records, so sometimes I take her to listen to them. They have two of the songs you sang with

Caspar Wells and that one you recorded with Lenor Felicity for that variety show."

"'A Friend Will Heal Your Heart,'" I said. The mention of Lenor wasn't welcome. When Colonel Erickson had come to collect my letters—one to my parents and one to Basil, telling him that though I wished him the best and wanted nothing more than to help him, I was detained by a worthy cause at home—he'd told me the news that Lenor had been happy to resume the tour in my stead. I'd known she'd agree, and yet the confirmation that she'd taken something so personal to enhance her fame felt like a knife in my gut.

Timothy snapped.

"That's the one," he said. "I grew up on Miss Felicity's music. Same as everybody else my age, I guess. Mama always sang her songs when she was scrubbing the laundry. I hear 'Dream of My Home' whenever I see anybody hanging clothes on a line."

"I know I'm younger than you, but I grew up listening to her too. She was my mother's favorite singer," I said, trying to rise above my irritation. "Mother nearly fainted when she showed up in my dressing room after my debut stage show in Columbus. When she asked if my parents would consider moving to New York so I could play her daughter in the mother-daughter act she was pitching to Willie Hammerstein, Mother couldn't answer, she was so awestruck." I laughed. It seemed like eons ago, and I suppose it was. This year marked two decades. I'd only been twelve. "When she did find her voice, Mother asked Lenor what she was doing in Columbus. Lenor started to explain that she'd missed a train, saw the theatre, and decided to take in a show, but I cut in and told Lenor we'd make the move. I couldn't risk her taking back the offer, and besides, the carriage factory Father worked for had shut down a few weeks before."

Timothy shook his head and whistled. "What a stroke of luck."

I'd thought so too, back when I was younger. Now I wasn't so sure.

"For Miss Felicity too," Goldie said. "I can't imagine the world without the two of you. It'd be awful dull."

"Well, ladies, let me get you to the Hostess House," Timothy said. "It's nearly one thirty. Sun'll be rising before you know it." He shut the door and walked around the front of the auto to the driver's seat and started the engine.

I looked out the window as we drove away from the hospital. The pine forest gave way to a clearing. In the near distance, strings of electric lights looped down from iron poles and a lake shimmered beyond them. A large white pavilion jutted out into the deep.

"Lakewood Park," Goldie murmured, noticing my gaze. "There's the Ferris wheel and the roller coaster right beyond that." Sure enough, the familiar sky-scraping metal circle came into view in front of a towering structure of white scaffolding. Beside us, right next to the road, was a large sign that read "Lakewood Park" in cursive red letters. Even in the dark, I was amazed by the wash of flowers—spring roses and pansies, zinnias and petunias—that surrounded the sign, providing a breathtaking entrance to the park. "When my brother and I were little, my parents would take us once a year to ride rides and see the diving horses that came every August."

"How interesting! Did you ever want to try it?" I asked. "I've only seen the act once, at Hanlan's Point Amusement Park in Toronto—my uncle lived up there for a time—and thought it would be an incredible rush to dive from the back of a horse." Pine forest eclipsed the view once again, and I settled back against the seat.

"Never," Goldie said, laughing. "Guy could barely convince me to get on the Ferris wheel when we visited a few months ago. Years back, the operator fell asleep and everyone was stuck on the ride for over an hour. The gas fumes got so bad, most people got sick. I know it's unlikely to happen again, but I can hardly think of it without my stomach souring."

"People are fascinating, aren't they, Goldie? Here you are, a nurse, able to endure blood, illness, death, and yet you can hardly bear an amusement ride, while I am a glutton for thrills but will most certainly faint the moment I encounter so much as a splinter."

"We're quite a pair. Say you'll go on the Ferris wheel for me next time and I'll make short order of the next splinter you see," Goldie said.

We laughed, and I realized, sitting there, that though I'd played a best friend in *The Sunshine Brigade* and though I'd had colleagues I'd enjoyed, I'd never had a true friend other than Caspar. Perhaps friendship only required ease and understanding and could come in the form of a nurse ten years my junior, who had grown up a world away from the home I knew, more easily than it had the fellow entertainers on Broadway. No one was truly looking for friends there, anyway. Even if you liked a person, they became your competition eventually and couldn't be trusted. I had Lenor to thank for that lesson.

"Here's your new home," Goldie said, pointing out of her window at an expansive two-story structure with a wide screened porch. "YWCA Hostess House" was spelled out in block letters against the second story. "I'll walk you in and get you settled, but all of your trunks are in your room, which has a lovely view of a field and some of the trenches. The Fourth Infantry regiment resides just down the way there." She tipped her head toward Timothy, still at the wheel. "Some of them have barracks instead of tents. Guy thinks they're the luckiest soldiers in the world." Goldie sighed and looked at the house again. "I know it's not the finery you're likely used to, but you'll feel right at home here. Promise you'll tell me if you have any concerns at all."

"I can't," I said, the mention of promises unsettling the merriment I'd felt moments before. "Promises from me mean nothing," I whispered, feeling the tremendous weakness I'd felt walking down the hall. "In fact, I'm breaking one by being here now." My chest heaved to sob, but I swallowed it down and opened my door to silence the noise. I'd never gone back on my word, not even to myself. I'd sworn to Caspar's memory I would push on to the front, but here I was, stuck.

Goldie caught my hand, stopping me.

"If you're breaking a promise in order to do something as worthy as cheering the soldiers who helped you, it's hardly cause for guilt," she said.

I nodded because it was the only thing to do. As much as I wanted to, I couldn't tell her that she was wrong, that I'd begged to leave this place, that I was practically a prisoner. Perhaps I was selfish. Perhaps I should serve here happily, doing what I'd told General Pershing I wanted to do: cheer the troops. But my heart was thousands of miles away on a French battlefield, and every day that I wasn't there, I heard Caspar's voice as I had moments before he departed. *"Don't you love me?"* he'd asked that day, a smile to his voice. I'd replied that I did, over and over. It was a game we played, a way to hear the words that brought us life. But now that question haunted me, its tone sterner and sharper each day I delayed.

"Yes," I nearly shouted, realizing as I said it that I was answering Caspar's question as Timothy inquired if I'd like a hand out.

"Welcome home," he said, and I stared at the darkened structure feeling nothing but shackles.

CHAPTER 5

The bugle call had sounded at 5:45 a.m. At first I'd thought I was dreaming and attempted to turn over in my surprisingly comfortable poster bed, but then the reveille sounded again, louder this time, and I'd flipped on the crystal lamp atop the oak bedside table with intricate barley twist legs and a rose engraved on its face. I watched the sun rise in soft pinks and golds from the picture window at the foot of my bed, casting the newly cleared field carved with a zigzag pattern of what I supposed were the replica trenches in dewy yellow. The trenches seemed to go on forever, hemmed in only by the barracks close by to the left and by lines of small white dots—the closest row of soldiers' tents—on the horizon.

The moment the sun rose in earnest and the ancient clock on top of the singed armoire on the opposite side of my room chimed six thirty, I'd watched the camp proper come to life. Men poured from the tents, looking to my eye much like scurrying ants. I could hear stirring in the house below me, the intermittent clack of pots and pans and a few hushed voices, but gave them no mind because it sounded just like home, like the apartment building waking up. The spectacle in front of me had been inspiring. I'd gathered the coverlet embroidered with lovely medallion lace trim around me, inhaling the scent of clean, sun-drenched linen, content to watch the boys start their day. Soon enough, groups of soldiers entered the trenches, hoisting what appeared to be sandbags, some close enough that I could see the mud from the recent rainfall clinging to their trousers.

It appeared that most thought it humorous. It was the perfect inspiration for a new song. I'd reluctantly peeled myself out of bed at that point and shivered across the old Oriental rug in my pink silk nightclothes to the armoire, where my notepads and pencils resided next to my gowns. I'd plucked the instruments from the armoire, then freed my long chinchilla coat from its hanger, slipping my freezing body into its cozy depths. The coat had been a gift from Caspar during our first winter in Liverpool. Despite growing up in Ohio and New York, I determined that American winters were no match for England's, and I was always shivering.

I'd eyed Caspar's wrinkled letter displayed prominently in the back of the armoire and Basil's envelope beside it. I'd decided the night before that I needed to find a way to write General Pershing himself and inform him that I was well again and quite ready to continue my tour. Then again, a letter requesting I continue on might make me appear either dimwitted or unable to comply with his orders or both. As much as it pained me, I would have to go along for now to remain in his good graces.

I'd closed the armoire, crossed to the little rocking chair in front of the window, curled in with my soft coat, and begun to write a new song—"Stuck in the Trenches (Even the Clay Won't Let Me Be)." By the time I'd finished the lyrics, I was smiling and laughing, in true high snuff for the first time in a week.

I yawned and shut my notebook. The boys would love the new song. I hummed the cheery tune and glanced at the closed door and then at the clock. It was going on seven thirty now. My stomach rumbled, craving a pastry and a cup of coffee. I wondered if the Hostess House employed servants or whether one was supposed to seek out their own refreshments. I was quite used to the latter— Mother, Father, and I lived a simple life—but when I stayed in hotels, service was often provided.

A knock at the door sounded just then, as if on cue. I hoped the interruption was the coffee and warm croissant I was dreaming of.

"It's me, Goldie," she said from the other side of the door. I told her to come in and she did. I gasped when I saw her. Instead of the ill-fitting nurse's uniform of starched stiff cotton, she wore a robin's-egg-blue dress of draped crepe de chine with a picture hat of brown taffeta and hemp wreathed with yellow buttercups. She carried a small silver tray boasting a steaming coffee cup, a little pitcher of cream, and a folded newspaper.

"You're absolutely stunning, and I could practically kiss you for the coffee," I said, walking toward her. Walking was still not easy, but the weight I'd felt in my legs the day before had significantly lightened.

Goldie laughed and set the tray down on my bedside table. "The house mother, Mrs. Kern, asked me to bring it up."

I practically lunged for the coffee.

"You seem much improved," she said. "Perhaps you only needed to be removed from the doldrums of the hospital."

She watched me sip the coffee and then glanced out the window. "They should be done by now," she murmured.

"What?" I asked, regrettably finishing the last of the coffee and setting the china cup on the tray.

"It's Sunday," she said. "They don't . . . We don't . . . work on Sundays. They're calling for rain tomorrow, so groups of men were asked to help reinforce the trenches with sandbags to prevent them from caving in, but they're supposed to be finished by now." Goldie looked at the clock. "It's almost eight."

I looked out at the field, still in awe over the elaborate maze set before me.

"The trenches are how many miles in all?" I asked.

"Five." Goldie looked at me. "General Liggett—the general over Camp Greene before General Alexander—had French officials come in with actual French plans to build them. Colonel Erickson helped too, since I suppose he lived in the trenches over there for months. It was important for the trenches to be as accurate as they could be to help the boys prepare for what they'll find on the front." She paused. "The trenches are just one small part of Camp Greene, though. It's 2,340 acres in all, built on mostly raw farmland. Our town fought hard to win it. And now there are forty thousand men training here—190 regiment sites plus brigade and divisional headquarters, a hospital, a remount station for the horses that is more than a hundred acres itself, the rifle and artillery ranges, and all of the recreational buildings like this one, the YMCA, and the Red Cross. The town is hoping the camp remains after the war ends. It's such a source of pride for us Charlotteans."

"It seems to be larger than most of the other camps I've been to," I said.

Goldie shrugged. "Perhaps. Large enough that Daddy had work for almost a year helping with the wiring and all that," she said. She glanced at the clock again. "And speaking of my daddy, I've got to get going in fifteen minutes or so. I only came by to make sure your move hadn't set back your healing. Church begins in a few hours, and I've got to meet Guy and catch the streetcar downtown. I'd offer to take you with us, and home to dinner after, but Colonel Erickson said you're not allowed to leave camp. Must be because you're a star, and without the watchful eye of a chaperone, you'd be swarmed." She smiled.

"I suppose you're right," I said. "But don't worry about me. I'm only accustomed to going to church on occasion, anyway—for Christmas or Easter or somebody's baptism. My family never went regularly."

"I still feel bad leaving you here alone. I could help you dress before I go, though, if you'd like. It might make you feel more yourself. I know from my other patients that the flu causes weakness in the strangest places—the arms, the fingers. Some find it difficult to do up laces and buttons."

I opened my mouth to reply that wasn't necessary, but Goldie had already walked over to the armoire and opened it. She gasped as she looked through my costumes, as though she hadn't deposited those very gowns in that very armoire the night before.

"Jacques Doucet, Paul Poiret, Burberry, Worth, Jeanne Paquin, Chanel." She read each label and then sighed. "I suppose I didn't realize what I was handling last night since it was so late. You don't understand how much a girl dreams of a collection of gowns like yours."

"You're welcome to borrow any of them. Most were gifts from the designers hoping I'd wear them on press tours and such," I said. "We look to be about the same size."

She whirled on her heel.

"I couldn't," she said, then smiled. "On second thought, maybe I could. The Poiret jupe-culotte at the next army dance at Lakewood? Guy would swoon."

"It's yours, but understand, it's the girl who makes the dress, not the dress that makes the girl. That's what Jeanne always says, and it's the truth. I'll wear the Chanel today, the third dress from the left, the white one with the silver apron, capped sleeves, and pink swagged garlands on the skirt."

Goldie found the dress and held it up, inspecting it.

"A work of art," she said.

"Indeed. I'll need a combination for this, the one at the bottom of the stack of undergarments just there," I said, pointing to the first drawer on the left side of the armoire. It occurred to me just then that I was asking for the very combination I'd been posing in in the photograph Basil had. I suppose I always gravitated toward it—fine fashion stood the test of time. "And then my corset in pink brocade coutil. It's the first one in the second drawer." Goldie hung my dress on the armoire door and began to rifle through my collection of chemises, drawers, and combinations. It was clear, watching her, that her calling was truly nursing and not a ladies' maid. "It's the white combination, the one made of cotton lawn with Brussels lace trim." She found it and held it out to me. I took it from her hands and studied it for a moment. "It's been thirteen years since Kirkland Ratchford gave me this," I said. "It's old but looks practically new. Perhaps because it's handmade. I wore it once for Kirkland, then he proposed—which was quite a shock— and I declined. I thought to throw it away after that, but it was made specifically for me and fits perfectly."

Goldie's blush deepened the more I talked, and she tried her best to look away from me. I realized then that I'd misspoken. It wasn't that I necessarily hid my affairs—I wasn't green in the slightest in that arena since Caspar and had no issue being honest about it with certain people I trusted—but Kirkland was a producer and failed fashion designer, not a lover.

"Did you . . . well, did you love him? This . . . this Kirkland?" she asked. Her voice returned to the meek whisper she'd used when we first met.

I laughed and her eyes widened. Something about Goldie settled me entirely, made me want to let her in on my life and who I really was.

"No. I suppose he thought he loved me, but he didn't know me in the slightest. He's a producer friend of Lenor's who had wanted to get into fashion—until he let his finances get ahead of him. He was hoping to design a line of women's lingerie when he saw me in *Flowers of New York* and asked me to be his muse. I happened to be out of work for some time after *Flowers* and Father was too, so I agreed. We'd only spoken a few words at most before he proposed, and he's decades older. I thought he was joking. It was very odd."

"Oh, I see," Goldie said, her normal tone and color returning. "Forgive my naivety, Miss Calla. I've only traveled out of the state once, just to South Carolina, and before Guy I'd only ever kissed one boy." The color returned to her cheeks, lighter this time.

"You should never apologize for innocence, Goldie." She handed me the corset I'd requested, and I motioned for her to turn around as I took off my nightgown, then stepped into the combination. I loosened the back lacing on the corset and unfastened the busk. She was right about the flu's effect on extremities. It felt like I was moving my arms through maple sap. I positioned it as I wished and then fastened the busk again. "I don't regret my life, not for a second, but I grew up much too fast—not with regard to men but about everything else. That's the way it is on Broadway. Would you mind lacing? I could do it myself, but since you're here?"

Goldie shook her head and grasped the laces, pulling up until the corset was snug.

"Thank you," I said when she was finished. "I appreciate your help, but you'd better get going. I know you have somewhere to be." I smiled.

"How do you know how to dress yourself?" she asked. "And I suppose you know how to arrange your hair too, since you haven't asked me to help. I thought—"

I laughed until I nearly cried.

"I'm sorry," I said, realizing my chortling was terribly rude. She was asking sincerely. "I might be famous and paid very well for what I do, but I'm not Alva Vanderbilt, nor am I a member of the British peerage. Occasionally, on set or when I'm going to make some sort of appearance, I'll have my costume and hair arranged for me, but most days it's simply me and Mother. See? We're not so different at all, you and I."

Goldie laughed.

"Even so, we're from different worlds, Miss Calla." She paused. "Speaking of other worlds, I nearly forgot. I meant to . . . Well, perhaps I shouldn't ruin the surprise."

She grinned and glanced at the folded newspaper on my bedside table. I pulled my dress over my head and did up the sashes. It felt good to wear something other than a scratchy cotton hospital gown.

When I looked up, Goldie was still smiling at the paper.

"Is there some news you'd like me to be aware of?" I asked. "And please stop calling me Miss Calla. I know you're my nurse, but I consider you a friend too."

"I suppose I'll come right out and say it," she said excitedly. "There's a big article in today's paper about you staying at Camp Greene, but there's an even larger article about Lenor Felicity coming to visit camp on tour three weeks from Saturday. Isn't it exciting? Your second mother coming to visit?"

I hadn't moved, no one had struck me, yet it felt like the wind had been knocked out of me, like someone had pummeled me in the stomach. The echo of illness prickled my skin, and I leaned down, grasped my knees, and pinched my eyes shut. The news that she was coming here took me by surprise. Her presence would be salt massaged into my deepest wound.

"Are you all right?" Goldie asked, her voice strained as she hastened to my side.

"I-I'm fine," I sputtered. "It's just . . . Lenor. I pretend that she and I are thick as thieves to keep up appearances, but that's simply not the truth. In recent years, she's done some unfathomable things, and now she's taking advantage of my stopping here for a while to take over the rest of my tour." I looked at Goldie. "Please don't say a word of this to anyone." Goldie nodded, her eyes crinkled in shock. "I still mean to go to the front, to perform there, and Lenor knows why—she knows about Caspar's letter and my request to General Pershing. But she also knows that my touring has garnered press, and she'll do absolutely anything to stay center stage, even poach my dreams." I took a deep breath and righted, but the moment I did, tears sprung to my eyes.

"Why don't you go then?" Goldie asked, her voice soothing. "You could perform here one more week as an extra thank-you and then move on to the other camps." Her eyes were watery, matching my own. "It was kind of you to convince Colonel Erickson to grant permission for Guy to play alongside you—and he was thrilled beyond compare when I asked him on your behalf—but I'll see to it that he plays music more regularly regardless somehow."

It was clear that Goldie thought Guy's music was a way to settle him here, to keep him out of confinement. When Colonel Erickson had come by the hospital to retrieve my letter to my parents, I'd asked him to allow Guy clearance to rehearse with me daily and accompany my performances on the weekends and he'd immediately agreed, echoing the same sentiments Goldie hadn't been bold enough to say.

"I'm sorry," she said. "Forget I said anything about Guy."

I'd only remained silent because I didn't know what to say other than the truth—that I'd been forced to remain—but I couldn't say that.

"I want to go, desperately, but I'm needed here," I said. "Colonel Erickson spoke of such a high concentration of despondent men in camp that I can't well leave them to go overseas depressed. I owe them. I owe all of you." I started crying.

"If it makes you feel better, everyone is positively tickled you're here," Goldie said. "Camp Greene's very own star. Is there anything I can do to cheer your spirits?"

I wiped my cheeks with the back of my hand and sniffed.

Beside us the clock struck nine.

"No. You've done so much for me this past week—and this morning," I said, forcing a smile. "You'd better go. You'll be late for church."

Goldie smiled. "You're not rid of me yet, Miss—I mean, Calla. I've been ordered to watch over you for the next week at least."

She winked, walked toward me as if she was about to embrace me, thought better of it, and tipped her head my way.

"Don't let Lenor Felicity derail you. Or anybody else, for that matter," Goldie said. "I'll see you tomorrow."

CHAPTER 6

I sat in front of the mirror in my Chanel dress, arranging my hair in a whimsical chignon at the base of my neck, wondering why I'd bothered to dress at all. It wasn't like I could hitch a ride on a streetcar and explore the little downtown Charlotte that Mary Pickford had been so enchanted with. She'd gone on and on about the loveliness of a department store called Belk Brothers that she claimed had the most extraordinary selection of hats. I also couldn't skip down the road to the Lakewood amusement park and beg someone to fetch me a cotton candy the size of my head or an ice cream cone—butter pecan, if you please.

I sighed and glanced out the window. The men were all gone from the trenches, likely off to the shower huts and back to their tents to ready for church and a nice Sunday dinner with a local family who would undoubtedly take them home from worship. The *Charlotte Observer* had detailed nearly every meal in last Monday's paper. I wondered what I was missing at the McGanns'. Likely something delightful. Last week some lucky soldier, Private Otis Burke, was taken in by Charlotte mayor Frank McNinch's family and served a veritable feast. The paper had outlined it all: the sugar ham, mashed potatoes, buttered lima beans, biscuits, pound cake, strawberry pie, and fresh roasted coffee served with cream from local cows. My stomach growled just thinking of it.

"M-Miss Connolly?" came a voice from the other side of my bedroom door.

"Yes?" I called.

"This is Francis Kern, the Hostess House mother. I don't mean to intrude," the voice went on, "and I know you must be exhausted, but I thought I would extend an offer anyway." She paused. I could tell she was nervous. "There's a simple breakfast laid out for everyone downstairs before we all depart for church — just biscuits, fried eggs, and pancakes. Coffee too. If you're hungry, please join us, or I'm happy to bring up a tray."

"I'm starving," I nearly shouted and stood on wobbly legs to fetch my hat—a darling silver tam-o'-shanter—from the stack of hat boxes set next to the armoire.

"Oh!" Mrs. Kern said, sounding as though my acceptance had taken her completely off guard. "Wonderful! Perhaps you already know where the dining room is, but if you haven't been fully acquainted with the building yet, simply follow your nose and your ears down the stairs and through the reading room. We're all situated there."

I fixed my hat on my head and opened the door before she could depart.

"Hello," I said, smiling at her. She was at least seventy, slight and short, with the warmest face I'd ever seen—though at the moment her mouth hung open. "It's lovely to make your acquaintance, Mrs. Kern. I'm delighted you asked me to dine with you."

At once she came to, as if jolted from a dream, shook her head, and nodded resolutely as if she'd determined I was a typical woman, the same as her, and she'd treat me as such.

"It's our honor. Follow me," she said. She led me down the dim hallway, past four other rooms and paintings and photographs of what I assumed were scenes of Charlotte on the walls. "I saw you perform once," Mrs. Kern said ahead of me as we started down the stairs. "I've loved the stage for as long as I can recall. When I was a girl, I wanted to be on Broadway, before I realized it's a long way between here and New York City." She laughed and glanced back at me as we stepped into the foyer. An enormous mirror framed by gold filigree flanked one wall beside the front door and a little table with a sign, "Welcome to the YWCA Hostess House," occupied the other. From here I could smell the sweet maple syrup and the buttery, fresh biscuits and hear a symphony of voices talking and laughing.

"Indeed. It was a long way from Columbus, Ohio too. I got to Broadway by a stroke of dumb luck. That's the truth," I said.

"Not entirely," she countered, grinning. "You're talented. Incredibly so. My late husband, William, took me by rail to see your show *The Sunshine Brigade* at the Walnut Street Theatre in Philadelphia for our fortieth wedding anniversary. What a show it was!"

I laughed.

"That was a landmark tour for me," I said. *The Sunshine Brigade* had been one of the most challenging productions I'd ever been a part of. The premise was that a group of mistreated circus performers decide to quit their tour and venture out on their own, bringing their act to the ill and poor who needed sunshine the most. The songs were beautiful and touching, and the play was splendidly written by Arthur Haviland—one of the best playwrights in history—but I played a trapeze artist, and the acrobatics required of me were the most difficult I'd ever done. "I learned to love tumbling during that run," I went on. "That's why I do so much of it in my variety shows now."

Mrs. Kern led me through the room to the right of the entry. It boasted great wicker chairs and couches with thick chintz cushions, an open fireplace, and walls covered entirely by books.

"You're welcome to come down and choose a book to read whenever you'd like," she said. "Sometimes the girls will even gather here and read together."

"It's a lovely room," I said. "And I must admit that I didn't pack many books. I thought I'd be too busy hopping from camp to camp, but now . . ." I couldn't finish the sentence. My throat tightened. By now I would have been in Camp Bowie in Texas and then on to the Louisiana camps, nearly halfway through my tour. I would have been alight with purpose carried over from the thrill of the stage every night. But now I would have to learn to find that feeling in my idle time and in rehearsals until the stage could spark me to life again, until I was freed from this camp.

"Well, there's so much here. Nonfiction, poetry, classic literature, Bible commentaries, even romance novels." She whispered the last bit as though *romance* were a naughty sort of word.

"I'm a glutton for romance. It's all I read," I said. Perhaps I could fill my days with fantasy worlds. That could possibly work to lift my spirits. I'd enjoyed reading for most of my life. I'd only stopped, I realized, after Caspar died, when my mind couldn't concentrate on the written word. I'd have to try again. "When the real world is filled with death and calamity and war, it's vital to fill your mind with happy things, don't you think? Everybody lauds the other genres, and I do understand it, but in my mind, Austen, the Brontës, Wharton, and even the dime novelists like Bertha Clay, Geraldine Fleming, and Laura Jean Libbey are just as worthy of praise. They whisk us away from these hard days to bask in possibility and excitement. It's hopeful, life-sustaining work they're doing, if you think of it."

Mrs. Kern only smiled and nodded in reply. I suppose my response had been rather long-winded, but the idea that the enjoyment of only serious and depressing works should be celebrated struck a nerve. My shows had been deemed a "trip to the candy store" and "an intentional disregard of the horrors of war." Both articles had intended to discount me as a performer worth little, but I'd read the criticism with a smile. Happiness was my intention. I may never be lauded by history as Sarah Bernhardt would be, but I'd be remembered for my cheer, and that was what mattered.

Mrs. Kern pushed the carved mahogany pocket door open and the chatter that had, moments before, been a racket suddenly stopped at the sight of me. The long dining table was full of women who all looked to be Goldie's age. Nine sets of eyes stared, frozen. I waited for Mrs. Kern to introduce me, but I suppose she'd temporarily lost her faculties too, so I broke the silence.

"Hi, everyone. I'm—"

"Calla Connolly." A pregnant woman wearing a yellow Grecian dress breathed my name.

I smiled. "Yes, that's me," I said cheerily. "It's lovely to make your acquaintance. I'm going to be here for some time, so I'm looking forward to getting to know all of you."

"Why don't you introduce yourselves while I have Rose fetch Miss Connolly a plate," Mrs. Kern said, finding her voice. She turned to me. "Have a seat right here." She pulled a heavy armchair at the head of the table out for me, and I sat down. The arms were made of thick walnut, carved intricately in a vine pattern. Though there was no spotlight here, I felt much like I was on display.

"I'm thrilled to meet you. I'm so glad you're recovered from the horrible flu that is claiming so many," the pregnant woman said. "And on a happier note, I'm very fond of your songs." She sat on the far end of the table, nearest the windows. "I'm Wendy, Wendy Wentworth from Portland, Maine. My husband, William, has been here since October, and I decided to come down last month so that he can meet his baby before he's deployed. There are five of us in similar spots."

Soft laughter came from the other pregnant girls scattered about the table.

"Nice to meet you, Wendy," I said. She grinned and went back to eating her pancakes while the other girls—Ruthie Pierce from Stowe, Vermont; Anna Regan from Concord, New Hampshire; Helen Clark from Boston; Mary Hines from New Haven, Connecticut; Dorothy Lee from Providence, Rhode Island; Margaret Baker from Bangor, Maine; Marie Lowder from Burlington, Vermont; and Elizabeth Barber from Worcester, Massachusetts—introduced themselves.

By the time Rose, a woman who could have been Mrs. Kern's twin and perhaps was, set my plate in front of me, I was famished.

I poured the maple syrup atop my warm pancakes and breathed in the steam before I cut them.

"Do you know Harold Lockwood, Miss Connolly?" Elizabeth asked abruptly. She was a natural redhead with the most delicate pale skin I'd ever seen. She blushed when she asked the question, then busied herself with her linen napkin.

"I suppose I do, but not well enough to write his mother," I said, laughing. "We were in a vaudeville variety show around twelve years ago with—"

"Lenor Felicity," Dorothy squeaked. "Did you see the news? She's coming to Camp Greene too. It's practically Broadway here."

The relative merriment of the later morning had eclipsed my anger and melancholy over the news of Lenor's expanded tour, but the feeling boiled up again, this time in a terrible rage I couldn't hold in. I swallowed a bite of pancake and forced myself to take a deep breath before saying something I'd regret. I pasted on a smile and hoped they wouldn't see through it.

"Yes, I did see that she was coming for a visit," I said finally.

"She's Mother's favorite, while you've always been mine," Marie said. "Do you hear that often? That you're this generation's Lenor Felicity?" Her doe eyes widened at something behind me, and the table silenced the same way it had when I'd entered the room. I went on eating my pancakes. Given recent developments, it wouldn't surprise me at all if Lenor had decided to pop by for a quick visit.

Mrs. Kern pushed through the swinging door from the kitchen with cups of coffee, then stopped abruptly and straightened.

"Colonel Erickson," she said, her voice flustered as it had been earlier. "To what do we owe the pleasure?"

I set my fork down with a clatter, noticing the girls' cheeks flush at the sight of him. I didn't bother to turn around, but instead took a sip of my coffee, watching the way the girls quickly looked away. It occurred to me then that I'd never seen him without a hospital mask covering the bottom half of his face, except when he'd made the announcement from the back of the theatre while I was on-stage. My recollections of that night were still quite hazy, and he'd been a long distance away. Perhaps it wasn't only his height and stature alone that arrested rooms.

"You're all near set to depart for church, I'm sure. I'm here to collect Miss Connolly. She'll be attending church with me," he said. His voice was gruff, and when I turned around to retort that I had no interest in going anywhere with him, I started at the sight. I'd seen Douglas Fairbanks and Wallace "Wild" Reid, Cullen Landis and Francis Bushman, the men whose presence could make the most sensible of women forget themselves, and yet all of them paled in comparison to the exquisiteness of Colonel Erickson. It took me a moment to comprehend it—those of us in show business were picked apart for our features, and his were the ideal combination: low dark brows, light green eyes, the perfect nose, full lips, and a square jaw. Had he possessed acting skills, he could have played any sort of role—a swashbuckler or a Casanova. He was wearing his uniform as usual, though with the high officer's boots this time.

"I don't wish to go," I said, collecting myself. Had he not made it clear that he thought my mission a frivolous one? Had his misplaced blame that morning in the hospital not have been the sole reason I was trapped here, I might have obliged. I might also have flirted. But since he was an enemy of my cause, I found no reason to comply. "I've only taken a few bites of my breakfast." I nodded to my plate and he surveyed it.

"Looks like another delicious meal, Miss Rose," he said loudly. A voice from the kitchen hollered back a word of thanks. "I'm happy to wait for you to finish, Miss Connolly," he said, turning his attention back to me, "but as we agreed when we spoke in the hospital, you aren't to be left alone. For your own safety," he amended. "And all of these women here are going to be departing in a matter of half an hour for the streetcar station to catch the trolley downtown."

I'd forgotten I was a prisoner.

"Could she attend services with us if she prefers?" Wendy asked.

"Afraid not," he said matter-of-factly.

Of course I couldn't. The army couldn't risk my spreading rumors outside of camp—or even the possibility that I'd make a run for it if they left me here unattended—although both options were ridiculous. If they'd only consider how desperate I was to make a good impression on General Pershing, the army would feel fully confident to let me do whatever I good and well pleased.

"I'll wait outside in the auto. We'll be late if we don't depart in ten minutes," he said, then turned on his heel, leaving the other girls gawking at his back.

CHAPTER 7

The wind threatened to yank the pins from my hair and my hat from my head. I grasped the top of the tam-o'-shanter and stared out at the farmland. Rows of baby tobacco leaves rustled in the cool May breeze.

"I suppose I shouldn't have made the decision to ride open air," Colonel Erickson shouted. "I didn't consider your hat. I apologize."

Colonel Erickson's auto was a Packard Twin Six touring of a few years age. The only reason I knew was because Father had one almost exactly like it, except Colonel Erickson's was black on the nose and white on the body instead of Father's all black.

"It's all right. I'm enjoying the ride," I said honestly. Father always kept his auto closed and it reeked of gasoline, oil, hot water, and cigar smoke. This was a welcome change. I'd thought to be snide the whole trip, but what was the use? I was stuck with him—possibly for months—and Mother always told me that you attracted more bees with honey than vinegar. "I'm a little disappointed that we won't be driving through town, though. It seems the place to be." There had been a huge crush of people at the streetcar station when we'd driven out of camp, all headed downtown to a variety of churches whose names began with First: First Presbyterian, First Baptist, First Methodist. What a proud moment it must have been for the founders of those storied sanctuaries when they were able to erect their signs, forever staking claim to the First. I wondered if there were Second churches and whether those congregations felt slighted.

"Most go down there with the hope of a meal afterward," he said, laughing.

"I don't blame them at all. Have you read the menus from some of these Sunday lunches? They're published in the paper. I'd give my right arm to be invited."

"They only write up the highlights. Last week one of our men came home from a dinner consisting of grits and baked hog livers."

I shook my head. "I'd have to excuse myself. I could endure the livers, I suppose, but the grits?"

"Grits are about the best we've got down here. I used to dream about them when I was—" He stopped short, biting back the rest of the sentence as he turned onto a tree-lined dirt road. Branches canopied the drive, and ahead several families walked together, Black and white. I was refreshed to see this country road operated much the same way as a New York City street: there were always certain neighborhoods that became predominantly one skin color, but the majority of the spaces I occupied were awash with different colors and different accents.

"Good morning, Jesse!" An older man dressed in a suit, holding the hand of a little boy, waved at Colonel Erickson, and he waved back. "Hey, is that—" he started when his gaze turned to me, but was interrupted by Colonel Erickson's return greeting.

"Morning, David."

"Jesse," I said, turning the name over in my mind as I looked at him. "I suppose you look like a Jesse. Though I thought you'd be named something else—like Archibald or Barrington, perhaps even Kensington. Something very serious and proper."

He glanced at me, his nose crinkling, as a small white church came into view. The church bells tolled. I'd made us late. Even so, there were others still filing in.

"It's Colonel Erickson, and you have an interesting perception of me."

"Yet it's exactly correct. It has to be. I know I'm not quite as popular as Mary Pickford or the like, but nearly so, and most people know at least one of my songs. You claim you know none. Which leads me to believe that you, a man whose name should have been Barrington, only listen to symphonies. You're a musical purist."

Laughter burst from his mouth despite his effort to control it.

"Just because I'm not familiar with your music doesn't mean I don't like popular songs. There have been times in my life that I haven't had access to a radio or any entertainment," he said.

He turned the wheel and stopped the auto next to an old Ford. Then he opened his door and walked around to mine, clicked it ajar, and held out his hand to help me down. I took it and stepped onto the dusty clay in the small channel of space between his auto and the Ford. I could smell Palmolive soap on his skin, feel the warmth of his chest against my arm, and immediately let his hand go.

He walked beside me as we started toward the open doors of the church. Inside, the organist was playing a hymn that seemed familiar but that I couldn't quite place. "You must think life would be boring without entertainment, but I didn't mind." He paused. "As I've said before, when you've seen what I've seen, Miss Connolly, you understand that almost nothing is more important than fighting for peace, for what is right, and any distraction from that goal is, quite honestly, unbearable."

Ordinarily I would have expressed my disagreement, but something stilled my spirit. I swallowed, recalling what Goldie had said about him, that he'd served in Mexico and Panama and on the front with the French, that he'd seen the same horrors Caspar had seen.

"Come on. We're in the third pew," he whispered as we walked through the doors.

Despite its clear age, the church smelled like new lumber and felt cool, much like a cavern. I followed Colonel Erickson past a series of stained glass windows depicting Jesus's miracles and past congregants who stopped singing and stared when they saw me. We filed into the end of the pew next to a sizable man with gray hair and a pretty woman possibly ten years my senior. They were clearly a couple. She leaned into him and held his hand.

After the first hymn was over, the church began to hum with whispers. It became so loud that the pastor, who looked to be at least ninety, clapped his open palm on the pulpit. When the church silenced again, he motioned for the organist seated somewhere behind him to continue playing.

"We'll need to leave right after the benediction or you'll be swallowed up," Colonel Erickson whispered to me.

I nodded. This hymn was one I'd heard before, from Easter services, "Fairest Lord Jesus," and as I sang, my heart swelled with the music. On the second verse, when harmony was encouraged, I heard a chorus of voices coming from somewhere behind and above me. I looked back, shocked to find the balcony of the church full of Black congregants while the floor was only occupied by whites. Even here, in worship, Black people were assigned a different space. It seemed so wrong, this separation, especially in a place where we were taught that God valued all human life equally.

I settled onto the red velvet pew cushion next to Colonel Erickson when the hymn was over and tried to focus. The pastor read a passage from 1 Peter, "'Each of you should use whatever gift you have received to serve others,'" and then spent the next hour emphasizing that a God-given gift wasted was a terrible thing, that God used our gifts to uplift the depressed, the lost, the weak. By the time he was finished, my body felt as though it had been set ablaze. I glared at Colonel Erickson, my previous commitment to pleasantries now tossed aside. Not only was his wiring General Dickman to tell him of what I'd overheard a terrible interference, General Pershing's orders had contained and stifled my gift, a gift absolutely needed both at other camps and at the front. I was sure I was meant to hear the sermon and that it meant I was to keep fighting—for the sake of my own soul's health, but primarily for the betterment of others.

The moment the benediction was given, I pushed past Colonel Erickson and practically fled up the aisle toward the door. My eyes teared and my heart pounded so hard I was sure it would seize. I heard my name being called by a variety of voices, none louder than Colonel Erickson's, whose bark floated above the others but whose person had been detained by the rest of the congregants in no hurry to depart so quickly.

I walked out of the church and into the quiet of the day, where the cicadas chirped and the birds called, but the day's peace did nothing to calm me. As I passed the final window, I saw Colonel Erickson embrace the older man who'd been seated beside us and ignore the friendly advances of the woman as she leaned to embrace him too. The older man's face materialized in my mind as I retreated toward the auto. He had the same frame, the same square set to his jaw as General Erickson. It had to be his father. But the woman, though she was possibly the man's wife, was certainly not his mother. She was much too young.

Voices sounded behind me and I hastened into the pine forest, following a worn path beside the few parked autos. I breathed deeply, trying to calm down. I attempted to name what I smelled—new grass, woodsmoke from far away, the loamy notes from the nearby river—but it didn't work. I felt bad for running away from everyone. Ordinarily I adored meeting people who loved my shows or my music, but fury still pulsed in my temples and sweat dampened my scalp and moistened my palms. In this state, I could speak out of turn, direct my anger where it wasn't meant to be.

The pines cleared and I stood at the edge of where the land dipped down a gradual clay bank to a full river. A small tree, roots and all, floated along, pushed farther away from wherever it had originated, wherever it belonged, by the force of gurgling rapids that supposed they had the right to control anything that fell into its depths. I was the tree, and the army, and Colonel Erickson, the rapids.

I whirled away from the view, unable to look at anything that stole others' gifts. If the water hadn't risen, the tree would have remained rooted in its purpose, its shade a favor to many. I walked back through the pines, glad to see that the churchgoers had dissipated as I neared. My name was called in Colonel Erickson's deep tone and the sound of it was like a match strike. I had no doubt he'd been looking for me these past minutes, but I hardly cared if he was worried. I emerged from the forest just as the pastor shut the church doors. Colonel Erickson stood, his hat in his hands, next to the pastor. They both turned around after the church was secured by an ancient skeleton key, and Colonel Erickson saw me.

"Where have you been?" he charged. His hands were balled into fists and his eyes tapered in a stern glare. The pastor clapped him on the back and nodded my way, then ambled back down the dirt road with his cane.

My body prickled and my face felt hot. I glanced around, and seeing that we were alone, I let my anger spill out unbidden.

"You ruined everything." My body pitched forward and I thought I might fall, but I steadied myself. "Everything," I said again. "I can't stay here. I am meant to—destined to—go to the front, but it seems that all is lost. I can't prove my worth to General Pershing when I am stuck here, and now Lenor Felicity is taking my tour, a woman who has done egregious things to me and doesn't give a fig for the soldiers except for the fame she'll get from entertaining them." I took a heaving breath, the aftereffects of flu stifling the depth of it. I knew I shouldn't have said anything about Lenor, but it was likely Colonel Erickson only vaguely knew of her too. "You heard the sermon yourself. If I'm not using my gifts for others, for those who need it the most, for those who are imminently facing death, I am doing nothing. I understand that all I have is my voice and my smile, but I want to use them. What good am I here?" The question ended in a shout, my voice ricocheting through the trees, echoing in the little clearing where the church resided.

"Has it ever occurred to you that I'm not there either? I'd give anything," he roared back, his gaze set on mine, his words low and devastating, like cannon fire. He paced toward me. "I was there, at the front in France. I was there for months. I've seen it. Men are dying minute by minute and the Allies need help. I am willing, I am able, and I am here instead, forced to stay behind as others deploy." The veins in his neck bulged and he stopped where he was, feet from where I stood.

"What happened?" The sudden realization that we wanted desperately to be in the same place calmed me, despite his hand in my plight.

"Pershing believes I'm insubordinate," he said. His jaw was gripped, his eyes glassy with fury.

"Why would he think that?" I asked.

He hesitated, his gaze still exhibiting rage. "Because I came to the aid of our allies before my country was ready. To do so indicates that I act on behalf of my own convictions instead of heeding the wisdom and interests of the United States first. Those were his exact words," he said.

"Did you go to France specifically to help the war effort?" I asked. As valiant as it seemed to cross the ocean to join a cause such as the one we were fighting now, I supposed I could understand that it might seem to the army that he'd been hasty to go ahead without them.

"No, and they know that. As I told you before, my mother was French. She moved back to Paris when my father had an affair." He said the words plainly, as I would have said them, as though these things were the consequence of life and not the societal scandal they were. "I decided to join her to study architecture after years of army service at the Mexican border and in Panama. Watching the canal being built only encouraged the interest in design and construction I'd had since I was young." He paused.

"I'd been living there for almost two years and had just realized architecture wasn't what I wanted to do after all when France entered the war. Nearly all of our friends and neighbors enlisted. It felt wrong to sit by and do nothing, especially because I'm a trained officer. So I enlisted. Mother cautioned me against it— for this very reason, actually—but I did it anyway." He paused again.

"They should understand why you did what you did," I said. "I was there during the call to arms in England. It was impossible to ignore. I imagine it was the same in France. To suppose you'd sit by and watch the other men risk their lives to defend a country you considered a second home, the native country of your mother, is ludicrous."

Colonel Erickson shrugged. "Yet they don't understand. They told me I should have come back to America when France entered the war and waited for instruction."

"Why did you return?" I asked.

His face paled and he shoved his hands in his pockets. At first I thought he might not answer.

"I didn't intend to. My division, the Seventy-Second, was called into battle first at Verdun. We were in a stalemate with the Germans, pushing hard but slowly against their line. I was leading a regiment of riflemen equipped with bayonets. At one point we came up against some Germans and the men charged before I gave the order. We were taken in a bad way. Some of our rifles didn't fire, so we were forced to use brute force. I knew my men were suffering, but I didn't realize how severely until it was over. I lost eight hundred and thirteen men that day."

He looked down at his boots. "I was injured as well. My leg was sliced from the hip to the ankle. I nearly lost it. I recall lying there in the trenches wondering if I was going to live, wondering if I wanted to live after what I'd seen." He shook his head. "I was taken to a military hospital in Paris, and when I was released, I found out that my mother had died while I was away. It was a quick illness, and the news was devastating."

I looked at him and my eyes teared. There was a deep sorrow in the tone of his voice, and his countenance appeared as though he'd only just lost her. I thought of my own mother, how horrible it would be if I came home to find her gone, and that on top of losing so many of his men. I didn't know how he stood, how he lived. The strength to breathe must have been something of a miracle.

"I can't imagine the heartache," I said softly.

"She'd written me a letter," he said, his eyes still fixed on the ground as though he hadn't heard me. "She said she was proud of me. She said that fighting for justice was the honorable thing to do and that my mission in this life was to continue toward it until my final breath—whether that was tomorrow or in eighty years." He looked at me. I wiped my eyes. "I got a letter in the mail the next week from my sister. She said my father was ailing and asked that I return home. I didn't want to. I'd planned to reenlist when my injuries healed. I hadn't spoken to my father since the affair, before I left for West Point, but I came home for her. She seemed desperate. By the time I arrived, my father had recovered."

"Do you suppose your sister wrote to you for another reason?" I asked.

"No. He'd actually been ill, some localized infection that had spread. But once I was here, I wasn't allowed to go back. I started working at the mill with my sister, and then, when America entered the war, I enlisted with the army. I told the officer who signed my enlistment papers about my experience in France. I thought it might be helpful, but then I was contacted by General Liggett. He scolded me, by order of General Pershing, in the manner in which I just told you. Instead of being dispatched overseas like I'd hoped, I was appointed here, to my hometown, to help a group of Frenchmen construct accurate drilling trenches at Camp Greene."

He cleared his throat and looked over my shoulder at the sliver of river that could be seen between the curtain of pine trees. "I thought that after I helped here I'd command a regiment on the front, but General Pershing made it clear that even after the camp trenches were complete, he planned to test my ability to take orders before I'd be allowed to go overseas. He assigned me to lead and train the 163rd Infantry Regiment at Camp Greene, and I assumed I'd be sent over to France with them. But when orders came for their deployment in November, I was told I had to stay and was reassigned to a regiment of General Alexander's Sixth Brigade. But now he's gone and I'm responsible for yet another group of men that could face—"

Colonel Erickson stopped abruptly and looked at me.

I knew what he'd stopped short of saying—that he was once again responsible for a regiment that would sustain a large number of casualties like the one he'd led in France.

"It's unfair to keep you from the front. If anyone knows the way to fight this, it's you," I said. "In a small way, we've been dealt the same hand, you and I."

His face hardened.

"I don't know what it's like to lead men into battle, to face the Huns and watch them kill your men, but I do know what it's like to receive desperate letters from the front begging for hope, begging for you." I choked out the last word and his countenance eased. "Just as you weren't being insubordinate in your desire to fight for peace, I'm innocent too. I know nothing of the mission you spoke to General Alexander about except for its danger. I don't even know the regiment."

"Perhaps you think you don't know anything important, but you do. If you tell someone you heard one of the regiments is slated for a dangerous mission, the news would annihilate the men's spirits. They would constantly wonder if the regiment is theirs. Surely you understand that."

"Surely you understand how desperately I want to get to the front. Why would I risk that to spread rumors about things I don't fully understand?" I asked, the earlier edge to my voice returning.

"You wouldn't mean to, I know that for certain," he said.

He sighed and started walking toward the Packard. I followed. He opened the door to the auto and helped me inside. When his fingers touched mine, he looked at me, and for a moment, I saw the man behind the uniform, the man, who, if this were another time, would likely be occupied by commerce and family and, at times, even entertainment.

"Maybe Pershing already knew the sorts of things I'm just discovering about you or had at least heard of the kind of person you are. You form attachments to people easily, Miss Connolly. It is part of your charm. And I'm afraid that makes you even more likely to warn a person of danger, even if you don't know the whole of it." His voice was low, and he didn't take his gaze from mine. I thought of the girls at the Hostess House, the men they knew as husbands and fiancés and brothers first, not soldiers. I

knew Colonel Erickson was right, that warning anyone of a gen-
eralization when there were sixty thousand soldiers living in a
confined space would only cause hysteria. But I wondered, if I
knew of the particular regiment, would I feel as though it were
my duty to warn them that their men may never come home, even
if it jeopardized everything I wanted? Something stirred in my
stomach, a crushing feeling in my spirit, and I knew the answer: I
would.

"Have you chosen the men? Do you know how many will be
included in this mission?" I asked. He let my hand go and gently
closed my door.

"I don't. A thousand or more, likely. And, no, I didn't have to
choose the men. I wired General Dickman back in Washington
and told him that I couldn't in good faith select any men to participate in this likely death sentence. I knew refusing might be another
strike against me, but I couldn't do it. Thankfully, he seemed to
understand and instructed me to send him the psychological reports
and the physical aptitude results. He said he would have his staff
choose on my behalf. I haven't received his orders yet." He stepped
into the auto, closed his door, and started the engine. "It will still
be an incredible burden to know those assigned, especially because,
though I'm training them along with the rest of the brigade, I
doubt I'll be allowed to go to the front with them. Then again,
I've been studying the war's progress closely. There's always the
chance the regiment's task could change if our intelligence is
wrong and Ludendorff is planning to achieve victory another
way. In that case, the regiment's danger would be the same as
the rest."

He paused and glanced at me as we followed the canopied road
back to the stretch of farmland that led to Camp Greene. "If I were
over there, I'd have a better understanding of the circumstances.
There is a tone of voice, a feel in the air, when you're on the ground
that no set of facts on paper can tell you."

We were silent for a while, and I watched the tobacco leaves dip
and rise in the fields. The sun washed them gold. I looked away for

a moment as the auto went around a sharp turn and noticed Colonel Erickson's hands were gripped so hard to the steering wheel, his knuckles were white. He was as desperate to be over there as I was.

"Is there anything I can do to help hurry your deployment?" I asked. "I know I'm just an entertainer, but I *am* well connected, and in some spheres my opinion holds weight. Perhaps I could write someone influential and have them convince General Pershing you're more than ready to go to France. Surely there's a way we can help each other find our way to the front."

"No," he said. He laughed and shook his head. "I appreciate the offer, but I doubt that anyone, even God himself, could convince Pershing I'm ready. With regard to you going to the front, I know why you want to go, but I wouldn't support you going there—even if I thought the men would benefit from the distraction of your shows."

"How could you not understand by now? You read Basil's letter. You heard the same sermon I did," I said, my voice rising.

We veered around another corner. The camp entrance and headquarters—a white colonial farmhouse formerly occupied by the Dowd family—loomed ahead.

"They need cheer at the front, where they're terrified the most," I went on. "For a man who's been there—"

"That's right," he countered gruffly, "I've been there. It's hell on earth. Men don't even look like men anymore. They're torn limb from limb; they're mutilated body and soul. Once you encounter it, you won't be the same. You won't be singing your cheery songs. You'll be singing funeral marches."

The auto skirted into the narrow drive that led past the Dowd Headquarters through camp.

"Colonel Erickson! Colonel! Thank goodness you're back." A private rushed up to the auto. His hair was soaked through, as were his fatigues.

Colonel Erickson pumped the brakes too hard and I jerked forward.

"I'm sorry," he said, reaching a hand out to steady me. "What is it, Private?" he asked, turning to the young man.

"Well, sir. There's a bit of a problem. You see, some of the men were bored—it being Sunday and all—and they've broken into Lakewood Park and are enjoying some of the amusements."

I laughed, and both men turned to stare.

"I'll take care of it right away, Private," he said.

"Yes, you should go see what that is about and shut it down immediately," I said, sobering.

"We will do just that," Colonel Erickson said and stomped on the gas.

CHAPTER 8

T he calliope music met my ears the moment we turned on Tuckaseegee Road. It was muted at first, but the closer we got to the entrance of Lakewood Park, the louder it became. "They're not even trying to hide it," Colonel Erickson said as he turned the auto onto the gravel drive. "They know they're going to be punished, a week in confinement, and they don't care." He struck the steering wheel. "What sort of army will we be taking over there? There is no regard for authority. None." We drove past the entrance sign and the silent trolley station, following the road through the great wash of spring flowers I'd admired the night before. The view in the dim light had been no match for the veritable rainbow of colors highlighted by the sunshine. I didn't know how to respond. He was right, and yet I felt deeply for the men who'd so desperately needed joy that they'd broken into an amusement park.

I took a deep breath, expecting sweet florals and buttery popcorn, but the popcorn wasn't to be.

I sighed and pushed back against the seat as we went through the wrought iron gate, past the empty ticket huts. The lake I'd seen on my midnight ride from the hospital to the Hostess House glittered in front of us. In the center spouted a huge geyser water feature.

"What is it?" Colonel Erickson asked.

"I was hoping there'd be popcorn," I said.

He laughed despite his clear anger at the disobedience he was tasked with correcting.

"Don't count it out just yet. They've figured out how to turn on the carousel, and I'm sure the roller coaster too. I don't think a popcorn machine would be any match for them."

To the left, a sign read "Zoo." Beneath it, labels with arrows pointed down various walking paths to monkeys, reindeer, black bear, ostriches, and zebra cow.

"What in the world is a zebra cow?" I asked as Colonel Erickson turned the auto in the opposite direction, toward the expansive pavilion jutting out into the lake.

Colonel Erickson made a dismissive sound and shook his head.

"It was all over the papers when the park bought it—a zebra cow, a rare, exotic species. It turns out that the carnival man the owner got it from had simply painted zebra stripes on the animal and convinced him that the cow was a genetic anomaly. How Mr. Cromwell believed the story, I'll never know. Some of the residents still insist it's real."

"How do you know it's not?" I asked.

He looked at me. "Because my father owns the hardware store where he's been buying the touch-up paint," he said, grinning. "They have to paint that cow every week."

"I'm sorry you know the truth. It's fun to believe in wonder now and again, don't you think? You haven't ruined it for everyone else, have you? And think of that poor cow if the rest of the town found out. She could go from star of the show to steak in moments."

The cow's possible demise was unsettling. It reminded me of mine. Especially with Lenor poking around.

"It's fun until you realize that the magic you've believed in all along is nothing but a lie," he said. "It's easier to face the reality of the world—the horror and the beauty—if you haven't been fed fantasies. It allows a person to marvel at real, honest-to-goodness loveliness rather than letting such things pale in comparison to gilded falsehoods. Perhaps that's the root of why I'm having trouble with your tour. I know you mean well and your heart is in the right place, but you appear on the stage like a fantasy, your happy songs suggesting that everything isn't as dire as it seems, but it is. The men have to understand that."

My hands balled, but I focused instead on the carousel music piping "Sidewalks of New York" as Colonel Erickson steered the auto toward a concrete tunnel that led to the amusements, according to the sign.

"As I said in the hospital, my shows are simply meant to lift a soldier's spirits," I said evenly. "They hardly have the power to make them forget that they're training to fight. If they did, General Pershing wouldn't have allowed my tour in the first place." I breathed and forced myself to calm. "And as much as I wish I were some sort of fantastical creature, I'm not. I'm just a red-blooded American girl from Ohio who likes to sing and dance and wants to make the soldiers smile so they won't lose hope," I said as the darkness and quiet enveloped us. There was a metallic smell to the air, and from time to time, droplets of water fell on my shoulders.

"That's where you're wrong," he said. His shoulder brushed mine and I scooted farther into my seat. "You *are* a fantasy. You may not be a painted cow or a fairy, but you're a fantasy all the same. Calla Connolly, the star, is the epitome of what a man desires and will never have, and what a woman wants to be. In every photo and in every role she is beautiful and confident, selling the idea that everything will turn out okay."

"But that's not who I really am. That Calla Connolly is only a character I play."

"I know. You're vulnerable and grieving. Sometimes you're angry and comical at the same time. You're more—"

The auto cleared the tunnel and the darkness that had allowed such honesty suddenly gave way to the sunlight. It dappled down through the trees onto his face. I wanted him to continue, for him to tell me exactly what he thought of me, but he didn't. The calliope was now playing "Turkey in the Straw," another carousel favorite, and I hummed along to break the silence.

"We'll come upon them in a few moments, just beyond this grove of pines. Please don't say anything while I deal with them," he said. "Remember, these men are in grave violation of conduct rules."

"Oh. That's too bad. I was hoping to reward them by offering to get the zebra cow out of its pen and do acrobatics atop it while singing along to whatever the calliope plays."

Colonel Erickson eyed me, his countenance indicating he thought me absolutely irritating, but he didn't bother to reply. At least he understood that I was joking, though given any other circumstance, I'd certainly put on a little show for the gents.

The trees cleared. An expansive whitewashed building was to my right—a movie house, apparently—and the carousel, void of any men at all, was going round and round beside it. In front of us, the Ferris wheel loomed, and the roller coaster before it. I could hear the whine and scrape of the metal tracks and see the slight shift of the wooden scaffolding as the cab made its way around a curve and then, in a few moments more, crested the highest hill.

Colonel Erickson stopped the auto as the four men on the roller coaster simultaneously plunged down the coaster's drop and noticed his presence. The blanched faces and complete lack of screams that typically accompanied such an activity were a clear enough indication that they knew they were in trouble.

"Stay here," he said to me as he got out of the auto and paced across the gravel expanse to a little white shed with a green roof situated up two flights of stairs that housed the coaster's controls and the docking and embarking of the cabs.

I got out of the auto anyway and stood beside it, watching the hand-painted horses and giraffes and dogs and cats leap and run as the carousel twirled.

I heard commotion from the shed, and though I knew I should remain where I was, I crept closer to the entrance to the roller coaster. The words *The Big Dipper* were painted in a cursive hand right below the roofline of the little structure. A red cab embarked, empty, on the voyage up a small hill. The tick-tick-ticking of the track made my heart race. I hadn't been on a roller coaster since my parents had taken me to visit Rye Playland the first summer we lived in New York, but I could still feel the weightless sensation in the pit of my stomach. I wanted desperately to ride it.

I climbed the stairs, and when I reached the platform, the five men sitting on the waiting benches facing the controls and a stern-faced Colonel Erickson turned toward me.

"I asked you to stay in the auto."

"Yes, I know, but I'm not here to disturb you. I simply wanted to watch the cab make its way around the track." I looked toward the coaster and away from the men before Colonel Erickson could erupt.

"As I was saying, I'll let General Cameron know I recommend that each of you receive a week in confinement, which includes labor duties on top of your regular drills. This week the refuse from the latrines needs to be burned," he said. "You'll enjoy grits and a bit of ham hock for each meal."

I scrunched my nose. That sounded like the worst sort of punishment.

"Aw, Jesse, I mean, Colonel Erickson," one of the men said. "We were just trying to have a little fun. General Cameron told us last week that our division is likely to be called to France soon, and we were sitting around in our tent with nothing to do but think of our own death. Hell, our view from our tent is the trenches."

"There ain't any Huns charging these, though, Mac," another man said.

"If you'd been at church, you wouldn't have been thinking of ways to get into trouble," Colonel Erickson barked.

I wondered how much of his tone had to do with his anger over their mischief or the reminder that he'd have to watch more men head to the front while he remained at camp.

"This is the reason the army insists on sending men away from home to train," he went on. "If it hadn't been for me begging General Alexander for an exception for you—"

"I would have been away when my father died. Yes, I know I am in debt to you for keeping me here," the man named Mac said.

He was speaking to Colonel Erickson as though they were related. Perhaps they were.

"Do the five of you understand that when you're faced with the front, which you will be shortly, any sort of disobedience is likely to get you killed or endanger thousands of others? If you can't follow the basic rules here, how do you suppose you'll fare over there?"

No one said anything, and the cab whooshed past on one of its final turns.

"When I was in France, I had one man climb out of the trench only two or three minutes before I was going to make the call, but those minutes mattered. He thought the enemy was closing in—which they weren't—and he was afraid of being ambushed. My men followed him. One after the other. Some were trying to stop the man in front of him; some thought, mistakenly, that I'd made the call and that they were following orders. Despite my screams, they went out anyway. I lost over eight hundred men that day. Only one hundred and thirty-one came back."

"I'm awfully sorry to hear that, Colonel, but there's no way I'm going out on my own over there," another man said.

"We all know how serious it is. That's all anybody talks about," Mac said.

I watched the cab idle in front of me and thought about climbing aboard, but there was no one at the controls. I recalled Goldie telling me about others getting stuck on the Ferris wheel and decided against it. The empty cab began its ascent again.

"I think about my death nearly every second. Am I going to be shot or slain with a bayonet? Am I going to be blasted away or flattened by an airman?" Mac continued.

His last comment made my skin flush cold and I gripped the rail in front of me. Caspar's body had never been found. There had been so much cannon fire that day that the men in his regiment assumed it had been obliterated. Yet the field in which he'd landed had been covered in enemy troops. Had he fallen atop another soldier?

"I'm not going to forget that I'm about to face death. But I've got to sometimes." Mac paused. "Everybody else was at church and we were just sitting around talking when Edgar here said he wished we could ride the Dipper today. That when he's zooming around in the sky, he's not able to think about being shipped off. I know I shouldn't have done it, but I worked here for years, Jesse, I mean, Colonel Erickson. And I never once took as much as a kernel of popcorn without paying my penny, but we were all in a bad way and I remembered how to switch on the controls and I remembered how to run the coaster and the carousel."

"I'm sorry you were having a hard day, but to break into Lakewood and—"

"We all find ways to reckon with our reality. Even you. With respect, Colonel, you've spent your day with Calla Connolly. We all know your mind hasn't been on the war," Mac went on.

The other boys started laughing and I felt the air shift. Regardless of whether or not what they said was true, Colonel Erickson deserved a certain level of respect. My presence, after he'd asked me to remain in the auto, was simply muddling things.

"That's—" he started, his voice stern, but I turned and interrupted him.

"Actually, he's been ordered to show me around," I said. "It's the last thing he wants to do. I don't believe Colonel Erickson is at all impressed by me or swayed from his tireless devotion to the war effort—even on his days off—in my presence. In fact, I'd say I'm more of a nuisance to him than anything else. He doesn't even know one of my songs."

"How is that possible?" Mac countered, staring at Colonel Erickson. Mac was a man of medium everything—medium height, medium build, moderately attractive. Clearly ten or more years younger than Colonel Erickson and me, he still had a baby face. It amazed me how many soldiers were barely older than children. "Uncle Gerald has at least five of her records."

"You know I don't visit," Colonel Erickson said gruffly, then turned to me. "This rabble-rouser is my cousin." He nodded toward Mac and then sighed. "All right, gents. It's time to reckon with today's infraction. Mac, you'll switch off the coaster and the carousel, and then you'll all line up behind my auto and march behind us to the confinement quarters."

I eyed the roller coaster longingly.

"You should at least offer Miss Connolly a ride before I turn it off," Mac said.

Colonel Erickson looked at me. "I hardly think she'd want to. It's a bumpy, winding ride. She's just recovered from the flu."

"Actually, if it would be all right, I'd like a turn."

"You should go with her," Mac said to Colonel Erickson. "When's the last time you rode it? Had to be before you left for West Point."

"I couldn't. It's wrong," he said, though I watched the way his gaze followed the cab around the curves and down the hill and knew he'd been struck with the same enchantment I had. He looked at the men and shook his head.

"They're not going to run off and get out of their punishment," I said. "Come on. It'll only take a few moments, but the exhilaration will last all day."

The cab stopped at the station and Mac beckoned me forward. I unpinned my hat and set it on the nearby bench, then walked toward where the cab idled.

"What an honor to help the beautiful Calla Connolly onto my humble ride," Mac said, grinning. I took his outstretched hand, stepped in, then sat down on the metal bench seat. "I'll never wash this hand again."

Colonel Erickson stood on the side of the track, hesitating. His gaze met mine and I smiled.

"Come along. Even colonels and Broadway singers are allowed a little amusement now and again."

Colonel Erickson stepped into the cab in one decisive movement and strapped the chain across our laps. The moment he did, Mac pushed a handle and we were off before the colonel could change his mind. The cab soared upward and my stomach flipped. It was enlivening and unnerving to be hoisted hundreds of feet in the air in a small cart held up only by what seemed to be a thicker version of a bicycle chain. The cab pummeled downward, and I screamed. My fingers tightened on the chain around my waist, and as we careened around another corner and dropped down another sharp decline, his hand clutched mine. The moment the track steadied, he let it go.

"I'm sorry." He turned to me, his face bright with merriment. It looked exactly like the faces of the men during my shows, an illumination in their eyes, a glow on their skin. Perhaps now he would understand that though Calla Connolly might be a fantasy, fantasies like this topsy-turvy ride we were on were essential too.

The cab rose again, higher this time than at the start.

"I won't fall out of this cab on the way down, will I?" I jabbered nervously. I considered the way the chain hung loosely around my hips. I could easily slip out and fall to my death. "I'm afraid these particular skirts aren't much of a parachute." I attempted humor. I always did when I was nervous.

"No. You won't fall out."

He grasped my hand again as the cab crested. Then we were falling, plunging down five stories. I clutched his fingers and screamed. My stomach turned and my head felt light by the time we reached the bottom, but I was alive. I felt like I'd just finished a show. I let go of his hand and breathed. The cab started back up to the reception.

"Who on earth designs these?" I asked. "Whoever it is must find immense pleasure in scaring the—"

My voice died and Colonel Erickson's face blanched as our cab stopped. I felt his body tense. There was an older man standing with the soldiers, his face the picture of fury.

"I shouldn't have ridden this," Colonel Erickson whispered. He unclipped the metal chain and stepped out of the cab, holding his hand out to me. It was a gesture of propriety for the sake of this angry man, whoever he was, but Colonel Erickson's glare clearly indicated that he thought his lapse of judgment riding the coaster with me all my fault. I ignored his outstretched hand and stepped out of the cab on my own.

"Mr. Cornwell," Colonel Erickson started, turning toward the older man whose face appeared much like a ripe strawberry. "I apologize for coming into your park without your permission."

"Imagine my surprise when I was summoned away from my Sunday dinner by a friend of Susan's who swore she heard the carousel music playing and the coaster running as she passed by on the way home from church," he said. "I told her she was mistaken. I even went back to my coconut pie, but something nagged at me to check." He shoved his hands in the pockets of his brown suit. "And imagine my complete and utter shock when I discover not miscreant children but a colonel in the United States Army riding round on my roller coaster. I will have to report your conduct, I'm afraid."

"Colonel Erickson's involvement in this mishap is innocent. Mr. Cornwell, was it?" I said, putting on my best stage smile. "This whole thing is my fault. You see, I am new to town, and not much of a churchgoer, if I'm honest. I got to walking around camp today, thinking up new ideas for my act—which I do hope you'll come see—when I happened upon Lakewood."

I stepped closer to Mr. Cornwell.

"Now, I must tell you that I've never seen such an immaculate park. Not in all of the places I've visited. Not in all of America or Europe."

Mr. Cornwell's anger seemed to drain a bit; his cheeks now burned only pink.

"In New York, parks like Playland and Coney Island are open on Sundays, so I innocently decided to walk in. Amusement parks cheer me so. But mistakenly walking in on a day you're closed is the only innocence I can claim, I'm afraid."

I smoothed my dress, which I realized had become quite wrinkled with the jerking of the coaster.

"I started walking around even after I knew the park was shut down for the day. You see, my uncle used to work at a little park in Toronto."

The claim was a complete lie, but in times like these, when a whole host of soldiers were about to be reprimanded, a lie was worth it.

"And I learned to sing along to the songs on the carousel. At that point I was so filled with nostalgia that I thought perhaps I should put on a whole show from a carousel. I walked over to the controls and they were so similar to the ones Uncle operated that I turned it on and rode it around a few times, singing along, before I noticed the coaster. You see, Mr. Cornwell, my audience likes it when I try something new. So I thought—what if I could do a series where I perform from various rides in your park? It would be different from a simple old stage." I paused. "In any case, I climbed up the stairs and noticed that these controls were no different from the carousel's, really, so I turned it on and got right into the cab and thought I'd take a few rides around. I got in before I realized that it was only me here and I couldn't turn it off. I began to panic and I started yelling. Thankfully, Colonel Erickson and these men here were out for a Sunday walk down Tuckaseegee and heard me. They came running, and Colonel Erickson valiantly flung himself into the cab as it came around to try to stop it."

Mac chuckled lightly under his breath but immediately sobered.

I continued. "But then we were both stuck. It was a miracle, pure and simple, that Mac here, who used to work at your park, was able to shut off the controls."

At first Mr. Cornwell said nothing, just looked from me to Colonel Erickson to the soldiers and back again.

"You're the Broadway singer, Calla Connolly, that my daughter likes," he said finally.

"Yes, sir," I said. "But it doesn't matter who I am. I greatly disrespected your park, and I will gladly accept any punishment you deem best. I promise I'll not come in here again regardless." I stood up straight and waited.

"I can't be mad at the niece of an amusement man," he said. His shoulders relaxed and he stuck out his hand to me. "I understand wanting to take a turn on a carousel when you've been starving for a ride for years. I'd be much obliged if you don't do this again, though. If you'd like to use my rides for a show, you're welcome to them, but please ring me first."

I tipped my head at him. "I thank you so much for your forgiveness," I said. "As to your offer, I tried to sing as I went. I truly did.

But I'm afraid the rides are too bumpy for my voice. I sounded like I had the hiccups."

He laughed and nodded. "I imagine that's right."

"Well, let's let Mr. Cornwell get back to his dinner," I said, retrieving my hat from the bench and prompting the men, who had been staring at me, to come to.

"Yes, yes, of course," Colonel Erickson said. "Come along, men. You'll march behind my auto. Let's get you home, Miss Connolly."

CHAPTER 9

"Your uncle was an amusement man," Colonel Erickson said under his breath. It was a question, but it didn't come out as such. The auto was rolling so slowly I was confident a snail could easily breeze by us. I blamed Mac and his comrades. They were marching at attention but barely moving. I knew it was the adrenaline crash. When it surged through your veins, you were invincible, but when it departed, it made you feel as though all of your strength had been swindled away.

"Not quite," I said.

I'd expected relief from Colonel Erickson after I'd smoothed things over with Mr. Cornwell, perhaps even a word of thanks. But he'd climbed mechanically into the auto, fixed his eyes on the road, and barked orders at the soldiers while pretending I wasn't sitting beside him.

I was certain he blamed me for his fated ride on the coaster, but I hadn't pushed him into the cab. He'd stepped in reluctantly but willingly, on his own.

"You were convincing."

"Yes, well, if I hadn't been, I imagine all four of you would be in a bit of trouble."

He didn't respond for a moment, but then he looked at me.

"General Pershing would have issued quite a punishment, I'm sure." He waved at a man in a Model T as it passed by. "I shouldn't have ridden the coaster with you. What example did I set for the men?" He lowered his voice, though I doubted the soldiers behind us would've heard anything anyway, what with the engine chugging.

"That they should allow themselves a bit of sunshine when they need it? You gave them a fine example today. You were one of them for once and joined in their trouble like an ordinary doughboy. You'll always recall it and they will too." I turned my tam-o'-shanter around in my hand. "And anyway, you're not letting them off the hook or encouraging them to do something this harebrained again. They're still going to be punished."

"I suppose you're right." Our eyes met. I could tell he wanted to say something but was hesitating. He opened his mouth and then shut it again and resumed his survey of the empty dirt road. The Hostess House was ahead, possibly two hundred yards away. It would likely take two hours to arrive.

"How often do you use your acting off the stage?" he asked. He didn't look at me when he said it, but studied his hands gripped to the steering wheel. "It's just it . . . came so quickly and easily to you back there and I wondered."

"I am not a liar," I said. I was shocked at how calm I sounded. "That's what you're asking, isn't it? And because I know why you're asking, let me be absolutely clear—everything I've told you about Caspar and this tour and wanting to go to the front, everything I've told you at all, is the truth."

I sat back against the leather seat and looked at the view to my right, away from him, at the neat rows of pines matching the precise arrangement of the tents in the distance. I'd only lied to protect him and his men. I'd figured their punishment would be worse than mine if Mr. Cornwell knew the truth.

"I apologize. I didn't mean to insinuate that you were in the habit of lying," he said, but I turned to face him and cut him off.

"Yes, you did. So let me explain. I have a quick mind. All day long it hums along, mostly presenting me with possible horrors and sad memories nowadays but occasionally amusing me with songs, jokes, and stories like it used to. From the time I was young, I would sit beside my grandmother, who was chairbound, and entertain her for hours. I make up nearly half of my shows on the spot. But I don't use my imagination to manipulate or lie." I paused. "Well, I suppose I've used it to lie a time or two, but rarely. The last time was ten years ago. A producer I was working with, a man in his late fifties known for his untoward behavior, asked a young girl of eighteen to try out for a part in one of his plays. I overheard him ask her and told him that I was sorry but she'd already been hired for the foreseeable future." I shrugged. "I saw it the same way I saw it today, that if I didn't step in, something bad would happen and it was worth the lie. I suppose I'm keen to help friends avoid dire consequences, especially if those friends are innocent, or at least nearly innocent, in the matter."

"Friends?" He smiled and I found myself staring at him, suddenly struck by his face like the girls at the Hostess House were. I felt my cheeks burn and looked away. I hadn't been talking about him, but given our situation, it made sense to be friendly in spite of our disagreements.

"I'm stuck here for quite some time, and you are too. I suppose, though you infuriate me and step in my way, you have told me enough about yourself that I understand you on some level above that of an acquaintance." My stomach felt like I was back on the coaster and I couldn't quite fathom why. The Hostess House neared, and I thought I might ask him to let me out so I could walk the rest of the way. Then again, the speed of the auto wouldn't outpace me, so I'd be forced to endure his company for the duration regardless.

"Okay. Friends. Now that I'm convinced all the things you told me before weren't just Calla Connolly yarns." He laughed, but I figured in the wake of my lie, he'd wondered if I was no better than Lenor, if I was using the war to bolster my popularity. "In all seriousness, I apologize for questioning your motives."

"If you didn't believe me, I was going to tell you to write my mother and ask for yourself." I grinned at him. "Another thing is—I'm an ace at most emotions when I act, but an absolute horror at pretending to be despondent. Arthur Haviland nearly fired me from *The Sunshine Brigade* because I couldn't cry on demand. I ended up having to douse my hands in rubbing alcohol before the shows and then rub my eyes right before the scene where Bridgette falls apart."

He steered the auto in front of the Hostess House, stopped, then motioned to the men behind us to stop as well. He came around to my door and opened it.

"I never doubted you were grieved or that you'd lost a great love," he said softly as I took his hand and stepped out of the auto. His eyes were sincere, and I let his hand go. "It was only that I wondered if you were honest about your reason for cheering the troops—if this tour was truly what you thought best for the whole of them or if you thought that . . . well, if you thought that perhaps the only way to say your farewell to Caspar was to convince Pershing to send you over to the place he left you."

My eyes teared and I looked down at my boots.

"It's been clear to me all along that it's both." I looked at him and he nodded. Most of my life I'd been putting on a show, wearing the persona of the star, Calla Connolly, on the stage and when I greeted people on the streets, but here, among Jesse and Goldie and Guy, it seemed I almost had no choice but to simply be me, the person I truly was—grief and joy and all. Perhaps I was only matching their sincerity.

"Caspar's final letter broke my heart. Every time I read it I cry as though it's the first time. Each letter he sent, from the week he was called to war and on, was riddled with fear. He was a sensitive soul like me, and though he was happy to serve his country, his spirits were dampened easily. For months he was told day in and day out about the horrors he would encounter, never knowing when he'd face them but supposing the day was imminent. Had he been gifted a moment on a roller coaster in the midst of it, or the fortune of attending a silly show, perhaps he could have found peace." I shrugged. "From his first letter I knew I wanted to bring a bit of relief to as many soldiers as I could. And yes, if in the process I found myself situated near the front in France, if I could see the field where he'd spent his final moments, then maybe I could stop wondering—hoping—that they were mistaken, that he was alive after all."

I swallowed my tears and sniffed. He cleared his throat.

"I'm sorry I upset you," he said. "I'll try my hardest to never do it again. Ever since France, I hear the voices of my men—the ones past and the ones in front of me. They're all afraid and I can't be, so I carry their fears like a yoke atop my shoulders. It's my job to protect them from everything—from false hope, from ill preparation, from untimely death."

I hazarded a glance at Mac and the other men. In the wake of their time at Lakewood and their merriment there, they seemed in good spirits. Still, I understood the way Colonel Erickson must have felt, the pressure to ensure he protect these men the way he figured he'd failed his men in France. I thought of the faces in the crowds at the camps I'd visited. Surely I'd cheered most of them, but there were some whose spirits I knew were so mired in panic that they couldn't even hear me.

"What happened in France wasn't your fault. You did your best to protect them, just as you're doing your best to protect these men. You will save men by your efforts, and you will lose men in spite of them."

He looked at his cousin and the others. "Yes," he said simply, then glanced at me. "Thank you for today."

"I should say the same. If you hadn't insisted I go to church with you, I would have been forced to lie around alone, reading from what I've been told is a paltry selection of romance novels Mrs. Kern is embarrassed about having on her shelves. So, officially, thank you, Colonel Erickson."

"Jesse," he said, a smile lifting his lips. "We're friends, remember?"

"Then I suppose it's goodbye for now, Jesse," I said and started up the front steps to the porch. "Do call if you find yourself in another pickle." I winked at him and he shook his head.

"I will, Miss—"

"Calla, please," I called back. I waved at Mac and the other men, opened the front door, and stepped inside.

I leaned against the door and closed my eyes. The house was silent and I listened to the auto chug away. We'd had heavy conversation most of the day. Argued too. Even so, my heart felt light. Nothing about Jesse was carefree, but I could feel the echo of his hand on mine when we'd pummeled down the last dip on the coaster. Regardless of our newfound friendship, I was fairly certain he still found me an incredible nuisance. Yet, the idea that I had not one but two friends in this place was shocking.

"Calla Connolly, as I live and breathe."

I jolted from the closed door at the sound of the nasally voice and came face-to-face with Mr. Crispel. He was wearing the same smug expression and ill-fitting trousers he'd always worn, though his graying hair had been made an unnatural black since I'd last seen him on the front stoop of our apartment three years ago when he'd come to offer me the role in London on Lenor's behalf. Back then he'd started by lamenting my misfortune at the rumor that had ruined my run on Broadway, though he knew full well he and Lenor and her director lover were behind it. Lenor herself couldn't be seen as the instigator or all of Broadway would likely see the rumor for what it was—revenge at my finding out she'd been stealing from me and taking my roles, revenge for my firing her—so Mr. Crispel had taken lunch with Mr. Davis, the go-to prop man for every big show in town, a man known for his loose lips. Mother had spied the two of them coming out of the submarine shop down the street from the Victoria Theatre. By dinner that day, my two starring offers had been rescinded, and by the time Mr. Crispel appeared at our front door two days later, it was clear all of the other shows' directors would take the same stance.

"What are you doing here? Is Lenor with you?" I asked. "If she's here to ask my permission to take my place, there's no need. The news broke in this morning's paper. She's already decided her course regardless of my wishes." My cheeks burned with irritation and my hands fisted. I glanced into the library but found only a bewildered Mrs. Kern sitting silently in an armchair next to a burlap sack that appeared to be full of letters.

Mr. Crispel laughed, jabbed his hands into his pockets, and smiled at me as best he could, though his grin did nothing to brighten his face. He'd worked for Lenor as long as I'd known her and had always appeared sinister. Most assistants were hired for their aptitude and general likability. Not so Mr. Crispel. I had no doubt Lenor had hired him early in her career because he'd scared her or possibly because he was the sort of person she was without the outward pleasantness required of our sort of fame. She admired those who intimidated others. That was likely why she'd never respected me.

"Why would she need to ask your permission? Last I checked, it was your decision to delay, leaving the poor soldiers on the latter half of your schedule high and dry. Stepping in is the patriotic thing to do, Miss Connolly. Miss Felicity is doing both you and General Pershing a great service."

"I have only delayed it to express my thanks to those who saved my life here. I haven't abandoned it forever. And she knows why I embarked on this tour in the first place and what it means to me. This is *my* tour, Mr. Crispel, not Lenor's. Now, where is she?"

I was nearly shouting by the final word and paced toward the library, toward Mrs. Kern still staring at us as though Mr. Crispel's presence had put her in a sort of trance.

"She's not here," he said finally. "She's on her way to Camp Upton to rehearse for her first show. And your tour was never yours, really, it was General Pershing's, and he asked Miss Felicity to continue it while you idle here and pay your respects."

I whirled around to face him. He was right. I was stuck here. It was horribly unfair, and now I was being forced to accept the lie that I was voluntarily setting aside my tour. The anger I'd forced away reemerged.

"I'm not idling!" I yelled. "And I've already visited Camp Upton." Tears sprang to my eyes.

"*You've* visited Camp Upton, but Miss Felicity hasn't. Can you imagine if those poor soldiers heard she'd overlooked them? General Pershing was thrilled to know she'd double back to the camps that hadn't had occasion to see her, a true artist."

I gritted my teeth and swallowed hard, forcing the emotion away. He was just trying to get under my skin as he always had. Ever since Lenor and I had been at odds, it seemed it was his mission to convince me I was lesser. I wouldn't allow myself to believe it. He took everything Lenor said about me as fact— perhaps he even still believed I'd made an advance at her lover all those years ago despite the man's public indiscretions—and it dictated the way he treated me. To him, I was an ungrateful enemy. He didn't care if her opinion of me was the truth because he was blindly and wholly in love with her. That was the only way to explain why he'd remained her secretary for so long when she paid him so little, and why he'd threaten to quit every time she took up with a new man.

"Plus, it's close to the city and Edwin Leathe has promised to cover the show for the *Times*," he went on. "By the conclusion of the tour, she'll be more beloved than she's ever been."

"Heaven forbid she perform without fanfare," I said evenly, staring down at Mr. Crispel, ignoring his prediction about Lenor's burgeoning popularity. "If she's there, then why are you here?"

"I'm scouting the various Liberty Theatres ahead of her arrival to ensure they'll be able to accommodate her set. She told me to locate you when I arrived at Camp Greene. She was sure you'd be happy to show me around, that the two of you had put the past behind you. I see I was mistaken. I did see a sign for a Liberty Theatre on my way to meet you, but it was affixed to a tent. That's not right, is it?"

"The theatre is a tent, yes," I said. "And if Lenor would prefer to skip over our camp because of it, she's welcome to do so." I prayed she'd pass it by. I couldn't fathom how I'd stop myself from pushing her from the platform. The thought of Lenor falling from the stage, layers of petticoats and tulle flying through the air, nearly made me laugh out loud.

"Of course not, though it is quite shocking. I suppose it'll just prepare her for her time in France. I doubt they'll have a proper theatre for her on the front."

"What?" The merriment I'd won at the imagining of Lenor's fall suddenly died and the room stilled. My heart crushed, an echo of the disbelief I'd felt when they told me Caspar was gone.

"You seem surprised, though General Pershing said you'd been asking for some time about performing on the front. If all goes as planned with Miss Felicity stateside, he mentioned he'd like to consider her service in Europe with the boys there."

Lenor being sent to the front wasn't a certainty yet, only a consideration, the same as Pershing had promised me. Surely I would be released from Camp Greene before she could get there.

"That reminds me that I should wire Jacques Doucet to tell him of the possibility. I'm sure he'd be obliging in creating suitable costumes for a French tour."

His thin lips turned up and he stared at me. My nerves singed.

"Get out," I said, and when he didn't move, I said it again.

"Oh, Miss Connolly, there's no need to get so—"

"I don't have time to show you around. Find someone else," I said, pushing him toward the door. I hazarded a glance at Mrs. Kern, whose mouth was hanging ajar, and at the sack of letters beside her. I'd forgotten she was there. "I have letters to respond to."

Mr. Crispel laughed as he cleared the doorframe and I slammed the door behind him, my heart hammering in my chest.

"Refusing to show me about won't stop her from coming, Miss Connolly," he yelled.

I pinched my eyes shut and tried to compose myself but couldn't. I felt much like I'd just eluded my own death. In many ways, I had, though my execution was only postponed. Lenor would come for her own glory, and in doing so, she'd take my purpose, the light I had left in my broken heart, and snuff it out.

"I . . . I'm sorry. I didn't know who he was," Mrs. Kern said from the library. Her voice was meek. I knew I should attempt to pretend that it was only Mr. Crispel I couldn't stand, that Lenor and I were dandy, but I didn't have the energy. "I always come back from dinner early to ready the beds for night, and I found him sitting on the doorstep. When he asked for you and told me he was Miss

Felicity's personal secretary, I thought you'd want to see him. I told him I thought you'd be dining at Colonel Erickson's. The colonel's family is in town, you know—has been for generations—though his father leaving his lovely French mother for that little woman no more than ten years the colonel's senior was quite a scandal." She was babbling, but that's what you did when you were unsure if you'd done something wrong. "It's not that the Ericksons are particularly society, not at least in this current time, but they have long roots here." Mrs. Kern sighed. "Anyway, I didn't know that man's presence would be unwelcome."

"There's no way you would've known," I said. I attempted a smile, but an urgency to find a way out of there burbled up and quickly died. There was no way to freedom. I was trapped.

"Thank you," Mrs. Kern said. She rose from the armchair and hoisted the sack of letters up with her. When she reached me in the foyer, she extended the bag toward me. "Here. They're all for you. Your many admirers."

I took it. I stared at the bulky sack filled with letters and was immediately heartened at the evidence that my work made a difference in the lives of so many. Back in New York, Mother, Father, and I would read through the letters together and split the responses into threes. We kept the replies simple, just well-wishes and thank-yous for writing, and we'd include my latest press photo in the envelope. Reading and writing letters might be just the distraction I needed at the moment. Otherwise, I was sure I'd be eclipsed by jealousy and desperation.

"Do you know when Goldie, Nurse McGann, will come again?" I asked, scaling the first step to my room. I wondered if I could convince Goldie to help me reply.

Mrs. Kern's face fell.

"Oh, Miss Connolly. I can't be sure." The words came out in the same soothing tone one used when apologizing for a dear one's loss.

"Whatever do you mean?" I asked. "Is she all right?"

"I'm afraid to tell you that she's in a bad way," Mrs. Kern said. "We were in church singing 'There Is a Balm in Gilead' when her fella, that soldier, started yelling. She was afire with fever. Her father wanted her taken to Presbyterian Hospital, but she insisted on being brought to the base hospital here. I suppose because Dr. Sheaff has nursed many back to health from this flu."

I could hardly breathe. Suddenly Mr. Crispel's intrusion seemed inconsequential.

"Take me to her, please," I said. "Do you have an auto?"

Mrs. Kern hesitated, and I dropped the letter bag and asked again, "Do you have an auto?"

"I'm afraid not, Miss Connolly, and anyway, it's not wise to visit her. You've just gotten over the flu yourself."

I pushed past her. My heart raced, the steady thump of it pounding in my temples as I ran down the steps and out on to Tuckaseegee Road toward Lakewood Park and the hospital.

CHAPTER 10

I was sweating by the time I reached the entrance to the hospital. I hadn't slowed since I left the Hostess House, and the distance to the hospital was at least a mile. My feet smarted in my boots and my lungs ached with the echo of flu.

I passed the small wooden officers' quarters where I'd spent my convalescing week and kept on until I reached the hospital's administration office. The office was a tiny one-room shack located on a square of green grass amid nine hospital buildings that appeared like barracks and were arranged in a U shape, with covered walkways connecting each building.

I swept into the office building, my heart drumming in my ears, startling a young private seated behind what appeared to be an old banker's desk. It was clear that flames had licked the sides of the desk as they had my armoire at the Hostess House, and I wondered how many fires the camp had had to endure.

"Hello, I'm here to see a friend of mine." My voice shook. "She's a nurse here but has recently been admitted as a patient. Her name is Goldie McGann. It's urgent, I'm afraid."

The private stared at me, his mouth going slack, before remembering himself and jolting toward a record book on the desk in front of him.

"I'm Calla Connolly," I said unnecessarily. The man nodded and began flipping quickly through the record book to the final page. "I'm looking for Goldie McGann," I repeated. His fingers trembled as he continued to peruse the book. I knew he couldn't help it, and yet my patience was wearing thin. My new friend, the woman who'd nursed me back to life, was in peril. When he finally reached the last page, he ran his index finger down the list of new patients, locating Goldie's name at the bottom.

"Y-yes, Miss Connolly. Goldie McGann is in building A2, just to our right, in room 12, though I must caution you, ma'am, she has the flu," he said. "We typically only allow physicians, nurses, and officers into flu wards. It's a risk, see."

"As I'm sure you know, I've already had the flu and recovered. I could have you ask Colonel Erickson for his stamp of approval, but I don't know Goldie's state and I worry I have limited time. Please."

Goldie couldn't die. Not after she'd saved me. Not after she'd become my friend. She'd endeared herself to me almost instantly and I hoped she felt the same of me. The world needed Goldie. The world was a better place with her in it. Tears watered my eyes.

"Please," I whispered, this time to God, I supposed.

The soldier didn't respond but reached into a drawer to his left and withdrew a cotton mask, the same sort Jesse and Goldie had worn during my time in the hospital.

"Thank you," I said, taking it from him and immediately wondering if his compliance had to do with the knowledge that Goldie's illness was severe. It wasn't often that people overlooked the rules, even for me. I turned and walked out the door, barely stopping myself from running.

When I reached the covered walkway, I started toward the first building. Even though I was out of doors, I could smell the stale odor of illness and my stomach turned. I envisioned General Alexander's lifeless body, recalled the swiftness with which everyone said he was taken, and quickened my pace.

I fitted the cotton mask over my nose and mouth, then opened the door to the building labeled A2 in sizable metal letters. Groans and cries surrounded me as I started down the hallway. My eyes filled, and I was thankful for the mask that hid my emotion from the

nurses bustling in and out of rooms with water pitchers and ther-
mometers and even the Tanlac Jesse had said the doctor in charge
had ordered to no longer be used. The last thing anyone needed was
a hysterical Broadway star adding to the desperation of this place.

By the time I reached room 12, I was sobbing quietly in spite of
my best efforts to keep my fear at bay. I could hear a man's voice
singing softly from the room, Harry Macdonough's "I Love You
Best of All." I knew it was Guy's voice despite the hitches and clear
emotion. He still sounded eerily similar to Caspar. I paused in the
hallway, listening to him, not wanting to interrupt. *Darling the
sunshine grows brighter, when you are by my side.* But when he
stopped singing and began to plead with Goldie to stay with him, I
burst into the room.

The sight shocked me. The ward was shared. Twenty identical
white iron twin beds stretched out on either side of an expansive
aisle. A quarter of the beds were occupied by other women—some
moaning, some sleeping. Though the blinds were pulled back, the
fluorescent lighting from three fixtures buried in the drop ceiling
washed the whole of the ward in dingy yellow light.

Goldie lay in the second bed. The youthful glow I'd seen earlier
this morning when she'd come to my room and helped me dress
was completely absent, replaced by an ashen pale that immediately
rendered me weak.

"What are you doing here?" Guy charged from his seat at her
bedside. He was completely disheveled. Even though he wore a
mask like mine, I could tell his face was swollen and his hair stood
straight up. He rose when I approached. "Don't come any closer.
This is your fault." His voice broke and he collapsed into his chair
and began to cry into his hands.

"I came the moment I heard," I said.

Goldie's eyes were closed, but her lips lifted just slightly at my
voice.

"If it was me," I said, "I'm sorry. I—"

"It was you. You're the only one she's attended to this last week.
No one else." His voice rose to a near shout.

"No," Goldie's voice sounded in an almost inaudible whisper. "Many others too."

Guy jerked toward her, his fingers desperately clutching hers. Goldie's eyelids opened to a slit. I recalled how tired I'd felt when I'd been infected. I'd wanted to try to claw my way back to consciousness, but I couldn't. I knew how much effort it took Goldie to open her eyes even a tiny bit.

"Rest," I said to Goldie. I looked at Guy, who was staring at her, willing her to come back to him.

"You saved me once," I said to Guy. "And she saved me too. I know she'll recover."

I said it mostly because I needed to believe it. I knew what Goldie said, that she'd been exposed to others with the flu. She was right, I knew that to be fact, and yet she'd primarily cared for me.

"She can't even open her eyes," he whispered.

"You likely don't remember, but I couldn't either," I said. "The illness makes every movement feel like raising an elephant above your head."

I looked around at the other women. None appeared quite as ashen as Goldie. Two of the beds were unmade but empty, and I wondered about the fate of those women.

"Gone." Guy followed my gaze.

A slight nurse who had to be close to Goldie's age stopped and lifted the quilts from Goldie's feet. I wanted desperately to see them, to verify that her skin was perfectly white and not blue, but I couldn't bring myself to hazard even a glance in case color indicated her demise. A look of concern passed across the nurse's face as she situated the covers again.

"I'm going to retrieve the doctor to . . . to s-see if he'd like to come take a look at Nurse McGann," the girl stammered.

Guy kept his gaze fixed on Goldie's face, not bothering to respond. A sob welled up in my throat, but I pushed it down. I closed my eyes and prayed with all my might to a God I barely knew. I begged him to save Goldie, that to spare me—if one of us had to go—had been a grave error.

"They should have done something to stop this flu," Guy growled under his breath. "But there are no warning signs, so they can't. One moment you're perfectly fine. The next you're—"

"'Same Sweet Heart,'" Goldie murmured. I opened my eyes, sure I'd misheard the words, but she whispered them again. "Sing for me."

"Same Sweet Heart" was another song from *The Bye and Bye Show*, a song Caspar had written for me inspired by our conversation the day he told me he loved me. I hadn't sung it since his death. I didn't feel that I could. But now I would make myself. It was the least I could do for a woman who'd become one of my only friends, a woman who'd saved my life at the cost of her own.

"There you are, across the stage. A perfect smile, a pretty face," I sang. My voice shook, but I focused on a bit of plain white wall behind Goldie's head and forced it steady.

"Here I am, an ordinary man. Not much to offer, still you take my hand." Guy's tone was such a near match to Caspar's that I stared at him, still hoping that Caspar was hiding somewhere and that this death business was all a big joke.

"Your mind is sharp, and you're adored," I answered.

"I failed Oxford and my name's ignored," Guy responded.

"But your heart calls to mine, dear, and it's the same as mine, dear." I barely finished the last word. Tears rolled down my cheeks.

"For all of time, dear. We'll have the same sweet heart," Guy sang.

After "Same Sweet Heart," Guy and I kept singing until the sun began to set. We sang "Midnight in the City," "I'm Not Ready," "I'm Always Chasing Rainbows," "The Way We Were," "It's Hard to Pick Just One." At times Goldie would smile, but that was her only response. Even so, singing was the only thing we knew to do. On a few occasions I'd instruct Guy in the correct key, but for the most part, singing with Guy was nearly like singing with Caspar again—except for the part where the man singing with me held my heart.

"How about 'You're Right Here'?" Guy asked.

I nodded and we launched into the song. Our voices were hoarse by this point, but it hardly mattered, and as we sang, I thought that perhaps I didn't need to be at the front or on the stage for Caspar to be with me. Perhaps he was here with us right now, in this desolate hospital in a town he'd never been to in his life.

"I'm sorry I was so delayed." An older doctor with kindly looking eyes and round spectacles interrupted us. "It seems the weekend has brought an influx of flu. I encouraged the town to consider shutting down for several days, but no one heard me." He stepped around Guy and me and leaned down toward Goldie's face. "Nurse McGann, if you can hear me, it's Dr. Sheaff. I'm just examining you for congestion." He pressed a metal stethoscope to her chest, made a satisfactory noise, and turned to us. "It doesn't do to treat the nurses as you do the patients. They have seen it all and are quite aware of the progression of this virus. Conceal their status from them and most will become agitated."

He walked to the end of the bed, and I watched him heave a breath before unveiling Goldie's feet. He smiled when he saw them and then covered them back up.

"Well, it appears that thus far, Nurse McGann is one of the fortunate ones, same as you, Miss Connolly," he said. "When she was brought in earlier today, her skin appeared with a tinge of blue, but now it has returned to its normal color, which is quite unusual indeed. Typically, when the blue sets in, it continues." Dr. Sheaff paused and looked from Guy to me and then back again. "The nurses have said that the two of you have put on quite a concert in here. Keep it up, if you will. These other women seem to be improving too. Perhaps music heals."

"I believe it," said Guy, whose eyes had brightened with the news of Goldie's condition. "It has the power to heal both body and soul. Even in the midst of this horrible war and all the drilling, when I sing or perform, everything falls away and I claim back a little of who I really am."

A peace I hadn't felt in some time swept through my spirit. I knew most of it was relief at Goldie's condition, but there was another feeling too, a settling sensation that came from being understood, from others confirming that music and joy held the restorative power I'd always felt. My pressing forward toward the front with my act was as vital as I'd known it to be.

"What shall we sing next?" I asked Guy.

"How about 'Give Me the Moonlight, Give Me the Girl'? I sang it to Goldie at the end of our first dance," he said.

"Strike it up," I said, and as Guy started singing, my eyes wandered across the room to find a hint of a smile on a sick girl's face.

CHAPTER 11

Nothing eluded newsmen, not even here. I eyed the paper rolled up in my palm with tremendous irritation. Someone named Judith Simons had taken it upon herself to tattle to the *Charlotte Observer* that upon accompanying her soldier back to camp after church, she'd noticed the roller coaster at Lakewood Park running—on a Sunday, no less. She'd walked closer, only to find a group of soldiers lingering on the platform and "Charlotte's own Colonel Jesse Erickson riding the coaster with Calla Connolly." The article went on to quote this Mrs. Simons, saying that she believed I was a poor example of morality and that if I had clearly influenced a high-ranking officer like Colonel Erickson to have a lapse of judgment, what sort of effect could I have over the other, more impressionable young men? The piece included a quote by Mr. Cornwell stating that I had simply been testing the rides for a potential future show and that Colonel Erickson had come to my aide to help me stop the ride when I'd been stuck, but that "truth" was eclipsed by sensationalism—as it always was.

At least it had made Goldie laugh. I'd been startled awake by the bugle call—a sound I'd initially mistaken for the city taxi horn occasionally blasted into the dark early morning to pick up our neighbor for his shift as an early Central Park watchman. After realizing my mistake, I hadn't been able to go back to sleep, so I'd gotten out of bed, dressed in the simplest frock I owned—a blush cotton voile with a floral panel overdress—and made my way to the hospital. Guy was sleeping in the metal chair beside Goldie's bed when I arrived, his neck lolling back toward the windowpanes. Goldie was still sick but awake and in good spirits, chuckling at the newspaper that sat atop her lap. When she saw me, she shook her head and handed it to me.

"You weren't joking about riding the coaster, were you?" she'd asked.

Although I'd laughed with Goldie in the moment, the article was a problem. If the town thought me a smudge on army morality, it wouldn't be long until others inside the camp felt the same, until word got back to General Pershing. I also knew Jesse would be beside himself to be mentioned in the paper this way, as though he were a blubbering fool around me, as though he could be manipulated. That sort of man would never get clearance to the front, just as the sort of woman who enticed men away from their virtuous focus on preparing for war wouldn't either.

Camp was a veritable hornet's nest today. Mondays were always jarring for most of the working sort, I supposed, a reminder that one was not the heir of a vast fortune destined for a life of ease but destined to use their limbs and brains to the point of utter exhaustion. I waved at men clambering out of the trenches and men doing calisthenics on the green and men retreating to the mess halls. Though they waved back, only a few had actually smiled. Perhaps they'd all read the newspaper and thought interacting with me might turn their sensibilities in a blink.

I passed a crush of motor trucks and horse-drawn wagons that looked to be joining others up ahead on the shoulder of Dowd Road. Beyond them, a train had just arrived, and the whistle blew as steam like a great cloud piped from the engine and hovered over the tracks for a moment before dissipating. I used to love the sound of train whistles as a child. We'd lived near the station in Columbus, and when the train came in, I'd watch the men and women board from my window and imagine all of the places they might be going. We'd never traveled outside our city before I made it to Broadway. Even now, with a little more money at their disposal, my parents never left New York. They were content. I'd never been. From the time I was young, I'd viewed life as a thrill—I wanted to experience it all. Father said I got my spirit from his grandfather, a man who'd followed the gold rush out to California and never returned. That didn't sound quite like me, but I supposed he was the only other Connolly who'd wanted to see what life was like beyond the banks of the Scioto River for near five generations.

A lone soldier passed me by, running in the opposite direction.

"Excuse me, sir?" I shouted.

The soldier slowed, just slightly. "Yes, ma'am?"

"I'm looking for the officers' administration building," I said. "I know what it looks like. It's just . . . I'm turned around, I'm afraid."

"Easiest way there is to keep on down to Dowd Road, exit camp, follow the road west until the entrance. It's right at the start of the drive."

"Thank you."

He tipped his head at me and kept running. After seeing the newspaper, I knew I needed to speak with Jesse, to apologize for my insisting on taking a ride on the coaster. Guy said Jesse often surveyed the drilling but tended to retire to his office in the administration building with the other officers while the soldiers scattered to the mess halls for lunch at noon. I figured I'd wait for him there with one of the romance books I'd borrowed from the Hostess House library. The book about an Amish couple courting wasn't exactly my normal fare, but I supposed it would be better than staring at a wall for the hours it took for Jesse to appear from making his rounds.

I was nearly at the exit to camp now, and after I passed the Knights of Columbus building and the post office, I noticed commotion on the front lawn of the Dowd House, the camp headquarters. The lawn, which sloped slightly upward toward the white farmhouse porch and was covered in centuries-old oaks, was situated at an intersection—the road I was on meeting a company road that ran past eleven regimental division tent quarters to the south. Soldiers lined the company road in two neat rows from the Dowd House to the horizon, it seemed. They were all dressed to perfection, led by officers in tall, brown leather boots that had clearly been shined for the occasion—whatever that was.

"Attention!" someone hollered.

The hundreds of men called out some sort of acknowledgment and stood stock-still. I stopped, too, mesmerized by the number of soldiers and the way they stood without speaking, without moving. I glanced at Dowd Road ahead of me and at the train still idling on the tracks. Men in overalls unloaded matching khaki linen bags from the trucks onto carts that other men pulled down to cargo cars at the rear of the long train.

At once the soldiers began to march down the street in my direction. One of the lines hollered, "Send the word," while the other shouted, "Over there!" I stood on the corner clutching my newspaper, my heart lurching into my throat as they neared. The men were heading for the trains. They were heading for New York, toward ships that would take them across the Atlantic to the front. I wondered if this was Mac's division. He'd said his general had told them they were going to be deployed soon. Still, this seemed abrupt. News of their departure hadn't even been announced in the paper.

Soldiers marched by grouped in regiments, the officers at the front. I watched for Mac and the others, craning my neck to see the regiments that passed on the far side of the street. The thought of them going filled my heart with a strange sort of desperation.

The men kept marching, their steps in perfect line, their gazes fixed on the shoulders of the men in front of them. The sight was moving and sobering, exciting and harrowing. I tried to smile as they passed me, to hold back the tears and capture all of their faces each time a regiment cleared and a new one stepped in front of me. It was the least I could do, to try to remember them. All of the men wore the same insignia on their shoulders: four ivy leaves pointing to the north, south, east, and west on white ground.

Somewhere in the distance, by the trains perhaps, someone shouted, "Fourth Division!" and now the insignia made sense.

The soldiers kept up their chant, "Send the word" and "Over there," and I began to sing.

"Over there, over there."

The men joined in, their chorus a deep swell that brought tears to my eyes once again. This time I allowed them to fall, but I smiled still; I had to.

"That the Yanks are coming, the Yanks are coming, the drums rum-tumming everywhere," we sang, the men's faces brightening with the mighty sound of their voices. This reminder of unity, this display of strength, heartened their spirits. I'd built my show on what I assumed would cheer a soldier, but now I understood what they needed most. They needed to underscore camaraderie. They needed to know they were not alone.

When the song concluded, I started it up again. I could see the last of the soldiers now skirting the little hill by the Dowd House and heading my way. There was a familiar face among them, a shock of red hair beneath a cap, and when he saw me, he grinned. Mac. I recalled his words yesterday, the way he feared the front, and yet, right now, he was smiling. The newspaper and the irritation that came with it dissolved in my hand. What if he wasn't going to the trains singing with his peers? What if he hadn't stolen a ride on the coaster yesterday?

"Will you kiss me, Miss Connolly?" Mac shouted as he passed. "As a send-off? We're heading to France, you know."

I laughed, but despite his grin, his eyes were earnest. Without thinking, I stepped into the road, pulled his face to mine, and kissed him. It was a deep kiss, a goodbye kiss for a man who'd be missed— for a year or forever. His breath hitched as his lips realized mine and he leaned into me in turn, pulling me closer. Around us, soldiers whooped, and when he finally let me go, I started sobbing. It was the kiss I should've given Caspar. The kiss that said I knew he might not be returning.

Mac's face was flushed red, nearly matching his hair.

"I'll remember it forever," he said over his shoulder, catching up to the others.

There was a chance I'd pay mightily for the kiss. I might be labeled promiscuous and my reputation could be further tarnished, but I knew in my heart I'd done the right thing. Mac would carry the memory onto the battlefield. He'd recall it in his darkest hours. I would have regretted refusing him. I wiped my eyes as I watched him go, vanishing into the train station with the last of the men.

Then all was quiet again, save the howling of the train engine. I looked toward the Dowd House, toward the place where the men had just been standing. Jesse stood on the porch, his tall, broad frame unmistakable, even from a distance. He was staring at the station, undoubtedly thinking the same thing I was—that I'd give anything to be among the men on that train.

I started to walk across the street toward him. He looked at me, and I thought he might come to meet me, but instead, he tipped his head and turned, disappearing into the house.

※ ※ ※

I wandered around, past the abandoned tents. The canvases had all been tied to their central poles, much like a sun umbrella when it wasn't in use, and the empty metal beds, stripped of their linens, gleamed in the spring sunshine. Nothing had been left behind—at least that I could see. No photographs or canteens or socks. Men weren't ordinarily this neat. I knew that from Father and Caspar. It was the army that left things so spick-and-span that there was hardly evidence there had been a thousand men housed here just hours before.

I'd thought to go up to the Dowd House and have a word with Jesse regardless of his clear desire to the contrary, but in the wake of the Fourth Division's departure and Mac's kiss, the newspaper article and its implications hardly seemed to matter. Plus, there would be other officers there—it was the lodging for many of them. I suppose Jesse lived there too. It occurred to me that I'd never truly considered where he lived before.

"Ma'am? I mean, Miss Connolly?" a woman's voice called out.

I whirled around, seeing no one, but realizing that in blindly following the company road while lost in thought, I'd found myself in the midst of occupied quarters. Here, full tents billowed, and the smell of gravy and yeast floated on the air from the mess halls beside me.

"I'm right here, Miss Connolly."

Just behind me, hidden in the shadow of a mess hall, was a small wooden house. A young Black woman stood on the porch in a smart yellow braided vestee, a short bolero to match, and a long tunic. I walked back toward her and smiled.

"I'm sorry. I didn't see you there," I said.

"It's no mind." She grinned, stepped down from the porch, and walked toward me. "I'd invite you in for a glass of tea, but down here it's against the law." She pursed her lips, and I shook my head. I'd forgotten too.

"The most ridiculous rules I've ever heard," I said.

Men began to pour from the mess halls, and I realized I'd made my way into one of the regimental quarters designated for Black soldiers.

"Indeed." She clapped her hands. "Well. I'm Juliet Duncan, just down visiting from Rhode Island for a few weeks. My husband is stationed here, so I'm back and forth until he leaves."

"Nice to meet you, Mrs. Duncan," I said. "I watched some boys ship off to France today and I daresay I sobbed like a baby."

"So did I." She smiled. "I called you over for a reason." She pulled at the ends of her jacket and met my eyes. "Some of the men, my husband included, are gifted musicians. Not to the level you are, mind, but they could be similarly wonderful, I think, if they were instructed." She paused. "I'll come right out and say it—do you suppose you would ever consider offering lessons while you're here?"

"Yes," I blurted, amazed the notion hadn't occurred to me before. "I'd love to. I am only performing once each week, and I've worried the past few days that I'll be terribly bored. Lessons would be a perfect solution. Colonel Erickson has put aside the YMCA Annex for my rehearsals, so I'm certain I could offer them there. And I'll need musicians to accompany my shows too." In the whirlwind of my illness and then the weekend, none of the particulars of when I'd conduct rehearsals for my shows or where I'd procure supporting musicians—other than Guy—had been settled. "What instrument does your husband play?"

She laughed. "The fiddle. That's what they call the violin down here, isn't it? And I'm fairly certain he wouldn't be allowed to enter the white YMCA, so perhaps you may want to inquire about a neutral space?"

"As much as I wish you were wrong, I suspect you're right, but I'm certain I'll find a solution. As to fiddle or violin, I've always thought them one and the same. I suppose it depends on if you're playing a country tune or Beethoven." I laughed. "When would he be able to start?"

"The day is over at 5:40 p.m. sharp," she said. "Sidney would be able to meet for lessons any day after his duties are complete."

"Sidney," I said. The name sounded familiar, and then I recalled where I'd heard it. "He's, I mean, the two of you are friends with Guy Werths. His fiancée, Goldie McGann, nursed me back to health at the hospital. I've heard of Sidney's talent."

Juliet's face brightened.

"He's quite remarkable." She hesitated. "There are others too—a saxophone player who puts Luiz Americano to shame and a trumpeter who rivals Louis Armstrong but who has been stuck playing only the reveille these last months."

"I'd love to hear them too," I said. "Have them write me at the Hostess House. In the meantime, I'll send a note to your attention as to where I'll meet Sidney for instruction, and if we get on well and if it suits Sidney, I'll see if I can convince him to be a part of my show. We'll perform every other week at the Liberty Theatre—so long as the army doesn't have a problem with the lot of us sharing a stage. It will be a knockout time, if I do say so myself."

✳ ✳ ✳

The conversation with Juliet enlivened me, and by the time we'd finished speaking, I was dreaming about training a veritable

Broadway band unlike any I'd ever had. Oftentimes I only had Mr. Keeghan's minimal piano accompaniment when I ventured away from the city. The simplicity was easy. But there was nothing like the way a band made your heart swell.

I started back to the Hostess House through the middle of camp this time, walking around the trenches, past the YMCA where a few men were playing basketball. It was midafternoon now and the sun was dipping just slightly, washing the neighboring tents in gold hues.

The men stopped dribbling when they saw me, nudging each other and pointing. I waved. I couldn't wait to rid myself of the newspaper and the novel. They were nothing but a nuisance and I'd been holding them for hours.

"Oh, I suppose it's time," one of the men said as I walked by, nodding at them over my shoulder. I heard the chug of auto engines and glanced behind me in time to see the beginning of a practical parade.

"What's happening?" I called to the men.

A short soldier who'd lost all sense of propriety and withdrawn his shirt grinned at me. "Charlotteans are allowed to drive through camp each day between four and seven."

Passengers in civilian attire waved and gawked from the windows of the autos as they breezed past me. I stopped and waved, realizing most of the autos were full of young women dressed to the nines in their finest costumes. Though some waved back enthusiastically, I noticed the way the women surveyed the men on the court and the way the men on the court eyed them.

"I wouldn't make a habit of standing here during the drive-throughs."

Jesse materialized behind me. His uniform was caked in hardened clay. "They might get used to it, and then everybody who wants a peek at Calla Connolly will descend on camp." He smiled.

Apparently his earlier melancholy at the other men going had cleared a bit, as mine had. There was nothing to be done now but hope they'd run the enemy down and return home in one piece.

"And I wouldn't make a habit of rolling in clay. You look like an earthenware vase," I said.

He laughed. "I can't exactly avoid it. The soldiers are so used to Alexander joining in, they call for me now when I make the rounds and I won't tell them no."

An auto full of beautiful women passed us. They shouted my name, but their gaze was fixed on Jesse.

We stood side by side, waving at the autos. It seemed like the line was never-ending.

"I hate to bring this up given our amiable moods at the moment, but—"

"I saw the article," he said, glancing at the rolled paper in my hand. "But only after the War Department's telegram arrived scolding me. Thankfully, General Dickman believed our story and wired Pershing's office to tell them that the woman quoted was mistaken, but it still threw my day off. And then I saw Nurse McGann's name among the ill listed on General Sheaff's report and was concerned, though I hear she's on the other side of things now."

"Yes, thank heavens. She's much improved. I saw her this morning," I said. "I intended to pay you a visit too, right after I left the hospital, to tell you how sorry I am that I asked you to ride on the coaster with me, but then I saw the men heading for the trains."

"And fell into the arms of my cousin. I saw the kiss. It doesn't threaten my reputation this time, but it does yours. Some people are keen to ruin everyone here." Jesse looked at me and then refocused on a decrepit Model T. Its hiccupping sounded as though it could give out at any moment. Perhaps that was the point. If it breathed its last here at Camp Greene, the ladies inside would be stranded among the charming doughboys for a few hours at least.

"He asked me and I couldn't refuse him, Jesse. We all hope they'll come back, but—"

"Yes, I know." He sighed.

"Is that why you saw me and went inside instead of greeting me? Did you think that being seen with me so soon after such a display would compromise your standing again? Or were you upset that I kissed Mac?"

He made a dismissive noise. "Of course I don't mind you mugging Mac. It was just a kiss. Though, as I said, some might make it out to be a scandal."

"You're right. It *was* just a kiss." I looked at him, deciding to leave out the reminder that I was versed at performing kisses, in case he'd question my sincerity in kissing altogether as he had my propensity to tell the truth. Most of the time kisses meant something. They still did to me in the context of love. Kissing for an audience and kissing because your heart demanded it were two different things entirely.

"Anyone who's matured beyond twenty would see clearly what it was. So, no, I didn't go to my room and punch my door because you kissed my cousin, nor was I worried my character would be questioned in your company."

We waved at more autos; this time a few held older folks. The change was refreshing. Then he held out his left hand and stared at the kaleidoscope of scratches and bruises visible along his knuckles despite the layer of clay.

"I did, as a matter of fact, punch my door because I could hardly bear standing there, watching my fellow officers and the other soldiers board the train that would ultimately take them to the front. I know they're not my men, but I've known most of them all the same. I've shared my experiences. Suppose they forget what I've taught them? Every part of me wanted to be on that train too."

"I understand," I said, recalling the manner in which my heart had burned with jealousy and anger at Mr. Crispel telling me that Lenor might be allowed clearance to the front, the very place I desired to go. "Lenor's secretary practically ambushed me yesterday at the Hostess House. He said he was passing through scouting the Liberty Theatres along her route, but I suspect he paid a special visit to me to let me know that Pershing mentioned possibly sending her to the front in my stead after her tour stateside. He's hated me since I fired her. Lenor doesn't care for the men like I do. She doesn't know what they need from a show."

The last auto chugged past us. Jesse faced me. "I'm sorry. It's excruciating to feel you can help in some way and then be told that you can't."

"We will get there," I said. "Both of us."

He shrugged. "Or perhaps we won't."

"Colonel Erickson!" A tall, lanky man appeared on the drive the autos had just departed, sprinting, followed by a group of at least ten more.

"What is it?" Jesse asked, reading their faces as I was. Something was terribly wrong.

"We're looking for some slackers," a large man breathed, his hands going to his knees as he paused in front of us. "Excuse us, Miss Connolly." He tipped his head at me.

"Slackers, you say? What are slackers?" I asked.

The men playing basketball abandoned their game and walked over to us.

"Men who've abandoned the army despite their promise to serve," Jesse said, an edge to his voice.

"Major Lindsey asked us to gather all the men we could. He has reason to believe William Robbins, Austin Zana, and Robert Light-ner slacked off right after lunch. Their things are missing and they didn't show for afternoon drills," the tall man continued. "We've searched nearly the whole camp but not the surrounding areas." He paused. "We're keen to find them, sir. They're just frightened. We saw the Fourth boarding the train while we were shooting at the range, and I suppose they got it in their head that our departure was imminent too."

One of the men, who had a baby face that made him look no older than twelve, kept glancing around as though the men would spring out from behind the YMCA building or perhaps a fold of a tent.

"If we don't find them, they'll . . . they'll," he stuttered.

"I know the penalty for going AWOL," Jesse said. "Have the mills been searched? Or the woods? I'll have officers in town look as well."

"No one's searched the mills, but the woods have been fairly well covered," the large man said.

"I'll call for the Tenth Field Artillery Regiment to route back to the mills and search there after Colonel Zachary is finished with drilling. As long as we locate them and bring them back within ten days, they'll only be subject to two weeks hard labor, most likely," Jesse said.

"And if they're not found?" I asked.

Jesse's gaze met mine. "After ten days, a warrant will be issued for their arrest and they could be sentenced to execution if General Pershing makes the order. Shirking the draft is a war crime. So far, Pershing hasn't followed the British policy that slackers should be shot on the spot, but he could. I'm surprised your fiancé didn't mention witnessing such things."

My heart stilled and I noticed that Jesse's face had paled.

"Do you . . . do you suppose he would do that, Colonel?" the baby-faced man asked.

"We are in a war, Private. It's Pershing's responsibility to ensure that the punishments required for justice are fairly administered." He paused, and as though he were reckoning with Pershing's own judgment on himself, added, "He's meticulous and thoughtful. He won't order a death sentence unless he feels he has to. Even so, we need to find these men immediately."

CHAPTER 12

I n the days following the deployment of Mac's regiment and the disappearance of the three soldiers, the nightmares I'd experienced after Caspar's death returned. I'd woken drenched in sweat twice, both times dreaming of peril. The first was a recurring dream of Caspar's balloon going down; only this time Mac was the one in it screaming for me to help him, that he needed to hear me sing to make it all go away. The second was of a man whose face was blurred, down on his knees in front of General Pershing, begging him not to order his execution, saying he'd only run because he was scared.

When two of the three men who'd gone AWOL had been found and returned willingly to camp two days ago, incurring an immediate penalty of confinement and two weeks hard labor, I hoped it meant the third man would be found imminently and my nightmares would cease, but that wasn't the case. As of this morning, he'd been gone four days. I didn't know the man, but still the worry that he wouldn't return and would be sentenced to death often threatened to arrest my mind.

I rubbed my eyes, forced my thoughts away from the missing soldier, and closed the cover on the old piano in front of me. Though I appreciated being allotted a space to rehearse and give lessons, the annex area, a sort of storeroom tacked on to the YMCA, might have had the worst acoustics I'd ever heard. From practically the moment the news of my giving music and acting lessons hit the soldiers' newspaper Tuesday morning, I'd spent four hours each evening in instruction, which gave me four hours in the day for my own solitary rehearsal. The distraction couldn't have come at a better time. However, the first day I'd wondered if perhaps the flu had somehow distorted my senses. Everything sounded sharp: my voice, Guy's extraordinary piano playing—a skill I had no idea he possessed—Sidney's fiddle playing. In addition to the warped notes, the whole room reverberated nearly as severely as if we were performing in a tunnel. Regardless, I knew it was the best Jesse could do. The annex had a separate entrance from the YMCA proper, and he'd made it clear to the other officers that Black and white musicians alike were to be permitted to enter it, calling it a performance space to get around the segregation laws. Performers of any color skin were allowed to share a stage, apparently.

"You said you're from Waterbury, Connecticut?" I asked, turning to my student, a saxophone player named Roland Tapley, who was taller and broader than Jesse. He shared a tent with Sidney, and they'd noticed their mutual love of music almost immediately. So far, Roland had played through almost all of Harry Burleigh's most popular songs, from "Deep River" to "Waiting" to "Little Mother of Mine." He'd been close to perfect at both solo performing and accompanying. His only instructible need was confidence. Each time he missed a note, he'd quit completely instead of correcting himself and moving on.

"Yes, ma'am," he said, setting the saxophone down on his lap. It was Friday and his olive drab, like everybody else's by this point in the week, needed a good wash and rest.

I pushed the metal partition that separated the annex from the YMCA lounge back a little and sat down on a stool next to it.

"How do you feel about 'Yankee Doodle'?" I asked. "The song," I specified. "Not the man. Then again, I don't know much about the man except that he's small enough to ride on a pony and enjoys feathers in his cap."

Roland laughed softly. He was a quiet sort. Most of my students were, save Sidney and Guy.

"I'm asking because I've had an idea swirling around in my head these past days and I wondered if you'd like to be a part of it." I hooked the heel of my patent leather boot over the wrung of the stool and pushed myself to a more comfortable position. "All of you men are far from home, so I wondered if my variety show next week could be something like a tribute to each of your states. It might cheer you all if you're feeling homesick. I hear 'Yankee Doodle' is something of a Connecticut state song. Is that correct?"

"Yes, though no one knows why. Folks say it was written in Connecticut, but there's no proof of that at all," he said.

"Is there another tune more suited or familiar to those from your state?" I asked. "I want to be sure everyone can sing along."

The sun was setting in the window behind him, washing the dull wooden mess halls in vibrant orange and gold. It had to be nearing seven.

"No. It's used all of the time—before the governor makes an address, when a building is dedicated, even before football games." Roland chuckled.

"Well then, how would you feel about playing it in my show next Saturday?" I asked.

In the hours I'd been unable to sleep this week, I'd thought of Guy's sentiments he'd shared at the hospital: that music and performance were his only respite, as they were mine. The more I got to know the men I was instructing, the more I realized they felt the same—they were no different from me or Guy or Caspar or Basil. Without an outlet in which to sing or play, without a goal to work toward, their light would be snuffed out by the promise of war that was to come. If I could involve them all in a show, if I could encourage their focus on dreams beyond the battlefield, perhaps I could help equip them to weather their worry. Perhaps I could serve a purpose even while I was stuck here, to give these men what I wished Caspar had been given—much needed peace, hope for tomorrow—and to help them the way I wanted to help Basil.

"I'm envisioning each state will be presented individually, in alphabetical order, so Connecticut will be first. If I can find costumes,

I'll have us all dress in colonial garb, perhaps even with powder guns. Betty DeWitt—the wife of a fabulous trombone player named Crowley—and Mary Hines, who live with me at the Hostess House, will help sing and square dance. Betty confirmed that the square dance means something to you Connecticut natives too. She also mentioned that Crowley has two left feet. So if you know anyone—"

"I'd very much like to be a part of it, but do we have to wear the guns?"

He picked at his fingernails, then looked at me and startled, as though he'd spoken out of turn. "I . . . I mean, I'd love to play on-stage, and if a powder gun completes the costume, that's fine."

"We don't have to have them. It was just an idea," I said.

I walked toward him. He'd been so calm while playing, his eyes closed to the music, his body swaying, but now his posture was straight and his face was drawn.

"You're an artillery man. You're handling guns day in and day out. If you'd like a break from them for the show, it's not a disappointment to me." I bent low in front of him, and he shook his head.

"No, Miss Connolly. That's not it at all. I enjoy my assignment, I really do." He said the words quickly and searched my face, doubtless in an attempt to ensure I believed him.

Over the last several days, the officers, keen to avoid more slackers, had been observing soldiers' sentiments with even more scrutiny than they had before.

"I didn't want to wear the gun for the performance because it might interfere with my playing. Anything attached to my belt could strike the saxophone," Roland went on.

I nodded. I could see straight through him to the fear that clutched his every moment except for the minutes when his mind and heart were enraptured by the music. I prayed that I could only see it because the thought of war horrified me too, that it wasn't so plainly recognized that the officers would notice. I hoped the show and the rehearsals required to put it on would help settle him a bit, to give him peace in greater frequency.

"I understand," I said. I'd given twelve lessons this week and only two of the men I'd taught were truly prepared to face the front. Souls attuned to music, to acting, felt everything more acutely: the diminuendo of a song and a life, the way a story could turn with the utterance of a word. If the world were run by such souls, perhaps we'd not know the word for war.

"I could work on arranging 'Yankee Doodle' as a square dance this week," he suggested, turning the conversation back to the show.

"That would be wonderful," I said. "If each state is allotted a song and a dance, a joke, and a little skit—and there are six states represented here at Camp Greene—we'll run right at an hour. Then I'll finish the show with a couple new songs I've written to tie things all together."

"I can't wait to write my mother and tell her I'm sharing a stage with Calla Connolly, of all people," he said.

"I wish she could be here to see you." I smiled.

I paused for a moment, thinking through the items I lacked for such a show. I still needed everything beyond the talent: backdrops, costumes, a light man, programs, permission. My breath caught, lingering on the last thought. I'd forgotten about having to get permission. I'd need Jesse to ask General Dickman for clearance for the men assigned to the Third Division and permission from Colonel Dawson for the 348th Battalion. For as much as I'd made progress with Jesse, I knew he still wasn't convinced the men were served well by being distracted with merriment. Although he'd agreed to lend me Guy, I wondered if he'd allow the others to participate. It would require regular group rehearsals beyond the half hour here and there, which meant more disruption from a singular focus on war.

Roland stood. "I assume we'll need time to practice. Do I need to ask Colonel Dawson?"

"I'll handle the officers, but I suppose I should start now."

I grinned at Roland, and he smiled back. He tucked his saxophone under his arm, and we walked out the door into the pleasant evening.

"I'll see you Monday at five?" he asked, turning south toward his tent.

"Unless you're going to be at the dance at Lakewood Park tomorrow. I've got a set list straight from Broadway, Guy will be tickling the ivories for me, and everybody will have on their glad rags—even the Charlotteans."

Roland shook his head, and I realized my mistake.

"Aw, Miss Connolly, I know it'll be a time, but we can't come."

I'd forgotten. "It's an absurd rule," I said. "Asinine, in fact. And not at all fair." I glanced in the direction of Roland's quarters where Sidney and Juliet also resided. "What if I come down and we put on a dance of our own?"

Roland laughed. "We hold our own dances each week—same time as the ones at Lakewood, only ours are out in the clearing in front of the mess halls. I don't know how it is to be over there, but every Saturday I have occasion to forget where I am. If you wrap up before we do, you're welcome to join us, so long as you won't find yourself subject to confinement for it."

I rolled my eyes. "I'd like to see them try," I said, though I knew full well I wasn't immune to the company police. They would make an example of me the same way they'd made an example of Guy and Sidney and the two men who'd fled.

✳ ✳ ✳

It was dark inside the Dowd House. I knocked again and peered through the beveled glass panes at the top of the old carved mahogany front door. Mrs. Kern told me just this morning that the house was the dwelling of four officers: Jesse, Major Gordon, Major Stone, and Colonel Zachary. It was strange that no one was home, especially at this hour. The sun had nearly set and the mess halls had closed hours ago.

I turned and started to walk back down the steps when a Packard appeared, coming up the hill. Jesse was at the wheel, three other officers occupied the rest of the seats, and they were all laughing. When the auto crested the hill and they saw me, they sobered.

"What's the matter? I'm not General Pershing," I called out as Jesse silenced the auto in front of the house.

"Clearly not," a slight man with a thick mustache in the back seat behind Jesse shouted back. "We all knew you were here at camp, and Colonel Erickson told us you were just like any other sort of girl, but seeing you standing on our porch . . . well, it's a little surreal, isn't it Mr. Gordon?" He tapped the man in the passenger seat on the shoulder.

"Like any sort of girl, eh?" Major Gordon chuckled as he got out of the auto. He looked to be older than Jesse by a few years and carried himself with confidence despite his height matching mine. "I'm not sure. We were surrounded by plenty of girls tonight and not a one seemed to be able to hold a conversation with a man without a gaggle of her friends, let alone seek out a group of officers." He glanced at me as he neared. "What can we help you with, Miss Connolly?"

"She's here to ask me for an elephant, I'm afraid," Jesse called out. He had just stepped out of the auto and was gathering what appeared to be a stack of glass casserole dishes filled with food from the back seat, while the other two men disembarked. One of them, a large man with black curly hair, seemed unable to look at me.

"Well, give her one then," the man with the mustache urged as he walked past Jesse toward me. "Whatever she wants. Just keep her here."

"Oh, don't you worry about me running off," I said. I forced laughter that sounded like chimes, just like Lenor taught me.

Jesse turned my way and his gaze leveled on mine. "The staff at the hospital saved her life. She wants to remain here as long as we'll allow it," he said, his voice matter-of-fact.

"Indeed," I said.

"I'm going to retrieve that letter from my desk, and then I'll go down to the office to get the correspondence from today, Erickson," Major Gordon said as he neared. He tipped his head as he walked past me.

"Good night, miss."

The other two officers seemed to lose their faculties entirely when they reached the porch where I stood. The one with the mustache, who had so easily conversed with me from the auto, stared, opened his mouth a few times, and then walked inside without a word, while the larger gentleman cleared his throat and said, "You're happy to meet me." It was clearly a mistake and he turned fire red.

"Thank you," I said. "I am."

By the time Jesse ambled up the porch with his food, the other men had departed inside.

He set the dishes down with a soft clatter on the seat of a ladder-back chair beside the front door. It looked to be platters of fried chicken and slices of pie. My stomach growled. Mrs. Kern, who knew I'd miss supper because of my lessons, had been boxing meals for me to eat when I returned home. Sometimes Wendy would come into the dining room from the library, where she practically seemed to live, and talk to me about her hometown or her wedding or her husband while I ate. I was accustomed to eating with my parents every night back at home, so the company was nice.

"I know you're not really going to ask me for an elephant, but you are going to ask me for some of the men, aren't you? I've passed by the annex and heard them playing. They're good." Jesse's voice diverted my attention away from the platters of food. He smiled when our eyes met. I was surprised at his mood given the stress of the past few days.

"Yes, I suppose I am," I said.

He was extraordinarily handsome tonight. I couldn't figure if it was his amiability or the way his green eyes that matched his olive jacket had been illuminated by the newly shining stars. He'd removed his hat—for supper, probably—and his dark hair was combed away from his face.

"Where were you? You look dashing." I said it without thinking and immediately gasped. It was a forward thing to say. It was something I would have said to a fellow actor I was keen to kiss or perhaps a handsome admirer who was so enamored with me that they'd kiss me straightaway, but not to someone like Jesse.

"I'm sorry," I said.

He laughed. He likely thought I said these sorts of things to men all of the time, that what I said had no meaning. Most of the time, it didn't. I straightened and fiddled with the brim of my sailor hat.

"I'll accept the compliment. Thank you," he said. "We were asked to come to the Selwyn Hotel for a Charlotte Women's Club gathering, to tell them of any needs the soldiers may have."

"I doubt you were only there to tell them that the soldiers could use more pairs of socks or more dinners after church. That sort of information can be expressed in a letter." I smiled.

"It could, but the Selwyn Hotel was catering. None of us really minded the turns around the dance floor with women aged twenty to ninety so long as we could enjoy a fine steak served with oysters and mashed potatoes followed with rum cake."

I eyed the casserole dishes that clearly weren't filled with such delicacies.

"If the hotel catered the event, then what are those?"

"Oh, well. The ladies always bring us dishes to take home. They worry we'll go hungry, I suppose. That's Miss Jacey Matthews's famed fried chicken and Mrs. Amy Baldwin's custard pie."

I noticed a bit of lipstick on his cheek when he turned his head to look at the dishes. I was unaware that proper Southern girls wore lipstick.

"No grits or corn bread?" I asked, ignoring the smear of pink on his skin. "I was supposed to stay at the Selwyn Hotel, you know. Mary Pickford told me of its charms and fine silk sheets. You could have at least smuggled poor old me a fine pillowcase as a consolation."

"Why would you want to stay at the Selwyn when you could sleep on army-grade cotton and cover yourself with handmade quilts?" he asked. He kept smiling at me, and it was enchanting. I wondered if he'd had drinks while he was away. I reckoned that was the reason for his unwavering stare and the reason we were flirting. *We're flirting.*

I stepped back, putting more space between us. We weren't all that close to begin with; it was simply that the more he smiled and held my gaze, the more I stared at his mouth and felt that feeling that I knew would encourage my leaning into his chest.

I cleared my throat and forced myself to concentrate on the reason I'd come. I wanted him to ask General Dickman for permission to secure the men for my show, and since he was in such an agreeable mood, now was a perfect time to ask.

"As I mentioned, I came by to ask if you'd wire General Dickman and see if he would let a selection of the men I've been teaching perform in my variety show next week. I was thinking of writing a skit that captured the spirit of each soldier's home state and then following that up with a patriotic finale to bolster camaraderie no matter where a soldier's from." I stared just beyond his shoulder at the porch light, though I could still feel his gaze. "It'll require two hours rehearsal time Monday, Wednesday, and Friday, I'm thinking, as well as the time for the show on Saturday. The rehearsals could be scheduled around training."

I glanced at Jesse. He was now leaning against the porch railing, studying me with his arms crossed, an amused expression on his face. For a moment, he said nothing. I thought to ask if he'd heard me. Then he shrugged and smiled.

"I suppose I'll grant it. General Dickman allows the camp commander to alter the men's schedules when he's away as long as the training time's the same."

"Really?" The word came out in a squeak and I stepped forward as though I'd embrace him. I stopped myself.

"Normally I'd be upset at the distraction, but for some reason I'm not. The men have mentioned several times during meals that you've hinted at involving them in your show, so I had an inkling that's what you were here to ask about." He sighed, but his countenance displayed no signs of distaste. "Their excitement convinced me. Although I'm still not sure that disrupting their focus is good for them, it's a better alternative than the entertainment the men have come up with themselves. Last week thirteen men in Gordon's division were sent to confinement for visiting the neighboring women who have set themselves up outside of camp. Twenty-four of Zachary's were caught drinking at a watering hole masquerading as a dry pool hall, not to mention my cousin's infraction at Lakewood."

"Regardless of your reason, thank you," I said.

He nodded.

"The War Department still isn't convinced I wasn't involved in the coaster incident," he said, his face sobering. It was a shame the merriment had to end.

"You said General Dickman set them straight," I said.

"Yes, but it's the way Pershing's aide is speaking to me. He's very short with me now. Different."

"Perhaps it's only that the action is intensifying and there's little time to add pleasantries to correspondence."

Jesse made a disgruntled noise. "The aides aren't on the front lines dodging rifle fire." He straightened from his leaning against the railing. "I imagine they'll send my replacement—or rather, General Alexander's—soon. They haven't mentioned it, but more men are coming in on the train Monday, this time from the West: Montana, Colorado, the Dakotas, and New Mexico. I suppose they could select a commander for the camp and the Sixth Brigade from those troops," he said.

"Or perhaps they're planning to nominate you for promotion and you won't be replaced at all. I think you're doing a bang-up job," I said.

"Not a chance." He grinned at me, but his expression was more melancholy this time. I couldn't well leave him this way, not after he'd had such a joyous evening otherwise.

"I know I came to ask about the men, but when you mentioned an elephant, it got me thinking. An elephant really would make my show memorable," I said. "Are you certain you can't get one for me?"

He shook his head. "Unfortunately, I can't. However, the Montana men have asked to bring their bear. It's their mascot, apparently," Jesse said, his mouth turning up.

"You're serious?" I asked, starting to laugh.

He nodded. "His name is Rocky."

"Are you going to let them?" I envisioned soldiers teeming from the trains, the final men pushing a bear. The town would go crazy for it. "It would be quite a spectacle. I imagine the Charlotteans would turn out in spades to greet the men. Do you suppose the bear likes donuts?" Laughter overtook me as I envisioned the Red Cross ladies of Charlotte pushing their signature fresh donuts through the cage to the bear.

He started laughing too.

"I'm sure he adores donuts. Who doesn't? But obviously I can't allow him here. The men can't stay out of an amusement park. Do you really think they'd manage to avoid getting into the bear cage? It's every boy's dream to conquer a bear, and these men aren't far off. Just last week Beau Huntington . . . Beau Huntington." He couldn't continue, he was laughing so hard. I was too. Before I knew it, tears were running down both of our faces. "Beau Huntington dared Sam Johnston that he couldn't pin the opossum that's been ravaging the mess hall trash each night. So Sam . . . he snuck up on him . . . and tried to pin him, but . . . the opossum bit him and ran off."

We couldn't stop laughing, so I reached out and grasped his shoulder to steady us. It was a gesture I'd done before, to Mother, to Father, but my hand on his body sobered him. His hand found the back of mine and then circled my wrist. He pulled me toward him.

"I don't have any costumes for my show," I blurted when my body met his. One second more and I would have closed my eyes and tipped my chin back and offered my mouth.

He stepped away, releasing me. I clutched my hands behind my back. Jesse looked down at his boots. I watched him swallow, and then he looked at me.

"My sister works at the mill. They may have some scraps you could use for costumes. I can take you there tomorrow morning," he said.

It was as if he'd never pulled me close. I wondered if I'd imagined it.

"I don't know how to sew," I said.

"We'll figure that part out. Perhaps one of the girls at the Hostess House could help."

I nodded. "I suppose you're right."

Jesse walked to the casserole dishes still resting beside us. "It's late," he said. "I'm sure you've missed dinner. Take these."

He started to reach for the dishes, reconsidered, and gestured to them instead. If he took them, he'd have to hand them to me. Our fingers would touch as they just had.

"I couldn't," I said. "They're for you."

"So are fifty others just inside. We get at least four dishes a day." He smiled.

I picked the dishes up and the buttery scent of fried chicken engulfed me. I walked down the steps to the lawn. It was so dark I could only see a few feet in front of me.

"Where are you going?" he asked, following me. He nodded to the auto. "You can't walk three miles home in the dark. Major Gordon will be along momentarily to go into camp for the mail. I'll have him take you back."

CHAPTER 13

I t was seven in the morning and already Guy and I had been rehearsing for two hours. It was his fault, really. He'd gone by Goldie's parents' house last weekend and borrowed her brother's tuxedo for the dance tonight—Jesse had given him permission to dress in civilian attire since he was performing with me—but he'd forgotten to try on the suit, and when he did, he discovered that it was two sizes too small. Now he had an appointment with the McGanns' tailor at nine all the way across Charlotte and didn't think he'd be back until close to showtime.

I yawned and asked him to begin the introduction to "Let Me Call You Sweetheart" again. Guy groaned and took a long sip of his cold coffee he'd abandoned on the piano bench beside him.

"Do we have to?"

I laughed. We'd been through all of my popular tunes and were now rehearsing a few numbers I couldn't claim as my own.

"I know I took the tempo too slowly the last time, but perhaps I'm onto something. What if we keep it that way? Turn it into a Bunny Hug?"

That was one marked place where Guy and Caspar were different. Caspar adored singing love songs. He said they made him think of me. Though Guy enjoyed performing my songs because he found them clever, he didn't quite enjoy the sentimental pieces like this one.

"The chaperones would be in an uproar, Guy. Think of all of those sweet Charlotte girls who greeted you at the train with donuts.

They would be scandalized. President Wilson has even attempted to outlaw the dance, he finds it so indecent," I said. The Bunny Hug was quite naughty in parts, especially when it was danced at a slow jazz pace. "We're already pushing the envelope playing the 'Grizzly Bear.'"

He laughed.

"The 'Grizzly Bear' is hardly sensational. I suggested we do the Bunny Hug to rattle things up a bit. It would be wildly entertaining," he said. "Even Goldie would be in favor of it, and she's the sweetest of Charlotte girls."

I shook my head, envisioning the headlines that would undoubtedly make it to General Pershing: "Calla Connolly Shocks Charlotte Ladies, Encourages Veritable Burlesque Show at Lakewood Park."

"Aw, come on, Miss Connolly. Most of the men stopped coming to the dances because they were so boring. The music was played by a rotating group of church organists, and the chaperones came around with an actual ruler to make sure you weren't too close. But everybody's coming tonight to dance to *the* Calla Connolly."

"And Guy Werths," I said. "At actual tempo, please." Guy groaned again and struck up the opening notes. "If it helps, imagine you're playing a dance called the frog hop or the horse canter."

The corners of his lips lifted. "I believe I've already done those. They were rather enjoyable. Particularly the frog hop," he said over his playing. He focused on shuffling the sheet music in front of him, and then his cheeks reddened and he burst into laughter, his hands lifting from the keys before he could get to the second line. Clearly something about my reputation allowed him to speak to me as though I were a fellow doughboy. I wasn't sure whether to be honored or horrified.

I cleared my throat. "Whatever do you mean? I've never heard of those dances," I said, pretending I didn't know what he was insinuating. For some reason my reply only encouraged his hilarity and he slapped the bench with his palms. I turned away from him, toward the window displaying a gorgeous pink sunrise over the camp, so he couldn't see me laugh.

He began to strike the opening notes once again, though this time they were swift.

"*Let me call you sweetheart, I'm in love with you,*" he sang at a ragtime pace. I turned to face him, irritated. We had such little time to rehearse, and though he was one of the most proficient musicians I'd ever worked with, he was not versed in taking musical instruction from another and it showed.

He sobered and slowed the tempo when he saw that I was unamused. I came in at the second line. "*Let me hear you whisper that you love me too.*"

I nodded at him to sing the next line. I thought it could be different, this back and forth. It wasn't often done in this song.

At once the remembrance of Jesse's eyes in the starlight the night before struck me, but before I could consider what that meant, Guy looked at me, and I was faced with Caspar.

I sang the last line but was overcome with tremendous guilt. Standing there last night with Jesse, I'd felt something I hadn't felt since Caspar. With the other men, there had been the thrill of their touch, of the way their kisses made me feel alive, of the way their adoration poured over me as though all of their hopes had been realized with each stroke of their fingertips on my skin. Caspar had seen through me from the start, and though we barely touched until our engagement, I'd been drawn to him, desperately. My soul had been compelled toward him in such a way that each time we were together, I felt the sensation of teetering on a grand precipice naked. It was a warning, I suppose. The flipping stomach, the sprinting heart, the weak knees, the impression that someone could see you, flaws and strengths. It had all returned last night on the Dowd House porch.

"I'm sorry for my humor," Guy said when he'd finished the song. "When I'm tired I tend to amuse myself rather easily, much to the chagrin of anyone in my company."

"It's all right," I said. "Let's play 'I Wonder Who's Kissing Her Now,' and then get you off to the McGanns' tailor."

Guy shuffled through the sheets on the music stand.

"Speaking of who's kissing her now," Guy said after he'd located the song. "Do you suppose you could manage without me for a song or two? Normally I'm with Goldie during the dances, but this time I'll be up onstage and she'll be down there in the crowd getting asked to dance by all the other men."

"Absolutely. How about this one? If you'll just strike the E for me, I'll start."

He gave me the key and I turned toward the window as I began to sing.

"If you want to feel wretched and lonesome and blue, just imagine the girl you loved best in the arms of some fellow who's stealing a kiss."

I stopped abruptly and began to cry. I couldn't allow myself to feel for anyone else.

A clap sounded behind me and I whirled around to find Jesse standing next to Guy at the piano bench. His eyes crinkled when he saw the dew on mine.

"They'll take lunch at the mill at nine. It's as good a time as any to ask after the fabric you need," he said. "That is, if you'd still like to go."

CHAPTER 14

"A re you sure you want to sing tonight?"

We'd just driven through Remount Station—the expansive stables that had to have been housing more than a thousand horses—and out of the camp property into a quaint mill village. The little clapboard houses were empty except for a few children playing on the porches, and small, freshly tilled vegetable gardens dotted the bit of earth between each house.

"Why would you ask me that?" I asked. He'd been stopped almost a dozen times on his way out of camp by soldiers and officers inquiring about various things and we hadn't had the chance to speak to each other. I glanced at him. I hadn't before, thinking it best to keep my gaze fixed ahead of us, and regretted doing it now almost immediately. The free-falling sensation I'd felt in my stomach the night before reemerged at the sight of him and I looked away.

"I've never canceled a performance—well, with the exception of the ones I was forced to cancel on this tour," I went on.

Up ahead, the mill loomed. Like every other mill I'd seen before, it was made of brick and sprawling, but this one wasn't tall, only four stories at most.

"Even so." He waved to a man in tattered overalls walking along the dirt road. "You were upset earlier when I walked in," he said. "I don't want you to feel like you have to perform if you're feeling unwell or blue. The cantor at St. Peter's Episcopal is more than able to step in."

I started laughing. "Guy told me that the local churches had been lending their organists for the dances, but I had no idea it was also the cantors. What sort of songs would he sing?"

"Hymns and wholesome songs, like that one about asking a girl to be your bumblebee." Jesse choked out the words and started laughing himself. "I suppose we shouldn't be surprised that most of the men don't go to the dances now, although some have kept coming regardless, in the hope that they'll meet someone to write when they're over there."

"Of course I want to sing tonight and spare the men the entertainment of the cantor. Nothing makes me happier than to perform," I said. "I was upset earlier because I'm failing Caspar. I promised to love him forever. To love someone means to walk alongside them as their wishes are realized. But he's gone, Jesse, and I'm here and men like Basil are marching into battle in despair."

"You would go if you could," he said. He drove into a circular drive in front of the mill and parked next to the only other auto, a Cadillac. Hundreds of bicycles were piled in front of the expansive wooden doors, and a few roosters waddled and flapped on the lawn.

"I could've been more persistent. I should have asked you to wire General Dickman to wire General Pershing again."

He shut the engine off and turned to face me. I avoided his stare and looked over his shoulder instead. It wouldn't do to be unnerved by him right now, to feel the sensations of last night and the guilt that followed.

"It wouldn't have mattered if I had. It wouldn't change his mind. You've done everything you could do," Jesse said. "Look at me, Calla."

I forced my eyes to his at the mention of my name. His gaze was serious now, nothing like the starlit joy of the night before, and yet I was transfixed.

"I know you still love him. You would put aside your whole life for him, yet I doubt he was the sort of man to ask you to do that. The way you love him is more than any man could hope for," he said.

"Yet at times I worry that I could stop loving him," I whispered.

Jesse shook his head. "Perhaps in time you'll find you have more heart to spare for someone else, but your love for him won't fade." His words were sure, as if he spoke from experience. I'd never considered his attachments, though I assumed he'd had plenty. We weren't in our twenties anymore, and most people our age had either been widowed or left behind in war if they were unattached.

"Did you—"

I screamed as one of the chickens took flight and landed in the back seat of the auto. It blinked at us, its jiggling waddle and proud crown daring us to say a word about its intrusion.

"I can't get you an elephant or a bear, but I can get you a fine chicken for your set tonight," Jesse said, gesturing to the animal. He grinned. "Perhaps he can strut around while you play that song, the 'Chicken Reel,' that was so popular a while back. My sister played it over and over on the Victrola when it was first released. It's set here in Carolina, you know."

"As long as you participate in the dancing." I smiled.

I couldn't imagine Jesse doing any of the animal dances. A waltz or one of the ballroom sort, most certainly, but any that required a silly flailing of limbs wasn't suited to his demeanor whatsoever. I, on the other hand, adored the way the movements of the Grizzly Bear or the Turkey Trot or the Chicken Reel made me laugh. The Bunny Hug was a little suggestive even for my liking, but the rest were great fun.

"Afraid not."

A bell rang from somewhere behind the brick wall in front of us.

"Sounds like lunch is almost over. Let's go in before the girls get back to work." Jesse opened his door and got out, then walked around the front of the auto and opened my door as well. The chicken remained.

"See you later, Liza Snow," I said to the rooster.

Jesse laughed. "It's a rooster," he said, walking toward the mill doors.

"So? That's the name of the girl in the song," I said.

He smiled.

"It'll be loud in here, even with the machines off."

He waited for me on the walk to the entrance and held out his arm. I hesitated and then took it. He'd said nothing of his clutching my hand and pulling me close last night.

The moment we walked inside, I thought I might vomit. I couldn't comprehend how the workers could bear the stench. It was sharp and suffocating. Little particles of cotton floated in the air like snow over rows and rows of spools that stretched as far as the eye could see. At the end of each line of spools was a weaving contraption that extended thread from at least a dozen spools toward a machine that appeared like a metal bed headboard in structure and flattened the thread with little pieces of wood or metal that looked like piano hammers. Finished surgical cloth lay in sheets on the other side of it.

I hazarded a breath and must have made a choking sound, because Jesse reached into his coat pocket and held a silk handkerchief out to me. I pressed it over my nose, but it did little to stifle the odor. I could still smell the horrid stink, only now it was joined by the fresh floral of Palmolive soap.

"Formaldehyde," he said. "So the cloth doesn't wrinkle."

I handed the handkerchief back to Jesse. He pushed it into his coat pocket, then knocked on a plain, closed wooden door with a small nameplate that read "E. A. Smith."

The answer was a grumble, and Jesse opened the door. When the slim older man behind the antique desk saw us, his eyes nearly popped out of their sockets and he lurched to his feet.

"C-colonel," he stammered. "And Miss . . . Miss." He stared at me as if I were an apparition, his eyes squinting as he appraised my face.

"Connolly," I said.

"Yes, yes," he said, finally coming to his senses. He ran a hand over his head that was mostly bald except for a thin halo of gray. "I read in the papers that you were staying here, but I didn't for a moment foresee you appearing at my mill."

"Oh, well, I hope it's not too much of an intrusion," I said. I couldn't tell if he admired my work or if he was of the mind that I was a floozy, as I imagined Jesse had once thought—perhaps he still did.

"No, not in the slightest, though if the girls see you, their focus will be diverted for the remainder of the workday and we've got a shipment of cloth scheduled to be picked up tomorrow."

"That's actually why we've come, Smith, to ask about some cloth. Calla here needs costumes for her variety show she's putting on next week at camp, and we wondered if you had any ribbon or cloth to spare." Jesse paused. "Just scraps. It would be another contribution to the army, and we'll be sure to tell the papers you donated."

Mr. Smith stuffed his hands in his pockets and nodded.

"Yes, certainly," he said. A bell rang from the other end of the mill, its shrill note blaring even in the confines of his office. "I'll have Robert round some up and bring it to . . ."

"The Hostess House in camp, if it's not too much trouble," I said.

"Not at all. Colonel, would you mind closing the door? In just a moment, the women will return from their early lunch and if they catch sight of you, Miss Connolly, all will be—"

Before he could finish his sentence, the door burst open and women streamed through the doors, laughing and talking. They all wore the same thing—crisp, white starched dresses with aprons—but I was amazed at the variety of them: very old, very young, white, Black, Hispanic. Before the war, most of these women had been at home tending house, and now here they were, taking commerce by the horns in their men's stead. They were quite brave.

I tucked myself against the wall to avoid being observed, but I realized very quickly that Jesse was quite an attraction himself.

Ladies greeted him cheerily while Mr. Smith hastened them onward. But one woman, a young girl with jet-black hair and skin that mimicked fine china, squealed and threw herself into his arms. He laughed and stepped backward toward Mr. Smith's desk as he caught her. I gaped at the affection, at the way the sight of her made his face brighten, at the way his arms wrapped around her as he bent to kiss the top of her head.

"What are you doing here, Jesse?" the girl asked when he put her down, her back facing me.

Mr. Smith took advantage of Jesse moving and closed his door.

"I'm helping a friend with something," he said. He glanced at me over her shoulder and then turned her around to face me.

She gasped and stepped back.

"You're Calla Connolly," she said.

"Calla, this is my sister," Jesse said.

"It's lovely to meet you." I grinned. Suddenly their mutual affection made sense.

"Your brother has been such a help to me here," I said, shocked to realize I was sincere.

"Well, that's a surprise," she said. She looked like Jesse—equally as stunning, with the same piercing eyes. "Ordinarily he's quite a grump." She looked back at him. "I'm amazed you even know who she is." She turned back to me. "A few months ago, when Charlie Chaplin and Mary Pickford came through, he told us he wanted to get away from camp because a mime and a short little lady wearing a doll costume and ringlets were visiting and the soldiers were in a tizzy. He couldn't figure out why, even though many told him they were movie stars."

She laughed and I did too. Even Mr. Smith was chuckling.

"You've never seen *Hearts Adrift, Poor Little Rich Girl, The Tramp?*" I asked.

"Can't say that I have." Jesse grinned. "It's not that I've never been to a movie house, but I don't go often—especially in recent years—nor do I necessarily recall the names of the actors. I've never been that interested in celebrity, as both of you know." He shrugged.

"Did you know who she was?" his sister asked, pointing at me.

"I doubt he did at first," I said. "He certainly didn't know any of my songs."

She shook her head, and her lips pinched. "He's been consumed by his duty every moment since he's been back from France. He rarely allows himself any fun, but he used to be the most amusing of us all—the first to jump into the river, the first to dance."

I glanced at Jesse. His smile had faded like his sister's, and he was looking down at his boots.

"Anyway, *I* know all of your songs," she said, her grin returning. "I have so many favorites—'I Have It All,' 'The Singing Man,' 'Find Me at the End of the Road.'"

"'Find Me' is awfully sad," I said. I'd written it after I'd received word of Caspar's death. I hadn't ever made it through the whole song without crying.

"That's precisely why we all love it so much. Sometimes when we're feeling blue that our men are away, we sing it while we work here in the mill," she said. She glanced at Mr. Smith.

"I don't mind it as long as you're working," he said.

"There are all sorts of songs about bravery and victory but so few about the reality that some we love won't return. I suppose it's comforting to know that even if the worst happens, they'll be waiting for us and that we'll be reunited one day."

I swallowed and nodded. "Yes, thank heavens for that," I said, though I often wondered how much I believed that I'd actually see Caspar again. Most of the time I found it impossible to accept the notion that he was gone, so perhaps that was evidence that he wasn't really.

"I'm Emma, by the way. Emma Erickson, but you already know my last name."

Mr. Smith cleared his throat.

"Well, I suppose I'll be getting back to work now, but it's been lovely to meet you, Miss Connolly, and all right to see you too, Jesse." She turned toward him and struck him in the chest with her elbow. Despite his momentary melancholy, he wrapped his arms around her again and then pushed her gently toward the door. "See you tonight at the dance."

"I'm sorry for the interruption," Jesse said to Mr. Smith as Emma disappeared into the mill. The machines were being awakened one by one. The chug of the motors and the mechanical click of the stitching built and built as one joined another and another. Before long, the noise was a roar.

"Don't think anything of it," Mr. Smith said loudly. "As I said, I'll have Robert see to the scraps and have them delivered to Miss Connolly's attention at the Hostess House."

"Thank you, sir." I tipped my head at Mr. Smith. "The men will be thrilled to know they'll have actual costumes for our show."

"We'll leave you to it," Jesse said, then held out his arm for me once again. I took it and we paced swiftly out of Mr. Smith's office, then the mill doors before the other women caught sight of us.

As we walked to the auto in the bright sunshine, I noticed I could see the few towering buildings of downtown Charlotte on the cloudless blue horizon. I thought of what Mary had mentioned about Belk Brothers Department Store and had an insatiable urge to go shopping for a new dress. Perhaps talking about costumes had prompted thoughts of mine.

"Do you suppose you could take me downtown?" I asked. "I'd like to buy a dress for the dance tonight."

Jesse looked at me. He started to say something but stopped himself.

"Sure."

I thought of what Emma had said about him never having fun. Perhaps she'd convinced him to abandon his office for the day.

"Looks like Liza Snow's left us," I said. The back seat of Jesse's auto was now abandoned except for a few wispy feathers. The chickens had all departed for greener pastures. I extended my bottom lip in my best pout. "Since I've convinced you to take me shopping, perhaps I can also convince you to ask Mr. Cornwell to let us use one of his animals tonight. I'd started to get excited about the idea of taking Liza with me and asking Guy to play the 'Chicken Reel.'"

"None of his animals have a dance," Jesse said, smiling. He held open the auto door for me and I stepped inside.

"But they could. The Ostrich Bounce, the Zebra Cow Shuffle. Just think of it, Jesse, Camp Greene could claim its own animal dance."

"A true legacy indeed." Jesse chuckled, then settled in the seat beside me and started the engine.

"Mary Pickford suggested Belk Brothers Department Store for their hats," I said as we motored out of the mill village to the north, passing another dozen little homes as we did.

"I thought you said you were on the hunt for a new dress." He took a right on a road marked Trade.

"I am. I suppose I assumed a fine hat selection equaled a fine gown selection. Is that not the case? I have a romantic chiffon in mind in either pink or possibly gold with a cluster of flowers at my waist. All the costumes I brought are too dramatic for a dance." I thought of the Worth number, the one with the black sequins and intricate braiding down the front. It was meant to draw the eye to me alone, and though, if I was honest, I would never not crave the spotlight, my purpose tonight was to blend in, to lend a backdrop to those keen on finding a love that would carry them through war and beyond. I sighed and sat back against the seat, surprised to find that though I was excited for the stage, I didn't feel the anxious desperation for it as I had so often these last years. Perhaps it was because, though I wasn't at the front where I desperately wanted to be, I was still cheering soldiers like Caspar every day with my lessons. He was with me in the midst of those too.

Jesse waved at a soldier coming out of a post office, an impressive brick federal building with a tower at the corner. I glanced at Jesse, wondering if he'd dance with anyone tonight or if he simply stood sentry at the corner of the pavilion, the doughboy's version of a chaperone. If the latter were the case, I was sure most of the ladies would find it a terrible shame.

"We'll go to Ivey's," he said. "It's where all of the Charlotte ladies buy their gowns."

I hadn't thought about the consequences of venturing downtown on a Saturday. The streets were crushed with autos and streetcars and pedestrians, and it seemed that the whole of them were keen to greet me as I got out of Jesse's Packard.

"Please, move back!" Jesse yelled as he swung my door open. A gaggle of young women and children and older men pressed forward instead. Jesse swore under his breath and then glanced at me, waiting for my shock, though I didn't respond. When it was clear the crowd wasn't going to abide his authority, I kicked off my shoes and stood on the auto seat.

"I am so glad to see all of you," I shouted. "It's a lovely day, isn't it? Colonel Erickson here has been given the horrid chore of escorting me into this fine department store for a new costume." I gestured at Ivey's Department Store in front of me. Even from the outside it was beautiful and looked nearly like Mrs. Astor's old place in New York, though this building was made of limestone instead of freestone. The picture windows boasted a gorgeous display of several mannequins dressed in soft chiffon finery having a tea party in a garden. "Though I would like to greet all of you and hold your hands and hear your stories, I'm afraid we're in a bit of a rush. You see, I have to get back to entertain the doughboys and many of your daughters at the dance at Lakewood Park tonight." A little girl in the middle of the crush began to cry. "Now, don't despair. I'll be here in Charlotte for some time yet, and when I have more than a moment, I'll be happy to say hello personally." I paused. "How about this? Let's sing a song together and then I'll pop into the store with Colonel Erickson?"

The crowd seemed to cheer at the mention of a song, so I thought fast. Everybody would know "The Caissons Go Rolling Along" by now, even if they didn't know my music.

I started singing, but by the time I made it to the chorus, "*Then its hi! hi! hee! In the field artillery,*" it seemed as if the whole town was singing. People stopped in the middle of the street, shopping treasures in hand, and joined in. Even Jesse was singing, and a smile painted his face in sunshine. I directed the town, hardly singing as they carried the song to its close.

"Now I must be off!" I shouted and hurriedly stepped down from the seat, pushed my feet into my brown leather pumps, and took Jesse's outstretched hand.

Much to my surprise, the crowd didn't persist in trying to reach me but went along their day, some of them humming the tune to "Caissons."

The noise ceased the moment we stepped into Ivey's and the intoxicating scent of bergamot and orange and rose wavered over me. A pharmacy and luncheon room were tucked away to the right of the entrance, but the rest of the floor boasted tables of perfumes in silver and gold boxes, hats of all shades and shapes atop stands of varying heights, ties in picture display cases, and baubles and jewelry locked in glass cabinets.

"You're amazing. The way you steadied that crowd was a lot like commanding a regiment," Jesse said.

"Not really. I asked them to sing. You ask them to fight. I imagine most are happy to lend their voices but not their—"

"Lives," he said, finishing my sentence. He squeezed my arm linked with his, then released me. I couldn't figure what the gesture meant. Perhaps only that he was letting me go. "The store has just opened its doors. I don't imagine there will be many shoppers around to swarm you."

"Welcome to Ivey's." A woman my mother's age with a thick French accent appeared from behind the perfume display, then turned to Jesse, wrapped him in an embrace, and began to speak in French. He laughed and said something back to her I couldn't understand. His command of the language was perfect, and I watched, in awe of him. I knew he'd been in France for a few years, but still, the way he slipped into the language with such ease indicated he'd been versed in it long before his time there. His mother had been French. Perhaps he'd been taught the language from his youth.

"Calla, this is my mother's best friend, Noemie. She's been working here at Ivey's since she and Mother came to America together. She helps the store find the finest fashion and the finest perfumes from France."

"Nice to meet you," I said. I smiled and she grinned back.

"It's lovely to meet *you*, Miss Calla," she said. "Jesse was right to bring you in. We have some lovely new dresses upstairs on the third floor. I'm happy to accompany you."

Before I could say that I could manage on my own, she turned to the back of the building and started walking toward a gilded elevator in the corner. I followed behind her and Jesse, watching the delicate sway of her hips as she sashayed past the hats and the gloves and the jewelry in her fashionable royal-blue basque and tunic. She was nearly as magnetic as Jesse was. I was sure that his mother had been similar, likely even more mesmerizing than Noemie, if Jesse's appearance was any indication. They chattered on in French and I noticed the elevator operator, a man about her age, staring at her until he noticed me behind the two of them and startled.

"You're . . . you're Miss . . . Miss," the elevator operator stammered.

"Yes, Mr. Tolar," Noemie said politely. "This is Miss Calla Connolly. While we're looking around upstairs, would you mind holding off any other customers? It will be difficult for Miss Connolly to appraise our selections in the company of adoring fans."

"Of course," Mr. Tolar said. I appreciated Noemie's thought to my comfort. It was true that I rarely shopped in public for this very reason.

"I'm pleased to make your acquaintance." I held my hand out to him and he took it and smiled. "Thank you for helping me up to the women's section today, Mr. Tolar."

Jesse clapped him on his back as we ushered into the elevator.

"Jeremiah had to endure a lot of mischief from me and Noemie's son, Phillippe, when we were young." Jesse laughed as Mr. Tolar pulled the grate across the opening and pushed the gold button marked 3.

"It's a good thing I enjoy my post," Mr. Tolar said, chuckling.

"When Father started the general store in Mount Holly, there was no one to watch Emma and me, and Noemie's husband had passed, so Phillippe was without care as well. Mr. Ivey allowed us to sit in the lunchroom and read or color as long as we could stay on good behavior. Well—"

"That didn't last very long," Noemie said. "They were into everything. They would try on the hats and the gloves and run around the upper floors. Camille, Jesse's mother, and I tried to keep them contained, but inevitably they'd find their way to trouble."

"Remember that time they shattered that bottle of Guerlain L'heure Bleue? Both you and Camille were beside yourselves, and the store smelled of neroli and carnation for months, but L'heure Bleue was sold in record numbers at this store because of it," Mr. Tolar said.

"We were never thanked for our contribution." Jesse laughed.

Noemie grinned and shook her head.

"You boys were true menaces, while sweet Emma read hundreds of books like a good little thing. The only upside to having you in the store was that you were both exposed to fine things and grew up to have taste. You're both fashionable men."

I wanted to ask after her son, but in times like these, you never knew if the inquiry was welcome. Perhaps he'd already been shipped to the front. Perhaps he'd perished.

"I'm not sure we're suited for the streets of Paris now." Jesse looked down at his olive jacket, and Noemie reached out and tugged at his lapel. His face clouded and my mind lingered on the word *Paris*. I wondered if the mention of that city, his second home, also made him think of the regiment possibly tasked with defending it, while he would likely be forced to stay behind here.

"I would say you're even more suited to those streets. Your mother would be proud of you. She always knew your heart was your strength, that you would live to champion others, and you have. You are."

Jesse looked away from her. My eyes teared at her words.

"It's not the truth," he whispered. "I hoped to be and then . . . there are things out of my control, *Tante*."

There were certain times when that day in the hospital over-hearing Jesse's words to General Alexander seemed like a dream, like that sort of mission couldn't at all be true and I had been held here for some other reason. But then there were moments like this one, when reality stomped upon contentedness, bringing us back to the war and the horror.

The bell dinged, and the elevator stopped.

Mr. Tolar pulled open the grate to reveal a polished white marble floor stretching toward mannequins draped in the finest soft chiffon and organza. I stepped out of the elevator but found I could barely stomach looking at the costumes. Asking Jesse to accompany me to a department store when there was so much work to be done at camp had been a selfish request.

"Does anything catch your eye?" Noemie asked. She stood beside me, surveying the same view I was.

"I suppose I'm not in the mood to look for a dress anymore," I said. I could feel Jesse on my other side, his shoulder nearly touching mine. "It seems inconsequential. What does it matter what I wear when men over there are fighting and dying?"

"I'm sorry," Jesse said, his voice low. "I've dampened your spirits. I was set on optimism today."

"It does matter, actually," Noemie said. She walked toward a purple chiffon and lamé dress with a gorgeous purple drape around the waist, pinched the fabric, glanced at me, and then made a dismissive noise and started toward another blush costume with silver rose stitching down the skirt. "My Phillippe is in an army training camp much like Camp Greene but in Illinois. Camp Grant, it's called. And my daughter-in-law, Natalie, sends for a new dress each week for his day off." She glanced at me. "Every day of a life should be special and celebrated, whether that day is a day in peril or a day in peace. When you first set out on your tour, the papers wrote about something you'd said that was marvelously true. You said that you intended to remind the soldiers of the joy of life even in the midst of war, to lift their spirits, because if a soldier's soul is crushed, they will find their strength to fight for justice crushed too."

"I believe that with all my heart, and yet at times even I need to be reminded."

"We can control so little of our lives. All that matters in the end is that we were compassionate and humble, that we loved as often as we could and tried our best to cheer those cast down among us." She emerged from a crush of mannequins with a costume so lovely and perfect it stole my breath. It was aqua silk with hand-beaded pink and metallic flowers that gathered and fell away in a diamond pattern down the length of the dress from bodice to skirt.

Her eyes fixed on Jesse. "We must press toward the light no matter our lot. Father always used to say, 'Au long aller, petit fardeau pèse.'"

"'On a lengthy journey, a small burden weighs,'" Jesse said.

"Imagine the weight of a large burden. We must throw them all off and cling to hope." Noemie walked toward me and held the dress up in front of me. "It's a Poiret. Just in from France." She appraised it. "Consider, the both of you, that the French are living with this war at their doorstep, yet they are still making beautiful things. They are not surrendering to the darkness, and neither shall we." She looked at me. "This will be absolutely stunning with your fair skin and dark hair."

I ran my fingers over the beading.

"She said she's looking for something light, a chiffon perhaps," Jesse said. I glanced at him. His attention was fixed on the dress. I was shocked he'd recalled my preference. Caspar, though I knew he loved me immensely, had a mind that flitted from one idea to another, his attention never settling too long on things that had no consequence to him—like the material I preferred in a gown.

"I thought I wanted a costume like that one there." I pointed to the purple chiffon at the front of the arrangement of mannequins. "But now that I've seen this one, I must have it. The color itself is wonderfully unique."

"And spring itself," Noemie said. "This sample is small enough, too, that it might just fit without much alteration. I fear that some of our selections would take at least a day to trim to your slim figure." She held the dress against my chest and I grasped the fabric straps to my shoulders. "This is a thirty-two-inch bust, but you're small in that area," she mused.

I could feel my cheeks burn. Mother had sizable breasts, as did Lenor and Evelyn Nesbit. I'd always envied the way they filled out a dress, the hourglass figure all the men craved.

"I'm quite built like a board." I laughed to hide my embarrassment, but neither Jesse nor Noemie seemed to notice. "My waist is twenty-five."

"And you're short, five feet"—she leveled her hand at her eyebrows where the top of my head stopped—"two inches. My. Just about the same exact measurements as Jesse's mother. Same as Ja—" Noemie stopped in the middle of her sentence and her gaze met Jesse's. "You're built much like a pixie," she said, turning back to me and laughing. She sounded like Goldie, all chime and no chortle.

"If only I could fly like one. That would be a fun addition to my shows, don't you think?" I smiled.

"You've already done that once, in *The Sunshine Brigade*, on the trapeze," Noemie said. "Phillippe and Natalie took me to see it in Columbus for my Christmas gift one year."

"My hometown," I said. "And you're right. I was scared out of my wits to do it at first and I was even held by cables. I can't imagine circus performers who are inclined to go at it without anything at all." I held the costume away from my shoulders. She was the second person in town who'd seen that particular show. It wasn't the most popular tour I'd ever been a part of, not even close, but I noticed at times that various towns had favorites.

"You were in an actual circus?" Jesse asked. His lips lifted in a smile and the atmosphere in the store seemed to shift, like the sun breaking through a wash of clouds. "All this time I thought we'd been joking about the elephants and the bear and the zebra cow, but now I know—"

"No, I wasn't in an actual circus," I said, laughing. "I don't have the skill."

"*The Sunshine Brigade* is a musical about a troop of dejected circus performers who decide to go into small towns and do shows for the downcast," Noemie said. "News of it was in all the papers. Miss Connolly here brought me to tears. When you sang 'The Clouds Broke Today' with that woman doing that beautiful routine on top of that white horse in the background, there wasn't a dry eye in the theatre."

"This explains so much. Calla's been begging me for an animal to accompany her acts," Jesse said. "She almost settled for a rooster earlier today, she's been so desperate for one."

"You caught me. Ever since *The Sunshine Brigade*, I've wanted a chance at performing with an animal. Never mind that Claudia Schubert, the woman on the horse, is a trained acrobat. And I would have settled for Liza the rooster, but my options would have been tremendously limited. I can't ride a rooster around the stage or do handstands on his back." I grinned, thinking of the absurdity of performing alongside a chicken—or even performing on the back of an elephant, for that matter. I was earnest in my awe of performers who could accomplish such a feat, but I would undoubtedly fall. "I think that Jesse should find me an elephant or an animal of similar stature, don't you think, Noemie? It would greatly cheer me—the boys too. They could take bets as to how long I'd stay on. I'm afraid there's quite a gap between my paltry skills and those of the Ringling Brothers performers." I started laughing. Without thinking, I swatted Jesse's chest, and he clutched my hand. He let go as quickly.

"Jesse hasn't only been tasked with accompanying you today, I gather?" she asked. Her expression changed as she beheld me. Before, she'd been lovely and accommodating, but now her eyes narrowed to something resembling scrutiny.

"Unfortunately for Jesse, General Pershing has ordered him to be my chaperone anytime I'm not in camp," I said. "It's a nuisance, I know."

"I wasn't happy about it at first," he admitted.

"I wasn't either."

"And now?" Noemie looked from Jesse to me and back again. Her face was drawn. She seemed worried about our arrangement. I couldn't figure why.

"We didn't have a choice but to become friends," I said.

"With Phillippe away, I was short one," Jesse said.

Noemie smiled, and her shoulders, which had moments ago been pitched upward, relaxed.

"Things tend to settle themselves with time," she said. "Now, let's go to the dressing room, Miss Calla. I'll pin it and then take it down to alterations." She took the dress from my hands and started walking toward the back of the store. "By the look of it, I doubt we'll need to do much, so the altering will only take an hour or so. While you wait, you may as well have a bit of refreshment in the lunchroom. My treat. I'll tell Mr. Jackson to clear the room."

"He doesn't have to do that. I don't mind greeting the Charlotteans. They've all been lovely so far," I said as we followed her back toward the dressing room.

I glanced at Jesse and found his gaze on my face before he looked away. Perhaps he was trying to figure out, as I was, if we were, in fact, friends.

CHAPTER 15

My hair resembled a soiled mop. I'd been singing for going on two hours—everything from "Pack Up Your Troubles" to "I Have It All" to "Same Sweet Heart" to "Let Me Call You Sweetheart," to even the "Grizzly Bear," much to the horror of the stodgy old chaperones who lined the edges of the expansive pavilion in ball gowns that mimicked their charge's.

The spotlight jerked a bit, and I nodded to Mr. Cornwell's jack-of-all-trades, Mr. Stanley Ackerman, who had been leaning on a twelve-foot metal ladder at the very back of the pavilion to situate the light just so. He had to be more exhausted than even I was. Four more songs and it would be nine thirty, only a half hour to curfew, leaving a half hour for the lovers to say their goodbyes. I'd need to wrap the show quickly.

The Lakewood Park pavilion was teeming with soldiers and ladies dancing, the ceiling decorated with electric bulb lights arranged in great swags across the entire expanse. If I squinted hard, I could see the glitter of the lake in the moonlight all the way at the back of the crowd in front of me and the dark spires of pine forest at the sides. Every inch of available space was covered by people. When Guy and I had first stepped onto the simple stage, I'd been shocked by how many guests Mr. Cornwell had allowed. The space was crushed with nearly four hundred. I'd heard it was only equipped to hold half of that. I'd felt the stage dip for a moment when I started "I Have It All" and wondered if the pavilion might snap from the little building it was attached to and sink into the lake.

"'I Wonder Who's Kissing Her Now,'" I turned and told Guy, who was sitting behind me at the bench of the baby grand piano Mr. Cornwell had had brought in by truck from his home in town. "Go get Goldie," I said.

"Are you sure?" he asked. He wiped the sweat from his brow with his handkerchief and stood before I could say I was. Goldie's brother's trim black suit fit Guy well and he looked the picture of a Broadway man. I decided then and there that he'd be a Broadway man someday. He'd return from this war whole and then wow the world.

"Have you seen her out there?" He looked over the crush when he reached my side and everyone cheered.

"Straight back, next to the ladder," I said. Goldie had been standing in the same place since we started, looking quite like a Hollywood darling herself in my gold silk costume inlaid with gilded stones. Soldiers had asked her to dance throughout the evening. I'd watched them approach her and then walk away disappointed as she smiled and declined. Guy wouldn't have seen it from his position behind me at the piano, but her devotion warmed my heart. The war would incite many love matches, but only a few would last. If I was a gambling sort, I'd put all my chips on Goldie and Guy.

Guy jumped down from the stage into the crowd, and a group of ladies in matching white taffeta dresses, who had occupied the space in front of the stage with various soldier dance partners the entire time, squealed. He smiled and pushed through to where Goldie stood.

"Let's give a round of applause for my dear friend, Guy Werths," I shouted, gesturing to Guy right as he tipped Goldie back to kiss her. "And his fiancée, Goldie McGann, who saved my life." The cheers rose and I cleared my throat. "These next numbers, I'm singing acapella—that means without Guy's marvelous piano playing—so if you know the words, do sing along."

I got halfway through "I Wonder Who's Kissing Her Now" before I spotted Jesse for the first time all evening. He was to the left of me, his arms wrapped around a pretty girl with auburn hair. He was wearing his dress coat and his hair was combed away from his face.

The girl put her head on his chest as I sang the second chorus, and something about the gesture made my muscles tense and my skin flush. I forced my gaze away and tried to focus on the beautiful sight of Goldie and Guy dancing together in front of me.

"*You have kissed 'neath the moon while the world seemed in tune. Then you've left her to hunt a new game,*" I sang.

Despite my intentions, my eyes drifted back toward Jesse. Now his hand was flat on the girl's back, encouraging her closer, and I had the insatiable urge to step off the stage and cut in. It wasn't as though he was mine—I'd only ever possessed one man truly—but after the day in his company, watching him hold someone was burning me through.

After I'd had my dress fitted, we'd retired to the luncheon room at Ivey's for tomato sandwiches and lemon meringue pie. We'd waved to the shoppers on the sidewalk from the picture window and poked fun at each other, and he'd reached for my hand when he escorted me to his auto. I'd thought, as we drove back to camp, that for the first time in my life I knew what it was like to be a normal girl dining with a normal boy. From the time I debuted on Broadway, I'd get stopped on the street, and the interruptions only increased when Caspar and I were together. But today I'd thrown off the shine of Calla Connolly, the darling of Broadway, as I always seemed to do in Jesse's company, and dined with a man who saw through to the woman I was.

I finished the song and considered continuing on with Guy's favorite, Harry Macdonough's "I Love You Best of All," but knew I wouldn't be able to endure watching Jesse hold this woman for another moment.

"We're going to switch gears a little, ladies and gents," I said. I snapped my fingers until the tempo was right, until the girl abandoned Jesse and another ebony-haired beauty took her place, then started into my song, "The Singing Man." It was funny to watch a crowd of people accustomed to formal dancing attempt kicks and hops and capers, and before I knew it, I was laughing and singing, having almost as much fun as the guests.

"*I love a lot of you and I'd marry you, Joe, but I want a singing man.*" I finished the song with a whoop and a bow, and the guests cheered louder than they had since the start of the dance.

"Miss Connolly has entertained us well all night, don't you think?" Guy was beside me on the stage again. This time Goldie stood just feet in front of us. I smiled at her, and she grinned back. The crowd yelled a smattering of affirmative noises.

"What are you doing? I have two more songs," I said to him, but he ignored me.

"I believe it's time for Miss Connolly to take a turn on the dance floor with a lucky doughboy or two, don't you think?"

"No," I protested, laughing. I'd promised them all a show, and to stop now to dance seemed like shortchanging them.

"Go," he said. When I didn't budge, he practically pushed me off the stage—right into the arms of Jesse, who stood at the left side.

"Would you dance with me?" Jesse asked. He offered his hand, and I took it, though I looked back at the stage, completely bewildered by this change in plans.

"What in the world is—"

"You deserve a moment's peace, same as the rest of us," Jesse said. I thought to tell him that being on the stage *was* my peace, but was silenced by his free hand capturing the small of my back and Guy playing the introduction to "I Love You Best of All." I felt my spine quiver at the whisper of his breath on my ear and the feel of his fingers on my body. "I suppose I should've asked if you had your heart set on dancing with some handsome soldier before I stepped in."

"I did. I'm already dancing with him," I said. I grinned and our eyes met. He held my gaze and drew me closer. I could feel his heartbeat and his eyes drifted to my lips. Guy's singing seemed far away, and the people who pressed in all around us disappeared. I recalled the way he'd held the woman he was dancing with before me. "I saw you with that other woman, the one with auburn hair. Did I take you away from her?"

"You couldn't have possibly taken me away from anyone," he said. "I've been mesmerized by you all night. We all are."

Perhaps this meant he felt it too—the racing heart, the urge to draw in, the knowing of a soul that wasn't yours.

A couple beside us jostled into me and I broke his gaze to smile at them.

"Calla." His voice was soft, and when our eyes met this time, he leaned in closer. "The moment you stepped out of my auto today and left me . . . This might seem odd to say, but I missed you."

There was a sudden commotion behind me, but I held on to Jesse and ignored it.

"I missed you too. I—"

"Forgive me," Jesse said suddenly. His face hardened and he let me go. I watched him push through the crowd toward the entrance to the pavilion where a girl in a white lace gown stood alone, her gaze fixed on Jesse. I felt the echo of his body pressed to mine, heard our whispered confessions, and at once, my heart shriveled. I'd betrayed Caspar's memory, his love. I'd allowed myself to get swept away, to feel for someone else. Tears sprung to my eyes and I vaguely heard voices asking me to dance as I wiped them away, stepped back on the stage, and joined Guy in the song.

"*I want you, I love you best of all,*" we sang. I tried to concentrate on bringing up Caspar's face in my mind as the music took over for my voice, but I pushed the recollection away as emotion threatened again.

Out of the corner of my eye, I could see Jesse bent low in front of the woman. He was furious, his face stony and flushed as he shook his head and appeared to shout. She was crying. I wondered what the conversation was about, but then again, he was the commander in charge of the camp. It could be any number of things. Everyone else seemed to ignore them and I tried to do the same, turning my back to them as I finished the song with Guy.

"What happened?" Guy whispered as we transitioned to the final song.

"I don't know," I said.

"How about a lullaby for the final number? 'Too-Ra-Loo-Ra-Loo-Ral'?" Guy winked at me, and I nodded.

"I do love that song. Did I ever tell you how comforting it was when you sang it to me the night I lost consciousness? My mother sang it to me as a child."

"No, but I guess the song came to mind for a reason."

He started playing the introduction. I turned back to the crowd.

"The night is almost over. Thank you for joining us. It's been the berries," I shouted. "Now, as a word of caution, you've all got about a half hour till the mean old curfew bell rings, so ready your kissers and make your plans and we'll see you again in two weeks—unless you're a Johnny, in which case we'll see you next week at the Liberty Theatre for a variety show you won't want to miss."

I smiled at the guests as they hollered and cheered and held their darlings close, then started singing.

Over the whispered goodbyes and Guy's playing, I could hear Jesse's angry growl from the side of the pavilion. I hazarded a glance. The girl was now clutching his arms and sobbing, but her distress didn't seem to stifle his anger. I recalled his confession that he missed me, that he'd been transfixed by me, but also the way in which he'd left me on the dance floor and the way he'd held the girl he'd danced with earlier. Perhaps this woman was one of his lovers and she'd been set into a jealous rage watching him dancing with me. Perhaps I'd been a fool. I thought of Caspar's face again and my heart settled. I could only hope that I was right, that Jesse was a philanderer after all.

"*Over in Killarney, many years ago,*" I sang.

The girl shouted, "No!" and the noise punctuated the song, but I kept on. I saw the last of Jesse's jacket as he disappeared into the shadowy pines at the perimeter of the pavilion, leaving the girl to crumple on the ground. A group of older women immediately gathered around her.

"*My mother sang a song to me.*"

The moment I finished the phrase, a guttural scream sounded from the woman on the ground and Jesse reemerged from the woods dragging a dirty, shivering man in tattered olive drab behind him.

"Calla!" Jesse shouted. "Miss Connolly," he amended, but Guy and I kept on. "Miss Connolly, stop the music." The demand boomed over me as it had the night I'd collapsed with flu. I stopped singing, realizing in that moment that the order was equal parts plea. "Major Gordon!" Jesse shouted again, and Major Gordon, who'd been taking advantage of the darkness to neck with an older woman in the corner of the pavilion, disentangled himself from her arms and hastened through the crowd toward Jesse. When Jesse was within Major Gordon's range of vision, he pushed the skinny, quivering soldier toward him and the man fell at the major's feet. "The last slacker's been found." Jesse's voice sounded over the silence. His shoulders squared and his large hands fisted. I nearly began to sob with relief. Only a few days more and he would have been charged; he could have been sentenced to death. "Deal with him appropriately."

CHAPTER 16

J esse had come by the Hostess House to collect me for church, but I'd refused to come out of my room, feigning a headache. My "illness" had required Mrs. Kern to stay home from church herself to attend to me, and I felt awful about that, but I couldn't face Jesse. In the wake of realizing what had actually happened—that the girl had been pleading with Jesse about something related to her entanglement with the slacker soldier—and that Jesse wasn't, in fact, an army Casanova, I was left with the implication of our dance.

I could still feel the warmth in the pit of my stomach when he'd held me and the way my spirit had lightened when he confessed he'd been mesmerized by me. I wanted to feel it both immediately and never again. I'd tried to distract myself by replying to the growing stack of letters from supporters and Mother and Father—they were relieved to know I'd recovered from the flu, weren't at all surprised to find me following my heart, and had just had a visit from Mr. Keeghan, who was well and about to set out to California to visit his brother—but since my letters were read by the army, I couldn't be myself in even my correspondence with my parents, and the distraction faded. Instead, I began to feel the presence of Caspar's letter in my armoire. I'd read it once again, I suppose in an attempt to find either forgiveness or permission in his words, but there was nothing. We'd never discussed his wishes for me if he died in the war. Neither of us believed he would, I supposed. I'd tried to close my eyes and conjure him. I'd envisioned telling him about Jesse, about the way we made each other laugh and the way he understood me, but even in my imagining, Caspar just stood there, a hint of a smile on his lips. He'd never been jealous, and even if I had developed feelings for Jesse, Jesse was right—it didn't take my love for Caspar away. Still, Caspar and I had left things unsaid.

"I'll have to borrow Roland and any other brass we can muster if we're settling on 'Second Connecticut' for the Rhode Island portion of the show," Sidney said, interrupting my thoughts of the morning. He was eyeing the sheet music in front of him. He set his violin down and laughed. "Marching band music doesn't have the same appeal on a stringed instrument."

"Should we think of another song?" I asked. Despite it being Sunday, I'd had Sidney and William Wentworth come over to practice the theme songs for Rhode Island and Maine respectively. Neither of them had dining plans after church and were more than happy to play for me rather than lie around in the tents with the other men.

"I'd love to find another one, but David Wallis Reeves is by far the most famous composer from Rhode Island, and there aren't many tunes that mention our little slice of paradise." Sidney laughed. "I could write one."

"Why don't you?" I asked. "Think of it—it could be quite a hit for you and the state."

"I'm not so great with words. That's Juliet's gift," he said.

"Could you come up with the tune and ask her to help you write the lyrics?" I sat down on the ledge of the window. It was gray today, threatening rain. I yawned. "I'd help you, but I've only been to Newport once, and I doubt Newport speaks for all of Rhode Island."

"The gilded set would like you to think it does," Sidney said. "I'll work with Juliet and see what we can come up with for a new song."

A knock on the rolling partition interrupted us. I called for whoever it was to come in, and Goldie appeared in a spring-green suit with a wide-brimmed khaki dress hat.

"I'm sorry to interrupt," she said. "Oh, hi, Sidney."

"Goldie." Sidney tipped his head.

"Mrs. Kern said I could find you here," Goldie said to me.

"I thought you'd be away all day," I said.

Goldie nodded. "Usually that's the case on Sundays, but to-day a group of us are planning to decorate the soldiers' graves at the cemetery downtown ahead of Memorial Day next Thursday." She paused. "I came to see if you might be able to ask Colonel Erickson if you could come along . . . and also have supper after-ward at the home of a distressed young girl who could use your cheer about now. I'd make sure Guy was there to protect you from any overzealous admirers that I know the army is worried you'll encounter."

"What's happened?" I asked.

Goldie glanced at Sidney—perhaps she was worried he'd over-hear some delicate detail—but he was tuning his violin, barely aware that there was a conversation occurring at all.

"We found out today at church. The girl from last night, the one who was crying over the slacker who was caught? Her family just moved to our side of town from the country, and they hardly know a soul, so Mother offered to bring them supper on account of her being so upset over her soldier. Her mother confided in Mother that the girl is pregnant." Goldie whispered the word, and it was sud-denly evident why she didn't want Sidney to overhear. Speaking of pregnancies, even within marriage, was considered poor manners in some circles. "Apparently he deserted when he heard about her condition. He didn't want to risk the baby growing up without a father." She shook her head. "I suppose he didn't think. She didn't know where he was until last night. Her mother said that he snuck out of the woods to find her just before the dance and Colonel Zachary saw him and went after him."

"What will become of that man? I read in the paper that he could face a worse sentence than the others since he was gone longer," Sidney said, now listening to the conversation.

"Not death," Goldie said. "They're hoping he'll get a month of hard labor and confinement rather than be jailed, but we'll see in the coming days."

"I sympathize with him," I said. "Imagine finding out you're going to be a father and then that you'll be overseas when the baby is born, that there's a chance you'll never see your child."

"The news from the front wasn't encouraging this morning either. Did you read that they suspect Germany is readying for another offensive soon? I know I'm supposed to be brave and reassuring, but I fear that means they'll need Guy—and you, Sidney, and all the rest," Goldie said. Her eyes began to tear.

"I didn't read the paper this morning," I said. My voice was weak. I'd been so consumed with thoughts of Caspar and Jesse, I hadn't given it a thought. Compared to the men on the front and the plight of the regiment that would be deployed to protect Paris if the rumored offensive was aimed that direction, my worries were inconsequential.

"Are you scared, Sidney?" Goldie asked. Sidney was staring blankly out the window and turned when she said his name. "Guy insists that he isn't, but I know he is."

"Not so much," Sidney said. "I don't want to die, but I suppose it's my belief in providence. If it's my time to leave, I'll go. Doesn't matter where I am. Could be here, could be there. When the Lord decides I'm finished here, I'll be finished." He glanced at me. "Don't ask anybody else that question, though. Ever since those boys went AWOL, the officers have been on the lookout for men who might do the same."

"I'd never say a word to Colonel Erickson, if that's what you're insinuating," I said.

"I'm not, but we should go now," Sidney said, retrieving his violin and snatching the bow from the piano's music stand. "Juliet wants to help decorate the graves, too, and we'll need to collect the ribbons and wreaths from our YMCA. Even the cemeteries are segregated here."

"I'm sorry," Goldie said. "It's how it's always been done around here, but it should change. It *will* change."

Sidney shook his head. "It's an archaic and ignorant practice. I'll see you at the cemetery, Goldie, and perhaps you too, Miss Connolly?"

"Calla, please," I said.

"What do you say? Will you come with us?" Goldie asked me. "And to dinner? She's quite enthralled with you but was obviously not able to listen last night because she was so upset about her beau being hauled off to confinement."

"I'd like to, but I'll need to ask permission from Colonel Erickson, and it's Sunday. I don't know where he is."

"He's at the Dowd House. At least his auto's there," Goldie said. "When Guy and I were walking home from the station after church, I saw it."

"Do we have time?" I asked.

She nodded.

"Very well." I plucked my hat from the stool where I'd discarded it, fitted it back atop my head, and followed Goldie out of the door.

✳ ✳ ✳

"Jesse!" I shouted his name as the engine roared to life. I ran toward the auto, leaving Goldie trailing behind me on the walk up the hill.

I reached his door right as he pressed the gas, and the sight of me startled him. He jammed the brake hard, propelling himself forward. A pile of ribbons and wreaths in red, white, and blue shades fell off the back seats to the auto's floor behind him.

"Damn," he swore, and then his eyes jerked to mine.

"I apologize, Calla. I didn't see you there. I just got done inspecting camp and am about to head downtown for the Memorial Day grave decorating. Has your headache improved?"

"Yes. It's gone now," I said. He stared at me for a moment. I didn't know what to say. My eyes drifted to his lips and I jerked them back to his gaze, hoping he hadn't noticed. I could feel my face flush. The weight of what we'd said the night before hung over us, making the man I'd thought so familiar only a day before feel foreign.

Goldie was still making her way up the hill and we were alone. He glanced at her and then back at me.

"I was hoping we'd have some time to talk this morning," he said finally. He looked down at the steering wheel, running his fingers over the leather. "Last night . . . I'm an ordinary man, Calla, hardly the sort you're used to. I meant what I said. Despite myself, I can't seem to stop thinking about you, but I know I caught you off guard and your kindness compelled you to say you missed me too in those hours we were apart." Jesse's eyes finally met mine. I shook my head. In the back of my mind, guilt persisted, but standing here in front of him, I could hardly deny the way I felt. His eyelids were washed gray, perhaps due to a night of dealing with the slacker, perhaps because he'd tossed and turned as I had, my mind fixed on the beauty of his face.

"I hoped you'd miss me so much you'd convinced Mr. Cornwell to let the zebra cow join my show, but it was not meant to be," I said. I smiled. Responding with humor had always saved me from exposing my heart. He looked away from me, and I cleared my throat. "And I am never compelled to say anything, Jesse. I did miss you, horribly so."

"All of that tumbling you do in your shows must exercise your stamina to an impressive degree," Goldie said, appearing at my side. "I suppose I'm not quite over the effects of the flu." Jesse's gaze remained on mine, looking like it held a question I thought I'd answered.

"Yes, indeed it does," I said to her.

"Did Calla ask you yet, Colonel?" She breathed hard and braced herself on the shiny black metal framing his door.

"Ask me what?" He was addressing me, but Goldie responded before I could.

"If you'll allow her to come to the grave decoration and then after to the . . ." Goldie paused and then seemed to steel herself to the struggle that would be her next request. "To the Knapps' home for dinner. Their daughter—"

"No." The word sounded in the back of Jesse's throat, a gruff refusal that made Goldie step back. The lines of Jesse's face sharpened and the color drained from his cheeks.

"But why not? You saw their daughter last night. She's in a bad way. You know that. Calla's presence would cheer her up."

"I'm aware," Jesse said evenly. "I know about her troubles. But Calla is in a delicate position."

He looked at me then and I figured he meant I was in a delicate position with General Pershing, and any news that emerged aligning me with anyone opposed to war would further delay my chances of going to the front.

"I won't allow it and Calla is in my charge," Jesse said.

Goldie's nose scrunched. "She'd be going to a private home with me. There would be little chance of Calla being hurt or abducted," she persisted. "Could you come with her?"

"I have other plans this evening, and I'm afraid even a little chance is too much. General Pershing was clear. I'm sorry, Miss McGann."

Goldie's shoulders slumped. I hated disappointing her, Miss Knapp too.

"I can, however, take you ladies to the cemetery for the decorating," he said.

Goldie brightened, just a little, at this news.

"That would be nice. Guy was planning to meet me down there with the other men anyway. I'll be glad to avoid the trolley. The ride to church this morning was absolutely horrid. For one thing, it was late, and for the other, by the time it came around to picking me up in First Ward, the stench of unwashed soldier was nearly unbearable."

Jesse laughed, shut off the engine, and climbed out of the auto.

"I assure you, I've bathed today," he said. "And it's required that the men visit the bathhouses daily, though some don't follow the rules." He grinned at us and walked around to the back passenger door. I hadn't been inside one of the bathhouses—long buildings that looked like a dozen attached outhouses—but I imagined they were dingy at best. Mrs. Kern cleaned our shared bath at the Hostess House every other day and still the tub could appear a bit soiled.

"I'll have to remind the men of that requirement at breakfast tomorrow," he went on. I could smell the Palmolive as he passed, the delicate scent of lily of the valley, peony, and musk. He ran a hand through his hair and I wondered what it felt like.

"Ladies." He opened the door and gestured for one of us to get in next to the crepe and the wreaths. Both Goldie and I stepped forward, wanting to allow the other to sit in the more comfortable seat next to Jesse up front.

"You'll sit next to Colonel Erickson, Calla. What would it look like if Guy's fiancée came motoring up to the ceremony next to one of the most eligible bachelors in town? It would cause quite a stir."

Jesse made a noise of disagreement. "I'd hardly call myself an eligible bachelor," he muttered, helping Goldie into the seat.

"Whether or not you call yourself that is inconsequential, Colonel," she said. "Most every girl in town has had their eye on you since the camp opened and you arrived on the scene—though I suppose you were already here before that." She paused. "Why is it that none of us knew of you before the war? You're from here like I am."

Jesse shrugged and started around the other side of the auto. I followed, unable to help staring at his tall, broad frame, his face that would make most actors pale in comparison. Someone so handsome would have been known by his town's girls by the time he was a teen.

"I grew up on the border of the county, near Belmont," he said. "And when I was old enough, my parents sent me to boarding school at Fork Union. I was only home in the summers, and even then, I was busy working at my father's general store."

He opened my door and held out his hand. I took it and the feel of his fingers on mine made my breath catch. I climbed into the Packard, and he let my hand go.

"After that, I was off at West Point—you were probably only thirteen or so when I went to college, Miss McGann, and then I served in the army and lived in France. I'd only been back home less than a year when the camp opened." He settled in his seat and started the ignition.

"That explains it, then," Goldie said. "Don't the two of you look the picture of glamour?" she went on as the auto motored down the Dowd House drive and past the administrative building to Dowd Road. The train station was empty today. Usually a supply car or two lingered.

"I didn't know I was going to the cemetery when I dressed," I said, only now realizing my gingham costume trimmed in lace was a bit too Broadway for the sort of occasion we were headed toward. "Should you take me by the Hostess House to change first?"

"I meant it as a compliment," Goldie said behind me. "The two of you look dashing together."

I turned around to glare at her and she was grinning. Clearly the whole thing—our dance the night before, our situation in the auto right now, Goldie complimenting Jesse in front of me so I'd understand his desirability—was a ploy by Goldie and Guy to endear Jesse and me to each other. Never mind that we were doing a fine job of it on our own.

"I think you look beautiful," Jesse said quietly as he turned the auto toward town. The clouds seemed to settle atop the buildings today, giving the whole atmosphere a somber feel. I supposed it was appropriate to the task set before us, but my heart felt the opposite.

The auto lumbered past limestone bank buildings and brick five-and-dimes and Belk Brothers tucked between them, finally turning between two prominent stone spires with an embedded sign that read "Elmwood Cemetery."

"The paper said that Reverend Albert Johnson from First Presbyterian was going to lead the service from the grounds tender's porch," Goldie whispered to Jesse, as though her voice would be more disruptive to the typical hush of the cemetery than the chug of the auto.

Jesse nodded.

A group of soldiers walked ahead of us and some local towns-people with them, carrying homemade wreaths and ribbons. When the road ended, Jesse turned the auto left, but I noticed a group of Black soldiers and Charlotteans heading right.

"Where are they going?" I asked Jesse as we followed the white soldiers toward a small log cabin structure that looked tremendously out of place among the grave spires and statues that dotted the manicured lawn beneath some of the oldest trees I'd ever seen.

"Toward Pinewood, the Black cemetery," he said. He glanced at me.

I turned around, trying to make out the opposite end of the road, but couldn't see anything but a paltry chain fence that ran across the land a distance away.

Jesse pulled the auto to the side of the road and shut the engine off. I leaned over my seat and began to gather the wreaths and ribbons on the ground next to Goldie, but she stilled my hand.

"There will be a short service first, and then we'll decorate the graves. You can leave them here."

I followed Jesse and Goldie across the small road to the little spot of grass absent graves in front of the log cabin. A decent amount of people, likely over two hundred in all, crammed together in front of a middle-aged man with a thin mustache who stood on the rickety porch in a pastor's robe adorned with cords that matched the American flag he held in his hand. Guy stood with a few other soldiers I recognized at the base of the porch, his back to us.

I heard whispers as the three of us settled at the back of the congregation and could feel eyes on me, but I kept my attention fixed on the pastor. Somewhere in the crowd, a few people were crying.

The pastor introduced himself and asked that we bow our heads to pray. He spoke of sacrifice and justice and eternal life for those who belonged to Jesus. He asked for strength and peace that passed all understanding and for faith for those who had none. All the while the spring wind blew and the birds chirped.

When the prayer was over, I opened my eyes to the soldiers standing in front of me and then looked at the hundreds of gravestones beside us. How many of these men would come back? How many would return to the earth? How many would be destined to die to save Paris, assigned to the task of holding off the Huns alone?

Jesse's eyes were still closed when the pastor instructed everyone to join him in singing the hymn "Kneel Gently Where Our Loves Are Sleeping." I didn't know the tune or the words, so I stayed silent as the voices of the others rose and quieted.

Tears fell from my eyes at the sound of the song and the sight of a nearby headstone carved in the form of a woman weeping. Caspar deserved such a stone, but there had been no body to bury. There was only a small plaque along an old wall in the churchyard in Liverpool. It was hardly any acknowledgment at all for the man he was and the life he gave.

Goldie began to cry at the second chorus, and when I glanced at Jesse, he also had tears in his eyes, but he reached into his jacket and handed me his handkerchief.

When the song concluded, we wordlessly walked to the auto and extracted the decorations from the back.

"The soldiers' stones are marked with a cross on top," Goldie whispered. Then she walked away from me across the expanse of the lawn to where Guy stood beside a grave nestled in the woods. It occurred to me then that Jesse had gone his own way too, and I found myself standing alone in front of a grave. It was thin and worn, tilting backward toward the gray sky. Lichen had made its home in the etched letters, but I could still make out the name:

SAMUEL KINZEL 1735–1780
BATTLE OF KINGS MOUNTAIN

I wondered who he'd been, who he'd hoped he'd be. I owed him that much, to think about his life before the battlefield and the life he'd dreamed he'd have after it. Had he been keen to fight for the cause like Jesse or terrified like Roland and Crowley? I looped the small ribbon wreath over the curve of the headstone.

"Thank you," I whispered. I pressed my hand to the name, then stood and began to walk down the road, away from the areas already covered by other decorators.

In the distance, past the chain-link fence and down a small hill beyond, I could hear singing and could barely make out the Black community gathered around a brick building that appeared a similar size to the log cabin structure we'd assembled in front of. I closed my eyes, listening to the faraway music, and a stillness settled on my soul. It was so serene, so peaceful in that moment, that I began to pray. I wasn't even sure I knew how, but my mind gathered words of thankfulness, petition, and hope. When I opened my eyes, the music had stopped, replaced only by the wind and the whisper of voices when it shifted.

I wandered toward a grave marked with a tall spire next to the fence line. The name read Edward Baird, a man of near seventy years who'd died fighting for the defeated Confederacy. Next to him was a rarity in the South, I imagined, a Union soldier of only nineteen. I held my remaining wreath and stared at the two graves. I wondered what had prompted a man of such advanced years to take up arms and what had prompted a man of such youth to take a stand that would force him to face most of his family and friends on the opposite side of the battlefield. The air around me suddenly felt heavy, and the peace that I'd experienced just minutes ago seemed to flee as an imagined vision of the front pushed its way into my mind. My fingers tightened around the wreath as I pictured men marching toward the battle, some crying as they went, some refusing to believe where they were headed. All around them, the sound of cannons and gunfire. They needed the sound of a song, of a voice. In my mind, the faces transformed to the men I'd come to know at Camp Greene—Guy, Sidney, Roland, Crowley—and a man's singing cut through the sounds of war, coming from the line of marching soldiers. At once I knew what I had to do. If I couldn't get there on my own in time, if I wouldn't see my Camp Greene men through to battle, I would have to ask a few of them to be my voice until I could get there.

I closed my eyes and the silence felt deafening. I began to sing "Amazing Grace." It was the only hymn I knew by heart. I simply couldn't abide the quiet. When another voice joined mine, I whirled around, finding that the other decorators had come closer in my moments of contemplation. By the third verse, most of the people in the graveyard were singing. Goose bumps prickled my arms at the sound. It was heavenly and reverent, perfect for the moment. Just to my right, I spied Goldie and Guy. Goldie's arm was around the shoulders of an old woman whose hands shook so severely she couldn't steady them enough to tie the wreath to the grave in front of her. Guy took the wreath from her hand and knelt down, pausing for a moment to run his hand over the inscription on the front.

Witnessing such a tender display felt like an intrusion and I turned around. As I did, my gaze leveled on Jesse and the Knapp girl who'd made such a scene at Lakewood the night before. They were standing in front of a simple headstone next to the entry road but facing each other, their countenances drawn in anger, their mouths moving in swift words, though nothing could be heard from this distance.

I looked away and stood between the two gravestones in front of me, studying the spire first and then the small square monument beside it. The hymn ended, but I knew I couldn't remain silent or I'd fall to melancholy imagining the names of the boys I'd come to know etched on a stone such as these.

"The Star-Spangled Banner" seemed an appropriate choice, so I started singing again. As I sang, I affixed the wreath around the top edges of the Union boy's grave.

I finished the last line of the song and stood back, my hands gripping my last bit of ribbon, appraising my work.

"You're standing on my grandfather." Jesse's voice startled me, and I jumped off the Confederate man's grave into the channel between the markers once again. I looked around for the Knapp girl, but she wasn't there, and it was only then that I realized we were among the last people in the graveyard. Jesse looked at the ribbon in my hand. "Don't put anything on his grave. He was a mean bastard who doesn't deserve a second thought, let alone a ribbon." I leaned down and added the decoration to the Union boy's grave, then righted. Jesse looked at me.

"Would you like to join me for dinner at my father's? I ordinarily pass. I don't like to spend much time with him, but it's Emma's birthday and I do adore her."

"I'd hate to interfere with a family affair," I said, though my stomach rumbled. Last night at the Hostess House it had been chicken broth with celery and carrots on account of so many of the newly pregnant girls feeling nauseous This morning had been equally bland—a slice of toast and coffee. I'd skipped lunch altogether because of lessons.

"Emma would be thrilled to have you there," he said, starting to wander through the maze of gravestones toward the road. "But if you'd rather me take you back home, I'm happy to do that too."

"I'd love to come." I watched the square of his shoulders as he walked toward the auto. Perhaps the heaviness of the afternoon had caught up to him. He opened my door, and I took his outstretched hand. When our fingers met, his gaze settled on mine.

"I'm sorry if this afternoon was a reminder of what you've faced," I said.

I settled into the seat and he looked away from me, toward the place where I'd seen him standing with the Knapp girl.

"Likewise. And it was, but not in the way you think. I'm glad you're here with me."

"As am I." I squeezed his hand, and he raised it to his lips and kissed it. The sensation of his mouth on my skin made my stomach flutter. "Jesse—"

"Colonel Erickson."

Jesse released my hand at the sound of his name. A middle-aged man in a gray overcoat carrying a large mail bag across his shoulders came around the side of the log cabin structure.

"I was just about to go by the Dowd after the service, but since you're already here, I thought I could hand these letters directly to you," he said, reaching into his bag and extracting a stack of at least a dozen envelopes. "I should have come by yesterday, but Helen's baby was born in the afternoon and I found myself occupied."

"No need to explain," Jesse said. "Congratulations. I trust Helen and the baby are healthy?" He took the letters from the postman's outstretched hand and paged through them. When he reached the third envelope, his face clouded.

"Yes, indeed. A baby boy named for me." The man beamed. "My first grandson."

Jesse stuck the letters in his jacket pocket and clapped the man on the back. "I couldn't think of a better namesake for a little boy, Hank."

The man teared up and shook his head. "Thank you, Colonel. That means a lot." He stared at Jesse for a moment and then said, "I'm sorry about Jacqueline. My new route is in town and I heard."

Jesse swallowed hard. "Have a lovely evening, Hank," he managed.

As he closed my door and walked around to his side, I watched his jaw bulge and wondered who Jacqueline was and why I'd never heard her name.

CHAPTER 17

W e'd been driving for nearly ten minutes without a word. I'd wanted to say something, to comfort him without forcing him to tell me things he wasn't ready to, but I couldn't seem to settle on the right sentiments. So I looked out at the cornfields and cotton fields washed in the gold hue of evening, watching the Catawba River play peekaboo at each break in the pine forests beyond.

We passed the drive to his church, and I stole a glance at him as we did. He must have felt my gaze because our eyes met. He sighed and loosened his grip on the steering wheel just slightly and the white across his knuckles eased.

"Hank was our postman in Belmont for years, and the Knapp girl, Jacqueline Knapp," he said, "she was my wife."

The words were said matter-of-factly, but they punctured something inside me, inside him too. His eyes teared and so did mine. Perhaps it was the sudden knowledge that I wasn't the only one who felt the sting of lost love.

"Was," I said softly. It wasn't a question. I didn't feel that I could ask what happened, though I wanted to. I could speak of Caspar, but if he was brought up at a time when I was particularly struck with grief, talking about him was unbearably painful. I wouldn't do the same to Jesse. Instead, the best I could do was acknowledge that I'd heard him.

"We fell in love the summer before I left for France. I was home here, working in Father's general store, when she came in with her father for some fencing boards. We spent every moment we could together, and in a matter of a few months, we decided to get married. We went down to the courthouse just the two of us. When her parents found out, they weren't happy. See, I was already set to go overseas, and Jacqueline said she was going to come with me."

He turned the auto to the right, past a sign that read "Welcome to Belmont." A little downtown stretched before us, a post office and then a clapboard general store with *Erickson's* painted on the white in royal blue.

"That's my father's store," he said. "Anyway, we found a little house just down the way here." He nodded to our right. "We lived there for two months until we were supposed to sail out. The morning we were set to leave, I found her sitting beside the bed crying. She said she wasn't coming with me, that she couldn't leave her parents. I was angry and offered to buy her parents tickets to go with us, but she refused. Instead, she said she'd wait for me." He shook his head. "A year later, right when I was about to be sent to the front, I got a letter from her saying that she wanted a divorce, that she'd changed her mind and couldn't wait for me. She said she didn't love me anymore."

"I'm sorry," I said. I recalled the way Noemie's expression had changed that day at Ivey's when she thought there might be something between us. She knew about his heartbreak and wanted to protect him from ever feeling that way again. I touched his shoulder, and he lifted his right hand from the steering wheel to clutch my fingers, then shifted our clasped hands to the space between us. I hadn't expected him to hold on to me, but I liked the way his fingers enveloped my hand, the rough warmth of his skin on mine. It felt right, a simple but vital measure of comfort, as though we'd done it forever.

The auto veered down a tree-lined street boasting sizable mansions with wrought iron gates and limestone veneers. I wondered if his father's general store was so successful that he'd obtained one of these, but Jesse kept on driving.

"I thought that she asked to divorce me because she'd fallen in love with someone else. But when I returned, I was shocked to find her still living with her parents. When she realized I was back, she thought we'd pick up where we left off and try again. It was as if she'd forgotten that she'd written that letter, that she'd left me. But I could never forget. I'd carried the grief of our separation through training and into battle. I was ashamed about the divorce and more stricken by the loss of her love than by the idea of my own death. At first she came to all the dances at camp, begging me to take her back, but I've known for some time that I'd never be able to try again. I don't think she ever loved me. Not truly, anyway."

He looked at me. "Do you think less of me? Because I'm divorced? I'll understand if you do."

"No," I said softly and squeezed his hand. His broken marriage wasn't his fault, and yet I knew most would see it as a smudge on his character all the same.

Jesse smiled and then his brow furrowed.

"You didn't leave Caspar when he went off to the front," he said. "You would have followed him if he'd asked you to perform with him at the ends of the earth."

I nodded, but the one thing I thought I'd pushed so far down into the recesses of my mind I'd forgotten, the one thing that threatened to paint our love counterfeit, intruded into the forefront of my thoughts.

"Yes, but I wonder if he'd do the same for me. He wouldn't marry me," I said. I turned away from Jesse. I felt the anger I'd suppressed with the news of his death singe the edges of my heart. I hadn't wanted to remember this part—the nights I'd cried, begging him to set a date, to marry me as he'd asked. I didn't want to recall the way my soul felt like he'd carved it from my very marrow when he'd fall silent, then respond that he loved me but nothing more. He'd never honestly explained the reason for his delay when I asked, so I'd assumed it was either because he didn't love me enough or because he thought he may find himself wanting to go back to the man he was before me, a man who found many women more thrilling than one.

Ever since his death, I'd been determined to hold fast to the good things, the memories I wanted to relive, the love I'd thought I'd never know again, the purpose I'd grasped hold of in the wake of my grief.

I sniffed and swallowed hard, forcing my emotion away. It was difficult to admit that the one man I'd ever loved, the man who'd asked for my hand, wouldn't actually swear his life to mine.

"But you were engaged," Jesse said.

"There were always excuses: his parents' awful marriage, his leaving for war, his apparent desire for a spring wedding. I'll never really know the truth."

I paused. Jesse squeezed my hand and I leaned into him.

"The day before he left, I asked one more time if we could marry quickly, but he told me we'd discuss it when he returned. Even though we kept two apartments, Mother knew I was playing house with Caspar and was against it. She said the sort of man who made a fine husband didn't do such things and married the woman he loved without delay." Jesse was such a man, I supposed. "She wondered what would happen if I became with child, if he would accept his role as a father or if he'd be as unable to accept that role as he was unable to accept the role of a husband."

"I know I shouldn't say anything, but I agree with your mother. You're magnificent, Calla, all around. I have no doubt that he loved you, but if he wouldn't marry you, then perhaps he knew he didn't deserve to be yours in the first place."

"She didn't deserve you either," I said.

He laughed under his breath. "I'm not so sure. When Jacqueline finally began to move on, when I saw her dancing with other men, I thought at first that I'd made a mistake by not trying again. But I kept reminding myself that I was going to go back to France eventually. If she didn't wait the last time, she wouldn't wait this time either. But now it's all water under the bridge. She's engaged again and having a baby."

"Do you still love her?" I asked.

He shrugged and turned the auto down a dirt road. Ramshackle clapboard houses dotted green fields on either side.

"As I told you, I don't believe you can ever truly stop loving someone you loved before. Despite your disappointment and grief, you'll always love Caspar, just as I'll always love Jacqueline. I was angry, but I still wanted to help her when she begged me to ask the company police and General Dickman for a lighter sentence. I agreed because I could see the same panic on her face that I'd seen the day she told me she wasn't coming to France."

"Do you suppose General Pershing would ever actually order executions for deserters?" I asked. "I find that terribly barbaric. The men are only scared."

"He might. As I said before, the British execute deserters routinely. It's a grave offense." He took a deep breath. "I've seen men gutted, men blown to dust, men shredded limb from limb, and yet they died to preserve our freedom and to uphold what is right. It's both cowardly and unfair to ask your fellow man to ready their rifles and die for you while you hide away. Every man has a mother or a sister or a wife or a child at home. It should be a man's greatest desire to protect those they love by winning this war." He pulled the auto into a narrow drive overgrown with grass. A little white house adorned with a porch all the way around its perimeter sat at the end of the drive.

"Is this where you grew up?" I asked.

"And where my father grew up," he said. He'd been right in telling Goldie that he'd grown up far from the city. There was nothing about this place that indicated it was near a town at all.

"If there wasn't a war, do you suppose you would have raised your children here too?" I asked. I studied him, considering his training and the confident, worldly manner in which he carried himself. He didn't seem the type to be content as a farmer or clerk in a general store, yet most would find tremendous peace living in a place like this.

"I thought I might when I was married to Jacqueline. We'd planned to settle here when we returned from France," he said. He stopped the auto and turned off the engine. The smell of bacon grease permeated the air. He let my hand go and faced me. "When

I came home, I wondered what I was thinking. Perhaps that's one of the reasons I didn't want to reconcile with her. I discovered when I was in Paris with Mother that I love the vibrancy of a true city. It's awake and thrilling and new and old all at once. I rarely think beyond the war, but there are times when I consider that if I walk out alive, I'd like to settle somewhere like that, where my children see possibilities all around them."

"You must," I said without thinking.

He smiled. "I must what?"

"Live to see the end of this war and far beyond it."

He reached for my hand again, but the slap of the front door against the wooden siding stopped him.

"Jesse, the chicken's nearly cold!" Emma's voice rang out.

"Come on," he said to me. "I should warn you in advance that Father's wife, Eleanor, will undoubtedly make you listen to her organ playing after dessert. She has no shred of skill and her playing can't be salvaged. When she mentions serving coffee, you'll suddenly feel feverish and I'll be required to take you home immediately."

He grinned at me, and for a moment, I forced myself to forget about the graves we'd just visited and our heartbreak and instead think of the contentedness I felt right now.

CHAPTER 18

The meal took a turn midway through my lemon pie. Until that point the mood had been merry. Jesse had even laughed with Eleanor—which, I gathered, was a rarity. Mr. Erickson had been telling me about Jesse's childhood, about how his propensity to round up neighboring children for a baseball game or a war reenactment inspired Jesse's mother, Camille, to encourage him to apply to West Point. But then he'd brought up Paris. He'd asked if Jesse had had any news from Camille's family still living on the outskirts of the city. The question had seemed innocent at first, and I'd kept eating my pie, content to be wedged into the corner of the small room at the end of the table because it reminded me of my parents and our nightly gatherings. But when Jesse didn't answer and set his metal plate down with a clatter, I did the same.

His father asked the question again, though this time he preceded it with a plea that he didn't intend to bring up Paris to upset Jesse but that he'd heard rumblings that the Germans might push toward Paris again. Jesse's whole body had tensed then, his hands balling into fists atop the table. I'd stared at him, hoping he'd reply. I knew what the action moving that way meant for his men. I'd recalled the letter he'd just received at the graveyard, the way he'd reacted to the envelope.

"To my knowledge, there's no indication the Huns will turn that way," Jesse had said finally after a few long minutes of silence where the incessant whistle of the teakettle on the stovetop behind him mimicked the rising tension in the room. "And I don't understand why you're concerned for Mother's family." The sentiments were the strike of a match.

"Most people with a heart care for people who were once in their lives," Emma had nearly shouted and then hesitated, looking at me, before continuing on. "You could learn a thing or two from Father. The way you've treated Jacqueline and her . . . her fiancé is horrid. She once meant a great deal to you. Surely you could have shown compassion for the man for her sake at least. Not everyone is as brave as you are, Jesse."

"I did!" Jesse had yelled the words and stood from the table. "If it wasn't for me, he'd be indicted for a war crime. Colonel Zachary and I brought him in so that he'd only be sentenced to hard labor. He still tried to run away twice on his way to confinement. And in any case, my bravery has little to do with my commitment to my country. My service is about doing what is right."

His father had attempted to calm things down then, but Emma's temper had been stoked and refused to cool.

"Doing what is right? Like following Mother after she left Father?"

I'd looked at Mr. Erickson, who was staring down at his plate. Eleanor leaned closer to him and grasped his hand.

"Father is an alcoholic. Mother went to live with Noemie first in hopes that he'd change, but instead, he took up with your teacher, and only then did she go back to Paris." Jesse's tone had calmed to a hiss, and he said the words in a low tone to Emma.

"But Mother left us too. I was only fifteen," Emma went on, her eyes tearing.

"She asked us to come with her," Jesse said.

"Neither of us were right," Mr. Erickson said finally, and the conversation stopped. After dessert, instead of settling in to play the organ, Eleanor retreated to the bedroom and Mr. Erickson went with her, after a short word of thanks to me for coming. Emma went to her room without saying goodbye.

"I thought it would be all right to visit just this once," Jesse said. We were driving back to camp in the dark, the auto's electric lights doing their best to illuminate the black of a cloudy night. "I'm sorry I got so angry."

"It's not the first heated meal I've endured," I said, trying to alleviate at least some of the tension of the evening. I felt terrible for Jesse on all accounts. It seemed he had no ally or even anyone who understood him—from his sister to his father to General Pershing. My mind drifted to his father's mention of Paris. That had been the first domino to fall. Worry tumbled in my stomach. I wanted to ask Jesse if he'd had any news from the front and what the letter said, but I wouldn't. Not following such a strained occasion. "Nearly every time Lenor came to visit, Mother and she would argue, though they swore ahead of it that both would set aside their differences. I sided with Mother because Lenor only visited when she wanted to talk me into a role or a deal that wasn't right for me. My mother always knew when to push back."

"You and your mother sound a lot like the way my mother and I were. We were cut from the same cloth, so to speak. She was a driven woman, worked at Ivey's with Noemie from the first day she landed in Charlotte, and kept the family afloat while Father drank his way through his days. She's the one who encouraged him to open the hardware store and bought the building for him. Regardless of what he says, Father resented her for pushing him to work." Jesse sighed and kept his focus on the road ahead. "What bothers me the most is that Emma doesn't know certain things and Mother asked me not to tell her, so she believes Mother abandoned Father, and her too. In reality, he hadn't been faithful to her nearly their entire marriage. Emma believes the best of Father and has been wrapped around his finger her whole life. She's as oblivious to his shortcomings as she is to the state of the world. If it's not occurring at her back door, she prefers to ignore it."

"I've known people like that, but I don't know how they do it. Can you recall a time where you had no worries at all?" I tipped my head back against the seat and closed my eyes, letting the cool late-spring air wash over me. The loamy smell of the river floated past now and again, but mostly it was the sweet scent of jasmine and early blooming honeysuckle. "I always think of this one particular morning, though it wasn't remarkable in the slightest. I was five, singing Lenor's 'Sweet Magnolia Sundays' in front of the picture window of our home. I was wearing my cotton nightgown with the lace trim that Mother made me for my birthday, and the graham muffins she was baking made the whole house smell like a bakery." I sighed. "That was before Lenor and the stage, before the pain and the fame."

"I think of the last day of September when I was eight. I'd organized a big baseball game in the field in front of our house and all my friends came after school. Everybody was barefoot—we didn't have to wear shoes to school until November—and we played until we couldn't see the ball anymore. The next day at school, one of my best friends found out his mother died in a mill accident, and when I got home, I found my father in bed with one of his old flames."

I opened my eyes and straightened in my seat. The electric lights shining from the entrance to camp emerged in the distance like fallen stars.

"It shouldn't be like that," I said. "Innocence and wonder should carry through our whole lives."

"Now, with the war on, hardly anyone can stay innocent long. These young men will never be the same," he said. "That's why the bleeding must stop as soon as it can and why I won't quit pressing forward to help until peace has been won."

We were driving through the pines now and the tall, thin spires blocked the moon's light and then allowed it, casting intermittent glow and shadow on Jesse's face.

"That is humanity's purpose, I think, to weed out wickedness, to fight for what the innocent have lost and return hope to tattered souls." We passed by the entrance to camp and then Jesse turned right on Tuckaseegee Road. "It's why I keep on singing too."

Lakewood Park was dark and silent on Jesse's side of the auto, the Ferris wheel and the roller coaster beaming white in the dim.

"I know I said I didn't understand it when we first met, but now I do, Calla," Jesse said. He glanced at me. "I want you to know that. I saw my training and contribution to the war as vital and yours as trivial, but it isn't. Just as I equip the men for battle— their bodies and their minds—you use your skills to equip their spirits."

"I have to do something, however small," I said, thinking of the men who would go and those who were in the trenches now, men who had been killed this very day on a battlefield far away. "I could hardly sit back while men were going into battle as despondent as Caspar had been." I paused. "And you, Jesse. How easy would it have been for you to withdraw after the terror you've lived through, and yet you give your life over and over again for the sake of men who will face death as you have, as you will again. Your suffering has made itself a part of who you are and yet you've chosen to use it for such valiant purpose."

He drove the auto onto the Hostess House drive and stopped the engine at the front. The house was dark, and as Jesse walked around to open my door, I realized I didn't want to get out. I wanted him to keep driving, to let the darkness and the comfort of his presence soothe my soul.

Jesse took my hand and helped me out. When I started to walk toward the door, his fingers tightened on mine and he pulled me back to him.

"Jacqueline didn't want to know the dark parts," he said. "Of me, I mean. When I returned, I had scars—from her, from war, from Mother's loss and Father's betrayal. When she asked me to come back to her, she asked me to forget them."

"That would be impossible." I searched his eyes as they held mine. His free hand rose to my face, his thumb resting on my cheek, his fingertips in my hair. My heartbeat quickened.

"For so long the darkness was all I could see. But you—"

He stopped speaking when I lifted my hand to the back of his on my face, intending to draw him closer, but then he removed his hand and stepped away.

"Mrs. Kern," he said, clearing his throat and strapping his arms behind his back. "I apologize if the engine has caused a disturbance. I'm bringing Miss Connolly back from dinner at my father's."

"That I see," she said. She was still in her housedress and looked at us disapprovingly, as though we were schoolchildren and not adults in our midthirties.

Though Jesse seemed composed, my heart was still beating fast. I glanced at his lips, wondering what it would have felt like to kiss him. I knew without doubt it would have stolen my breath. His touch nearly did as much.

"I . . . I'll see you later, Colonel Erickson," I said, walking up the steps toward Mrs. Kern. Jesse grinned at me. If we hadn't been in the presence of Mrs. Kern, I would have run back down the steps and kissed him then and there, but as it was, a smile was the best I could do.

"Sweet dreams, Miss Connolly, Mrs. Kern," he said. He withdrew to his auto, and I followed Mrs. Kern into the house.

The moment we crossed the threshold, I was struck with the pungent scent of baked cabbage and thanked my lucky stars I'd agreed to go to Jesse's father's for dinner despite the quarreling. All the lights had been extinguished except for one in the little library. Wendy Wentworth sat in a tufted leather chair next to the light, reading what appeared to be a riveting book on laundering. I'd have to tell her about my favorite romances.

"I went by the camp office yesterday to retrieve our mail and received another batch of letters for you," Mrs. Kern said. She walked into the sitting room and opened a large secretary, then extracted a stack of envelopes.

"Not too many this time," I said. "I've only had time to read and respond to half of them so far. I'm relieved to find they're slowing."

Mrs. Kern smiled at me. "I'm sure you are," she said simply, handing the letters to me. She stood there, staring at me for a moment before she spoke again. "I thought to bite my tongue, Miss Connolly, but I've decided that to do so is unwise. I must tell you something unpleasant about Colonel Erickson that I just discovered, in case you find yourself attached."

I laughed. "I'm afraid I don't attach myself to anyone," I said, but the moment the sentiment was out of my mouth, I knew it wasn't true.

"Even if you don't, you must know—he's been divorced," she whispered, looking over my shoulder to make sure Wendy hadn't overheard a room away. "He was married to the Knapp girl. There was talk about it at the grocery today."

"Yes. I'm aware." I grinned at Mrs. Kern, who was looking at me as though I hadn't heard her correctly. "He was married before and now he's not," I said, reiterating the words so she knew I understood. She continued to stare at me "Well, I suppose I'm off to bed. Thank you, Mrs. Kern."

I was halfway up the stairs before I heard her call, "You're welcome."

I undressed slowly and closed my eyes, my mind still fixed on the almost-kiss. I wondered if he would have kissed me softly or if his mouth would have met mine with passion. I wondered if his fingers would have captured my hips and pulled me closer. Other than Caspar, men I'd kissed hadn't given kissing much thought. They'd been more focused on what came after. Kissing was meant for people who sought each other from the heart.

I flung the discarded gown toward my armoire and did the same with my corset, then settled on the bed in my combination. I flipped through the envelopes from California and Utah and Texas and Virginia and England. My hand stilled on the letter from England. The return address said Duchess of Westminster Hospital. It had to be another note from Basil.

The letter was sealed tight, but I ripped the envelope open without bothering to get my letter opener. My head rushed with panic. I hoped he hadn't been called back to service yet, that I hadn't failed Caspar by failing to arrive in time to save his friend.

Dear Calla,

I greatly appreciated your reply, though I do hope you'll alter your plans after you've read what I have to say. I've been meaning to write you again for some days, but today, one month before the second anniversary of Caspar's untimely death on June 1, I finally found the time.

I stared at the letter. Surely he was mistaken. When they'd told me of Caspar's death, they'd said he'd died on June 8, I was sure of it. The date had been seared into my mind for nearly two years. I'd gone over and over what I'd been doing that day when the army men told me. It had been a rainy day and I'd missed Caspar terribly. I'd gone into town to the bookstore to look for something to cheer me but had come up short. Later, when I looked back on that day, it seemed to me that I'd known deep down in my soul that he was gone. I was already mourning. But now everything I thought about that day was in question. Perhaps I'd forgotten the real date like I'd forgotten Caspar refusing to marry me. I couldn't recall what I'd been doing June 1 two years ago. What if I'd had a lovely day without an inkling at all that he'd perished and had simply chosen June 8 because of my melancholy that day? I forced my attention back to the letter.

I've thought often on the contents of my last letter to you and it left out much. I didn't tell you of Caspar's final moments, but after watching a comrade tell a fellow soldier's wife the specifics of her husband's valiant death here in the hospital and seeing the peace it brought her, I felt that I needed to write. I felt that I owed you—and Caspar too—the particulars.

As you know, Caspar and I were dispatched at the same time. I was on the ground, in artillery, and he was to be in the balloon, but we were still sent to the front together. I thought I might be more attuned to bear the burden of war than most of the men in our regiment during that first battle. I suppose it was my upbringing in a family with a history of army service. I'd heard countless stories from my uncle and father, so facing the Huns seemed but another face on an enemy I knew well. The rest of our regiment, Caspar included, were filled with anxiety. You could smell the fear on them as we marched to the front.

I stopped and put the letter down, not sure if I could go on. It was one thing to be comforted by a loved one's final hours if they were peaceful, but Caspar's clearly were not. I wiped my eyes and continued. This was Caspar's story, and I loved him regardless of the messy truth of us that had burbled to the surface today. I had to face it for him.

It was clear from the start that we were going to be obliterated. The men we joined weren't as well trained, and the enemy had just been renewed with forces that hadn't seen action at all. A mile from the trenches, Caspar turned to me and asked me to sing him a song. I started singing and he started singing and before you knew it, everybody was joining in. We sang all your tunes from The Bye and Bye Show— *"Same Sweet Heart," "I Have It All," etc. We sang until all the men were grinning. Even when the colonel ordered our entrance into the trenches, and even a few days later, before Caspar left in the balloon, we sang through it. The last I saw him, he was waving over the edge of the balloon, the last line of "I Have It All" on his lips.*

He died with a song in his heart, Calla. Your song.

And now I suppose I should tell you that I have a request of you too. The same as I had last time, only this time it's more urgent. In three weeks I'll be considered fully healed and will have to reenlist. I'm not the same brave man I was in that first battle. I'm terrified and desperately blue. I know you said you're serving in America and that you can't go about as you please, but I can't help but doubt your words. You are a star, one of the best-known figures in the world. Surely that affords you privileges us ordinary sorts don't have. I need you here. I'm begging you to abandon what you're doing and come help me. If you were coming with the promise to let me perform by your side, I would still face death, but I'd be facing it with hope that when the war was over, I'd be whole. Please come find me. I'm begging you. I will not be able to go on if you don't help me. If Caspar hadn't gone down in that balloon, I know he

*would have come to my aide. I know he would have honored
his promise. Please, Miss Connolly. He told me the two of you
share the same heart. I want to believe it.*

Caspar's friend,

Pvt. Basil Omar

I folded the letter, clutched it in my palm, fell to the bed, and cried myself to sleep.

CHAPTER 19

My, do you have an eye for talent." Mr. Spaulding, the Liberty Theatre manager, said beside me as we watched Sidney and Guy conclude a moving postlude to the full band's rendition of "Second Connecticut," written by Rhode Island's most famous composer. After the strength of the brass fell away, only Sidney's strings and Guy's voice and Juliet's words of green pastures and salty seas and the feeling of the wind in your hair remained. It nearly made me long for Rhode Island and I'd only ever been there one time. It also confirmed that asking Guy and Sidney to lead their respective regiments in song at the front if they were to be sent over without me was the right thing. They'd both balked at the request when I'd asked them after rehearsal a few days ago, as though the concept of them actually going was unfathomable, but then they'd steadied and accepted the responsibility solemnly. They both knew how powerful song could be, how much it could improve morale.

"Thank you. Mother had them switched out when I was young," I said to Mr. Spaulding. "The old ones couldn't tell Arthur Fields from the milkman."

Mr. Spaulding looked at me, confusion playing on his weathered face before his mind caught up to my joke. On the stage, Sidney instructed Guy to go through the last few lines and the song again.

"This show is shaping up to be something remarkably special," I said, listening to Sidney and Guy and recalling the excellence of the other states' performances before them. All of the men and women had been such naturals at singing and acting and dancing. Roland and Crowley still lingered on the side of the stage, watching their friends. I smiled, recalling the Connecticut square dancing and the way Betty and Mary had embraced their parts with glee. After that had been William and Wendy Wentworth for Maine, and Guy's friends, Samuel and John, who played the fife and drums for Massachusetts, followed by Walter and Jones, two fiddlers from New Hampshire who borrowed Sidney to join them in playing a traditional Celtic reel while two local YWCA girls, decidedly not from New Hampshire but talented all the same, danced a jig. Vermont proved to be a difficult state to represent as it seemed none of the musically inclined fellows were from there. So I recruited Ruthie and Marie from the Hostess House to read an old Vermont poem, "The Independent Farmer," by Thomas Green Fessenden, and then I joined Guy onstage to sing the Revolutionary War-era composer Justin Morgan's "Amanda," a setting of Isaac Watts's poem based on Psalm 90.

"It certainly is," Mr. Spaulding said, disturbing my mental review of the show. He leaned on his cane. "I daresay some of these musicians are better than those I've seen on Broadway—and I've had occasion to see many in my eighty years."

"Indeed, they are," I said. "I wish I could show some of my contemporaries right now, though it's impossible, I suppose, with the war on."

"Not entirely. Your dear friend Lenor Felicity is coming next week. Perhaps you could persuade her to stay on for a day or two and gather the men and women to give her a private show," he said.

"Is it really next week?" I asked. I'd tried my best to forget about Lenor's intrusion, but the rest of the city was counting down the days.

"It's hard to believe, isn't it? We've just received a shipment of her posters. If we show her a warm welcome like we did you, she's liable to stay and hear the men, isn't she?" Mr. Spaulding pressed. "She's done so much for the doughboys. Surely she'll be receptive. Can you imagine if some of the men were given the news that they'd have a chance on Broadway when they got home? They'd go to the front heartened indeed. If they could obtain both your endorsement *and* Miss Felicity's, it wouldn't be out of reach in the slightest for them, would it?"

"No, it wouldn't."

I thought of why I'd involved the men in my shows in the first place. It was for this very reason—to encourage their dreams for the future to occupy them amid the horror of war. I eyed Guy and Sidney and then the stack of new poster tubes gathered at the foot of the stage. At the moment, my image still occupied the dozen frames lining the linen walls. I'd become a part of Camp Greene. Because of that, I wanted more than anything for the talented soldiers I'd discovered here to accompany *me* back to Broadway, not Lenor. I knew the thought was selfish. When it came down to it, I knew I'd give up my own pride if Lenor's support would mean the soldiers' chance at the spotlight, and yet Lenor had taken so much from me, possibly even my ticket to the front. I didn't want her to have my men too.

The thought of the front made me think of Basil's letter. It had been five days and still his words haunted me. They'd had an edge to them this time, a desperation I knew came from fear. If I'd been able to speak freely in my correspondence, I would have tried to say something hopeful to calm his nerves or promise I'd get there as soon as I could, but I'd already said all I was allowed to. To reply once again that I wasn't coming because I was serving where I was and had no agency as to my whereabouts seemed more callous than ignoring him. If he never received a reply, perhaps he could hope I was on my way—which I always hoped I was. I hadn't slept more than a few hours each night. The moment I fell asleep, a vision of Caspar singing our song as he drifted into the air, and the image of his balloon being shot down, played over and over.

If Lenor hadn't stepped in in my stead, perhaps General Pershing would have acquiesced to my continuing on earlier. There weren't many performers keen to dodge bullets and sleep in huts. If she hadn't interfered, I could have reached Basil weeks ago.

I took a breath and forced calm. Perhaps it didn't matter, really. If Lenor went to the front instead, men like Caspar, like Basil, like Guy and Sidney would still be brightened by music. Perhaps I could even convince her to give Basil his shot—then again, if he truly didn't have a voice, as Caspar claimed, it wouldn't work. Lenor didn't do anything charitably. But my Camp Greene men were exactly her sort—talented, adaptable. If she felt inclined to sweep them away to Broadway, to claim them as her discoveries to retain her relevance, then at least the men would have the chance at the main stage. Despite the considerable length of my career, I didn't have the connections she did after going away to London for those years. My spirit settled at the thought of giving up the struggle against Lenor so long as it solidified the joy of others.

Guy and Sidney finished the song once again and Roland and Crowley clapped from the side of the stage. I supposed the rest of the performers were still situated in the green room behind the curtain.

"Well done, men!" I shouted. Though the theatre was set up like a real theatre, with rows of chairs and a sizable stage, the canvas roof didn't quite lend the acoustics I was used to, so I shouted again, louder this time. "We're almost through all of it. Let's get Goldie and Juliet out here to recite Jesse E. Dow's Rhode Island poem and you will be free to go."

"Goldie's not here," Guy said.

He shook his head and pushed his hands into the pockets of his pants that were covered from knees to boots in a layer of thick dried clay. His newly assigned regiment—whatever number it was, I couldn't recall—had been ordered to march to the rifle range nearly fifteen miles away and back in the soaking rain today. Jesse had accompanied them apparently, though I hadn't seen him, even in passing, since he'd dropped the remnant cloth from the factory off at the Hostess House on Monday. Even then he'd been in the company of Mr. Smith's mill man, so we'd barely had a chance to speak. Upon his departure, I'd stopped him in the library for a moment to tell him of Basil's letter and asked him if he thought asking General

Dickman to wire General Pershing on my behalf might help convince him to let me go over there, but he'd seemed distant and we'd been interrupted immediately after he agreed by Mrs. Kern, who clearly didn't approve of my fraternizing with a divorcé.

"The flu withered for a while, but now there's been an outbreak in the Seventh Machine Gun Battalion," Guy went on. "She's been at the hospital for two days straight, since Tuesday night. Eleven men have succumbed so far."

"That's terrible news," I said.

"It's due to the dip in temperatures, she thinks. When the weather's fair it seems the flu calms."

"I'm praying everyone recovers immediately. It's horrible." I thought of the way I felt those first days in the hospital. I'd not known my head from my feet, the flu had muddled my mind so. "If she can't break away, I'll read the poem with Juliet."

Juliet appeared onstage at the mention of her name. She was wearing a simple butter-colored dress and yet she looked more glamorous than Lenor looked on her best day.

"I don't mind reading the whole thing, Calla," she said. She grinned at me. "Now that I know we won't have to wear the colonial costumes you were suggesting at first."

I'd settled for sashes bearing the emblem of each state after appraising the cloth scraps we'd been given. Most of the cloth was leftover surgical grade, the worst sort of linen to work with, according to Wendy and Mrs. Kern.

"I can still have a powdered wig made for you if you'd like," I said, laughing. "Or a buckle for your shoes."

"My granny is white-haired and mighty gorgeous still, but I'll wait until I'm eighty," Juliet said. "Now, where would you like me to stand?"

I instructed her toward the middle, where I hoped I could display the six state wreaths Ruthie was supposed to be finishing today. Juliet started reading, and I was moved. Her voice was full of emotion but also smooth and nearly hypnotic. In the middle of the reading, Mr. Spaulding began to unroll Lenor's posters. The first displayed a colorized photograph that was at least twenty-five years old from Lenor's role in *The Fine American*. The photograph had been taken from her profile, a determined expression on her face. Her hair was blonde and curled perfectly, her full lips painted a cherry red. On the side of the poster, her name was spelled out in cascading block letters.

Mr. Spaulding held the poster over one of me smiling with Caspar on *The Bye and Bye Show*, then removed the frame from the wall, opened the back, and instead of replacing my poster with Lenor's, simply placed Lenor's face over mine and closed the clasps. The peace I'd felt earlier swiftly disappeared, and another vision of Caspar singing as he was swept away in his balloon struck me through.

"That was lovely," I said when Juliet was finished reading. "From here, you all will be free to sit with the audience and I'll finish the show with a few patriotic numbers—it makes everyone smile to sing along together—and a few jokes too. Guy, would you mind asking everyone to come out to the stage so I can instruct them on tomorrow?"

Guy disappeared behind the curtain, and when he returned, the rest of the cast followed him. I surveyed the men. Guy, Crowley, and William must have been assigned the same regiment because their uniforms appeared as if they'd been submerged in a bog. Sidney's and Roland's olive drab appeared more beige than green, coated in a film of dust. Perhaps they'd been working with the tanks today. Regardless of their assignment, they were all in good spirits. I smiled, knowing it was the stage that drew out their excitement.

"Colonel Erickson and Major Dawson will allow you men enough time to visit the bathhouses after your training tomorrow, won't they? You all look like moths in comparison to these beautiful ladies beside you," I said.

The men chuckled and grumbled a little in agreement.

"Wonderful," I said, then clapped my hands. "You're dismissed. Remember—report directly here after you're through with assembly at five forty. The doors will open promptly at six thirty and we'll be through by eight thirty, leaving you lovebirds plenty of time for goodbyes."

Guy and Sidney snickered and grinned at me. Juliet elbowed Sidney in the ribs and he sobered. I knew they were insinuating that I was wrapping the show earlier to spend time with Jesse, but their reaction demonstrated their age. I felt like a schoolmarm whose students figured her affection for the principal. I thought to bring it up to dispel the rumor, but I supposed there was always the chance I'd find myself in Jesse's company after all. I'd replayed the moment beside his auto repeatedly since we were interrupted on Sunday, hoping I'd settle on being relieved that the kiss didn't occur, but each time I was swept away, wishing I was in his arms again. When he'd left the Hostess House on Monday, he hadn't reached for my hand and he hadn't attempted to see me since. In fact, it seemed as if, despite his busyness, he could be avoiding me.

Guy jumped down from the stage as the others disappeared out of the side of the tent. "I have a favor to ask you, Calla," he said when he reached me. "Goldie was supposed to ask you tonight, but seeing as she's not here and we don't have much time, I thought I'd ask instead." Guy ran a hand through his hair. It was straight, smooth, and light brown with hints of gold—exactly like Caspar's. "Goldie and I were talking at dinner after the cemetery. We've decided to get married in two weeks. I know we said we were going to wait until after the war but . . ." Guy shrugged and the light in his eyes that always sparked when he was performing or speaking of Goldie dimmed. He cleared his throat. "The truth is that I don't know for sure if I'll return, and if these moments are all we have . . . well, we're wasting time."

I was speechless for a moment. Not because of his news but because of his willingness to marry quickly—something Caspar had refused. I'd thought Caspar and I had been as in love as Goldie and Guy, but perhaps that wasn't entirely the truth. Caspar loved me, but he hadn't loved me enough. The honesty felt like a knife plunged into my heart.

"You'll be back," I said, fixing my mind on Goldie and Guy as tears pooled in my eyes. I clutched his hand and his gaze met mine. He couldn't die. Goldie couldn't lose him like I'd lost Caspar. Because even if Caspar wouldn't marry me, even if he hadn't felt for me like I'd felt for him, it didn't matter. He'd loved me as best he could and I'd loved him with everything I had, and until recently, until Camp Greene gave purpose to my days, until Jesse and Goldie and Guy and the rest had given me some of my heart back, I'd lived with the ache of that loss every moment I was absent the stage.

"I pray I will." Guy straightened and shook his head. "But we wondered if you'd consider singing at our wedding. It'll just be the two of us and Goldie's parents at First Presbyterian. You've become such a dear friend to us both."

"Of course I will," I said.

"Do you suppose you could manage 'Same Sweet Heart'?" he asked. "I know when we sang it in the hospital you seemed shaken, but we made it through it at Lakewood."

"I was upset at the hospital over Goldie's condition and it was the first time I'd sung it since Caspar's death. Now that it's been done, I have new memories of the song. It'll become just as much yours and Goldie's as it is ours."

"What an honor," Guy said, smiling. "I'd better go tell her you agreed."

"Be safe around the hospital," I said.

"I haven't been contaminated yet and I sat by Goldie for three straight days. I imagine I'm all right, but thank you anyway, Calla."

He walked up the aisle of the theatre toward the front doors. I watched him go, Mr. Spaulding slowly tacking Lenor's face over each of mine in my periphery. I recalled what I'd said about the song being Guy and Goldie's like it was mine and Caspar's and prayed that though they shared our song, they wouldn't share our fate.

CHAPTER 20

Nearly all of camp had come to see us. The theatre had been filled to capacity and the doors had been left open to accommodate those latecomers who'd been forced to sit on the lawn. The crowd had been riotous, clapping and shouting and singing along, standing on their chairs at the Rhode Island finale when the doughboys and the women were done with their part, and climbing back atop their seats when I concluded the show with "Stuck in the Trenches," followed by "Over There." I'd been able to tumble about quite a bit in another of Lydia Bambridge's signature costumes—pantaloons overlaid in a skirt—during the final songs because of the soldiers singing along, and was heartened to know that I could still do my usual series of cartwheels followed by a back handspring without fainting. I hadn't done it since contracting the flu, and doing my full set, flips and all, felt like I'd been revived.

At the end of the show, soldiers and townspeople and newspaper writers alike had clambered backstage for a chance to speak with us. When the reporter for the *Charlotte Observer* asked if I was as impressed with the men and women I'd recruited from camp as I was my Broadway cohorts, I answered wholeheartedly in the affirmative, saying truthfully that I'd do anything in my power to get them on the stage in New York when the war was through. The reporter followed the initial question with an inquiry into how long I planned to stay in camp, and I'd recited the script Jesse had instructed me to say from the first day—that I owed my life to the women and men of Camp Greene and that I was going to reside there as long as they'd have me.

I'd looked around the crush for Jesse as I answered the writer's questions but didn't see him. There was always the chance he'd been called off to handle some duty or another or resolve a conflict between men—they always seemed to arise on the weekends when flasks of liquor hidden in army jackets were more readily overlooked.

Goldie, who had been granted a few hours leave, had approached me after the reporter departed and said that Mr. Cornwell, Lakewood Park's owner, had loved the show so much he'd offered to keep the park open later, until curfew, for anyone who'd like to take a ride on the carousel or the Ferris wheel or the coaster. She'd said that she and Guy were planning to go and asked that I go with them.

I'd agreed, and now, here I was, my head tipped back to the wind, the red, white, and blue sequin tassels affixed to my bodice striking me in the neck as the cart pummeled downward.

I screamed and Ruthie, who had reluctantly agreed to go with me, clutched my arm so hard I thought she might break it.

"I'm going to die!" she shouted as the cart jerked to a slow and rounded a curve quickly.

I laughed and smiled up at the stars. The velocity of the cart had ripped my hair from its pins, and I pushed the stray strands back behind my ears.

"Isn't it glorious?" I yelled as we ticked upward, the sound like a striking of a grandfather clock.

"No," Ruthie said. "No. I am never trusting you again, Calla Connolly." The last syllable of my name was uttered in a loud squeak as the cart tipped down again, catapulting us to our final descent before the track steadied and deposited us at the little depot.

Goldie and Guy stood at the railing, and Goldie took one look at us and laughed.

"You should've come with us, Goldie," I said. "We had quite a time."

"It would have been a time you would have hoped to forget had I come along and vomited on your pretty dress," she said.

Ruthie and I climbed out of the cart, and two young soldiers I'd never seen before blushed at the sight of me and hastened into the seat in our places.

"Guy and I have just come by to say that we're going to walk home. Would you like to accompany us, Calla? I suppose we all forgot that you're not supposed to be out of camp proper without a chaperone."

I felt my face blanch. She was right. I'd been so excited by the success of the show that I hadn't given a thought to trotting over to the park with Goldie and Guy. I supposed I'd also assumed that Jesse would have joined us by now, that he was somewhere milling about in the crush, but if he wasn't and came to the Hostess House to find me gone, as unlikely as it was, he could assume I'd run off. Though I doubted he'd be so hasty, I couldn't afford for him to think I'd disobeyed orders. I thought of Basil's letter. Now, more than ever, I needed General Pershing to have confidence in my loyalty.

"I forgot that I was out of camp," I said. "Thank you for reminding me. Yes, I'd like to go."

I gathered the bulk of my sequined skirt in my fist and made my way down the stairs to the grass behind Goldie. The park was crammed with soldiers, but I noticed, once again, that Sidney and Juliet and Roland weren't among them. As vital as they'd been to the show Mr. Cornwell touted as exceptional, it didn't matter. They weren't allowed in. It wasn't fair.

"How long did it take your dressmaker to construct that costume?" Goldie asked, looping her arm through mine.

I waved at the doughboys laughing and pretending to ride the elephants and ostriches on the carousel as though they were cowboys, and at the couples leaning into each other as the Ferris wheel looped up to the sky and back again.

"Months," I said. "Lydia Bambridge made two patriotic costumes for my tour so I could alternate them each night. I wore the other one the night I fell ill here."

We walked past the popcorn stand and Guy handed the man a nickel in exchange for the largest bag he had. Guy clawed his fingers into the bucket, extracted a handful, and passed the buttery treat to me.

"I'm sure you saw the pantaloons underneath," I went on, munching the popcorn. I handed the bag to Goldie. "The beading alone must have taken weeks." The costume was fashioned as an American flag in sequined beading. At the sides of the skirt were two slits that I untied for my shows to allow for tumbling, and then when the show was over, I tied them back. Pantaloons were fine enough for the stage, but most still found them improper for regular wear.

We walked down the main concourse and under the tunnel to the entrance where a Closed sign was affixed over the directional placard toward the animals.

"Someday I'm going to see the zebra cow," I said.

Guy laughed. "It's ridiculous looking. The paint is chipping off the poor bovine's hide, but still, if you ask Mr. Cornwell, he swears the cow was born that way," he said.

"Jesse said that he buys the paint for the cow from his father's hardware store in Belmont," I said.

"So he won't run into Charlotteans." Goldie grinned.

"Speaking of Jesse," Guy said as we walked into camp. He pointed to a single light in the upper right corner of the administration building ahead. "That's his office. He's still working. I wonder why. I didn't see him at the show either." The rest of the building was dark. Unease flipped my stomach as though I were back on the coaster in a downward plunge. Goldie and Guy began to walk past the building toward the YMCA and Guy's regiment's tents.

"I'm going to go see if he's all right," I said.

"That's a good idea." Guy smiled and took Goldie's hand, doubtless thinking I was planning to meet Jesse for a romantic rendezvous.

"We'll see you tomorrow," Goldie said, and they left me standing in the road alone.

I glanced at the light in the window, hesitating. Perhaps my presence wouldn't be welcome. My heart was racing despite my standing still and my skin flushed with goose bumps. I couldn't care less if I was an intrusion. I could feel it. Something was terribly wrong.

I paced down the dirt walkway and then up the two steps to the porch. I reached for the doorknob. The metal was cold in my palm, chilled by the night, and I turned it, shocked to find it unlocked. I went inside. The sound of the latch echoed in the nearly empty building, closing me in darkness. I could barely see a foot in front of me.

I held my hand out and shuffled forward until my eyes adjusted to the dimness. To my right and left were closed office doors, and spiral stairs twisted upward ahead. It was unusual to see such detail in the buildings here and I wondered why they'd made the effort. Perhaps General Alexander had requested it.

My boots clacked on the hardwood steps as I made my way up to the second floor. When I reached the landing, I realized the light we'd seen from the road had been extinguished. I stood, squinting into the darkness for any sort of indication that Jesse was still there, but I couldn't even make out the doors. I walked down the hall, passing three closed rooms before realizing the door to the last office was open. I stepped over the threshold. The space smelled like whiskey, like the grainy, woody scent of the amber liquid my father always drank after a difficult day. Jesse sat in an armchair cloaked in shadows, his back to me. I heard him stifle a sob and then heard him sniff.

"Jesse."

He jumped up when I said his name and whirled around to face me, holding an empty crystal glass. Even in the dark, I could see that he'd been crying. The moonglow from the window behind him highlighted tears on his face and the tears in his eyes. My heartbeat hummed in my ears.

"What are you doing here?" he asked, his voice barely above a whisper.

"What's happened? Where have you been? I noticed you weren't at the show," I said. I stepped toward him.

"Too far away," he said. He turned and plucked a telegram from his desktop but didn't hold it out to me. "I received this as I was leaving for the show. Many are lost, Calla." His voice broke on my name, and I reached to touch his arm. "Many we loved," he choked out. "My cousin among them."

"Mac?" My mind whirled and at once I thought I might faint, but I swallowed hard and forced myself to focus on the rough sensation of Jesse's jacket on my fingertips.

Jesse nodded. "I should've been there. They were between Reims and Soissons. They were greatly outnumbered and taken by surprise. The Huns reached the Aisne in under six hours and blasted through eight Allied divisions, pushing us back to the Vesle River. No one knew the attack was coming, not even Pershing. I know that area of the country. Colonel Rue had never left Iowa before now. Had I been there, had I been allowed, I could have tried to reroute the men. I could have tried to save Mac." His voice rose in a growl, and he pulled away from my grasp. "Damn it!" He threw the glass against the wall. It shattered. My chest convulsed, and I began to sob.

"They're gone. Gone forever, Calla, and—"

"It can't be true. He was just here."

He stood before me, his eyes pouring tears as mine were, his chest heaving, his gaze searching beyond me for somewhere to go, for some way to right this terrible wrong.

"Jesse," I whispered, thinking other words would come, but they didn't.

At once his eyes steadied on my face, and he paced toward me. He grasped my hips and pulled me to him as his mouth found mine. I reached for him, threading my hands in his hair as I deepened the kiss. He tasted like whiskey and warmth and tears, and as his tongue swept mine, my fingertips clutched his back. He groaned and lifted me to the top of his desk. I closed my eyes, intoxicated by his touch as his hands skimmed my ankles and then my knees and then my thighs, until all of me trembled for him. I leaned back against the desktop and pulled him to me, kissing his neck and the lobe of his ear, but when he found his way back to my mouth, his fire cooled and his lips were gentle. His mouth broke from mine, and he wiped the tears from my cheeks, then lifted off me and situated my skirt back over my knees. My body still shuddered, hoping he'd resume his pursuit, but my heart knew he shouldn't, we shouldn't.

"I'm sorry. So very sorry," he said. "I'm desperately sad and furious. I lost control, but I've wanted you so badly. I didn't mean it to be this way."

I stood and he looked down at me. He cupped my cheeks in his hands and then withdrew his touch. I caught his hands in mine.

"I don't mind it. Kiss me again," I said, but he shook his head.

"It's not right," he whispered, glancing at the broken glass. "I've thought of the way I would kiss you so many times. I've dreamed of it, Calla, and for it to happen this way . . . I've disgraced you, and Mac's memory too."

"No, you haven't," I said.

"Would you mind if . . . As much as I'd like to take you in my arms and forget what happened, I can't." He choked out the words and ran a hand over his face. I walked forward to embrace him, but he stepped back. "I'd like to be left alone, just tonight, if it's all right with you." He sat back down in his chair. I thought to argue with him, to tell him that my company might soothe him in his grief, but the arguing would only trouble him further.

"I'll agree if you promise me that after tonight you'll allow me to bear this pain with you," I said. "You can't go through this alone." He muttered some sort of agreement, and I gripped his shoulder once. He pulled my hand to his mouth and kissed it, then let me go.

"This wasn't your fault. You've tried your best to get there," I said as I walked toward the door, knowing that regardless of General Pershing's restricting him from the front, regardless of the fact that he likely couldn't have done a thing to stop it even if he had been present, he'd find a way to blame himself for Mac's death. In so many ways, as ridiculous as it was, I blamed myself for Caspar's, for not knowing that he'd needed me, for not moving heaven and earth to follow him. How easy it was for a sliver of a possibility to bury a person in guilt. How easy it was to both underestimate and exaggerate our role in another's fate.

Jesse began to cry again, and the sound of his heartbreak nearly broke me. I stood there in the doorway, unable to move, unable to leave him.

"Please, Calla," he whispered, and I turned and left him in the darkness.

CHAPTER 21

My legs felt like they'd been overtaken by two great millstones and my spirit felt hollow. I slogged down Company Road past the silent YMCA building and the post office. Beyond them, the rows of white tents situated in front of the trenches were equally void of life. It was early, barely sunup, but I'd been awake for so long it seemed as though it should be evening at least.

I'd been jolted awake by a scream and a guttural sob outside my door at a quarter past five. When I emerged seconds later, still in my nightgown, I found Ruthie on her knees in front of Mrs. Kern, who was crying herself, holding a note. I recognized the handwriting immediately—it was Jesse's. Ruthie's husband was one of the men who perished with Mac and now he'd never meet his baby, due in two weeks. I'd sunk down beside her on the floor and wrapped my arms around her. I'd been alone when they'd come to tell me about Caspar, and I hadn't been able to get off the ground for hours. I also hadn't been with child. I couldn't fathom the pain of knowing that the baby you'd created with the man you loved would never know him.

When she'd composed herself enough to speak, Ruthie lamented that she'd stayed at the Hostess House upon his departure because she had nowhere else to go—both of her parents were dead and now her husband. She said that Jesse had allowed her to stay and had found her the post as a finisher at the Chadwick-Hoskins Mill until her husband returned. I'd felt a pang of regret at this information that I hadn't known even though I'd been living with her. Between lessons and practices, I was rarely at the Hostess House.

When Mrs. Kern and I had helped her off the ground, she told us that she couldn't go to the mill to work today, that she didn't have the strength, but she knew Mr. Smith wouldn't tolerate her absence. The mill was supposed to ship out a large order of surgical cloth on the evening train. I'd thought of what I'd planned for the day—reading letters and rehearsing with Guy—and decided right then that I could stand in for her. So I'd offered to go to Jesse and beg him to let me work in her stead. Ruthie told me enough of the post to know it was entry level and only required adding dye or water to the machines to ensure they kept running smoothly.

"Miss Connolly. Whatever are you doing up and about this early?" Major Gordon appeared from around the edge of the Knights of Columbus building, his hands fisting a steaming mug of coffee and a biscuit. My stomach growled, but I wasn't hungry.

"I need to speak with Colonel Erickson. Have you seen him?" I hoped he had, that Jesse had returned at some point to the Dowd House for rest. I'd tossed and turned all night, wondering how he was doing. "I'm terribly worried about him," I went on. I knew I looked a fright. Not only were my eyelids swollen, but I'd selected my most plain day dress—a faded gray costume with lace trimming that I'd only packed for instances when I'd have to perform or travel in the rain—and a blue felt hat that I figured would undoubtedly be white by the time I was finished with the twelve-hour shift at the mill.

"Afraid not." He pressed his lips together and shook his head. "It's such a shame what's happened to Mac and the others. And only days after arriving." A breeze swept over us, disturbing the ends of his gray mustache. "They were fine men."

"They were so young. They had their whole lives ahead of them." My throat was tight, and I swallowed the tears away.

"I know," he said gently.

"Do you suppose Colonel Erickson is at the Dowd House or in his office?" I asked. "I'll need his approval to work at the mill today for a woman at the Hostess House whose husband was lost with Mac."

"The mill? It's hard work, Miss Connolly."

"Yes, I'm aware. My father used to work in a buggy factory and is now a ribbon mill man. I'm confident I can stand in for the day at least."

The sentiment seemed to satisfy Major Gordon's doubt in my abilities, and he nodded.

"His room was empty this morning when I woke," he said. "He could be in his office. I know the notices he'd written went out to next of kin before our secretary, Mrs. Simpkins, could have sent them. If he's not there, he might be in town, telling his aunt about Mac's loss."

"Thank you," I said. I started toward the administration building, recalling the joy on Mac's face when I'd agreed to a kiss. My fingertips found my lips, still a bit swollen from Jesse's mouth. Those kisses had been desperate and beautiful all at once. I wondered, when Jesse saw me again, if he'd take me in his arms. My knees felt weak at the thought of it, though my heart still held a tremendous heaviness I could hardly bear.

"Jesse?" I shouted as I opened the door to the administration building. It was as silent as it had been the night before. I called his name again, but there was no answer, so I scaled the stairs and walked toward his office. This time the door was shut. I knocked, but there was no reply. At once I felt that I had to see him, to know he'd managed the night alone. Perhaps I shouldn't have left him. I tried the knob and it opened. The office was vacant. I stepped inside. It smelled like him, like the lily of the valley in his soap and the woodsy backdrop of whiskey. The pieces of broken glass and a pile of papers he'd obviously swept from his desk lay scattered on the floor.

I knelt down and collected the shards in my palm, turning them into the wastebasket beside his desk. Then I began to gather the papers one by one. I reached to retrieve a letter that had slipped under the desk and stared at it, recognizing the looping handwriting.

It was the letter he'd received at the graveyard. The handwriting on the envelope was the same. The sight of the return address alone had drained his face.

Despite knowing I should put it away, that the knowledge of army secrets was the reason I'd been confined here to begin with, I skimmed the first line and my mind fixed on the words *Surmelin Valley*. My skin washed cold, my thoughts immediately going to the assignment that could mean the end for a great number of men. I sat down on the ground, my eyes sweeping swiftly over the words, hoping I could read them quickly and find they held nothing of consequence.

The letter was from General Pershing's aide, further outlining the requirements of the regiment if the Huns attempted to push toward Paris again. Once in France, if the Germans launched the offensive as intelligence was suggesting, the Third Division would be sent to reinforce the line with the French and British troops who had already been fortifying and protecting Paris at the front forty-five miles away. The letter said the 543rd Infantry Regiment, the regiment made up of men from Jesse's Sixth Brigade, men who would be sent over without Jesse at the helm and replaced with a commander who hadn't yet been assigned, would be stationed in the Surmelin Valley, the gateway to Paris, a space the Allies knew the Huns would strike the hardest, a place where the French troops there were already tired. The valley couldn't be given over to the Germans. If the other Allied troops withdrew in their exhaustion, the 543rd would be ordered to remain and fight no matter their losses so that the other soldiers could safely retreat.

My eyes teared. The mention of the mission that day in the hospital felt like a year ago, and though I'd known it was still a possibility, the further removed from it I became, the more I thought it might not occur. But here it was, detailed in black and white. If the Germans came for Paris, men—our men—would die.

My mind stilled on the mention of the 543rd. I'd heard the number mentioned recently by one of my men, one of the music men. The letter went on to say that the regiment had been selected carefully by

General Dickman's staff, as Jesse had requested, using the physical and psychiatric evaluations. I swallowed hard.

Below the letter's conclusion, the names and descriptions of at least a thousand men were listed in alphabetical order broken into companies from A to E. I skimmed them and their reason for selection. The first in Company A, Jamie Ackerman, was selected because he had a keen sense of awareness and followed instruction but had been a bed wetter since childhood. I kept reading until my eyes stilled on Crowley DeWitt. "Crowley DeWitt—small, undersized, is a farmer, precise in firing procedures, at times insubordinate." Nausea churned in my gut and fear rushed through my mind. "William Wentworth—complains of frequent headaches, overconfident, organized, adept in ensuring ammunition supplies are well maintained. Guy Werths—proficient marksman, arrogant, violates discipline."

I doubled over and gagged as my eyesight failed. Everything swirled around me. I forced my fingertips to the grain of the hardwood floor and pinched my eyes closed. Surely I was mistaken. Surely Guy and William and Crowley weren't truly listed among these men. They were the kindest of men, men whose hearts bled deeply for others, whose talents were so remarkable they were a marvel. I looked at the paper in my hand once again. Their names were there. I read the letter again, thinking fleetingly that if I tore it up, perhaps they'd have no record of the men comprising the 543rd, but that was ridiculous. This was simply a copy of the official record.

"If the Germans attempt to cross the Marne," the letter began. I stared at the word *if* and forced a deep breath. There was always the chance the Germans would attempt victory by going another direction. In fact, it was quite likely they would. I didn't know much about the workings of war, but I did know the tide could turn at a moment's notice. I plucked another paper from the floor and set it atop the letter and then another, until the correspondence was buried in a stack of others. I would have to do the same. I would have to bury this knowledge deep. Otherwise the terror of the possibility would cripple me. Otherwise I knew I would warn Guy—Crowley and William too—and subject us all to treason. I remembered how swiftly the four soldiers had run away after watching the Fourth Division board the trains. There had been no terrible mission prompting their fleeing. I thought of my men, all sensitive enough to feel the soul of each note they sang or played. If they knew they were assigned to such a task, they would undoubtedly run, and in that running risk certain death rather than the high probability their place in war offered.

I set the stack of papers on the desktop and blinked back tears, recalling Jesse's arms around me only hours before. How I needed an embrace at this moment, a chest to sob into, but I couldn't go to him with this either. I couldn't let him know that I'd seen the letter, in case he'd feel compelled to make General Pershing aware. Perhaps if both of them thought their secret safe with me, they'd ship me off to France along with the Third Division. Perhaps in that case I could somehow see to it that my men returned safely. I shook my head at the thought. Of course I couldn't do that. But I could see my men to war with a song in their hearts.

I walked around Jesse's desk and opened the top drawer. Neat stacks of white paper and fine silver pens occupied the space. I extracted a clean sheet and wrote Jesse a note saying that I was going to the mill to work Ruthie's shift in her stead and that I hoped he would have approved it. He'd come to his office eventually or run into Major Gordon or speak to Mrs. Kern and know where I'd gone. I hoped I wouldn't be scolded for the gesture, for leaving camp without him, but I hardly had a choice. I had to help. Perhaps helping would get my mind off the letter too. I had to forget about it somehow.

I started out of the room but was caught for a moment by a small miniature in a frame set on a secretary against the wall. The raven-haired beauty in the photograph was clearly Jesse's mother. She had the same enchanting smile, the same mysterious, tapered eyes.

Mother. I blinked back tears. She had always been my rock, my shoulder to cry on, and I'd missed her terribly in the time I'd been away. Before England, she'd accompanied me everywhere. I thought of Jesse. Though I hadn't been able to write freely to Mother and Father, I'd return home one day soon and see them again, but his mother was gone forever, and the family he had left didn't understand him. Jacqueline had abandoned him. It was no wonder he'd seemed so stern when we'd first met or even that he wished to be alone last night. He'd become accustomed to fighting through life on his own. He had no one to lean on. Perhaps from now on, things could be different. Perhaps from now on, that person could be me.

CHAPTER 22

B y the time the bell rang for lunch, my costume was completely soiled. Indigo dye and bleach ran down the front of my bodice in equal measure from my first attempts at pouring them into the machines, and the rest of my dress had been moistened through by extracting the water from the well outside and by my sweat. My legs, which had already been taxed to begin with, ached, and my lungs felt heavy from breathing in the cotton dust and bleach. The only consolation to the day had been working alongside Emma, who had been temporarily switched over from weaver to finisher in order to ensure the final rolls of surgical cloth would be ready to add to the evening's shipment.

Despite Mr. Smith being utterly taken aback by my appearance and request to work in Ruthie's stead, he'd allowed it. He'd even granted me permission to sing and tell jokes while I worked after I kept going on and on about his generosity in donating the cloth for last night's show. The hours had passed quickly for everyone as we laughed and sang. I was thankful for the distraction. Working with my hands and entertaining the women didn't allow me to concentrate on the deep melancholy I felt over the men assigned to the 543rd. Each time the reminder of their assignment intruded into my thoughts, I imagined the call to arms for them would never come to pass.

"Tell one more joke as we switch off the machines," an older woman named Eunice shouted from across the mill as I climbed up a small ladder to hang my bucket in its resting place.

I wiped the sweat from my face with my sleeve and nodded.

"All right," I said. "There were some soldiers stationed in Zurich that decided to go to a café. There was another fellow there who had a German civilian companion with him. Noticing the soldiers' uniforms, the German asked the soldiers if they'd fire on the Germans if they came to America. One of the soldiers said no, so the German ordered glasses of beer for him. Then he asked the soldier if his friends would fire on the Germans, and once again, the soldier said no, they would no more fire on the Germans than he would. So the German once again ordered beer, but this time for the whole table. Finally, the German found the courage to ask if all Americans were really as fond of the Germans as he was, and he replied that he doubted it, that the only reason he wouldn't fire on the Germans was because he was in the band."

The ladies laughed heartily, and I climbed down from the ladder and joined Emma as she walked outside with her lunch pail.

"Calla, meet my friend Winnie," she said, nudging a short girl who'd just come up from the weaving machines behind us. Winnie's cheeks blushed, and she waved at me. "We all eat on the hill just here." Emma pointed to a bank a stone's throw from the mill. Already several dozen girls were sitting down, their lunch pails spilling open to reveal sandwiches and apples.

"You've seen Ruthie, Miss Connolly?" A woman who appeared to be only a few years my senior asked. She was sitting on a yellow threadbare blanket she'd spread out and had a half-eaten egg salad sandwich in her hand. "I heard of the tragedy in the papers this morning and I immediately hoped her Lincoln was spared. I was crushed to find that he was among the lost."

Emma sat down in front of her, and I followed suit, leaning back to address the woman.

"Yes, she's beside herself. It's the worst sort of feeling you can imagine, knowing your love and the life you've dreamed you'd have are gone forever."

Grief passed over my spirit like a shadow, threatening to cripple my strength and turn my mind to terror as it had for years, but somehow I only felt the memory of it. The realization that Ruthie was caught, as I had been, watching the palm of the reaper close around the man she loved most was the thought that brought tears to my eyes.

"And to think that she's nearly due with her child too," the woman said. "Can you imagine if you had been with child when you lost Caspar Wells?"

I wiped my eyes and shook my head. "No, I can't," I said simply. "I didn't get out of bed for a week and it was only me. War is devastating."

I glanced at Emma. Though Mac had been her cousin too, she'd barely seemed to tear up when I told her I was sorry for her loss. She'd said that she hadn't been close to him, but that he'd idolized Jesse ever since she could recall.

"Lincoln, Ruthie's man, didn't seem suited to war," Emma said.

"I don't know why we're fighting in the first place," a woman to Emma's right said. "It's all the way across the ocean, yet President Wilson says we need to be involved."

"There are rumors that Wilson is secretly working for the Germans and that the plan is for them to overtake our country and give Texas and New Mexico back to Mexico in some sort of exchange," someone whispered behind me.

The sentiments scared me. It wasn't that I hadn't heard such propaganda before, but here, so close to camp, the women's words could infiltrate the minds of the men, and they could even be charged with treason.

"I'm glad our local boys are still mostly in training up north. Hopefully they'll stay there until the whole war is over." A woman who was clearly in her sixties nodded her head resolutely at the end of her statement as though she'd willed it so.

"We're losing our men for nothing. We're just fine here." The woman who'd asked me about Ruthie shut her metal lunch pail with a sharp clang.

"Or keep a low profile until the draft is through," Emma whispered. She'd turned away from me completely, as though doing so would prevent me from hearing it. I couldn't believe what she was insinuating. "There are many ways to do so, you know, if a man is scared or ill-suited to war."

"I've visited many of our army training camps as well as seen the ripple of the conflict overseas firsthand," I said loudly, hoping to stop Emma's dangerous conversation and Ruthie's friend's hurtful comments. I noticed several women had remained quiet and figured they were the ones who were loyal to the country, who understood the reason we'd entered the war: to ensure freedom and justice for all people. "War is evil and should be avoided at all costs, but innocent lives have been lost at Germany's hand. Should we continue to allow their plundering of towns and taking of civilian lives in order to retain our own peace? It seems rather selfish to do so. For as horrible as war is, our men aren't fighting in vain. Mac and Caspar and Lincoln didn't die without reason." By the time I stopped speaking, I was furious. My hands shook. I knew they likely didn't intend it, but to insinuate we'd involved ourselves in a war we shouldn't have been in seemed to me a discounting of the lives we'd lost fighting it, the lives our men had saved fighting it. They had died protecting the innocent. They were heroes.

"You sound like my brother," Emma said, turning back to me. "War has marred him beyond repair and yet he champions the effort as if it is solely his own."

"It's all of ours to champion," I said sharply. "It's about care for humanity, about the sanctity of human life."

"And yet we're sending innocent men to die to protect innocent men," the woman behind me said.

"They are dying to protect us, to protect the women and children both here and there." My body tingled, my fury stoked by every notion that our men were losing their lives for nothing. "They are willing to make the sacrifice because of their great love for others."

"I suppose you're right about that," Emma said. "Jesse has always been one to feel deeply for certain causes. What he respects, he loves. It's easy to see it in him. He loves to fight for what is right. He loves freedom, he loves this country, and he's on his way to loving you."

I stared at her, my anger giving way to confusion, wondering if I'd heard her correctly. We were speaking of the war, not of me and Jesse, but a smile pulled at the corners of her mouth.

"What?" I asked finally.

"He's on his way to loving you, just as he loves what he's fighting for," Emma said again. "I saw it at dinner on my birthday. He looks at you the same way . . . Well, he's been in love before and—"

I laughed. It was the only thing to do when you didn't quite know if something was true. It wasn't that I doubted he felt affection for me, but I suppose I found it difficult to tell whether he was falling in love with me. If he was, what would that mean for us? We were at war.

Emma was staring at me, a bemused look on her face. Perhaps this was only her way of digging into my heart, of attempting to expose the longing to be near him I'd hoped to bury until I could speak to him about his missing me, wanting me, kissing me.

"Are you sure he's not looking at me the same way he appraises a splinter in his heel?" I asked.

I recalled when we first met, when he'd said as much. We hadn't understood each other then, but now we did. Now he knew my heart and I, his. We knew each other's greatest pains and most desperate aspirations. And yet there was the chance that what Emma perceived as love was not. Perhaps Jesse had only found himself enchanted by my appearance or proximity, and when he went away, he'd find his feelings no longer present. There was always the possibility that Jesse, like Caspar, would find he didn't love me enough, or at all.

"Yes." She said it simply and opened her lunch pail. She extracted a chicken salad sandwich and handed me half.

"Thank you," I said. The sandwich was divine. Perhaps it was because I was so hungry, but the bread was freshly baked and the dressing was creamy and cold.

"You know, I can prove he's falling in love with you even beyond my observations about the way he looks at you," she said.

She grinned, then turned her sandwich over in her hands and took a small bite.

"Mr. Smith tasks me with telegramming duties for work, so I go down to the camp office at open each morning—otherwise my shift is too late—and do you know who I see every Monday?" She paused to chew. "My brother. For weeks he refused to tell me why he was there so often. Ordinarily he sends one of the secretaries to wire on his behalf." She took another bite. "Finally, last week he gave in and told me that he's been sending telegrams to the War Department in both DC and at the front, telling them of the regular things he's required to keep them apprised of but also of your exemplary conduct here in hopes that when you're through paying your respects to those at Camp Greene, you'll be permitted clearance to perform for the soldiers over there."

I set the sandwich on my lap, not entirely comprehending. I couldn't believe he'd gone to such effort for me.

"That's what you want, isn't it?" Emma asked.

I nodded. "Are you sure? He's quite busy."

"I think I know my brother when I see him. He went himself because he didn't want the secretaries to notice his praise of you and start rumors," she said. "Perhaps you'll be cleared to go together. I know it's killing him to be here when he wants so desperately to fight to end the war over there. Either way, that's how I know he's smitten with you, Calla."

At once her face sobered.

"Perhaps he simply wants me out of his way," I said, though I knew the moment I said it that it wasn't the truth.

"I know that millions of men believe they're in love with you," Emma went on, not acknowledging what I'd just said. "I'm certain you're used to the adoration. And although Jesse and I don't always see eye to eye, he's my brother and I love him."

I took a bite of my sandwich, still stunned at the revelation that Jesse hadn't only been fighting for our country, he'd also been fighting for me. Around us, the other women weren't paying us any mind. They'd moved on from discussing the war and were now laughing and talking about the dress patterns just released for the summer season.

"You've remained here in Charlotte for nearly a month now. You've more than paid the nurses and soldiers back for saving your life." She looked at me. "Perhaps it's not only your desire to say thank you that's keeping you here. There's a chance that you've stayed this long because you don't want to leave him, because you're falling in love with him too."

The truth remained that I couldn't leave if I wanted to, but when I envisioned going, leaving Jesse—Goldie and Guy and the rest too—a warning pang of sorrow filled my soul.

"I think you're right," I said, this time without a hint of laughter, my heart laid bare.

CHAPTER 23

B y the time I made it back to the Hostess House, the sun was setting and I could barely stand. My dress was transformed to white from the cotton dust and I could smell nothing beyond the pungent scent of bleach that coated my nostrils. I didn't know how Ruthie could bear a day of work pregnant. I'd only made it through because my mind had been elsewhere—on entertaining the other girls, on Guy and William and Crowley in the quiet minutes, on Jesse and the telegrams he'd sent—and not on the way the bleach burned beneath my fingernails and the spilled water on my gown heated to sweaty dampness in the humidity of the mill. I still couldn't believe Jesse had been sending telegrams to the War Department on my behalf. A part of me wondered if Emma was mistaken.

"Hello, ladies," I called as I breezed through the door and unpinned my hat. I hung it on the coatrack and cotton particles rained down like snow to the floor. I'd have to obtain a broom from Mrs. Kern later.

From the smell of it, dinner was some sort of beef dish. Last night's offering had been braised tongue. I had never been partial to that and was thankful I'd been able to discard the plate Mrs. Kern had left out for me rather than leave it untouched at the dinner table. I'd been too exhausted and worried after finding out about Mac to eat anything anyway.

I walked through the library, heartened to see that Wendy had been taking my advice. Geraldine Fleming's *How He Won Her* was

sitting on the little carved cherry table beside Wendy's usual armchair by the window. I'm sure Mrs. Kern was beside herself with
irritation that I'd encouraged the girls to read romance. But it was
equally as important as any sort of nonfiction, in my opinion. There
seemed to be plenty of women who went into marriages blind, settling for the sort of husband who was amiable enough to shuffle
through life with as their mothers had done before them, without
any notion that they shouldn't settle at all. Many unfortunate hearts
who'd never experienced the intoxication of true desire were quick
to dissuade women from reading romance novels, painting them
as mere fairy tales in hopes that others would join them in their
dutiful boredom.

I certainly wouldn't abide such a match. Perhaps Lenor's only
redeeming contribution to my life, besides her discovering me, was
introducing me to romance novels as research for my role in her
starring show, *The Midnight Princess*. From that moment on, I'd refused the advances of various solid but uninteresting men and knew
the mark of true love when I found it with Caspar. I glanced into the
dining room and surveyed the women, hoping they were all tied to
men who made their souls blaze and their hearts soften. At once I recalled Jesse's mouth on mine, the way he'd reached for me because
something in his soul understood that I would catch him. We were
the makings of the characters in Ms. Fleming's novels.

"You look a fright," Mrs. Kern said when I entered the room.

Wendy and the others started laughing.

"Oh," I said, taking my seat at the far end of the table, my mind
still fixed on Jesse's kiss. "Yes. I've just finished my shift at the mill. I
look like I've been tarred and feathered, don't I?" I grinned. "Should
I go up and change?"

"No need," Wendy said across from me. I could barely look at
her, knowing what I did about William's regiment. I'd have to com-
mit to forgetting what I saw. It was the only way forward, the only
way to help the men face their troubles with their minds focused on
the promise of their lives when they returned from war. If I became
mired in the possibility of what they would meet at the front, I'd

never leave my room. I wouldn't have the strength to conduct lessons or put on shows that allowed them respite from thinking of the battle to come. "We've all nearly finished and there are ladyfingers for dessert. If we have to wait for you to go upstairs and change, we'll have to wait for them." She winked at me and licked her lips.

"Very well. I apologize for my appearance, Mrs. Kern. It won't happen again."

Mrs. Kern shrugged and then stood and walked into the kitchen.

"Thank you," Ruthie whispered from across the table. Her eyes were still glassy, but she attempted a smile. It was a valiant effort. I'd gone days without smiling after Caspar died. So long, in fact, that when the gesture first happened—at the market ten days later—I'd immediately burst into tears.

I stole another glance at Ruthie and thought of Mac, who had likely died at Lincoln's side. I could still hear his laugh, Caspar's too, in fact. It was one of the things that made me believe that perhaps there was more after this life, that the Creator had given us the remembrance of a loved one's laugh to impress a bit of joy into our sadness. When I died, would those left behind recall my real laugh, chortle and all, or the feigned stage laugh Lenor had taught me?

"It's hard work," I said, turning my attention back to my day at the mill. "I don't know how you're able to do it in your condition."

"I work in a rubber factory at home with no windows," she said. "Chadwick-Hoskins is heaven in comparison."

"Still, I'm happy to go again tomorrow as long as I can be back in time for my lessons with the doughboys," I said.

Mrs. Kern deposited a bowl of beef stew in front of me. A slice of crusty bread was angled into the broth.

"Thank you." I grinned at her and lifted my spoon, hoping the bits of beef in the stew weren't leftover tongue from the night before. I tried my best not to appear as though I was examining it and then took a bite, immediately relieved to find that the meat was tender.

"Thank you for offering, but if I don't go, I'll—"

"Never leave your room again?" I asked.

Her eyes widened in surprise, as though she'd thought her grief entirely foreign to everyone else. "Yes."

"I left our flat two weeks and two days after I found out about Caspar and sailed back to New York. The day after I returned, I was on the stage rehearsing for Albert Hoffman's *Milkweed in the Wind*. If I didn't work, I knew I'd simply dissolve."

"Mr. Smith allows me to sit while I work," Ruthie explained. Her voice was hoarse, and I recognized the sound acutely. At once the echo of my sorrow settled on my shoulders. I never wanted to feel that way again, and yet, didn't the possibility of love require it? I supposed it was worth the risk.

"If you ever need me to go again, you know I'm capable now. I've learned all the tricks—only fill the buckets halfway or they'll slosh, and have one of the girls hold the ladder for you."

I dipped my bread farther into the stew and took a bite.

"Don't take breaks without informing Mr. Smith or else you'll be forced to work the extra time," she said. "In case you ever need to know."

It occurred to me just then that Jesse hadn't come for me. Either he'd found my note or received word from Major Gordon and thought my going to the mill unchaperoned was acceptable, or he didn't yet know I'd gone and come back.

"Did Colonel Erickson come by at all?" I asked Mrs. Kern, who was collecting empty bowls around the table.

"Yes, just about lunchtime. I told him where you'd gone, but it seemed he already knew. He left you a note, but I was planning to let you eat before I gave it to you."

I wished he would have come by when I was here. I wished I could have seen his face, tested his expression against the words Emma had told me, the words my heart agreed with.

Mrs. Kern walked slowly toward the kitchen, balancing the dishes, and suddenly I couldn't take it anymore.

"Where is the letter, Mrs. Kern?" I asked, rising from my seat and setting my napkin next to my bowl.

"In the letter stand next to the door," she said, nodding over her shoulder to the library and the foyer beyond.

Wendy cleared her throat and stared at me pointedly as I exited the room.

"Has he read *How He Won Her?*" Wendy called out. "When he came by today to deliver the letter, he looked quite dashing. It seems something that Ian would do."

Ian Johnson was the hero in the novel. To woo Violet to his side, he brought her gifts each day to prove he knew her heart.

"Not a chance," I said back, plucking the letter from the stand. "Colonel Erickson doesn't do much of anything but train and study his craft. He doesn't know what to do with entertainment."

The girls in the dining room laughed.

"Perhaps that's how he used to be," Wendy said. "But he told us today that he bought some of your records for the YMCA and that the boys have played them so much he's learned all the words."

I ran my fingers over my name written in his hand and smiled. Perhaps Emma was right.

I opened the seal and extracted the letter.

Dearest Calla,

I saw you leave my office today from a distance and read the note you left only minutes after you departed. I thought to ask if you'd like me to drive you to the mill to begin such a valiant day of service for your friend but was stopped by Major Gordon, who arrived to accompany me as I went around to visit with the local fallen's families. I told my aunt of Mac's death this morning. She vomited immediately and then walked out to the field without so much as a word. Many of the families we were forced to tell reacted the same way. I can't stop alternating between fury and melancholy. I am either crying or searching for something to throw. Despite others' words to the contrary, I know I will never entirely re-cover from losing Mac and the rest when I could have been by their sides, when I could have redirected them along a safer route.

Along those lines, as I said last night, I am deeply sorry for the manner in which I treated you. I thought of it for hours, wondering how I'd face you again. I still don't know how. I know that I reached for you so desperately and kissed you that way because I was grieving, but even so, I can't pretend that I haven't wanted to take you in my arms for weeks or that I'm not captivated by knowing what your lips feel like on mine.

I fear that there are only two choices moving forward—to stoke the flame set blazing last night or snuff it out entirely. As for me, I want to continue on, to be close to you, but I don't know if you feel the same. You're Calla Connolly, after all, and I don't trust my perception of others' feelings toward me anymore. How can I after I was so mistaken with my former wife? All I know is what I feel. I have never met a person whose heart aligns with mine like yours does and whose spirit shines light into my darkest moments. I know that you're still in mourning and that my agony might have been the only reason you allowed me to hold you, but if I'm wrong, I'd like to spend more time with you at next leave. However, if you feel nothing beyond friendship when you think of me, we'll never mention this again. I will take your lead.

I'll be occupied with the men tonight, tending to their spirits as we all mourn the fallen, so don't worry that you'll happen upon me if you don't wish to see me and venture out for a walk.

Yours,

Jesse

I folded the letter back up and leaned against the wall. I closed my eyes, remembering the taste of his mouth, the warmth of his kiss, the way my body had cried out for his touch and my heart for his. I wanted to go to him now, to tell him that his thoughts of me were my thoughts of him, to tell him that I knew he'd been sending telegrams to General Pershing on my behalf, to tell him that I would help shoulder his sorrow. I wanted to be consumed by him, to feel his arms around me once more, but I couldn't, not tonight when his duties were tending to grieving men and to mourning himself.

I walked upstairs, barely aware of the girls calling to me from the dining room, telling me that the ladyfingers were being served. I opened my armoire to extract a nightgown and my gaze stilled on Caspar's letter. My fingers curled around the paper in my hand. A part of me wanted Jesse's words to seem trivial in comparison to Caspar's, for Jesse to matter less to me than the man I'd loved first, and yet my soul yearned for them both in equal measure. I wondered if Jesse felt the same when he saw Jacqueline and me. A wave of unease filtered through me. It was one thing for me to love two men when one was gone, but Jacqueline was still here and at one point he'd sworn his life to hers. Then again, she was with child by another man, nearly married again.

A knock disturbed my thoughts and I set Jesse's letter on the shelf next to Caspar's, snatched the silk nightgown with Brussels lace trim, and called out for whoever it was to enter.

Goldie stood in the doorway in her nurse's uniform and immediately began to laugh.

"I had to see it with my own two eyes," she said, walking into my room. "Everyone at the hospital was talking about how they'd seen Calla Connolly walking home from the mill and that it looked as if she'd been working. I didn't believe it."

"And why would you? Dust isn't my usual choice of costume decoration." I grinned, though the vision of Guy's name printed on the list selected for the 543rd, for possible ruin, pressed into my mind. An urge to tell her, to warn Guy, nearly persuaded me to risk treason, but then again, their fate wasn't set in stone, and if Goldie knew, if Guy knew, there'd be a chance he'd desert and risk certain death. "How is everyone faring at the hospital?"

"This wave seems to be subsiding. We lost two men yesterday, but fifteen are recovering. No new admissions today, the first day with no new cases in a week."

She walked over to my armchair by the window and sat down. Goldie appraised me, her lips turning up in a grin.

"What?" I asked, beginning to undo the buttons down my back.

"Nothing. It's only that with your hair covered in dust and that old dirty gown, you almost look like a normal girl. I suppose all of us believe that even dressed in rags, you'd glitter."

I rolled my eyes. "You've practically seen me on my deathbed."

"And you looked better then than you do now."

I laughed. "Remind me not to die in the cotton mill."

"Well." Goldie stood and grasped one of my shoulders. "Besides coming by to confirm the rumor of your descent to the ordinary, I wondered if you'd have time tomorrow morning to come with me and some of the Red Cross girls to the Tuckaseegee rail station. New troops are arriving, and I know your presence would both thrill them and make them feel welcome."

"Tomorrow?" I asked. My heart began to race and my chest felt tight. Though I knew that the new troops were going to occupy the space formerly used by the Fourth Division, I wondered if new arrivals indicated that the Third was closer to receiving orders to go.

"Yes. Colonel Erickson confirmed that there will be around five hundred set to arrive tomorrow morning at seven and another two or three trains coming in over the next week," she said. "There was supposed to be a replacement for Colonel Erickson aboard too, but apparently that's not to be. I saw him today and he said his replacement was called to the front at the last minute to step in for another colonel who passed away from flu in transit from New York." She paused. "I thought Colonel Erickson would welcome the news, that he was enjoying his post—and perhaps he does—but he seems greatly disturbed by Mac's passing. I know it's not even been a full day since the news broke, though."

"He and Mac were very close," I said. "He also had to go around to the local families to tell them about the deaths of their children today. I suppose that, coupled with his own sadness, is a great burden to bear." And without a replacement to shift him back to his old responsibilities, he'd be chiefly responsible for commanding the

Sixth Brigade until they were given the orders to the front. He'd have to carry the knowledge of the 543rd Regiment's possible demise entirely alone, looking each soldier in the face and pretending they were as likely to come home as the next man.

"Indeed. I feel horrible for him. Mac was a bit of a troublemaker, but all the girls growing up were crazy for him." Goldie shook her head and then looked at me. "I'm going to try to get clearance to go to France with Guy. They're in dire need of nurses, and I don't care what injuries I'm forced to see as long as I'm with him."

"I think that's a perfect idea," I said.

The thought that Goldie could be there, so close to where Guy was fighting, settled my spirits just a bit. I prayed he wouldn't be lost, but if our nightmares came true, at the very least she wouldn't be left wondering about his final days. Though reality was a horror, imagined reality could be worse. I knew that firsthand. Before Basil had detailed Caspar's final moments in his letter, I'd thought up countless scenarios where he'd perished entirely alone. Even now, what I didn't know, what I hadn't seen, haunted me. Women like Ruthie would forever be stricken with the dread of the unknown, the worst possible scenarios of her husband's demise playing out over and over in her mind. Jesse's assignment meant he wouldn't be in harm's way, at least not yet. As much as he wanted to be over there, it was a mercy to realize I likely wouldn't find myself mourning him the way I mourned Caspar.

"I'm glad you agree." Goldie smiled and started to walk out of my room. "Seven o'clock sharp at the train station."

CHAPTER 24

The train was delayed. I reached into the box I'd been handed by Goldie and her Red Cross friend, Sue, and took a bite. The dough was still warm, the slight sugar glaze heavenly, and I closed my eyes as I chewed. Each of us girls was allotted one donut, but I'd hesitated before eating mine. What if there weren't enough for the men?

"More Charlotteans have arrived," Goldie murmured beside me. I opened my eyes and glanced behind us at the grassy area at the front of the station, swiftly looking past the stack of coffins tucked by the station office. Goldie said those coffins held the men who'd passed from flu and were not incoming bodies from the Fourth. Those, she said, would be escorted back home by boat and then direct rail. Logically I knew that, and yet I couldn't help thinking of Mac and the others when I saw them.

"I think it's nice," Sue said beside Goldie. She was a tiny thing, wearing a robin's-egg-blue dress emblazoned with a red cross at her breast and a white apron around her waist. Most of the fifty or so Red Cross girls wore the same sort of uniform and were situated in a line stretching from where I stood by the stairs all the way down the platform to the other set of steps. "The men will receive quite a warm welcome with the townspeople, us, and Calla Connolly here." She looked around Goldie at me.

I smiled. Over the past half hour, a little crowd had gathered, huddled together at the side of the stairs. Most were women dressed in their finest, holding homemade cookies and pastries. I supposed I didn't feel quite so guilty for eating my donut.

"You'll sing when they arrive, won't you?" Sue asked me.

"I'd love to. What do suppose I should start with?"

"Do you know 'You're a Grand Old Flag'?"

"From the musical *George Washington, Jr.*? It's one of my favorites," I said, laughing. "Lenor played Evelyn Rothburt. It opened at the Herald Square Theatre the day before my musical, *The Storied Streets of New York*."

"Lenor Felicity?" Sue's eyes widened. "You know her? I mean, of course you know her, you're Calla Connolly."

She stopped talking abruptly and I forced a grin and nodded. "Yes, she's my mentor or second mother, depending upon the day."

On the way to the train station, Goldie and I had passed by Liberty Theatre. The posters beside the marquee had heralded Lenor's arrival, and as we'd walked through camp, the men lackadaisically waving at us, I began to feel deflated. I was becoming old hat, and when Lenor arrived, she'd burst onto the scene with fanfare and awe. I'd had a moment where anger flared at Lenor for stealing my shows, but I knew the emotion was pointless. Despite my irritation at Lenor and regardless of her motives, she was doing the soldiers at other camps a great service. It was more important for the soldiers to be cheered by someone—even if that someone couldn't be me—than to be left despondent.

"You can't be serious." A girl I hadn't met, standing on the other side of Sue, peered around her. "You're that close to Miss Felicity?" She squealed the last words, and I nodded once again. "She's coming to perform Saturday, you know," she went on as though I might have somehow missed this bit of information.

"Yes. It would be impossible to be unaware of it. Lenor's arrivals are much like volcanic eruptions, notifying the cities by earthquake months in advance of the explosion," I said.

I focused on the train tracks in front of me but could feel the girl's surprised expression. As much as I tried, I couldn't altogether squash my exasperation with Lenor. In the distance a whistle blew, and thankfully the girls' attention turned to the incoming train.

A few seconds later the engine appeared, its smokestack piping black coal smoke into the cerulean, cloudless sky. My heartbeat quickened and I straightened and smoothed the front of my frock, running my fingers down the embroidered pink roses impaneled on white linen between a blush vest front that extended from neck to hem.

I wished it wasn't a weekday and that I could have brought Roland along to accompany me on the saxophone. There was nothing so cheery or soothing as the sound of a saxophone. I'd have to tell him that when I saw him later for our lesson.

The train squealed to a stop and the steam sighed in three long exhales. Porters hastened from the ticket office to the train doors, and the line of Red Cross girls stepped forward. I was the last in line next to the stairs that would lead the men down to the lawn and Major Gordon, who would situate them into groups to march to the field behind the administration building for evaluations. The thought made my heart fill with sorrow. I recalled the scrutiny with which Guy and William and Crowley and the others had been appraised and hoped all of these men would avoid such harsh assessments. In the next two days, the new soldiers would be put through psychological and physical tests to determine their place in the army, but their place in the army was hardly their worth to the world, and that was the problem. They were evaluated on their ability to fight, but I believed a person was truly formed for the opposite purpose.

The train doors were opened, and the men began to pour out. My skin prickled and my eyes teared at the sight of them. There was something moving about the bravery exhibited by these men, regardless of whether they were keen or terrified to go overseas.

I began to sing and was glad the girls joined in. It was immediately clear that these doughboys were proper cowboys from the West. Beneath my singing, I heard a series of "thank you, ma'ams" and watched as the men took the girls' hands and kissed the backs of them before accepting a donut.

I was midway through "It's a Grand Old Flag" when the first soldier passed me by. He dropped his donut and gasped.

"You're Calla Connolly," he said when he found his voice. I smiled and handed him another donut from my box.

It went like that for half an hour, me singing through every patriotic song I knew, from "The Star-Spangled Banner" to "My Country 'Tis of Thee" to "America the Beautiful" to "Yankee Doodle" to "Battle Hymn of the Republic" to "Over There." Each time a soldier saw me, his face brightened and the sight of it touched my heart, reaffirming the reason I'd started this endeavor in the first place. I did my best to acknowledge each one, smiling at them all and even reaching my hand toward the men whose bodies visibly quaked with nerves.

The last soldier finally reached me. He looked no older than fifteen, and when he saw me, he smiled widely.

"Some of the men said you were here, but no one believed them," he said. "My mother sang me one of your early songs as a lullaby when I was a child and I've loved your music ever since."

"Which song?" I asked.

"'The Wonder of Children,'" he said.

The song was the second I'd ever sung onstage. It was part of Lenor's variety show. When the curtain closed on the show, I'd never sung it again. In fact, no one except for this man had ever mentioned it.

"I'm not sure I recall all the words," I said. "Would you like me to try?"

He shrugged and looked down, clearly embarrassed to ask anything of me, but I sang it anyway, my voice low, and to my surprise I recalled all the words. Tears blurred his eyes, and he wiped the moisture away when the song was through.

"Thank you," he said. "I'm homesick already, I'm afraid."

"If you ever need a bit of home, come see me and I'll sing it to you again," I said.

"I will."

The other girls had mostly made their way out of the station and had joined the other Charlotteans, who were now watching the soldiers being corralled into groups.

I started down the stairs. Major Gordon stood on a flimsy-looking wooden platform next to his auto, pointing and yelling off names from a portfolio he held in his hand. Men hustled to attention when they were called and hurried to their specific area.

I looked over the group, noticing the unfaded olive of their new uniforms—a symbol of naivety that wouldn't last long in the practice trenches or on the rifle ranges. On the far edge of the crush of soldiers, a familiar face caught my eye. Jacqueline. I hadn't noticed that she'd been among the Red Cross girls, but then again, Goldie and I had arrived late and there were more than four dozen women on the platform. She skirted around the outermost groups with her box of donuts and finally stopped in front of a man who'd just emerged from Major Gordon's auto. When he turned toward the men and took the donut from Jacqueline's outstretched hand, I realized it was Jesse. I froze on the step, watching as Jacqueline reached to hug him. I waited for his head to dip to hers, for his arms to pull her closer, but he didn't. When he withdrew from her embrace, his face was friendly but without the longing I'd seen in his eyes when he'd kissed me.

"Calla!" Goldie shouted my name, pushing through the other Charlotteans gathered to the right of the soldiers. Jesse's head jerked toward me when he heard it and his eyes met mine. He stared for a moment, clearly unsure of the way I'd respond to his letter, but I smiled as he started to look away and he grinned back. He waved and my gaze stilled on his hands. I could still recall the grip of his fingers on my hips. At once my stomach felt like I was in free fall, and I swallowed hard and clutched the railing.

"Calla," Goldie said again when she reached me. "Do you think you could lead us in a song to see the boys off? Perhaps 'Keep the Home Fires Burning'?"

"Of course," I said. "Though give me a moment. I have to tend to something."

Goldie followed my eyes and laughed. "Some*one*."

I walked past her and through the maze among the groups of men to where Major Gordon stood on the platform and Jesse stood at the foot of it, now speaking with a young major I'd never seen before. I looked around for Jacqueline but found she'd departed.

"Hello, Colonel Erickson," I said. He stopped talking and looked at me. His lips turned up, though beneath his pleasant demeanor, melancholy weathered his face.

"Calla Connolly," the young major said. I supposed he'd exited the train on the opposite end and hadn't encountered me yet.

"Yes, hello, Miss Connolly," Jesse said. "Allow me to introduce you to Major Keller, just in on the train from Montana. He'll be heading up our mechanical engineering division."

I held out my hand and he took it. His palm was clammy.

"Lovely to meet you," I said, then turned to Jesse. "Goldie asked that I sing a song as the soldiers march out to camp. Would that be all right with you?"

He nodded. "Yes. I believe Major Gordon's got them nearly organized."

"Wonderful," I said. I glanced at Major Gordon's auto. "I know your day is quite busy, but I was wondering if you'd mind stealing Major Gordon's wheels to drive me back to camp—or wherever you're going—after this."

Major Keller's eyebrows rose. Jesse's stoic expression didn't ease. Clearly, he figured whatever conversation we were going to have had equal chance of going either way.

"Certainly, Miss Connolly. Major Gordon and Major Keller are planning to march to camp with the men and I'll be passing by the Hostess House on the way to the rifle range."

Major Gordon jumped down from the platform and landed next to Jesse. "We're set, men," he said. Then he noticed me. "Miss Connolly."

"Miss Connolly is going to lead the men and civilians in a song to see them off," Jesse said.

Major Gordon nodded and extended his hand to me. I took it and climbed up on the platform. The moment I did, whistles and cheers rang out.

"Welcome to your home away from home!" I shouted. I smiled at the men. "You know, I'm not from here either, but the moment I stepped off the train I realized this town is a special place. I have no doubt you'll be happy here, and the locals are eager to make it so." I paused as the men cheered again. "Now, you're about to head off to camp, so we thought we'd sing you down the road. Many of you know 'Keep the Home Fires Burning,' I'm sure, and I expect you to sing along as you march, all right?"

Whistles sounded and then Major Gordon and Major Keller assumed positions at the front two sections of the horde. The men arranged themselves in perfectly straight lines and began to march as I started the song.

"Keep the home fires burning, while your hearts are yearning, though your lads are far away they dream of home."

When the last group of men marched away from the station and up Dowd Road to the camp entrance, the civilians began to amble away as well.

Jesse held his hand up to me and helped me down from the platform, but when I reached the ground and his fingers loosened, I kept hold of his hand.

"Major Keller's been here all of five minutes and is already begging me to reconsider allowing him to send for their mascot— the bear," he said. He looked over my shoulder at the lingering Charlotteans and I let go of his hand.

"Please let them," I said. I thought of the possibility of a bear amid the rigid structure of camp life and the serious training and drilling and began to laugh.

"The bear apparently has a friend who is the mascot of another regiment set to arrive here later this week," he said. He walked around the auto and opened my door. I got in, and then he settled in the seat beside me and started the engine. "He wants clearance to bring them both. Can you imagine? What if they got loose and mauled someone?"

"Could you convince Mr. Cornwell to keep them at Lakewood? Think of the tickets he'd sell."

"Perhaps," he said.

We fell silent for a moment. Nerves flipped in my stomach, and I could feel his unease. Ordinarily he'd rest his arm on the seat beside me. Ordinarily he'd make some quip about the men wrestling the bears or about starting my circus again.

"How are you feeling today?" I asked. As much as I wanted to talk about his letter without delay, asking about his spirits mattered more.

"I'm all right. I have no choice but to be. We must continue to push on," he said.

"Yes, we must, but we're also allowed to be blue over our losses."

Jesse made a wry noise and shook his head. "I am, but I force myself forward, to carry their memories on to peace. They will always be with me, but I can't honor the fallen by falling myself."

"I know," I said simply.

The lines of soldiers marching ahead of us turned right into camp, and Jesse waved at an officer on horseback who sped past the auto to follow the soldiers as they marched. I supposed there was always the chance a doughboy or two could try and make a run for it if they were situated toward the back of a group without an officer's watchful eye.

"I read your letter," I said.

He didn't look at me but kept his eyes fixed straight ahead, toward the next intersection where an empty supply train lingered on the tracks.

"I love Caspar. I . . . I'll never be able to tear my heart completely from his, even though I don't think he loved me the same, even though he's gone now."

I swallowed. My throat felt dry, tight, and at once my chest followed to the point that I thought I might not be able to keep speaking. Up ahead, wagons containing ammunition rolled across the street. Jesse slowed the auto. I pushed my fingers into the leather seats, willing myself to continue regardless of the discomfort. I stared at Jesse's face and wondered if I could simply kiss him instead, if the gesture would tell him all he needed to know. That was what Caspar had always done. He'd had a difficult time with words. Then again, he'd been British, and the British were often reserved when it came to expressing affection verbally.

"As I said, we can simply go back to the way it was before. It was only a kiss, after all." His voice was low, and he continued to stare at the wagons' progress. The last wagon pushed across the road in front of us and he accelerated the auto. There was no way to get out of it now. I needed to say it.

"I don't want to go back to the way it was. A part of my heart will always be Caspar's, but my heart is yours too. I feel for you as you feel for me," I said.

Jesse's hand jerked the wheel, nearly running the auto into a ditch. He stole a glance at me as he steadied us and then again as we turned toward Tuckaseegee Road.

"Are you sure?" he asked finally. "Anything you've said before has only been in response to something I've confessed. I ruined your chances at going to the front, and anyway, Calla, I'm no star. I'm an ordinary man from this little town."

"Pull over, please," I said. "Just there."

I pointed to a little strip of trees bordering the road and he complied. When the auto settled, I drew close to him and pulled his hands from the steering wheel to hold mine. I stared at his beautiful face—at the full lips, at the strong square jaw, at the hooded blue eyes that had captivated me long before I wanted to admit it. But it had been his heart that had made me fall.

"I'm falling in love with you," I said.

His gaze settled on mine. One of his hands lifted to my face and his thumb traced my lips.

"I don't know if we're meant to be," I went on. "War has taken that away from us." Tears filled my eyes with the realization that he might not be mine forever. "But the fire you spoke of—I want to let it burn as long as it can."

He said nothing. It was as if he hadn't heard me, not truly anyway.

"I know about the telegrams you sent," I said, simply to eclipse the silence.

"It was nothing. I'd do anything in my power for you," he said softly. "I'm falling in love with you too."

I rose up on my knees on the seat beside him, took his head in my hands, leaned down, and kissed him. His lips were soft, and his mouth opened mine to his warmth. My tongue brushed his and his hands pulled me closer. My fingers stroked his neck as our kiss deepened. I was entranced by him, by the feel of his solid body against mine, by the hum of his heart that I knew beat for me, by the taste of his mouth.

When his lips broke from mine, he kept me close and kissed my forehead.

"You're wrong about one thing," he said. "War might tear me limb from limb, but it will never take away that I am yours, Calla, and you are mine."

CHAPTER 25

Lenor had sent the camp's head secretary, Mrs. Simpkins, instructions in advance of her arrival. I'd heard of her demands on Tuesday when I'd run across Jesse on my walk to the YMCA for lessons. He'd been on his way to survey the new men in the trenches after a surprise visit from two generals in from DC, but had pulled the auto to the side of the street when he saw me, got out, led me into the shadows of the Knights of Columbus building, and kissed me. When he'd finally forced his lips to break from mine, he'd told me of Lenor's ridiculous demands—how she'd insisted that the secretaries help fluff her prop feathers and set up six wagonloads of stage decorations according to detailed drawings.

I watched out my window as the wagons carrying Lenor's things caravanned toward the Liberty Theatre and lifted my fingers to my lips. Jesse had been occupied from early morning until late at night with acclimating the new men, and I'd busied myself with rehearsals for next weekend's performance. Though I hadn't seen him much, he'd made a point to find me every day, if just for a moment, to kiss me and tell me he'd been thinking of me. He'd come by after my lessons or while I was walking in camp or early in the morning at breakfast. Despite appearing so weathered he seemed he could collapse, he always thought to bring something along: a flower or a dessert from one of the Charlotte ladies.

The purple iris he'd gifted me this morning smiled from a little crystal vase I'd borrowed from the kitchen. Though it was Saturday, he'd had to escort a dozen just-arrived men to confinement. They'd already been caught sneaking out of camp after final taps and into two of the little houses just past Remount Station whose lady occupants were known for entertaining lonely men.

The faraway sound of the Charlotte veterans' brass band drifted through the window from the train station. Either Lenor had just disembarked or she was being sent off to prepare for tonight's show in her room at the Selwyn Hotel. The only reason I knew anything about her stay here in Charlotte was because of the paper. It had printed a complete itinerary of the day. She was to arrive on the nine thirty train in her private rail car. Lenor's car was cloaked from ceiling to floor in red velvet, and every piece of furniture from the chairs to the bar cart was rimmed in gold leaf. It was pretty but terribly stuffy. I'd loathed riding in it.

When she arrived, the Charlotte veterans' band was going to play a selection of her most beloved songs and the mayor was going to say a word of thanks to her for visiting before she'd be whisked off to the Selwyn Hotel in a Crane-Simplex limousine. The whole charade was much more fanfare than they'd doled out for the new doughboys. The mayor had originally asked Jesse to give Lenor's welcome address, but he'd refused on the grounds that he was much too busy, when he was really steering clear of her for my sake. Instead, he'd sent Major Gordon as an army representative. Major Gordon would also accompany her into camp for her performance at six o'clock sharp. I wondered if Lenor would find him attractive. For someone so famous she wasn't at all picky in her conquests.

I sat down on my bed and stared at my flower. Perhaps Jesse and I could sneak away during Lenor's show. I certainly had no interest in seeing her myself. Then again, I owed it to Guy and the others to convince her to experience their talent, and I'd have to face her to ask.

Someone shrieked downstairs. I lurched from my bed and opened my door to find Lenor standing in the hallway.

"Calla dear," she said. Below us, in the foyer, Mrs. Kern was leaning against the wall, her hand over her mouth in shock. "I suppose

I gave that poor woman quite a fright. That happens sometimes when Lenor Felicity shows up on your doorstep unawares." She laughed, that irritating, high-pitched tinkling she'd cultivated over years of covering up her snorts.

"What are you doing here, Lenor?" I asked, ignoring the way she reached for my hands. I knew I should be amiable and remind myself that regardless of her motives for the tour, she was doing the good I could not, but standing before her, my fury raged. She wore a ridiculous costume for travel—a pink-and-gold brocade silk gown with gold sleeves fashioned like butterfly wings that started at her wrists and cascaded to the floor. Her brown hair had been colored an unnatural auburn, and her face bore such thick paint that her wrinkles were invisible.

"I'm performing tonight. You know that."

"I meant here, in my room. I assumed you'd breeze in and out after stealing my tour, but I suppose you believed I'd simply pretend to forget about the way the jealousy lit up your face when you first heard the news I was going around to the camps, just like you assumed we'd gloss over your stealing from me, lying about me, attempting to blackball my name on Broadway. I'd say I was surprised you had the nerve to show your face, but I'm not. What would you like me to give you this time? A lock of my hair? A vial of blood? Or perhaps you're here to give me a poisoned apple." I laughed despite myself and turned away from her. I was shaking. I pinched my eyes shut and forced calm. I'd never win an audience for my music men by letting my anger reign.

She didn't respond but followed me into my room uninvited and closed my door behind her as though I were a small child pitching a fit that I'd momentarily get over. She glanced around at the simple poster bed and the singed armoire and shook her head. "My. This is shabby." Lenor crossed to the mirror and appraised herself, smoothed her lipstick, and then looked at me in the reflection. "Whyever are you staying here in this hovel like a regular army wife when you could be residing in luxury at the Selwyn Hotel?" She paused. "I know you can afford it. I asked around. You were paid generously in London and in the city before you set out on this tour. I was the one who told Mr. Shubert you should be paid top dollar."

I walked to the armchair and sat down. I wanted to tell her that she was mistaken, that the funds for my army tour came from my savings and that by the time the London staff was paid, Caspar and I had only made enough money to afford new clothing for the season and our flats for six months, but decided against it. She'd taken a large part of my income for a decade. If I didn't have much money, it was partially her fault.

"Surely your lover . . . whoever he is . . . could visit you there."

My breath caught.

"You've been speaking to my mother?" I asked. It was the only way she would have known. Though my parents and I had only exchanged a few letters—it was too difficult to mince words for the censors—I'd been more detailed in my description of the man I'd fallen in love with the last time I'd written.

"Just once. She refused to answer the door for Mr. Crispel or reply to my letters inquiring about whether she still had my Worth shawl I let her borrow for the premiere of our variety show way back when, so I went over to see her last week when I was in the city. Your father was on his way out to the mill and let it slip that you had a man here."

Lenor turned to face me. I could feel the heat on my cheeks. It wasn't that it mattered if Lenor knew what I'd told my parents, but I worried that she'd told others, that my reputation was at stake. It was one thing to pause your tour for the sake of appreciation and another entirely to cancel it because you'd fallen in love. I didn't know why, but calling off a tour to enliven the soldiers who would fight and die for me in order to stoke the flames in my own heart seemed extraordinarily selfish. I knew without doubt others would agree.

"Don't you worry, dear. I didn't say a word to anyone." She walked closer to me, her sequined heels clacking on the wood. "I didn't believe you were staying at one camp indefinitely just to show your appreciation anyway. Love is what set you out on the road and now love compels you to give it up."

She shrugged and I stood abruptly. I fisted my hands at my sides.

"I've not given it up," I growled. "After I'm through with shows in the American camps, I plan to go to the front—and I will. I simply don't have clearance to go yet. The moment General Pershing allows it, I'll be on a ship. I promised Caspar. There are so many men begging for a little merriment." My voice softened at the end, thinking of how desperately I wanted to go. Even though I'd found purpose here, even though I'd found love, I still owed it to Caspar's memory and to the soldiers imminently facing death to push forward.

"Well, isn't that nice." Lenor ran her hands down one of her sleeves and then let it fall to the floor. "I'm planning to go over to France too, you know. The papers have been calling me the 'Darling of the American Expeditionary Forces.'"

"Is that right?" I stepped forward, thinking I'd slap her, but something stilled my hand. This was what Lenor always did. She knew exactly how to get under my skin. I would settle down instead. Perhaps then I could ask her to hear my men, she would agree, and then take her leave.

I sat back down in the armchair and took a deep breath. I closed my eyes and envisioned Guy, Sidney, William, Crowley, and Roland safe and on a Broadway stage, then called up the faces of the men on the front smiling up at a performer I couldn't see. Calm flooded through me. As I'd told myself before—as much as I desperately wanted to go, if Lenor was sent instead, at least the men would be cheered.

Lenor wandered back toward the mirror. She fiddled with the pins holding a low chignon in place. "Where is your lady's maid? I loathe this style. I asked Geraldine if she supposes me to be seventy, but she keeps telling me that it becomes my face and makes me look youthful. She promised to try a new style for tonight, but I don't entirely believe it'll be any better."

"I don't have one. I've never had one. Only Mother," I said. "We couldn't afford one. You know that. Speaking of tonight, Lenor. I've met a great number of men with extraordinary talent here and I'd love it if—"

She snapped her fingers at me, interrupting. "I should hire your mother," she said, as though she hadn't heard anything I'd said beyond that Mother did my hair. She appraised me and her nose wrinkled. "It's clear she's not here. I hesitated to say a word, but you look a fright."

Ordinarily I'd remind her that only moments before she'd assumed I'd employed a lady's maid, but I trained my gaze out the window and ignored her.

"I'll need to let Geraldine go before I go to the front, and procure a more suitable maid," she went on.

"Why do you want to go over there?" I asked. The question gnawed at me, but I knew the moment I asked it that it was a mistake.

"I don't really. General Pershing saw how the country took to my shows here and asked if I'd consider it because apparently you'd mentioned it to him before you were sidetracked by your devotion."

I wanted both to scream at the injustice of her clearance in my place and cry with relief at the same time.

"I told his office I'd go so long as he guaranteed me a two weeks' respite headlining on Broadway between the American camps and going overseas. I can't have the city forgetting about me now." She smiled. "I told them I'll be playing the lead role of the vixen and not someone's mother, as is Broadway's ridiculous leaning these days. He agreed he'd make the necessary arrangements." She paused. "It's been incredibly rewarding for my reputation too. I watched the response the country had to your little tour and figured, when he asked if I'd resume yours, that it wouldn't hurt."

"You knew how much the tour meant to me."

"Yes, but you walked away from it, so now I'm doing you and the army a favor in keeping it going." A hint of a grin lifted her lips. "He must be quite a man."

I wouldn't tell her about Jesse. I hoped she'd never see him. If she did, there was a chance she'd try to seduce him. Her charms wouldn't work on him, as he wasn't at all impressed by her, but she'd done it before with a few men I'd accompanied to dinner or to a show. Our relationship was much like Snow White and the Evil Queen. If there was any inkling I was more famous, more beautiful, more beloved, she felt compelled to prove that I wasn't. For some time after I fired her and she continued to push her way into my life, I'd wondered why she kept her thumb on my pulse, but then it was clear: my success served as a sort of benchmark for her. Fame was all Lenor had ever wanted, and if she could remain more famous than me, then it meant that Nina Napier and Ida Crispi and the rest weren't worth worrying about.

Lenor sauntered to the window. "It must be dreadful watching the men drill all day long, preparing for war. I don't believe in it, you know. Neither do most of the men. Even the generals. An officer I had occasion to spend the evening with last night in Greenville told me some dreadful things when we retired to his quarters."

"War is awful, but these men are heroes. America can hardly stay on the sidelines while our civilian comrades in Europe are under such duress. Caspar didn't sit by, and I won't either. Sit by and we're no better than the Huns."

"I've heard the Huns have a lot of money." Lenor grinned. "If the rumor is true, perhaps I'll go entertain them instead."

"How could you possibly say that? Not only is it disrespectful and alarming, it's treasonous."

"Perhaps. The way I see it, war is nothing but a cockfight."

Lenor sighed. My veins seethed with rage.

"Get—" I started to tell her to get out, to leave my room immediately and never speak to me again, but she interrupted.

"I do hope those ladies are setting my things up to my specifications at the theatre. We had a bit of an issue with the secretaries in Alabama a few nights back. The place looked more like a pool hall than a grand Parisian salon."

She turned away from me, walked to my armoire, and opened the door. I thought she might comment on Caspar's letter, but she said nothing. At once I thought of Lenor's solo shows she put on for the Fifth Avenue set and for private parties—the dripping glitz, the overbearing glamour. They were nothing like mine. Mine were light, filled with humor. Despite not being able to go anyway, I hadn't had one invitation back to Broadway since I'd embarked on the tour. Perhaps it was only that everyone knew of my determination to be off with the army men or perhaps I'd return and find that Lenor had started another rumor and finally snuffed my star out, that there was no room for a lighthearted songbird on the New York stage. Perhaps General Pershing was of the same mind when it came to the front.

"I think you should—" I attempted to ask her to hear the boys once again, but she cut me off.

"Did you not bring any of your Worth gowns?" Lenor asked.

"No. They're beautiful, but I can't tumble in them."

"Why you ever set to flipping around the stage, I'll never understand. It's very juvenile. In any case, I suppose this green silk Doucet will do." She plucked the costume from the armoire, appraising the silk panels laced with silver and pearls.

"For what?" I asked.

Lenor pursed her lips and tilted her head, looking at me as if I should already know the answer.

"I'm bringing you onstage tonight, of course. For 'A Friend Will Heal Your Heart' and that little ditty we did when you first came on tour with me—'Elder Sister Knows Best.' George Sigmond and Edmund Wilson, those writers from the *New York Times*, have decided that they wish to cover this particular show." Her gaze momentarily shifted to a glare before she realized her emotion was showing and she smiled. "I told them it was practically the same song and dance at each stop, but they said they hoped to catch us together."

Perhaps I wasn't yesterday's news after all. Still, Lenor had chosen one of the worst songs I'd ever performed for the show. I hadn't sung "Elder Sister Knows Best" since I was twelve. She'd obviously selected it to make me appear lesser. Then again, it didn't matter which songs she wanted me to sing. I wouldn't share the stage with her. Not after she'd taken so much from me.

"I'd rather not," I said.

Lenor rolled her eyes. "'Sister' is a cheery old song, and that's what you're about, is it not?" she asked, misinterpreting my dismissal of the stage entirely for my disapproval of her song selection. "What about 'We Have the Same Love' instead of 'Sister'?"

The former song was the last we'd ever performed together, about two women vying for the eye of the same man. It was quite spot-on—if the man was really Broadway. Roland and Crowley had requested I teach them to play it during our last lesson. The thought of them encouraged an idea, and suddenly, sharing the stage with Lenor seemed like a good choice.

"Yes, I think that will work. As long as you agree to allow a few of the doughboys here at Camp Greene up onstage with us during those numbers," I said. "The talent here is unbelievable, Lenor, and they adore you. They would dream of this night forever."

My tone changed entirely, but Lenor didn't seem to detect it. Instead, she looked in the mirror once again, tilting her head this way and that to appraise her own beauty. If licking Lenor's boots was what it took to get Guy, Roland, Sidney, Crowley, and the others noticed by the newspaper men and subsequently Lenor and Broadway, I'd steel my tongue and clean them all.

"They can actually play?"

"Yes. Sing and act too. Better than most of our contemporaries on Broadway," I said. "There's a man named Guy Werths whose voice rivals Caspar's. He could sing Dennison's part on 'The Same Love.' We haven't included his part in years."

"So that's how he caught your eye. You've always nearly fainted at the sound of a smooth baritone." She wiggled her brows at me, and I shook my head.

"Guy is engaged to a dear friend of mine, the nurse who saved my life."

"But he is a musician, this love of yours," Lenor said.

I wasn't sure if Jesse had any sort of musical acumen. At this point, I doubted it. He'd not so much as hummed in my presence this past month, even during hymns at church.

"Have this steamed." Lenor held my gown out to me. I took it from her but knew the garment would be worn as is. I didn't know if anyone in camp owned a steamer.

"No, he's not." I answered her earlier question and she smiled.

"That's even better. I've found that men who have no clue are more adoring, more struck by the glitz of a girl like us on their arm."

"He was not adoring at all when we first met," I said. "In fact, he loathed that I was here. He said I was only a distraction and he didn't know any of my songs."

I laughed, thinking back on my first days in camp. Those days had been hard, and yet when I thought of Jesse and me, it was nearly miraculous to think that we'd gone from loathing each other to loving each other.

Outside, a woman in a plain brown dress ran across the road carrying handfuls of feathers.

"Good lord. Those are part of my stage swag. They were all boxed together. What on earth is that woman doing?" Lenor walked toward the window and leaned into the pane. "I must get to the Selwyn at once and get ready so that I can arrive at the theatre early. Would you mind going down to supervise this madness?" She looked at me and then gestured out the window. "I know the stage will be perfect if you're overseeing it."

"Sure," I said. I smiled. Ordinarily I'd be irritated that she was bossing me around as if I were her assistant instead of her equal, but she'd agreed to let the men play, and I had to go tell them the news. I'd go to the theatre directly after and dress there.

Lenor sighed. "Then I'll see you at five o'clock sharp to warm up. Doors open at six thirty." She turned on her heel and breezed toward the door. "And don't forget the bonnet headpiece that accompanies that gown." Lenor pointed at the gown I'd laid across my bed. "I saw you wear that costume without it when you returned from England, and I could've passed you on the street without knowing at all that you were someone to look at. The bonnet commands, *Look at me*."

I nodded, shocked that she'd recommend I draw attention to

myself at all. Lenor tipped her head at me and left my room. Another shriek from Mrs. Kern indicated she'd cleared the front door, and then I heard the chug of the limousine's engine as it roared to life.

"Miss Connolly? Telegram for Miss Connolly?" I heard a young man's voice sound from the foyer where Mrs. Kern was likely still reeling from her interaction with Lenor.

I opened my door and walked down the hall to the stairs. Mrs. Kern had revived as best she could and was standing in front of the telegraph boy. He looked up at the sound of my footsteps and his face blanched.

"Hello there," I said. "Do you have something for me?"

"Y-yes," he stammered. He handed me the envelope and I grinned at him.

"Thank you."

Mrs. Kern didn't say a word but stared out the window to the drive, doubtless wondering if Lenor would reappear.

The boy walked out the door and I started back up the stairs to my room. I slid my finger into the seal of the envelope and extracted the telegram, then closed the door behind me.

The telegram was from England.

> Heard you were still at Camp Greene from a fellow patient American STOP Reenlisting order scheduled for two weeks STOP Come before I go STOP Otherwise will share photo with uncle to give to GP and press STOP No other choice
>   Basil Omar

I couldn't believe he'd stooped this low. I stared at the paper and at once felt as though I might vomit. I sank to the floor. I couldn't go to England at my leisure. I couldn't help him as he'd been begging me to. And if General Pershing saw the photograph, if the press got ahold of the photograph, my reputation would be smudged and my chances would be ruined. I'd never be allowed to go to the front. My days on the stage would be a thing of the past. A rumor could be overcome eventually because there was no sure way to prove it true. But a suggestive photograph couldn't be falsified. It was unmistakably me, my breasts and body barely covered in silk and lace.

My hands began to sweat and I let the paper drop into my lap. After the show, I would find Jesse and beg him to wire Basil and tell him that by order of the United States, I couldn't help him. Surely Basil would understand then and it would all get sorted.

CHAPTER 26

*H*e'll *decide the fate—the incredible, awful fate—of this same love."* My voice closed the song, following the final wail of Roland's saxophone. The crowd's shouts and claps thundered over us. Guy stood beside me in his trim black tuxedo and Lenor stood beside him. We waved and bowed, and when the applause died down, Jesse scaled the steps to the stage.

"Thank you, everyone, for coming out tonight for such a wonderful show!" he shouted. "Thanks to Lenor Felicity, to the band—including some of our own, Guy Werths, Crowley DeWitt, Roland Tapley, Sidney Duncan, and William Wentworth—and last, but absolutely not least, to our own Camp Greene star, Calla Connolly."

Jesse turned to face me when he said my name. His eyes met mine. I grinned at him, but I could tell in the seconds we stared at each other that something wasn't right. Perhaps Basil had wired him too.

I could feel Lenor's eyes on my face, and when I looked at her, she was smiling knowingly. I forced a deep breath and kept my attention fixed on Jesse's back and the crowd in front of him. Jesse had had a strenuous week. There was a chance nothing was wrong and he was only exhausted from his camp and command duties and mourning Mac and the fate of his men of the 543rd. I wished more than anything I could tell him I'd seen the letter, that I lived with the knowledge of it too, but I couldn't. I wasn't supposed to see it and he'd undoubtedly worry that I'd break down and warn the men I spent so much time with.

"Next week we'll be back at Lakewood Park for a dance accompanied by Miss Connolly and her band. Until then, enjoy your hour of freedom, men, and turn in on time."

Everyone cheered again and we bowed once more. Jesse walked back down the steps and into the crush instead of accompanying me backstage. I started to follow him, but Guy stopped me.

"This is what I was meant to do," Guy said, looping his arm around my shoulders and leading me behind the curtain to where the rest of the musicians were lingering.

"I know. Everyone else will know now too."

The other men were laughing, their faces radiant.

"That's about the most fun I've ever had," Sidney said. He was perched on a stool by a long row of mirrors Lenor had brought in so she could stare at herself before curtain. A little feather that had drifted up from the stage swag was stuck in his hair, and I reached to extract it.

"You were all fabulous," Lenor said, catching up behind me. She walked over to Roland, who was sitting in a small armchair next to Sidney, his saxophone still clutched in his hand. "Especially you." She sat on his lap when she said it, and Roland froze. I'd noticed Lenor's attention on Roland during the show, but now she made her intentions perfectly clear. At least he was the oldest of the group—almost thirty-one, but Lenor was still twenty years his senior. I wondered if he would accept her advances. There was nothing I could do if he did. They were both adults and able to make up their minds on such things.

"We're thinking of going to Johnny Clements to play pool," he said to Lenor, clearly in an attempt to steady himself from her sudden attention. He leaned toward her face, which was already tilted toward his.

"They have drinks there too, Miss Felicity," Crowley commented from beside Sidney.

Guy shook his head. "It's a hovel masquerading as a pool hall," he said. "Hardly a place to ask Miss Felicity to accompany us to—if that's what you're insinuating, men, and we couldn't be all together there anyway. Roland and Sidney would be ushered into the other Johnny Clements pool hall next door."

Lenor yawned and shook her head, then looped her hand around Roland's neck.

"I'm much too tired to play games tonight, I'm afraid," she said, her gaze not breaking from Roland's face. "I wondered, Mr. Tapley, if you would mind walking me home?"

"But you're staying all the way at the Selwyn Hotel in town," Sidney said, clearly not catching on to the fact that an innocent walk was not at all what Lenor had in mind. "He won't make it back in time for final taps."

Lenor rose to her feet, took Roland's hand in hers, and began to lead him out of the tent flap. I could hear voices just beyond it. Ordinarily the crowd dispersed out of the main entrance, but I was certain tonight that some Charlotteans and soldiers had gathered to have one last look at Lenor Felicity up close before she was whisked off to her next tour stop.

I left the other men and ran after Lenor and Roland before they reached the exit.

"Roland, I . . . I wondered if you'd like to stay behind for a moment. I was hoping to have a word with all of you. What a wonderful performance you put on tonight."

I wanted to give him an excuse to stay if he didn't wish to be Lenor's entertainment for the evening, but he smiled at me, glanced at Lenor, and shook his head.

"Can we discuss it tomorrow?" he asked.

At once the tent flap opened, and Jesse appeared.

"Oh. Miss Felicity, Roland," he said. He tipped his head at them and Lenor immediately giggled like a girl of twenty, whispered something to Roland, and let go of his hand. She stepped out into the night, and he followed behind.

When Jesse and I were alone, I reached for him, and he pulled me close and kissed me. When his lips broke from mine, I looked up at him.

"What's wrong?" I asked. His eyes were tired and glassy, and he shook his head.

"I came to ask you if you'd come with me. I need to speak with you," he whispered.

Before I could answer, before I could tell him I needed to speak with him too, he took my hand in his and led me out of the tent. In front of us, the crowd was so enamored by Lenor—who had paused her pursuit of Roland to greet fans—that they didn't notice Jesse and me as we made our way into his Packard parked beside the tent.

"Jesse, what is it?" I asked when he'd settled into the seat beside me.

He glanced at me and his eyes teared. "Would you come have a drink with me?"

I squeezed his hand, and he started the auto.

"Yes, of course." My heart began to race. Not knowing what he was about to tell me was a torture. Not knowing how he'd react to the news that Caspar's friend was blackmailing me was a similar sensation. Perhaps he'd decided Jacqueline was his true love after all, despite the baby. Perhaps he realized his heart couldn't belong to a woman who belonged to the stage. Perhaps he'd refuse to help me settle Basil's threat.

We drove behind the regimental tents, out of the way of the dispersing crowd, to the Dowd House hill. The engine seemed to protest as we ascended the drive to the front.

By the time he shut off the auto and came around to retrieve me, my hands were clammy and my chest was tight. He leaned down and kissed me, then took my hand and led me into the house.

It was a traditional four-square farmhouse and the air smelled like expired cigar smoke. A little electric lamp was ignited on a small table in the foyer, casting a bit of glow into the darkened study to our right and the dining room to our left. The dining table was significantly smaller than the expansive fourteen-place situation in the Hostess House.

"Up here," Jesse said. We walked up the stairs, our hands still clasped together, and entered a large bedroom at the back of the house. I closed the door behind me as Jesse flipped on a lamp atop a weathered mahogany desk in the corner. An old tufted leather armchair was situated in front of it and a sizable metal bed occu-pied the other half of the room. The bed was adorned with a simple white quilt, but it had been made up perfectly, without a wrinkle.

I stood, frozen, as Jesse began to rummage in the bottom drawer of his desk. He finally withdrew a bottle of amber liquor and two glasses. He poured a generous amount into each glass and handed one to me. I stared at it. I barely drank alcohol at all. I didn't enjoy what it did to my inhibitions, and yet I felt that if I didn't take a drink to settle my nerves, I'd either collapse or explode.

Jesse dropped into the leather chair and put his head in his hands.

I walked toward him, set my glass on the desktop, and sank down on the ground next to his knees. My request for help was on the tip of my tongue, yet I couldn't ask it, not when he was clearly so distraught already.

"Darling, please. What is it?" I asked. I reached up and grasped his forearms gently. When his fingers were twined in mine and his gaze fell on me, I asked again. "If it's that you don't feel for me anymore, I—"

"No." He lifted me up and pulled me to him in one solid move-ment. His palms grasped my cheeks, and he kissed my forehead. "I love you."

"I love you too," I whispered. "But you have to tell me what's troubling you."

He nodded and looked away from me. "I will. It's only . . . I need a moment." He swallowed hard. I kissed his cheek and stood. Jesse tipped his glass to his mouth and closed his eyes.

I left him alone in the chair, retrieved my own glass, and wan-dered around his room. I studied the photo of his parents atop the little table by his bedside and the stack of books—Robert

Frost's *Mountain Interval, Democracy and Education* by John Dewey, Edgar Rice Burroughs's *The Son of Tarzan*. With every second of silence, the walls seemed to shift and close in. I tried to breathe—to breathe in the lingering smell of Jesse's soap, of the fresh sundrenched linen of his bedclothes—but my neck and chest had tightened to the point I couldn't.

Finally, Jesse cleared his throat, and I turned back to look at him. My eyes filled, though he hadn't said a word. He twirled the whiskey in his glass.

"There's no other way to say it." His voice was gravelly and his eyes were red, and at once he appeared more haggard than I'd ever seen him. "As you know, I was visited by a few generals from the War Department this week. They alluded to imminent movement for the Third Division and said they'd notified General Dickman of the same, but last night I received a telegram confirming what I feared. The Third Division has been ordered to France on Monday next week. The Germans are moving from the Chemin des Dames, and it's believed their attack is looming, threatening Paris and the Allies' rail line. Our number has been called. Most of the regiments will join the British and French at the front and support their efforts, but the 543rd will be sent to the Sumerlin Valley where they'll carry out the mission they've been assigned."

My fingers trembled around the glass, and I stumbled toward Jesse and sank down on the foot of the bed. Our knees touched and I could feel his own quaking. Tears ran down my cheeks.

"I'd hoped it would never come to this. Jesse . . . I saw . . . that day when I came to your office, I picked up the papers on the floor and saw the list of the men assigned to the 543rd. My friends. Guy and Crowley and William. I know I wasn't supposed to read it, but I saw the mention of Paris and I couldn't stop myself."

Their faces tonight, so full of joy, appeared in my mind. I pressed my hand to my chest, sure my heart would give out. I waited for Jesse to be angry that I'd read the letter, but he wasn't.

"I thought you might have." Jesse was looking down. "I can hardly bear to look at them. I'm not guilty when it comes to their task, but to know what I do and keep it silent is agony, as I'm sure it is for you."

"Goldie and Guy were supposed to get married," I whispered. My cheeks were soaked with tears. "And you and I will simply have to wait and pray for news that they've survived."

Jesse sniffed and shook his head. His gaze was trained on his hands. A little clock ticked from his desktop, a rhythmic accompaniment to our emotion.

"Calla," he said finally. He leaned toward me and threaded his fingers through mine. "Pershing is sending me too."

Surely I'd heard him wrong.

"I'm going over," he continued. "When we reach France, the Sixth Brigade will be assigned a new general and I'll be commanding the 543rd. Most of the time officers stay out of the action, only forced to take up arms if they must, but knowing what I do, I figure I'll be fighting along with the others." He ran his thumb over my finger. "I suppose Pershing still finds my early involvement in France problematic, a mortal sin along with the faults they've noted in the others. But if being given over to such a fate means I'll be with my men, it will work out as I've hoped. I'll do my best to protect them like I couldn't protect Mac."

"I know you wanted to go, but not this way. Not this way, Jesse," I managed to say before my chest heaved and I began to sob. Jesse's arms wrapped around me, and he carried me to the chair and held me there. I buried my face in his jacket and cried until I couldn't anymore.

"I'm at peace with it," he whispered. I could feel his breath, his tears in my hair. "My men won't face this alone."

I held on to him, my fingers clutching the heavy fabric against his back with all the strength I had. I tried to memorize the sensation of his arms around me, the sound of his voice. I would lose him too, just like I'd lost Caspar. Everything suddenly felt desperate, and my heart felt hollow. I began to cry again. His fingers drifted through my hair.

"When I get there, I'll speak to Dickman and Pershing about

sending for you. He clearly doesn't think much of me, but if I can convince him, perhaps we can be together until they send us to the trenches."

I sat up and he wiped the tears from my eyes. The gesture hardly mattered. The terror I felt at this revelation saturated my face, replacing the sadness he'd cleared away.

"If he doesn't agree, Jesse," I said, barely able to make the words sound, "what will I do?"

"He might permit it."

"No, he won't." At once I recalled Basil's telegram and began to sob again. "I received a wire today from Caspar's friend, Basil. He's threatening that if I don't involve him in a show before he reenlists in two weeks, he'll send the photograph to General Pershing and leak it to the papers. Pershing will never allow me over there if I'm made out to be a veritable strumpet, and you'll be at the front without me, tasked with this terrible mission." I started sobbing. My world was unraveling and I couldn't bear it. "Perhaps if you were to wire Basil and explain that I've been ordered to remain here, he'll reconsider. If he doesn't, I—"

"I'll do it," Jesse whispered. "First thing in the morning. And Pershing won't ever know of the photograph. The moment I arrive I'll speak to him about sending for you. I promise. I . . . I need you near me."

"But you'll still go before me. What if he won't give me clearance? I don't want you to go without me." My lips quivered and my heart broke. "I was a fool to fall again. I can't lose you. You cannot . . . you cannot . . ." I couldn't manage to say *die*.

Jesse kissed me and his eyes welled.

"The minute I got the orders, I thought of you. I'm glad to go, to die if I must, but my only regret is leaving you. I shouldn't have told you how I felt. It was selfish."

"I would have loved you regardless of your love for me," I said. "And I'll telegram General Pershing every hour if I must, but I'll follow after you as quickly as I can. I can't bear the thought of you going into battle without me nearby."

"You will be with me, with us, whether you're in France or only in our hearts." Jesse's breath hitched and his hands dropped to the small of my back. I leaned into his chest and kissed his cheek, tasting the salt trails of his tears, and then his neck. He tilted his head back and whispered my name.

When my lips reached the collar of his jacket, he caught my chin in his hand and drew my face to his.

"If I live, would you consider marrying me? The moment I return?"

The question hung in the air as my heartbeat rushed in my ears. Now, if he perished, I would forever bear the weight of two broken loves, two shattered futures. If I lost Jesse, I knew I'd never love again. I'd loved Caspar desperately, but this love I felt for Jesse was consuming.

"Yes." The word barely sounded and he smiled, then kissed me deeply.

"I'll do everything in my power to have Pershing send for you and use every bit of my strength to come back to you and bring the others back with me," he said. "But tonight, will you stay? Perhaps I'll die, but I'll dream of the vision of waking to your face, of holding you in my arms."

I nodded and another tear escaped my eyes. The thought of leaving him tonight was impossible. I stood and he did in turn. He switched off the electric light atop his desk, leaving only the illumination of the crescent moon from his window.

He removed his jacket, then pulled his shirt over his head and took off his trousers. His body was shadowed in darkness, and yet the sight of his long muscles, his bare skin, made my knees weak. He climbed into bed, pushing back the quilt. My fingers trembled as I unclasped the buttons at the back of my dress. Jesse was watching me, his gaze serious and trained on my hands as they pushed what remained of my gown from my hips and undid my corset. I pulled the pins from my hair, letting the strands fall to my waist. My silk chemise felt cold against my body as I walked toward him.

"Come here," he said.

I laid down and wrapped myself around him. His skin was warm, and he pulled the quilt over us as my hands explored his body— the bulge of his shoulders and the lines of his stomach. He barely breathed as I touched him, but when I turned my head on the pillow, he kissed me. His fingers drifted down my thigh, catching the hem of my chemise and urging it up my body until all that was left was me and him, until all that mattered was our love and this bed, this night and this moment.

CHAPTER 27

"A re you sure you're all right?" Wendy whispered. Her breath smelled like maple syrup. I nodded and forced myself to take a bite of my breakfast. I couldn't look at her. I didn't know how I'd face any of the men or women who would be impacted by the approaching fate of the 543rd. It was the worst sort of secret to be forced to keep, but there was no alternative, really. Even if I told them all, nothing would change save obliterating their spirits or encouraging them to desert. They would still have to march into battle. Their orders would undoubtedly remain the same.

"Coffee?" Mrs. Kern asked me.

"Yes, please," I murmured, handing my empty china cup to her.

"Wasn't last night magical?" Betty said from the other side of the table. "Lenor was everything I thought she'd be, and you, Calla, were just perfect. The other men too."

"Thank you," I said. It seemed as if the show had been a year ago. So much had changed in the hours following it.

Jesse had driven me back to the Hostess House before daylight, before the bugle call, before Mrs. Kern would notice I'd never returned home, saying he was going straight to the telegram office to wire Basil. I yawned and rubbed my eyes. I hadn't slept. Instead, I'd silently cried and panicked in alternating measure all night. Jesse had fallen asleep for a few hours at least. I knew, because at one point I'd felt his body ease and still beside me and his breathing slow. But for most of the hours, we laid in each other's arms whispering promises we couldn't keep between long moments of silence where I was certain our minds battled the same demons. When his clock chimed four, he'd pulled me to him one more time, then kissed me long and deep and told me that we had to go but that he wanted me to know he'd love me forever. I'd never forget that kiss or the way he looked at me.

My eyes teared, and I hurriedly picked up my coffee cup to distract the others from noticing. We had only been separated for a few hours and he'd promised to take me to church with him, but I knew that last night had likely been our final moments truly alone. Despite it being the weekend, preparations to leave would begin today and he'd announce the departure news to his men tomorrow.

"Calla!"

Goldie shouted my name from the foyer at the same time the front door slapped against the wall, shaking the house.

I rose from my chair, my skin washing cold with panic.

"Calla!" she screamed again. This time a sob punctuated the end of it.

The other girls began to chatter, and Mrs. Kern burst from the kitchen as I hastened from the room. Goldie's footsteps hurried up the stairs and she continued to call my name.

"I'm here!" I yelled back. I was out of breath by the time I reached the landing and ran down the hall to my room.

"What is it? What's happened?" I asked. She stood beside my bed, her cheeks damp with tears, in her Sunday best—a cream dress embroidered with vines in green silk thread. My stomach churned and I felt as though I was going to vomit. Whatever had happened was horrible, and I didn't know how much more horror I could bear.

I closed my door behind me and began to reach for her, but she sank to the floor and sobbed into her hands. I curled my fingers into fists, forcing myself to feel the sensation of my nails digging into my palms. It was the only way I could keep from collapsing myself.

"Miss Connolly, is everything all right?" Mrs. Kern called from the hall.

"Yes," I lied.

I dropped to my knees next to Goldie.

"Tell me what's happened," I whispered.

She shook her head and then finally looked at me. Her face exhibited confusion as she noticed mine, splotchy with spent tears like hers.

"What's the matter?" she asked. It was exactly like Goldie to think to care for me first.

"Nothing at all," I lied. "I didn't sleep."

"Guy and ten others are missing." She choked out the words. I froze.

"What . . . ? How?"

I took her hands in mine. They were shaking. I could feel the moisture gathering in my palms, the primal urge to run, to help, coursing through my veins, but I had no idea where to go.

"I came by the hospital this morning to check on a few flu patients before church." She heaved a breath. "When I got to my quarters and unlocked my desk drawer to retrieve my patient files, I saw a note from Guy on top of the stack—he knows I keep the key under the desk leg. He said—"

Her eyes met mine and she began to sob again.

"You can't say a word of this to anyone, Calla. No one. Do you understand me? Not Colonel Erickson especially."

I nodded, not knowing at all whether I'd regret this promise later.

"The letter was written in haste, but he said that he was going to . . . that he and a group of other men were going to abandon, that they'd been told in certain terms, by a reliable source, that the army was planning to ship his division to France next week and that his regiment's mission was a perilous one, that they alone would be forced to stay and fight the Huns while other troops drew back."

I gagged and the room seemed to spin. I forced my head between my legs. As far as I knew, Jesse and I were the only people to know their fate here in camp. If Jesse had decided to tell the men of their mission, he would be subject to treason, a serious war crime. I couldn't imagine he'd done such a thing.

"Calla," Goldie said. Her fingers were freezing, and they grasped my arm. The shocking feel of them steadied me, and I met her eyes and nodded for her to continue.

"He said he couldn't stay knowing he'd most likely die over there and leave me." She let me go and began to cry again and tears filled my eyes. "He said he was meant to be my husband and meant to be a musician and he'd rather risk being punished than go and face certain death. He said he'll come for me in a few months, because if he comes back too soon and gets caught, he'll be sent over anyway."

"We have to find him," I said.

"I know. And yet I don't know if that's best either. If he's found, he'll die at the front, and if he stays away, he could be sentenced to death." Goldie sobbed. "Either way, he's doomed."

I shook my head. "There has to be another way," I said, but the sentiment was only a wish. "We need to tell Jesse. We'll need help finding him."

"No." Goldie nearly shouted the word, then shook her head and cried silently. "Not yet. I . . . I need to figure what is most likely to keep Guy safe. If he's brought back now, he's right. He'll most certainly go. Perhaps if the others are sent off and he turns up afterward, he could avoid charges and avoid the fate of his division."

"Or he could be expedited quickly and assigned a calling more dangerous than the one he's been given now."

I rose from the floor unsteadily and gripped one of my bedposts.

"You can't tell a soul," Goldie whispered as she stood. She wiped her cheeks. "Promise me."

I hesitated and she lunged for my arms.

"Promise," she hissed. "Everyone will notice they're gone soon enough, but it's Sunday, and in case abandoning is the right choice, this will give them a bit of a start."

I looked into her eyes and saw the fear and panic and heartbreak that mirrored mine. "I promise."

She released her grip on me and stepped toward the windows. "We were supposed to be married," she murmured.

"I know," I said.

"Mother even ordered a cake with buttercream frosting." Goldie wiped her eyes. "But now his name will be in all the papers, and he'll be labeled a slacker." She sniffed. "We'll have to settle somewhere else entirely. I'd hoped to settle here." She wasn't talking to me, not really, but I understood the need to vocalize the could-have-beens war stole, the disappointments. Jesse and I had done the same throughout the night. At one point he'd said that if there hadn't been a war, he would have taken me downtown to choose a ring, and I'd said I would have telegrammed my parents to let them know I was going to be a wife. The things we'd once thought ordinary were really blessings, miracles even, and war had taken them away.

"Don't lose hope," I said, as much to myself as to Goldie.

"I suppose I should go to church," she said suddenly. "I imagine you'll attend with Colonel Erickson, but would you mind walking me to the station first? It will only take a few minutes. I feel quite weak right now."

"Of course," I said. I walked toward her, looped my arm through hers, and led her out of the door. Thankfully, the other girls were still downstairs. I could hear their distant chatter.

"If anyone asks why I came by in such a state, say there's been a death in my family—my cousin, who's just died of flu but who loved your music. I came by to tell you and ask if you'd sing at her funeral," Goldie whispered. "The news will be out soon enough, but I can't bear the questions right now." She stole a glance at me as we walked down the stairs and out of the front door. We started down the little company road that ran along the side of the Hostess House toward the trenches and camp proper.

"I forgot that you were rather desperate-looking before I told you about Guy," Goldie said as we walked between regiment tents and the trenches. "I know you said it was nothing, but I don't believe you. What is it that made you so sad?"

"Nothing of consequence." I looked away from her, toward the maze etched into the ground on my left. I studied it—the long stretches of fortified ground, the sharp turns, the muddy footprints scattered on the steep knolls.

"You went away with Colonel Erickson last night. That's what Guy said right before he kissed me good night at the edge of camp." Her voice broke. "I wonder if Guy knew then. But he couldn't have. He told me he'd see me at church in the morning." She sniffed. "I'm sorry. Did something happen with Colonel Erickson?"

"I suppose. I fell in love with him."

"Aren't you glad? It's clear he feels the same for you. Did he not tell you as much?" Goldie seemed to stabilize when speaking of my melancholy instead of her own, so I continued on despite feeling my heart tearing end to end.

"He did." I didn't know what else to say. I couldn't tell her he was leaving too, that I'd known the men were going before she did, so I shrugged. We passed the YMCA and the Knights of Columbus. Both were silent. "I'm terrified I'll lose him like I did Caspar."

She didn't say anything to the contrary. She couldn't. We passed the administration building and were about to walk out of camp to the streetcar when my eyes caught a crush of men on the Dowd House hillside.

"Something's happened," I said. Goldie and I nearly ran across the road. Soldiers chattered in an angry-sounding murmur that rose to a roar as we pushed through the crowd and neared the Dowd House porch. A few men stood in front of the door, pounding on the wood until it groaned, yelling for Jesse and Colonel Zachary.

I'd nearly reached the foot of the stairs with Goldie close behind me, to ask the men at the front what they were doing, when the door opened and Jesse emerged.

He glanced at the men in front of him and then at the crowd gathered beyond. His face looked like mine, awash with regret and heartbreak, but the bulge of his jaw suggested he'd decided he had no other choice but to face it, to fight his way out of it the same way he'd fight his way out of battle and home to me. When his gaze began to shift back to the soldiers at his door, I tried to catch his eye but couldn't. The soldiers around us surged forward.

"Is it true?" I heard one of the men ask him.

"We heard that our regiment, the 543rd, will start to France next Monday with the rest of the Third Division, but that we'll likely be placed in a perilous part of the front with weary French forces and abandoned to hold off the Huns when the French can't go on," another said.

My heartbeat quickened, the blood rushing through my veins.

"This is a death mission," the first man said.

Jesse shook his head and instructed the men to come to the edge of the porch alongside him. I watched him move. His skin was flushed, his shoulders rigid, his hands curled into fists, his eyes glaring.

"Gentlemen!" he shouted, his voice like a detonated bomb. The crush around us pressed in to hear him and their height blocked my view. Despite some claiming the contrary, fear had a smell, and the acrid stench of it radiated from the bodies of the men around us.

Goldie was crying again, though this time she barely made a sound.

"I was planning to address this in the special assembly I called tomorrow morning, but it seems all of you have lost your heads," Jesse went on. "I'm unsure where you heard these half-truths, but they've already poisoned your regiment. Eleven slackers are at large as of this morning. Colonel Zachary is already searching along with twelve other officers, and I'm confident the men will be located before deployment. If they aren't, I fear General Pershing will be more likely to exercise his right to sentence these men to execution. Let me remind you that resisting service is a war crime."

Goldie gasped and her knees buckled. I lunged to grab her arm. The men were unnervingly quiet.

"The truth of the matter is that we are going to be sent over there in a week. We're boarding the trains Monday morning at 8:20 a.m., to be exact. All of the Third Division will be reporting to New York City first and then directed on a boat to France. As to the rumor of the 543rd regiment's mission, there's no reason for fear." I heard his voice falter. He was going to lie to them. He had no other choice. "When we arrive in France, another general will be placed over command of the Sixth Brigade and I'll be commanding you, the 543rd. We will go together."

Chatter rippled through the crowd. I glanced at the faces I could see. Most appeared relieved that their beloved Colonel Erickson would be alongside them in battle. I suppose it was also the knowledge that Jesse appeared calm in the face of his assignment.

"I know France well. I have lived there; I have fought there. We'll be given our assignment once we're there, and we'll face it with strength and valor. I will guide you as brothers and friends, and I promise you I'll do everything in my power to bring you back to your loved ones when we've claimed the victory."

He paused and the men cheered. I waited for the shouts to subside and the men to start asking questions, but they didn't.

"Now, as to the men that have gone AWOL. We'll need your help. As I said, they're in grave danger if they desert entirely. As you go to church today and around town, keep your ears and eyes open for these men." Jesse paused and then cleared his throat. "Samuel Aberson, Crowley DeWitt."

I started at the sound of Crowley's name. I'd just been with Betty this morning at breakfast. She didn't have a clue.

"Malcolm Frank, Christopher Highmont, Douglas Litten, Thomas Powell, Heath Sewell, Kenneth Simpson, James Thompkins, William Wentworth, and Guy Werths. You're dismissed."

Goldie swallowed another sob and tears rolled down her cheeks. All of the musicians except for Sidney and Roland, who weren't in the same regiment as the others, were AWOL. I thought of Wendy. She was almost eight months pregnant. I couldn't fathom how she'd react when she found out William had abandoned.

"We'll find him," I whispered. "We'll find all of them."

The men began to disperse.

I looped my arm back through Goldie's and began to walk down the hill toward the station with the men.

"Poor old Chris got it all mixed around," I heard a soldier say. "Who'd he say told him?"

The talk of starting rumors made me feel dizzy. It hadn't occurred to me, listening to Jesse's address, that he could assume I'd been the one to leak the information, but of course he did. Watching him speak, it was clear he hadn't spread the word, that he didn't welcome the knowledge among the soldiers. I was the only other person who knew.

"I'll be fine from here," Goldie said when we reached the bottom of the hill and the entry road that led to the streetcar tracks. She wiped her eyes and attempted a smile. "I'm going to go to church and pray he turns up there. At the very least, I'll clear my head."

"Are you certain?" I thought to go with her all the way to the streetcar, but the idea that Jesse could think I was the one to reveal the army's secrets made me anxious.

"Yes, though I'll come by and get you later, if you wouldn't mind searching around with me."

"I'll search with you until we find him," I said.

She turned away from me and began walking with the men toward the streetcars that would carry them downtown.

I had just started up the hill when I heard my name from the street. An older man with an extraordinary mustache I'd never seen waved from a Model T auto just beside the drive up to the Dowd House. I waved back, but he called my name again and gestured for me to come over to him.

"I'm in quite a hurry!" I yelled and began toward the house. Midway up the drive, the auto caught up to me.

"Miss Connolly, I need a word," the man said. He stopped beside me, and I turned to face him. The haze of morning had burned away and now the sun and the exertion required to climb a hill encouraged sweat to gather on my brow.

"As I mentioned, sir, I'm in a hurry. I'm on my way to speak to Colonel Erickson."

"Colonel Erickson is otherwise occupied," the man said. He stuck out his hand. "Colonel River Tucker, just in from DC."

I shook his hand. "I assume your folks enjoy the water."

"Indeed," he said. "As do I. Now, Miss Connolly, I'm going to politely and quietly let you know that you are under arrest. Please do get into my auto."

I stared at the man, sure he was mistaken. I even started laughing.

"Do you suppose revealing information about a classified mission to young men about to be sent to the front is humorous? On the contrary, Miss Connolly. It is a serious crime, one that might cost you your life."

The man's eyes were cold, steely, and at once the sunshine darkened to midnight and the birds stopped singing and my heart threatened to fail me.

"B-but, Colonel Tucker, I didn't say a word of it," I stammered.

I opened the auto's door and got inside without thinking. He sped down the drive and through camp without replying. I thought, belatedly, that I could've made a run for it, that I could've absorbed into the crowd jumping onto the streetcars, but that disappearance would have only been temporary. I was Calla Connolly. Sooner or later, someone would recognize me, and I knew without doubt my punishment would be more severe if I eluded it—though I hadn't done anything to be punished for.

The auto jerked to a stop in front of what looked like ramshackle barracks tucked away through a bit of pine forest behind the Dowd House. There had been a fire in the structure at some point. The roofline was singed and some of the wooden exterior exhibited holes from the blaze.

"Where are we?" I asked.

"Confinement," he barked. He got out and opened the door for me.

"I told you, I didn't say a word," I said.

He pursed his lips. "There were only two individuals privy to the knowledge of the assignment here at Camp Greene. An officer and you."

"And I've kept the mission secret all this time," I said, my voice strained.

He shook his head. "You're a trained actress. Come with me."

I followed him into the building. There was only one window in the entry and the light was dim. The stench of mold permeated the air. A soldier around my age reclined at a worm-eaten desk in a ladderback chair. A stack of ledgers sat in front of him. When he saw me, he gasped.

"Calla Connolly." Then he cleared his throat. "I mean, excuse me, ma'am. It's only, while the others have been going to the dances and your shows, I've been here, see, so I haven't had a chance to say hello."

"She's not here to sing you a song. Last I checked you were company police. She's your newest ward."

The young police officer's face went slack. "Miss Connolly?"

Colonel Tucker groaned. "Yes. She'll be occupying room 1211 and is to be given three meals per day until she is transported for trial."

The man behind the desk gasped.

"Trial?" I asked. Reality consumed me and I began to cry. "I told you, Colonel. I said nothing. I did nothing wrong."

The door opened, pushing a gust of fresh air into the room, and another man I'd never seen before walked in. A few moments later, Jesse appeared behind him. Relief rushed through me.

"Jesse—I mean, Colonel Erickson. There's been a terrible misunderstanding. This man, Colonel Tucker, believes I'm guilty of—"

"Leave us, Eldridge," Colonel Tucker barked to the young soldier at the desk. Eldridge jerked from his chair and exited the room in haste.

When he was gone, I looked at Jesse. He stared at the warped hardwood floor.

"Colonel Erickson, please tell this man that I've done nothing wrong."

"I thought . . . we all thought we could trust you," he said finally. His eyes lifted to mine, but his gaze was hard, the love that had softened them only hours before completely absent.

I burst into tears.

"Perhaps you regret it now?" Colonel Tucker sneered.

"I didn't," was all I could muster, but I couldn't peel my eyes from Jesse's face. He was looking away from me, at the adjacent wall. "Jesse!" I screamed his name. I was being accused, rejected. I was losing him, and he didn't believe me. He glanced up at the sound, just for a moment. "I didn't do this."

"Come along, Colonel. You're this way," the man standing next to Jesse said. At once I realized it wasn't only me they were faulting. They'd arrested both of us, unsure who was to blame. Jesse followed the officer down a hallway just feet away from me and disappeared. The sight of him being led away like a criminal ignited something in me and I wiped my eyes and squared my shoulders.

"I kept the secret, though it killed me to do so." I sneered in Colonel Tucker's face. "I didn't say anything, and Colonel Erickson didn't either. It has been our sole desire to prove to General Pershing that we belong at the front, and to think that we'd jeopardize that in any way is ridiculous."

Colonel Tucker held up his hand and shook his head. "Save your breath for your hearing. Follow me."

I complied, following Colonel Tucker down the same dank hallway I'd seen Jesse go before me. Solid matching doors with a small rectangular opening facing the hall at the top stretched as far as the eye could see. My heels thudded on the spoiled wood floors. We stopped in front of a room marked 1211, and Colonel Tucker extracted a key from his pocket and opened the door. A small metal bed occupied one side of the room and a cracked, dirty chamber pot sat in the corner. There were no windows. The only light came from a tiny skylight in the hallway. I stepped inside.

"I am not an animal. This is filthy."

"It's not the Ritz, like you're accustomed to, but traitors can hardly be treated to luxury," he said.

His voice echoed. I wondered where they'd put Jesse, if this was the only hallway or if another corridor connected somewhere farther down from my room.

"I told you, we're innocent. Someone else must have heard the information."

Colonel Tucker began to close me in. My heartbeat drummed in my ears.

"You might claim so, but what about your sympathies to the men you've taught in your lessons? They've abandoned the cause."

"I—"

"According to General Pershing himself, there were only two people who knew about the 543rd's mission here at Camp Greene, and both of those people were unaccounted for much of last night, leading us to believe you were busy spreading the word of the 543rd's operation to the others. Major Gordon said he didn't see Colonel Erickson return home from the show, and according to the Hostess House mother, you didn't come back until four in the morning, when Colonel Erickson brought you home. Only an hour later, at bugle, we find eleven men gone, all from the tents of your musicians."

"Colonel Erickson and I weren't going around camp warning the soldiers. We were . . . we were . . . in his room. Major Gordon must not have seen us come in. It was before taps. Perhaps he was still out." I felt my cheeks burn but hardly cared. "I love Jesse, Colonel Erickson."

Colonel Tucker laughed. "That would be a convenient alibi, wouldn't it? Though I find it hard to believe that a Broadway star has fallen for the likes of an army officer with no musical ability after being engaged to *the* Caspar Wells."

"You enjoyed Caspar's music?" I asked.

"Yes. Yours too, but it will hardly help you. Though I find myself rather endeared to fine music and performance, I am absolutely married to our country's cause."

"See? One can find themselves in love with two different but wonderful things. You love music? I do too, and I've loved a music man. You love our country? I do too, and I love an army man, the most devoted to our country I've met."

I stepped toward him and my eyes teared. "You have to believe me, Colonel. If you don't believe that I'm innocent, at least believe that Jesse is."

"It doesn't matter what I believe. I'm not judge or jury. I was told to bring both of you in to confinement. That was my order. And that's what I did," he said. "I must be going, Miss Connolly. There are slackers to find."

"Will you—"

I started to ask if he'd tell me if they found them and if he'd tell Goldie where I was, but he closed the door and locked it.

I sat down on the hard metal bed and cried until I couldn't anymore. I cried for Jesse, for Goldie, for Guy and William and Crowley. I even cried for Basil, for the desperation he'd feel when he received the wire that I couldn't help him—if Jesse had sent the wire at all—and for what he might do to make my situation worse if he never received it. I cried for Caspar too, and then I cried for myself and the stage that I was afraid I'd never grace again.

All was lost.

CHAPTER 28

Madness began in places like this. I stared at the plain white ceiling bathed in dim light from the window in the hall. It was hard to tell the time or the day. There were almost no noises except for the snores at night and intermittent coughs coming from the small opening at the top of my door. The bugle call, which had been so piercing even from the Hostess House, sounded like a whisper. I'd only been here two nights and yet the damp stink of my clothes from the unchecked humidity hung heavy in the air over the permeating stench of sewage from the unemptied chamber pots.

There was no reason to rise from my quilt. There was no reason to move at all, really. Yesterday, upon waking, I'd been taken to a closet-sized room where Colonel Tucker and the man I'd seen with Jesse, a Colonel Meyer, interrogated me like a common criminal. They'd asked me why I'd gone on tour in the first place; they'd asked about Caspar's sympathies. They'd asked me about my parents and their opinion on the war. They'd asked me about my music and if I'd given the men who'd gone AWOL false hope. They'd accused me of embarking on the tour because I was against the war effort after Caspar's death and wished to lead men away from the cause. They'd accused me of seducing Jesse in hopes that he'd fall away, in hopes that he'd turn from our country's mission. They'd told me I was an enemy to my country. They'd asked me where Guy and the others had gone. I had refused to accept their accusations and refused to reply to questions I didn't know the answers to. I'd insisted on my innocence, and Jesse's too. When I finally became angry after nearly an hour of forced composure, they both smiled and led me back to my room.

In the hours after my interrogation, I'd gone over and over their questions in my mind. I determined that there was no real point to them, only the hope that they could convince themselves I had reason to reveal classified secrets so that they could tell General Pershing they'd contained the problem. After the worst dinner of diced tongue in gravy and hard lima beans, I ruminated on how someone else could have learned of the 543rd's assignment. I'd thought of the stack of papers on Jesse's desk. Perhaps someone had gone through them and read the same notice I had. That was a logical conclusion. It wasn't as if Jesse's office was heavily guarded or his correspondence locked in a safe.

"Miss Connolly. Breakfast." The young man I'd met at reception peered into the little opening at the top of my door. I sighed and rose from the lumpy mattress. My back ached. I pulled the faded patchwork quilt off the bed and wrapped it around my dress.

The soldier unlocked the door and handed me a metal tray. I looked down at it and began to laugh. Grits were slopped on one side and corn cakes were piled on the other.

"Does the army's protocol demand that those in confinement have their stomach lining exfoliated?" I asked.

The soldier looked confused.

"Everything on this plate has the consistency of sand."

He shrugged. "I don't know, ma'am. I've always been fond of grits and Johnny cakes."

"I suppose they're better than tongue and parboiled lima beans," I said. I took a bite of a corn cake. It was still warm and tasted like corn bread without the density. I actually enjoyed it.

"I'm sorry for the food, Miss Connolly. If you must know, it's the scraps from the mess halls. I asked for this plate special." He looked at me.

"Thank you," I said. "Truly. I'm sorry for appearing ungrateful. The Johnny cake is quite good."

I touched his arm and he jumped. "Yes, well." His face reddened.

"Are there any newspapers available? I'd like something to read if you have it," I said.

He shook his head. "We're not allowed to give out any amusements."

He stared at me for a moment as if he wanted to say more.

"It's all right. I imagine the news would only depress me anyway. Unless the men have been found?"

"I'm not at liberty to say," he said.

"I understand. Thank you again for breakfast. It means a lot that you'd go to the effort to get this meal for me." I turned back into the room and sat down on the bed to finish my meal. He closed the door and locked it.

"Have a . . . have a nice day, Miss Connolly," he said.

I heard him walk down the hall and open another door, converse with another prisoner. I listened for Jesse's voice but knew he was likely far away from me.

My heart ached for him. He was certain I'd been the one to reveal the secret. I could see it plainly in the way he'd looked at me. I imagined him sitting as I was, on a hard metal bed, all of his years of service, of training, wasted. He'd lived his life to right injustice, to fight for his country. It was his purpose, and yet he was locked here, accused. I'd read enough of the newspapers to know that if I was indicted for treason, I'd be sentenced to years in prison. But if a colonel was convicted of treason, the end was much more dire. The end was death. My skin rippled with cold, and my chest seized as I pondered the possibility. I wouldn't allow it to happen. I'd lie and admit to telling the soldiers if it meant he'd be set free. I would lose everything—his love, my name, my music—but at least he'd not be executed as a traitor. I knew without doubt that that fate was the worst he could imagine.

I took a bite of the grits, amazed the texture no longer repulsed me. Mrs. Kern would see that development as a victory. What I'd give to be back at that dining table in the Hostess House with the girls. I wondered how Wendy and Betty and Goldie were holding up. I wondered about Guy and Crowley and William and the others. I worried they wouldn't consider turning back regardless of the risk, that they, too, could be sentenced to death. Then there were the others, the men who hadn't run. They would be shipped to France without Jesse, thinking the rumor they'd heard was false. Most wouldn't return.

I set the metal tray down on the floor with a soft clatter and curled into a ball, hugging my knees to my chest. Despair rushed through me, stealing my strength, stealing my hope. I couldn't save any of them. Not totally, anyway.

I closed my eyes and forced my mind blank, but the voice of Jesse's pastor somehow pushed its way in.

"Each of you should use whatever gift you have received to serve others."

"How?" I said the word out loud. "Do you see where I am?"

I recalled the hymn the church had sung after that sermon. I didn't know all of the words, but still, I began to sing and the lyrics came back to me.

"Fair are the meadows, fairer still the woodlands, robed in the blooming garb of spring."

Strangely, the acoustics were perfect in here, and as I kept singing, I recalled the little room behind the stage in London where Caspar and I would sneak away to practice before the shows. I imagined he was singing with me now, giving me strength in my weakest moment. Or perhaps it wasn't Caspar at all but God.

"Jesus is fairer, Jesus is purer, who makes the woeful heart to sing."

"Stop!" Jesse's voice ricocheted down the hall. It was distant, but still it struck through the melodic sound of my singing. "Stop pretending!" His voice broke on the last word, and in that moment, all I could see was his face in the dark of his room when he'd told me the news he was leaving. I'd thought he'd appeared melancholy then. I could only imagine his face now. He thought I'd betrayed him; he thought he'd lost everything, and perhaps he had.

I heard a guard shout for him to be silent.

"I didn't do it!" I screamed as loud as I could muster. "I would never."

Moments later, the young soldier who'd brought me my break-fast unlocked my door and beckoned me forward.

"You're being moved."

CHAPTER 29

I'd been wrong. There were worse accommodations than the room I'd initially been assigned to. I'd been moved to quarters located through the reception and down another hall. No one occupied this area, and it was for good reason. The rooms were tiny, only large enough for a small bed topped with an old-fashioned straw mattress that itched terribly. The chamber pot had to be stowed under the bed because there wasn't enough room to leave it sitting on a stand.

It had been days. I'd lost track of how many. Recently I found myself laughing for no reason at all. Perhaps I was going insane. Now a large older woman brought my meals instead of the kindly young soldier. She refused to speak to me but knocked on the door, unlocked it, slid the food in on the floor, then closed me back in.

I'd asked for paper and a pencil one day. I thought I might write a song or perhaps a few jokes to pass the time but had been denied the privilege. So I'd taken to sleeping all day. My eyes were swollen, and it hurt to encounter the light at all — not that there was much to be had. My mind was sluggish, and the moment I woke, I turned back over and tried to sleep again. If I slept, I couldn't torture myself worrying about Jesse or Guy or Goldie or Crowley or William. I couldn't wonder when I'd get out of this place or if Jesse's wire had ever reached Basil. I couldn't worry that the newspapers were splashed with the photograph Basil had threatened to disseminate, muddling the public's perception of me before I stood trial.

I turned over on my pillow. The scent of chicken gravy from my discarded dinner hung heavy on the air, making my stomach turn, so I pressed my nose into the fabric. I closed my eyes and tried to fall asleep again, but I couldn't. I ran my hand through my hair as Mother used to do, as Jesse had done the night we'd spent together, but my fingers kept snagging the matted tangles.

"Miss Connolly."

My door was pushed open, and I jerked upright, rubbing my eyes. Colonel Tucker stood in the doorway. His gaze drifted over the paltry space, and he shook his head.

"To what do I owe the pleasure, Colonel?" I asked. I realized then that I hadn't spoken in days and cleared my throat. "Am I being removed to live in the latrines now?"

He cleared his throat. "I'm glad to tell you that your name has been cleared."

"How? You were so certain it was me, Colonel."

He shook his head. "I never said I was certain."

I sat up straight and spread the quilt over my legs.

"I can't say how we determined your innocence, Miss Connolly, but I can tell you that one of the slackers led us to the source of the information. We located most of the missing men the day after they deserted. They'd been smuggled out in textile crates from the Chadwick-Hoskins Mill by a group of slacker sympathizers. The owner, Mr. Smith, is innocent. He was outraged. The soldiers were on their way to New York when we caught up to them."

I gaped at Colonel Tucker, my day working in the mill playing out in my mind. I could hear the propaganda I'd heard from the workers as clearly as if I were sitting next to them now. I wondered what would become of the women who had orchestrated such an act. I prayed Emma wasn't among them.

"What's become of them?" I knew I couldn't ask if Guy, Crowley, and William were among those found. He wouldn't answer me. "The sympathizers and the slackers?"

"The group that smuggled the men away was a cluster of four older ladies. I'm unsure how they'll fair," he said. Emma wouldn't qualify as an older lady. I exhaled just a little. "The soldiers are being dealt with. They should be thankful they were found so quickly. But mention of New York reminds me of what else I've come to tell you." He paused. "We're sending you home."

I stared at him.

"What? I thought you said my name was cleared."

"It has been," he said, and then he sighed. "Miss Connolly, we arrested you and Colonel Erickson quietly for a reason. We couldn't let the others in camp know the two of you were under suspicion for disseminating classified information involving the soldiers' mission on the front. Therefore, everyone in camp has been led to believe that you've simply left town. That's why you haven't been permitted to go outside and why you were relocated over here, away from the others in confinement."

"But what about New York?" I asked. "Why must I go there?"

Colonel Tucker looked confused. "Isn't New York your home?"

"Yes. I mean, I suppose it was and sometimes still is."

"To explain your absence, General Pershing told us to tell everyone you had been called back to Broadway for a new show."

I began to laugh.

"You expect people to believe that? Being cast in a new show would require an audition. I've been here this last month, Colonel, and haven't spoken of returning to New York to anyone."

He shrugged. "No one but your type understands the particulars of Broadway. With the men shipping out in a matter of days, Pershing believes it's best to send you back. The revealed secret was thankfully dealt with and soldiers' spirits have eased, but their operation hasn't come to pass. He worries—"

"That I could decide to warn the men? That I could muddy the waters? Even after all of this?" I stood in my foot of empty space between my bed and the wall and gestured around me.

"I suppose," he said, almost apologetically.

"And if the men look me up? Which show will I be starring in? I daresay I don't think General Pershing thought this through. I know he has much bigger fish to fry, so to speak, but still."

"Surely you know that Broadway is a friend of our cause. General Pershing spoke to the Shuberts and they've agreed to assist you in putting on a show at the Casino Theatre."

"What sort of show?"

"We suggest a variety show like the one you put on for the boys at the various camps. Something patriotic. As you may know, Lenor Felicity was supposed to finish her American tour by running a similar show at the Casino for two weeks. Although it was her idea originally, the War Department thinks it's a good one, a way to improve civilian morale, so it fits perfectly. General Pershing has asked the Shuberts to clear the space for the next three weeks."

"Was? Did she change her mind?" I vaguely recalled Lenor mentioning a return to Broadway, but the timing was indeterminate, depending on her clearance to the front. I wondered if the reason Lenor had changed course was because she'd forgone the Broadway opportunity to go to France. That didn't quite sound like something Lenor would do, but perhaps she'd been convinced.

"I can't say exactly, though I can tell you that Miss Felicity will not be involved in AEF activities from this point forward."

I stared at him, and he only shook his head. I wondered what she'd done, but then again, when it came to Lenor, one never quite knew. Still, the news she'd been removed from service to the soldiers had to have been devastating to her, though her motivation had only been to further her fame.

"You'll be on the midnight train tonight, in a private car. A captain from Montana, Winters, will be accompanying you there. When you arrive, another officer will keep an eye on your behavior in the city. Do understand that you're being chaperoned because the classified information you were asked to keep quiet is still privileged and requires your discretion. I don't suppose I need to remind you of the consequences if you decide to talk."

I shook my head.

"Wonderful. In a few hours we'll have the showers cleared of men and we will take you to them discreetly, so that you can get ready for your departure. We'll have one of your trunks brought around for fresh clothing as well."

The news was welcome, but still my eyes teared. "I'll be sad to leave."

"Really?" Colonel Tucker glanced around the room, and I laughed.

"Not this room, of course."

"Ah yes. Well. All things must come to an end." His eyes widened. "Oh. As the show will need to open rather swiftly, I'm supposed to ask you for a list of musicians and staff you require. Pershing will allow anyone civilian or enlisted within reasonable numbers, as long as they're not of officer rank. We will gather them quickly and send everyone to you as soon as we can. Hopefully in the next day or two."

He put a hand into his jacket and withdrew a small piece of paper and a pencil. He handed them to me.

"I could ask for some soldiers from here?" The idea that I could save the men who meant so much to me and introduce them to Broadway at the same time made my spirits rise. "Even if they might have been sent to confinement and ordered to hard labor for desertion?"

"Yes," he said. "In that case, they'll join you when their punishment is complete. As I said, you can ask for anyone except men of officer rank. Any enlisted you choose will be reassigned to Broadway for the time being and told that their services are required for a show endorsed by the army to boost civilian support for the war effort. After it's over, they'll be ordered to another station."

I smiled. I could hardly believe it. Perhaps I hadn't made it to the front, and I couldn't save them forever, but I was protecting men like Caspar just the same. I hoped he'd be proud of me, that he would know I'd tried my best to honor him. I started to press the pencil to paper but then paused. Jesse's face materialized in my mind. I'd been set free, but what had become of him?

"Has Jesse been released as well?" My heart skipped in my chest, and I could feel my skin prickle. The urgency to hear that he'd been deemed innocent, too, consumed me.

Colonel Tucker's face sobered and the sight of it filled me with dread. "I'm not at liberty to discuss another's fate, miss."

I thought of the way Jesse had looked addressing the men on the porch of the Dowd House the morning of our arrest, of the way he'd refused to meet my eyes when he'd seen me in the reception area. I recalled his emotion when he'd told me his regiment had been called up and the promise to do what he could to save his men. Fear gripped my heart. Perhaps something had transpired. Perhaps he'd been the one to tell them after all. With the soldier's confession, I knew I could no longer take the blame. The truth had been revealed and they knew I'd had no part in it.

"I wasn't lying to you when I said I loved him," I attempted. "Please, Colonel. Won't you tell me if he's all right?"

"I'm bound to remain silent on the matter," he said. His lips pressed together, and his gaze met mine.

"Is he going to die?" The question came out in a whisper and tears filled my eyes.

"Miss Connolly," he said gently. "The truth is that I don't know."

I nodded and swallowed hard, then turned my attention to the blank sheet of paper in front of me. I wrote down Guy's name and then Crowley's and William's. They would be safe, at least for a while—if they'd been among the found. I wrote down Sidney's name next and then Roland's. So far their regiment hadn't been called to the front, but it could soon enough. I scribbled the names of my favorite conductor, Marshall Fitzwater; my costume designer, Lydia Bambridge; and then listed some musicians I admired to fill in the instruments the army men didn't play. Finally, I wrote Goldie's name. She wasn't going to be in the show, but what did Colonel Tucker know?

"Here. Thank you," I said. I handed the paper to Colonel Tucker, and he took it. He looked over the names and nodded. "I assume the three men listed first have been found?"

"Yes," he said. He folded the paper and put it back in his jacket pocket. "Well then, on behalf of the United States Army, we're truly sorry for the trouble." He sighed and ran a hand across his face.

"One more thing, Colonel Tucker. I know I'm required to go to Broadway, but I wonder if General Pershing might see to it to permit me clearance to the front after the show's run," I said. "It was Caspar's wish that we go to the front and cheer the troops together. I'd hoped to honor his memory by going myself."

Even as I said it, I realized the shocking stab that typically came with acknowledging Caspar's death had become a painful bruise. I thought of Jesse's proposal. The realization that I had no idea how he fared made my stomach turn and my soul cry.

Colonel Tucker nodded. "He had a feeling you'd ask about that," he said. "I don't know that he'll grant your request, but I'm happy to pass it along. I must be off, but I'll be back to retrieve you at nightfall."

He started to close the door, but I caught the handle right before it shut.

"Perhaps you can't tell me what's become of Jesse, but if you've ever experienced love before, Colonel, you'll find a way to tell him that I love him, that I was innocent in this, and where I'm going."

Colonel Tucker tipped his head. "I'll see what I can do, Miss Connolly," he said and then closed the door.

CHAPTER 30

T he little makeshift tent city I'd learned to call home, the place that had healed me and filled me with purpose, passed me by from the window of the Model T. Camp was silent, as one could expect at midnight, and yet my memories filled the scene with music. My memories played that way sometimes, like a silent movie accompanied by the most beautiful songs you've ever heard. We passed the Liberty Theatre, which was still heralding Lenor's arrival, and then the YMCA building. I thought of all the soldiers and Mrs. Kern and the women at the Hostess House. I knew they thought I'd left them behind without bothering to say goodbye. There was nothing I could do to make it right or explain what happened. The tune in my mind was melancholy, nostalgic, and I couldn't help but hum it under my breath as my thoughts filled in the words. Perhaps I could write them a song. Maybe then they'd understand how much they'd meant to me.

"*Found myself in an army camp, my task to tame the dirt. Found myself homesick, afraid of being hurt. Found my strength growing, found my spirits bright. Found myself in knowing only love could tame the night.*"

Just ahead, the administrative building loomed and the Dowd House hill next to it. A few more moments and I'd leave camp for the last time. I squinted as we went, scanning the landscape for Jesse's auto on the hill, for any evidence of him. Had he simply been set free and restored to his role without anyone knowing? Or was he still assumed to be guilty and locked away? There was no way to tell.

"That was a pretty tune you were humming just now," Colonel Tucker commented from the driver's seat in front of me.

"A new song about camp life," I murmured, my gaze still fixed on the Dowd House as the auto left it behind.

Jesse's little window at the back of the house was dark like the rest, but I imagined it was occupied, that the starched white quilt was warm from the heat of his body, that the crickets just outside his window were loud enough to accompany dreams but not intrusive enough to wake him, that the air smelled of the Palmolive soap in his hair. I ached to be there with him, tucked against his chest. I ached to know where he was. Then again, even if we hadn't been arrested, in a matter of days I would have lost track of him anyway. I would have had to face the notion that he'd likely die in battle.

My chest tightened and I pushed my palm to it as though I'd just been shot and was trying to stop the bleeding. There would be no such mercy. That much I knew from losing Caspar. If Jesse died, I would wear a festering wound the rest of my life.

"Is that so? I'd imagine most would dream up something that sounds like Beethoven's Fifth Symphony for such a camp." Colonel Tucker chuckled, forcing me back to the moment. "The reports from Greene to DC made the place sound like a swamp bog, hardly worthy of the gentle tune I just heard."

"I suppose that's a matter of perspective, Colonel. If you're an alligator or turtle or snowy egret, I imagine you'd think of a bog in a rather dreamy manner, don't you?"

"Which are you?"

"A turtle," I said.

Colonel Tucker turned the auto on to Tuckaseegee Road toward the rail station. I looked back at the welcome sign and my breath hitched.

"Not the egret? I would guess you were more inclined to the grace of such an animal."

"No," I said, turning toward his back and shaking my head. "At first I thought I would simply remain on the banks sunning or retreat into my shell, but that was before I was plunged into the bog and realized what a journey was to be had there."

"I see," Colonel Tucker said.

"Would you do something for me, Colonel? Would you tell everyone in camp goodbye for me and that I didn't intend to leave them so abruptly? Will you remind the men to sing as they march to the front and sing when they're scared?"

My eyes blurred. I could tell Colonel Tucker didn't know what to think of my request, especially the last part, but now that my song leaders, Sidney and Guy, would be coming with me, I needed the men to keep their spirits up until I could get over there.

"I can do that," he said finally.

"Thank you," I whispered.

Up ahead, the rail station was mostly dark except for a small electric streetlight beside the stairs leading to the platform. A gray car idled on the sidetrack, waiting to be hooked to the incoming train.

"The train is set to arrive in thirty minutes. It looks like no one is on the platform waiting to board yet, which is perfect. Captain Winters is already situated in the private car," he said. He pulled the auto to a stop in front of the station and shut off the engine.

When he opened my door, he held out his hand, then withdrew it.

"Would you mind pulling your hood on as we discussed? I know it seems that no one is around, but there are railmen here, and even one set of eyes is enough for tongues to begin wagging."

I nodded and pulled the hood of my thin cotton cloak over my head, then got out of the auto on my own.

Colonel Tucker began to walk up the steps and I followed. A young man wearing Carhartt overalls stepped out of the station. I turned my face toward the shadows as Colonel Tucker greeted him.

"Thank you for arranging the private car on such short notice," he said in a low tone to the railman. "As I mentioned, this woman was staying at the Hostess House out at camp and just received word that her husband was killed. She asked to be transported back to her home in New York immediately but couldn't bear to be around any other passengers who might ask about her loss."

"I understand," the young man said. "You know, Colonel, I'd be out at the camp or over in France if I could. It's just this bad leg." He tapped his left leg, and the sound was a hollow noise. "Lost it in a mill accident four years ago." It was obvious the man felt compelled to let Colonel Tucker know he wasn't shirking his duties but rather hadn't been permitted to fight.

"You're doing enough for the cause right here," he said.

"Well, thank you kindly. If the young woman would like to step down to the tracks, I can escort her over to the car."

"That's quite all right, sir. You have an incoming train to ready for."

Colonel Tucker stepped down another set of stairs and I followed him over the tracks to the car. He knocked on the door and a man with a scruffy beard wearing trim olive drab—an oxymoron if I'd ever seen one—edged it open. He stared when he saw me, and his mouth gaped a bit.

"Winters!" Colonel Tucker barked. "Get ahold of yourself."

Captain Winters flinched and then blinked and stepped out of the doorway.

"I apologize, Colonel, Miss Connolly," he said. "It's just that I assumed you would look different from the pictures, see. Miss Felicity did, I thought, and so I only figured you wouldn't be as beautiful as your likeness either, but you are."

"Will you be able to control your awe around Miss Connolly or do I need to send for a replacement?" Colonel Tucker asked.

I smiled at Captain Winters and edged around him into the car.

"We'll be quite all right, I'm sure," I said.

All in all, the car was comfortable enough. The windows were draped with sheer crepe and the car's warm electric lights made the oversized chintz armchairs and matching couch appear almost as cozy as my parents' living room. I wished I had asked for a few novels to read on the twelve-hour ride home.

I sat down on the couch. "When we arrive at Grand Central—"

"Ah yes," Colonel Tucker said to Captain Winters. "I forgot to tell you. When you arrive at Grand Central, you'll be greeted by a Captain Pitt. He's nearly seven feet tall with an unsightly mustache that appears as though he's affixed two mice beneath his nose. You won't be able to miss him." He turned to address me. "Miss Connolly, Captain Pitt will escort you to your apartment above the Casino Theatre and will stay in quarters just down the hall from yours. You've been appointed spacious accommodations according to the manager."

"What? I thought you said I was going home. My parents are just in the Bronx, Colonel Tucker, and that's where I live when I'm in the city."

He shook his head. Disappointment dampened my spirits. When I heard I was being sent to New York without knowing where Jesse was, I'd assumed I was at least going to my family home where I could speak freely as I'd been so unable to do in my letters. Mother would make me tea and let me cry after a long day of rehearsals, and when night came, I'd tuck into my little bed adorned with my grandmother's patchwork quilt. But that wasn't to be.

"Not this time," he said apologetically. "Until the show wraps, you're subject to monitoring by the army. Your parents can visit, but the story is that the show requires you to stay on-site. You are the producer, writer, and performer, after all."

"I don't understand," I said. "You said I was free."

I began to say that I was cleared of wrongdoing, but Colonel Tucker waved his hand and looked pointedly at Captain Winters, who was now sitting in the armchair across from me, picking at his cuticles. Clearly he didn't know why I'd been in confinement, though he had to know I'd been there these days instead of in the city.

"When your show wraps, certain missions in France of which you were informed will have likely been completed if they're going to at all, and you will be able to do as you wish. The chaperoning is simply a continuation of the care you received here at Camp Greene."

I swallowed hard thinking of the Third Division, thinking of all the faces that would march to the trains in a matter of days and the faces of the 543rd Infantry that I'd failed to save with music. His words *"if they're going to at all"* lingered in my mind like a prayer. I hoped the operation would never come to pass. There was always the chance.

"I hope that will be the case," I said. "You know what I wish to do afterward, Colonel."

He smiled. "I do. I told you I'd elevate your request. I think you're the most persistent woman I've ever known." He turned to Captain Winters. "Take heed."

"And of the message I requested you pass along to Colonel Erickson."

"I'm not a simpleton, Miss Connolly, nor do I have the memory of an ant." He began to turn back toward the open door but stopped. "Your trunks have already been loaded. It was a pleasure knowing you, Miss Connolly, despite the trouble." He grinned and I smiled back.

"Likewise, Colonel, though don't suppose if you come upon me in your auto again that I'll join you next time."

He chuckled. "I can't say I blame you," he said, then disappeared into the night.

From somewhere close by, a train whistle shrilled, and Captain Winters rose from the chair to close us in. Exhaustion drew over me like a blanket and I lifted my legs to fill the expanse of the couch, pulled a cushion behind my head, and fell asleep.

I woke to the sun beaming onto my face, the train gently rocking back and forth. It was no wonder I'd slept so well.

"Would you like coffee?"

I started at the sound of Captain Winters's voice. For a moment I'd forgotten he was there. I sat up and smoothed my sky-blue silk satin bodice that seemed to have been quite attracted to the couch's upholstery—bits of lint clung to it in an effect that made it seem like I'd walked out into a snowstorm.

"Yes, that would be nice," I said.

He hastened to the front of the car, extracted a bag of coffee and a delicate glass French press from a little cart, and then reached beneath the cart for a thermos. When he unscrewed the lid, steam poured out.

"Did you bring that boiling water from Charlotte?" I asked.

He turned to face me. In the light, he looked to be Guy's age, though beards aged even the youngest men.

"I did. I figured you might like a warm cup of coffee and, well, when you grow up on the ranges of Montana, you learn two things about the time you learn to walk: how to keep coffee warm and how to fight off a bear."

The mention of a bear made me laugh and then nearly cry, thinking of Jesse and me joking about the Montana men bringing my circus animals.

"Do you belong to the group that hoped to bring your bear mascot with you to camp?" I asked.

"Yes. Ditty is as essential as one of us. She's been like a pet for nearly five years now, and it's a shame they wouldn't let us bring her." He paused to pour the fresh coffee into a dainty china teacup. "You would've loved her."

"I know I would have. I tried to talk Colonel Erickson into it—there's a zoo on the edge of camp that she could've gone to if he didn't want to house her in camp proper—but he said having a bear around was liable to get some boys in trouble."

"Maybe, if you're talking about the other bear the Eastern Montana doughboys wanted to bring. He's named Rocky. Ditty's just a tame old girl."

Captain Winters handed me my coffee with a shaky hand, and a bit of it drizzled onto the skirt of my gown.

"I'm so sorry," he said, lunging back toward the cart for linen napkins as his face blazed red.

"It's nothing to apologize for," I said. I took the napkin from his outstretched hand, dabbed my skirt, then pushed the crepe curtains back from the window beside me.

"We're somewhere in Maryland, according to time," he said. He glanced at an old wristwatch. "Nine thirty. Three more hours to go."

From the look of the farmland out the window, we could have been anywhere. Mother used to say that city folk lamented about missing particular cities, while country folk simply said they missed space, and that because of that, farmers were lucky—they could find home much more easily than a displaced New Yorker.

I couldn't wait to see my parents, to fling my arms around Mother's shoulders and kiss Father's cheek and tell them how much I'd missed them.

"I've never been to New York City," Captain Winters said after he took a sip of his coffee. "I don't suppose I'll see much of it this time either, but at least I will be able to say I've been there."

"It's a city full of tremendous possibility, and tremendous hardship too. Regardless, there's nothing like it. You should visit when the war's over."

He nodded and then looked out the window beyond me.

"If I make it back home, I surely will," he said finally.

I wanted to tell him that he would find his way back, that he'd have all the time in the world to see the bright lights of the most glorious city, but that wasn't necessarily the case when death partnered with war to meet men at equal measure at twenty-two as it did at ninety-five.

"When you do visit, be sure to write me a letter. I'll get you a front-row seat to any show on Broadway you'd like," I said.

"Do you suppose you could spare two seats when I come?" His lips turned up in a grin. "If I make it home, the first thing I'm going to do is find my girl and ask her to marry me. We had a terrible row right before I left, but she's always been keen to see the bright lights of the city. Think she'd forgive me if I asked her there?"

"I think she'd forgive you if you asked her anywhere," I said. "Just do your best to make it home."

CHAPTER 31

D eparting the train at Grand Central Station had felt something like climbing in my childhood bed. I'd been absolutely crushed by the number of passengers pushing toward the exits or toward the departures, and the energy of so many vibrant souls all together had lifted my spirits tremendously, to the point that, for a moment, while strangers called my name and asked me for autographs, I forgot there was a war at all.

The wake-up call came at the base of the magnificent limestone stairs in the form of Colonel Pitt. Colonel Tucker had been exact in his description of him, though he hadn't mentioned that in addition to his height and mustache, he was also stoic and irritatingly boring. Captain Winters had balked when he saw him, and it was in the seconds after, as I watched Captain Winters push through the crush to the train that would take him back to Camp Greene, that I realized the lively crowd I'd thought so typical and dynamic moments before was almost entirely void of young men. I'd forgotten. Any able-bodied male between eighteen and forty-six was off training or fighting or dying.

I'd followed Colonel Pitt to a limousine he required we take despite my request to ride the streetcar or take the omnibus to Broadway. He deflected any well-meaning New Yorkers' greetings or requests of me with a strong shake of his head. He even turned away a small child no more than eight who approached me on my way into the auto.

From there the day's happenings proceeded to decline. I'd cranked down my window to better see the city and the people and breathe the crummy, stale air that had always been the backdrop to my dreams coming true, but he'd complained the whole time that he could hardly bear the stench of it.

Then, when we finally turned on Broadway, the sight of theatres as far as the eye could see, making my heart leap with joy and fond memories, he ordered the driver to take us to the Casino directly. I'd argued with him. Couldn't he see that *Listen Lester* was playing at the Knickerbocker and it practically required a stop? John Dool, one of Lenor's favorites, was playing the lead. Or perhaps he'd enjoy *Ziegfeld Follies* at the New York? Kate Covey, who'd played my sister in *The Sunshine Brigade*, was a Follies Girl this season.

He'd grumbled that he was hungry, that he'd only eaten a cracker on his way from Camp Upton to chaperone me, so I'd asked if perhaps we could go to the famed Reisenweber's Cafe, renowned for its beefsteak dinner. The manager, Louis Fischer, loved Broadway almost as much as food and always seated me immediately, though the rest of the city required a lengthy wait. Captain Pitt declined that idea, too, saying he'd simply go out to the market later and cook something in his apartment's kitchen. When the limousine squeaked to a stop outside of the Casino and the electric lights at the Winter Garden next door heralded the night's entertainment, *Monte Cristo, Jr.*, I attempted one last time to convince Colonel Pitt that he was on Broadway, for crying out loud, and that Mary Adelaide, arguably the country's best burlesque performer, was playing the Countess of Shamokin, but he refused. He said he didn't abide burlesque shows and that he was a married man. I wondered, in that moment, how he'd possibly wooed anyone. Mrs. Pitt must be a bore too.

We'd been ushered into the darkened Casino theatre lobby where Jacob Shubert stood with his pocket watch in his hand. I supposed we were late. I hadn't seen the youngest Mr. Shubert since before I left for London — he'd been away in South America when

I'd returned—and despite my forced enthusiasm at encountering him again, his excitement seemed to match that of Colonel Pitt's because our tardiness had made him late to dinner with a new belle at Delmonico's.

Mr. Shubert had told me he'd organized meetings with my conductor, Marshall Fitzwater, and my costume designer, Lydia Bambridge, for the following afternoon. Lodging for the army musicians would be in apartments above his other theatres, the Winter Garden and the Imperial, whenever they arrived.

After outlining our arrangements, Mr. Shubert ushered us up four flights of stairs and toward the corner tower, where he'd directed Colonel Pitt to a small apartment that overlooked Broadway and me to a fifth-floor apartment at the very top of the dome. The circular space was cramped at best, not the sizable apartment I was promised. It was clear that before my occupation it had been used for storage and boasted only an antique bed, a lumpy couch and tea table, one electric lamp, a chest of drawers, a threadbare China rug, a tiny washroom, and an equally tiny kitchenette. The one magnificent concession, however, was the view. From the windows that circled the entire space, I could see all of Broadway. I suppose if I had to be stuck in a tower, like a Broadway Rapunzel, at least I could marvel over the loveliness of the city.

Mr. Shubert had left me in haste with instructions to "write something good and we'll speak in the morning." In the next hour, while our chauffeur worked to lug our trunks up the narrow stairwell, I sat down and read a week-old *New York Times* that had been left on the bedside table. The news was absent my indecent photograph, thankfully, though full of developments about the war, and I hurried past the stories quickly. I could feel the melancholy bubbling up in my heart and knew that if I as much as read a word of the devastation in France or the need of our troops, I'd plunge into worry for Jesse, for the others again, completely snuffing out the brief ember of happiness I'd obtained since departing the train. I knew it would come, that in the night my heartache would overtake me, but soon enough, Guy and the others would turn up here and

I'd need my heart to be light enough to spend the evening writing the start of a bang-up show that would draw crowds and solidify their careers on Broadway. I couldn't let the purpose I'd grasped during each day at Camp Greene depart me now.

I turned my attention back to the paper and paused on a headline on the fourteenth page: "Lenor Felicity, the Darling of the AEF, Cancels Tour." The article was short, simply saying that Lenor had had to cancel the remaining tour stops and her Broadway show due to a sudden illness, but I knew it wasn't true. She'd done something wrong, something untoward, I was certain. I wondered what it was and if she was back home in her town house on the park. Since I was still a practical prisoner of the army, I couldn't wander down there myself, but I'd certainly have Mother poke around for me.

About seven thirty, Broadway had begun to buzz, as it always did. The sidewalks were jammed with old men in tuxedos and women of all ages in their finest and brightest summer silks. The autos and omnibuses and streetcars contended for mere inches of space as they attempted to make their way to this theatre or that. I watched from my tower windows as all of New York seemed to usher into various theatres. In that moment I was certain that if the world was New York City's Broadway, there would never be another war. People were too merry here to resort to violence. I wondered, as I watched the guests filter into the Winter Garden just below me, who they all were, and I began to make up stories about their backgrounds. One large man in a gray suit was a stockbroker who had just spent his entire year's paycheck on a new Pierce-Arrow. The older woman in an ambitious sun-yellow silk gown was a fashion designer who operated under her husband's name. Then I spied a soldier. He was standing on the corner and had just climbed out of the streetcar. It occurred to me that in the midst of war, men seemed to lose their personhood to the uniform. They were soldier first and who they truly were second.

A song had burbled up in my mind then, from the perspective of the soldier telling of the explorer he truly was and the explorer he hoped he would be after the war. I kept on with the theme of it until the variety show poured from my heart. It would be titled *They Call Me Soldier*. It would start with soldiers drilling and training, but then in the evenings, they'd enter a sort of dream world where each man would be transported to complete an alternate mission based on the person he truly was. One had to climb Mount Everest, another had to gain entrance to New York's Philharmonic, another had to teach a class of unruly children how to read, another had to keep his family's restaurant from closing, and another had to lead the war effort all alone. At the finale, each soldier would use the lessons he'd learned from his adventure to win the war against the Huns and the show would conclude with an overture of patriotic tunes.

At one point Colonel Pitt had come up to bring me a baguette, some cured meats, and a bit of cheese he'd procured from a nearby market, but I'd barely looked up from my paper. The show would be simple but fantastic, a smash hit, I was sure of it. It would speak to our colorful individuality that unified in war to create unbeatable military strength. I'd fallen asleep with my pencil completely spent and my notebook full of ideas. The moment I woke, I'd come down to the stage to put it all together.

"Calla Connolly, as I live and breathe." The delicate voice echoed from the back of the theatre, startling me. I glanced up from the piano's music stand and the manuscript paper boasting half of a song, squinting past the jewel-laced velvet stage curtain, past the boxes detailed with arabesque patterns, down the center aisle beneath the ceiling decorated in filigrees, fans, and arches. The theatre was dark. I hadn't been able to locate the electric light switches.

"I ran into Mr. Shubert early this morning ordering a dozen bagels at Weisner's on Hester Street, and he mentioned you'd arrived back from North Carolina over a week ago to open a show here, taking the spot of that washed-up Lenor Felicity." Tabitha Scherrer, arguably Broadway's best set designer, appeared from the shadows. She was wearing a fabulous pair of wide-leg trousers and a lace shirtwaist, carrying the most glorious sight I'd ever seen: a box of Weisner's bagels.

"I told him he must be mistaken, that I'd heard of no such thing and everyone in the business knew it was a foregone conclusion that I'd work on any show my dear Calla Connolly was attached to. Why haven't you called for me yet?"

My delay would have been easier to explain had Mr. Shubert and I not been required by the army to pretend that I'd departed Camp Greene a week ago instead of a day. The army insisted on the difference in order to explain away my time in confinement to anyone who might inquire where I'd been.

"I planned to call today," I said, meaning it.

The moment I'd realized my error in leaving her off my list of needed reinforcements, I would have begged Colonel Pitt to accompany me to her studio on West Twenty-Ninth. She'd done all the set work for my earlier variety show and it was fantastic. When I'd been writing the night before, her sets were all I could imagine.

"The arrangement was terribly swift. I nearly have whiplash."

I laughed and then sobered, thinking of the last time I'd felt such a thing. It was on the coaster at Lakewood right after Jesse and I had caught Mac and the others, before I knew all the twists and turns of the ride. I closed my eyes around the memory and recalled Mac's face that day and then again a day later when he marched with the others to the train. I would never forget the way he smiled after I kissed him. But soon enough, the men of the Third would be marching the same way as the Fourth had, and no one would be there to sing them off to war or kiss the random young man terrified to leave. My mind began to think of all of the possibilities of where Jesse could be, but the options were endless. I took a deep breath, inhaling the scent of the theatre—musty velvet from the drapes and resin-coated wood—and forced myself to settle.

Tabitha climbed up the stairs and sat down beside me on the piano bench. She didn't wear a hat. She never did, and her wild, gray curls spilled down to her shoulders. She'd always carried a bit of a scandal along with her, never adhering to the dress code of a proper woman. She hardly minded. She wore the badge proudly, as eccentrics often did.

"Have a bagel. There are several poppyseed. Philadelphia cream cheese too." She gestured to the white box she'd set between us and I opened it, extracting a warm bagel, a flimsy metal knife, and the block of cream cheese wrapped in foil. I sighed.

"They eat corn for breakfast in the South," I said as I slathered the bagel with cream cheese and took a bite. It was perfect. Doughy and chewy with a crackly crust.

"Corn? On the cob?" Tabitha laughed. "You must have been terribly thankful for their part in saving your life to endure that."

"No," I said, grinning. "They eat grits and corn bread and corncakes."

"Oh yes. I recall grits. One of my former artists was from Virginia. He made them for me once and I didn't hate them."

I took another bite of my bagel. "Still, nothing compares to the heaven of bagels."

Tabitha glanced at the notebook sitting beside my manuscript paper on the stand. "Is that the show?"

I nodded. "Yes, a sort of variety show like before, but a different theme. Of course, I'll need to meet with the musicians and have the songs all arranged, but the general structure is here."

I handed the notebook to her, and she flipped through it.

"I'd like the opening to be in an army training camp, much like the one I just left."

She pointed at the page. "Tents?"

"Yes. Strangely enough, many of the men in Camp Greene live in them. I suppose the camp population grew too quickly to construct proper barracks."

Tabitha made a face and kept reading, then she whistled.

"This is a tall order for only two weeks' lead time. Mount Everest, the Philharmonic, a classroom, a restaurant, two battlefields, and New York City—though we can use the buildings we constructed last time for that."

"I suppose I could ask after Gregory Cogar," I said and waited.

"Don't threaten me. I brought you bagels." She closed my notebook and handed it back to me. "Would you like to come with me now? I could sketch out some sets and we could look through what I have in the studio."

I hesitated. Colonel Pitt was sitting just outside the stage door and had instructed me that I wasn't permitted to go around the city without him. The requirement had induced a strange disorientation. I was home, but not really. I couldn't wander down Broadway as I often did and look at the new show posters. I couldn't pop into Weisner's for a bagel or browse the shelves at Wannamaker's as I'd begun to do to fill my idle time and distract grief when I'd returned from London.

Perhaps it was just as well. Despite the familiarity of the city and my unyielding love of Broadway and the stage, I wasn't the same person I was when I'd set out on tour. I'd realized last night, as I was writing the new show, that before Camp Greene, I'd seen all my hours, even the hours performing for the troops, as idle time filled by waiting. I'd seen performing on the front as my sole ambition and, in many ways, my sole purpose. But Camp Greene had changed my perspective. It had brought me back to myself. My time spent in the army camps wasn't irrelevant. It had been necessary. I was meant to intervene in the lives of the men and women I'd come to know and they in mine. I was meant to return to Broadway at this very time to write this show for them. I was meant to fall in love again.

The thought encouraged a burning sensation behind my eyes, an urge to cry over Jesse, to torture myself over his whereabouts, but I couldn't. Not right now.

"Calla," she pressed.

"I'm sorry," I said, bringing myself back to the stage. "I'm afraid I have to meet with Marshall in just about an hour with regard to the music, and Lydia about the costumes after," I said, taking another bite of bagel. "I trust you, Tabitha."

She stood up and dusted off her trousers. "I'm leaving the bagels, but never speak of Gregory Cogar again," she said. "*Monte Cristo, Jr.* tomorrow night? It's a beautiful show."

"Perhaps," I said. "Come by on your way and I'll see if I can break free. I'm staying here in the apartments above."

"Not with your parents?"

"No. With the swift turnaround for this show, I need to eat, sleep, and breathe it," I said.

"Understood. I'll call later to tell you what I've unearthed in the studio."

She started back up the aisle the way she came. I ripped a page from my notebook and wrote out a telegram for Colonel Pitt to send to my parents, telling them I was in the city and asking them to visit later after my meeting with my conductor and costume designer.

I rose from the piano bench and took the bagels with me to the stage door where Colonel Pitt was sitting in an old ladderback chair—asleep. I shook his shoulder and he jerked, nearly sending the bagels flying from my hand.

"Have a bagel and then pop down to Western Union just a block away to send this telegram to my parents, if you have the time," I said. He blinked at me and yawned. "I'd accompany you, but Mr. Shubert has arranged meetings with my conductor and costume designer. It's a terribly swift turnaround for the show. Ordinarily it takes three months at least to get things set to open and we only have two weeks." Colonel Pitt shook his head and I sighed. "I'm not going to run off and tell the world about the army's classified secrets. I've been in confinement and I'm not keen to repeat the experience. You have my word that I'll stay right here."

"Very well, but if I return and find you absent, understand that I won't hesitate to wire General Pershing and have you thrown in jail and brought to trial."

"Understood," I said.

I opened the stage door and went back inside the theatre. The new song I'd thought up on my midnight ride out of Camp Greene pushed into my mind and I stood in the very center of the stage where I'd sang countless times with Lenor at my start and sang it with all of my might. My voice was strong, and the acoustics carried the timbre of it perfectly, even the delicate way my emotion wavered the words.

"Found myself in an army camp, my task to tame the dirt. Found myself homesick, afraid of being hurt. Found my strength growing, found my spirits bright. Found myself in knowing only love could tame the night."

I kept going, adding on to the song. I knew without doubt it would be a beautiful finale, a tribute to the men at Camp Greene and the men fighting at the front.

"Found the news alarming, the trouble everywhere. Found myself out marching, wondering if the world would care. Found my answer in a letter, found that I was, in fact, held dear. Found myself a world away, but my heart still living here.

"Found myself wondering, Would I make it back alive? Found myself considering that my mind was full of lies. Found myself remembering Camp Greene, the others too. Found myself in knowing that my truest self was found in you."

I wiped a tear from my eye as the last of my voice echoed and died in the theatre.

"Where are you?" I whispered to the nothingness, to Jesse wherever he was.

The door at the back of the theatre opened and then slammed shut.

"I'm up here, Marshall!" I shouted, though he'd know where I was. The stage was always washed in at least a little light from the stained glass windows around it. The back of the theatre was the blind spot.

I heard the door open again and this time there was chatter.

"Who is it?" I called.

The moment they stepped out of the shadow of the mezzanine, I began to sob. Guy and Goldie appeared first, holding hands. I ran down the steps and down the aisle, then flung my arms around Goldie. She laughed and hugged me in turn.

"You saved him," she whispered in my ear. "You saved all of them, and me too."

When I stepped back, I noticed they were all present: Guy and Roland and Crowley and William and Sidney, still in their weathered olive drab. The sight of them here, in New York, in the Casino Theatre, felt much like a dream made manifest.

"How can we ever thank you, Calla?" Guy said. His eyes were fixed on the stage in front of him. A hush fell over the group, and Sidney set his fiddle case down with a quiet thump.

"We'll be performing here?" he asked in awe.

"I've never seen anything like it," Roland said.

I cleared my throat, hoping to dispel the emotion; otherwise I'd never stop crying. They were here, safe, not boarding trains to get to the boats or wielding rifles they'd never been fit to carry. Perhaps in a month or two they'd be sent over, but not now. Right now they were here where they were always meant to be. I looked at their faces and suddenly had that feeling again, that peaceful, settled sensation that had come in fits and starts since I'd disembarked the train at Grand Central. My heart was shattered by Jesse's absence, and I hadn't yet made it to the front—there was a chance I never would—but I had pushed as hard as I could and I had loved Caspar and Jesse with all I had. I hadn't accomplished what I set out to do, but perhaps life had turned out as it was supposed to—on Broadway, with a troupe of talented soldiers primed to face the ear-splitting sounds of applause rather than cannon fire.

"You'll never comprehend how relieved I am to see you all, but I'm going to warn you ahead of time—I'm putting my name on this show, and my reputation depends on the success of it. There's a chance you'll be begging to go overseas rather than work as hard as I'll have you working these next weeks."

"I'll sleep on the stage if it means a chance to be here doing what I love instead of going over there," William said. "Wendy is . . . well, she stayed back to situate herself in our apartment at the Winter Garden with Betty, but she's beside herself with gratefulness."

I smiled.

"When they ushered us onto the cars early this morning, no one told us where we were heading. Finally, about Virginia, a Captain Winters, who apparently accompanied you the week before, told us that we'd been given new assignments on Broadway. We all thought he was joking," Sidney said. "Juliet's back in Rhode Island with her family, but she'll be over the moon when she gets my wire."

"When we abandoned, the women who tucked us into the boxes asked where we wished to go," Crowley said, his voice barely above a whisper. "We said New York City because we all hoped to get to the stage someday, but I know now that without you, Calla, we'd be doomed altogether. We'd never have made it."

"You deserve to be here," I said.

"The others in our company ship out in only two days. It's difficult not to feel guilty that they'll face war and we won't, at least not yet," Guy said, his face void of the joy I'd seen moments before.

"I don't want to deny you the chance to fight if you want to," I said.

He shook his head. "I don't. Of course I don't. I was running from it," he said. "But I'll feel guilt all the same. Colonel Erickson wouldn't run."

My heart lurched in my chest at the mention of his name.

"When did you see Jesse last?" I asked. My voice sounded choked.

Guy looked to Goldie and then back to me.

"The same day you left for Broadway, when he made that big pronouncement on the Dowd House porch. Colonel Tucker said he'd been reassigned. We thought you knew."

"Oh," I said.

I swallowed hard and then forced a smile. This moment was a joyful one, not one I'd allow to be tainted by the deep melancholy of losing Jesse.

"Did something happen between the two of you? We thought that's why you'd both gone," Goldie said.

"No. I got the call that Lenor was unable to do the show she and the army had been working on with Mr. Shubert and they needed a replacement urgently. The show was meant to boost civilian morale and support the war effort. They were desperate, so I told them I'd do it," I lied. "I had to leave right away, without saying goodbye, and it killed me. Especially when it came to you, Goldie. You'd been so upset when I saw you last. But when they told me I could ask for soldiers to round out the show, I knew it was meant to be." I reached for Goldie's hand and she squeezed it. "I tried to wire Jesse and tell him what happened too, but—"

"Miss Connolly!" A deep, bellowing voice interrupted me, and Marshall Fitzwater appeared behind the group.

"Everyone, meet our esteemed conductor for our show, *They Call Me Soldier*, Mr. Marshall Fitzwater," I said.

Roland's eyes widened and Crowley's face went white.

"Marshall Fitzwater?" Sidney whispered in disbelief as he turned toward Marshall making his way down the center aisle. Marshall was a stereotypical conductor through and through. He had flowing white hair to his shoulders and wore black tuxedos whether he was walking to the market or conducting a great orchestra from the pit.

"I've heard nothing of your show besides the name just now, Miss Connolly, and Mr. Shubert's man is already putting the announcement up on the marquee." Marshall puffed. His face turned an unsightly shade of red.

"You're in good company. As I just told Tabitha Scherrer, I was asked to put this show together only last week on behalf of the army. It's not my fault that Lenor has taken ill and that her variety show can't go on. If I didn't swoop in and help the army and Mr. Shubert, you would be out a show, would you not?" I asked. "I know Lenor is as loyal to you as I am. Surely you were on her call list."

Marshall hesitated and then nodded.

"These are the men I've recruited from Camp Greene to be your solo players. They'll be acting and singing too," I said.

Marshall glanced at the men still dressed in olive drab and scrunched his nose.

"They are better than most of your musicians and will be wildly popular. Let me prove it to you. Gentlemen," I said, turning to the men, "I told you that I'd work you hard. Head up to the stage. We're going to play 'I Have It All' for Mr. Fitzwater here."

✳ ✳ ✳

We'd remained onstage for the next five hours. We'd played through a few old patriotic numbers after "I Have It All" until Marshall was so impressed, he'd stopped interjecting advice and sat down in one of the theatre seats next to Goldie and just watched. After that, we'd gone through each scene of the show and assigned parts and figured the number of songs to be written. Roland would play the explorer, Guy the musician, Sidney the teacher, Crowley the restaurateur, and William the true army man. I'd narrate and lead the patriotic songs at the end. We'd fill in the background vocals with the girls in Marshall's chorus. Following assigning roles, I'd taught the men "Found Myself (A Song of Camp Greene)," and all of us teared as we sang it. We went over it and over it, and about the third time, I noticed that Kate Covey, the star of Flo Ziegfeld's *Follies*, was sitting in the front row with Mary Pickford. Kate, Mary, Marshall, and Goldie had risen to their feet and clapped for a full two minutes after our last run-through. The sight had thrilled the men. When my peers rushed over to me and asked where I'd found such talent, the men nearly collapsed with joy—exhaustion too.

I slogged up the four flights of stairs to my apartment, my feet feeling like cement had been poured over them. Even so, I couldn't help but smile at the way the day had turned out. I was excited for the show and excited for the futures of my friends. Even if they had to fight after this, they would go knowing they'd wowed Broadway and had a bright future to return to.

I unlocked my door, edged it open, and nearly burst into tears. My parents were sitting on the old lumpy couch across from my bed. When she saw me, Mother put her cross-stitch down on the tea table in front of her and rose to her feet. Father, who had been rereading *The Count of Monte Cristo*—I'm sure as prelude to seeing *Monte Cristo, Jr.*—set it down on the cushion next to him.

"Calla," Mother breathed, meeting me in the middle of the room. She threw her arms around me, and I dipped my head to her chest, noticing as I did that she was wearing the Worth shawl Lenor had wanted back. "I've missed you," I said, my eyes filling.

She smelled like home—morning coffee and the oatmeal cookies she baked every other day for Father.

"We thought we'd lost you to Carolina forever. You barely wrote," Father said from behind her.

His voice was strained with emotion, and I disentangled myself from Mother to hug him hard. Mother missed me when I was away, but Father took my absence the hardest. He worried that something ominous would happen to me apart from him.

"I know. I didn't mean anything by it, but the army read over every bit of correspondence and I couldn't say what I wished, though I needed you both desperately." I pulled back from his embrace and noticed a bit of dark oil from the ribbon machines still lingered on his cheek. He must have changed hurriedly after work. I licked my thumb, then cleared the oil from his skin. "There. Handsome as ever."

I grinned at him and then glanced at Mother, who looked the picture of glamour with her silver hair done up in a high, modern coiffure with a marcel wave. I touched a hand to my hair reflexively, recalling the way Lenor had balked at it upon her visit. I'd done my best to pin my thick waves in a becoming manner, but I knew Lenor had been right—it looked nothing close to the way Mother arranged it.

"You learned marcelling," I commented to Mother, disentangling myself from Father. "It's absolutely striking."

She reached to hold my hand and smiled.

"I did. What else was I supposed to do with you gone?" she asked. When I'd been away in London, she'd taken up crochet and had become such a marvel at it that the young wives in our building had asked her if they could order placemats.

She squeezed my hand. "I don't want to press you, dear, and I know you've got to work on this show, but, Calla, why don't you come home? There's a lovely view here, but the other furnishings hardly declare a New York welcome," Mother said.

"I would love nothing more, but as I said in the telegram, I can't. I've got to open this show in two weeks' time and my key musicians have just arrived on the rail this afternoon."

Mother nodded and sat back down on the couch. Father followed and I sat on the edge of the bed across from them.

"But just as soon as we wrap the show, I'll be back in the cheery old Bronx," I said, though the moment it crossed my lips, I realized that as wonderful as it would be to reimmerse myself in my old life, I still hoped I'd be called to the front. I supposed I'd always hope for that.

Mother's gaze leveled on mine, but then she looked away and busied herself by plucking her cross-stitch from its discarded place beside her.

"Mother, what is it?" She was biting back words. I knew it. "You're nearly as obvious as a full moon. Spit it out."

"Don't feel that you must tell us, but what happened in Carolina, darling? As your father said, we barely heard from you—and I suppose now we understand why—but we hoped your infrequent writing only meant you were happy, that you'd found true love again after the tragedy that befell poor Caspar."

I swallowed hard and looked out the window at the Winter Garden sign just illuminated for evening. I watched it blink on and off, on and off, on and off before I met her eyes once again. I didn't quite know what to say. We hadn't fallen out of love. We hadn't decided to go our separate ways. I thought of the last time I saw him, the way he'd looked at me. He'd been so angry, so sure I'd betrayed him, that I'd been the one to tell the men of the mission.

"We had a misunderstanding," I said. It was the truest thing I could say. I blinked to dispel the emotion burning behind my eyes. "And then the opportunity came to help the war effort by putting on the show here and I decided I would take it, that it was time for me to go." These half-truths were painful to articulate. Even now, sitting in front of my parents, I couldn't be entirely honest with them as I'd always been.

"Better now than later I suppose," Father said, his kind eyes softening. "Life is long and it shouldn't be spent with someone who doesn't understand you to the soul."

I sniffed and rubbed my eyes to keep from crying. If I disagreed and said that he did understand me, that he knew me better than anyone I'd ever met and that I loved him desperately, they'd ask why we didn't reconcile. That was one of the questions I wasn't permitted to answer.

Father continued. "We're glad you're back regardless. We assumed that if something fractured with the love you'd found, you'd go back on your tour and then push toward the front. You seemed so set on that course when you departed. We were certain we'd be without our dear girl for years."

"I'm sure she simply decided that she doesn't want to go to the front anymore, Paul," Mother said softly to Father as though I wasn't there. "I see it as a sign that she's healing from her loss. People change, you know, and she's been offered quite an opportunity here. The Shubert theatres are the most successful in all New York, and our girl is being given the chance to highlight the myriad of her talents here, endorsed by the army no less."

"I do want to go to the front," I said, finding my voice. "More than anything. Nothing at all has changed in that regard. I took this opportunity on Broadway because it was a good one and because I met some extraordinary musicians at Camp Greene who I wanted to make much of here. As you both know, General Pershing permitted me to tour the American camps and promised that he'd consider my request to go to France, but he never said it was a guarantee." I paused to find the right words, honest words that wouldn't reveal what I wasn't allowed to say. "I've asked for clearance several times along my tour and particularly when I demonstrated my loyalty and appreciation to Camp Greene for saving my life, but have so far been denied." I paused and picked at my nails. "I can hardly think of the men over there going into battle so horribly forlorn. I received a note from Caspar's friend, Basil, when I was in Charlotte and he begged me to come. I promised I'd continue to try, to honor Caspar's memory as he would have wanted, but I also have to make peace with the realization that I may never be allowed over there and that what I've contributed in cheering the men stateside is a testament to his memory too." Thinking of Basil reminded me that although my photograph wasn't circulating in the papers yet, it still could.

I hoped Jesse had sent the telegram and that Basil had just been speaking from a place of fear and would not truly expose something that could do so much damage.

"You're absolutely right," Mother said. She reached out and patted my knee. "I know without a doubt he would be so proud of you and honored that you'd lent your talents to the men on his behalf, even if it doesn't take you to the front."

My eyes welled and a tear fell from my lids. I swept it away and nodded, wondering why I'd imagined Caspar's anger or disappointment in my efforts all this time when he'd never been that sort. Perhaps it was only the memories of our arguments at the end. Perhaps somewhere deep down I thought that if I lived his dreams for him, I could eclipse his uncertainty about marrying me, that I could prove myself worthy of being his wife.

"Thank you, Mother," I said finally.

I glanced out the window and thought of Jesse. I wouldn't let the last time I saw him overshadow our love. I knew without a doubt that we'd loved each other entirely.

"Now, Calla, I know you're exhausted," Mother said, sitting up straight, "but that droll Colonel Pitt, who said he's been charged by the army to watch over your show since it involves their men, has somehow come upon fabulous tickets for the four of us to tonight's *Monte Cristo, Jr.* We thought it rude to decline. Would you like to go?"

I was shocked. Either Colonel Pitt was more interested in Broadway than he let on or he had a more compassionate side than I assumed and knew a show would brighten my spirits.

"I'd love to," I said. "I've heard wonderful things about it. Tabitha asked me to go tomorrow night, but I'm not sure I'll have the time." There was no way Colonel Pitt would allow me to go without him.

"We'll wait outside while you change," Father said, rising from the sofa.

Mother followed him, then stared across the room into the simple armoire that the chauffeur had crudely jammed my gowns into the day before and pointed. "Wear the green Doucet, the one they sent you right before the tour. The other guests will notice you're there, and you'll want the papers to herald your wonderful return to benefit your upcoming show."

I nodded, barely aware of them leaving my room. I stared at the green silk, at the panels down the sides glittering with silver and gold beads. I'd worn the gown the night I'd performed with Lenor, the night I'd spent with Jesse. I could still feel the weight of his gaze as I pushed the costume off my body, and then the all-consuming fire of his love in my veins, the way our melancholy punctuated every touch, every promise.

I took a breath, stepped toward the armoire, and retrieved the dress from its hanger. I gathered it to my chest and then to my face, longing for the light scent of Palmolive, for evidence of the night we could have relived forever had we not fallen in love during a war. I laid the gown on the bed and started undoing the pearl buttons of my shirtwaist, my mind fixed on the memory of Jesse's face. Perhaps, in a way, wearing it would be like having him close to me again.

CHAPTER 32

The musicians were playing the overture in the pit, but you could barely hear it over the chatter of voices. Mr. Shubert had said the tickets for *They Call Me Soldier* were sold out for the shows through the week, but I couldn't quite believe it. I pinched the edge of the heavy velvet curtain and pushed it back an inch to reveal the crowd. There were the usual theatergoers in crisp tuxedos and couture gowns, but up in the mezzanine and in the balcony, I noticed spots of olive too—soldiers on twenty-four-hour leave from nearby Camp Upton. At the edge of the mezzanine, dressed in the manner of an ordinary soldier, I noticed a familiar frame and a considerable amount of fluttering around him. My stomach flipped with nerves. I'd only met Irving Berlin twice before in passing, though we'd rotated around each other for the last ten years. He was the greatest songwriter of our time, that was certain, and suddenly the songs we'd written for our show seemed silly in comparison to his "Alexander's Ragtime Band" or "Down in My Heart."

"Do you get nervous anymore?" Roland asked, startling me. He was wearing his costume, an elaborate cloak made of white fox fur, thick hiking trousers, and black boots, and holding his saxophone. Lydia had crafted each of our costumes with such care that they were truly works of art. I looked down at my blue bodice awash with stars outlined in paste diamonds and at the red-and-white-striped skirt that billowed around me. She'd fashioned my gown so that I could remove the skirt to reveal trousers of the same design at the end of the show.

"Only when the likes of Irving Berlin are in the audience," I whispered.

"Irving Berlin?" Roland murmured, and his eyes widened.

I beckoned him closer and let him peek through the curtain as I had. Beside us, the enormous depiction of Mount Everest that Tabitha had crafted of papier-mâché, oil paints, and an elaborate scaffolding system Roland would use to "climb" Everest was shadowed by the velvet drape.

"Middle of the mezzanine, right at the edge. He's a slight man with black hair wearing olive drab like the rest."

"Well, I'll be," Roland whispered, then let the curtain drop back into place. He chuckled. "Now I understand how Miss Felicity felt each time she played here. She told me that the Casino stage was the most exposed, that the seats were arranged so that everyone watching could see the entirety of the show no matter the vantage point. I hope I'll make you proud, Calla."

"You will. Of course you will," I said, but my mind was stuck on what he'd said about Lenor. I'd seen them go off together, but I'd assumed they'd done little talking the night of her show at the Liberty Theatre. "How much did you actually get to speak with Lenor? I assumed the two of you were only—"

"Oh, quite a bit, actually. I don't mind the kissing, Calla, but I find anything beyond that in poor taste outside of a commitment," he said. "She lured me into my tent saying that she wanted to hear me play just for her, that I was an incredible talent. I played for her, sang a little too, but I quickly realized that's not what she really wanted. The longer I played, the more clothing she removed. When she was down to her corset and I wouldn't touch her, she figured out she couldn't seduce me into laying aside my better senses. She started crying at that point, saying she wasn't beautiful or desirable anymore. I told her that wasn't the case, but she kept asking me to prove it."

I gasped. "I'm sorry, Roland."

He shrugged. "It turned out all right. We went back and forth for a while, though. She started begging me to . . . to . . . lie down with her. She said she was going to help me, after all. I told her I didn't know how she figured she would help me—you had been the one to do that, Calla—but she told me she'd tell me for a kiss, that it might be the last one I ever had. That scared me something awful, so I kissed her. She told me she'd been with a man the night before, a general at Camp Wadsworth, who'd ruined their fun by crying all night over the news of Camp Greene's Third Infantry Division being shipped out and the 543rd assigned to a perilous operation."

"What?" I asked, barely able to breathe.

"The general's son was stationed with us at Camp Greene, I suppose. Miss Felicity wouldn't tell me his name and said he didn't have any idea that he was going to be among those involved in such a mission, but she said she'd taken a liking to me and wanted to make sure I wasn't in harm's way. After I heard that news, I couldn't keep it to myself and let my friends die. I . . . I'm the one who told Guy and the others. I'm the reason they fled. When they were caught and asked why they'd deserted, Crowley told the company police that Miss Felicity had told a few soldiers that the 543rd was going to be involved in a dangerous mission. Please don't tell anyone I was the one who told. Miss Felicity never said to keep the news quiet and I trusted her word. I didn't know it was false information I was spreading, honest."

Everything seemed to still. I could barely hear the orchestra. "I won't, but you've done nothing wrong in any case. The blame lies with Lenor and the army knows it. Perhaps that's why Lenor was removed from her touring duties," I said.

Beyond the curtain, the electric lights dimmed and brightened, urging the guests to make their way to their seats.

"The Third has been in France three days now according to the ship schedules," Roland whispered. "No matter what action they see, they're risking their lives. I can hardly think of it without the possibilities consuming me. I suppose that's why I'm not suited to join them. But here I stand, doing nothing."

I grasped his arm. "You did something remarkable. Perhaps you don't realize it, and I can't tell you exactly what you did or how I know, but you are a hero," I said.

If the rumor hadn't emerged, I wouldn't have been confined, Lenor would have continued her tour, and there would have been no need for a new Broadway show—the show that saved Guy and Crowley and William for now, and likely Roland and Sidney too.

Still, there were so many others I couldn't spare with the show, and the 543rd's solitary stand was likely still the plan if the Germans pressed on toward the Allied rail lines and Paris. I closed my eyes and prayed for God to protect the other men of the Third and Jesse, wherever he was.

"When we get on the stage, we must think of those brave souls we call friends who are marching through France," I said to Roland, who was studying his saxophone as though he'd never seen it before. "When you play tonight, when you say your lines, pretend you're performing for those about to meet the Huns, the boys at the very front who need cheer."

The overture grew louder as the crowd silenced. The other leading men and chorus girls came to stand at their places on either side of the curtain. I smiled at Guy across the stage, who appeared much like he always did when we performed, though Lydia had designed a black-and-white floral vest to wear beneath his black tuxedo jacket. I'd forgotten that the Philharmonic men were permitted a piece of celebratory clothing once in a while— for various holidays or for special performances.

The last notes of "Found Myself" were playing, signaling that the overture was nearly through.

I walked onstage from behind the curtain to riotous applause and Guy met me in the middle. The spotlight was glorious and bright, and I couldn't see a single face in front of me, but I waved as though I could and encouraged Guy to do the same.

"Welcome, ladies and gents—and the finest of the gents, the doughboys!" I said.

Whoops sounded from the balconies, and I smiled in their

direction and blew them a kiss, forgetting on purpose about Irving Berlin being among them.

"Before we begin, how about a round of applause for the inimitable Calla Connolly? She's written quite a show!" Guy shouted. "Break a leg," he whispered. Then he winked at me and exited the stage the way he came.

"As many of you know," I said, pacing down the left side of the stage, "I had the absolute pleasure of spending a little over a month in one of our army camps in North Carolina, Camp Greene, after the brave men and women saved me from the Spanish flu. While residing there, I found some of the most talented musicians and actors I've ever encountered, and it's quite an honor to be sharing the stage with them tonight. It certainly won't be the last you'll see of these magnificent boys from Camp Greene. Without further ado, let's get this show started. Thank you for coming to see *They Call Me Soldier*."

Marshall signaled the prelude to the first song, a song Guy and I wrote the second day of rehearsals. We called it "My Soldier," and it had a fun tune that made you want to skip around when you sang it, so I did—as best I could in a gown. The crowd clapped along without prompting, the sign of a successful show already.

The chorus girls strode out from stages right and left and met in the middle. Half wore army fatigues while the others wore gowns. The girls in gowns acted like they were just meeting the soldiers on a rail platform as I sang the song. Genevieve Franklin, a choreographer friend of Marshall's, had been kind enough to write up a few steps for each number.

"*I met him on the train, that soldier of mine, though when I met him the world was fine. I was on my way to work at the textile mill. He was on his way to work on Murray Hill. He had pretty blue eyes and a smart black suit. He made me laugh and said I was cute. He said he'd soon be off to sail the seas—the Arctic, the Atlantic, the Caribbean too, and would that be attractive to someone like you?*"

The chorus girls coupled up, then joined me on the chorus.

"We were meant to roam, together at last, but now my man is in a soldier's cast. He crossed the sea, though not with me, and his boat's still docked onshore. But Soldier's not the name of a man, it's only what he does. So when he returns with the Huns at bay, he'll go back to what he loves."

Then the curtain opened and Roland stood atop Mount Everest with his saxophone. He spoke his lines as though they came from the heart, as though he'd always wished to explore, but perhaps that was because he did. The crowd silenced at the melancholy tune he played as he made his way down the mountain. When he reached the bottom, he set his saxophone down on the last step and removed his costume to display his army uniform beneath.

Guy's character was next. I couldn't help but laugh from the side of the stage as he pretended to learn the piano. It clearly took considerable effort to intentionally muddle the tunes he was trying to play, but he did a fine job, and when Goldie emerged as a male conductor to assess his tryout, the guests chuckled heartily. He finished his part with a song he'd written five years ago, "Music Is the Beat of My Heart," and the crowd stomped their feet and clapped as he lifted one hand at a time from the keyboard and encouraged them to sing along.

I pushed the painted image of the inside of Carnegie Hall to the other side of the stage with the stagehands and sat down in a desk deposited in front of a tableau of a classroom. Sidney emerged from stage right carrying a stack of books, a notebook, and his fiddle tucked under his arm. He said his lines—that he'd had no teacher starting at ten, that he'd found early on that the answers to life's questions could be found in a book, that he'd never wanted others to feel as starved for knowledge as he had. Then he pretended to teach me, and I pretended to ask questions. At the final question he lifted his fiddle to his chin and began to play his lively tune, this time one I'd written called "Two Plus Two." I sang, pretending to think and write at my desk as I did.

"Two plus two is four, and four plus four is eight, but the most important lesson is to lean into your fate."

The chorus girls appeared in feathers and did a number in which they tossed and tapped books to the music.

At the end of the song, the girls twirled off the stage and I stood, plucked the desk from its place, and left the spotlight just as one of the stagehands wheeled a giant plate of spaghetti to the middle of the set. The schoolroom backdrop was replaced with a scene of white linen–dressed tables and fine chandeliers. Crowley emerged in a chef's apron, bellowing on his trumpet and calling out suppertime. The chorus girls came back out with empty plates, and I emerged with the largest ladle I'd ever seen that we'd borrowed from Mr. Shubert's friend, Daniel, who owned Barbetta down the street. I spooned the noodles onto the girls' plates as Crowley played. At one point, I looked out at the crowd, and as the spotlight was squarely on Crowley and not on me, I was able to see the faces of the guests in the first row. Wendy and Betty and Juliet were among them, their smiles bright with joy.

I disappeared behind the curtain once more as the set was transformed yet again, this time to a child's bedroom. William sat on the floor in children's pajamas—which elicited much glee from the audience—playing with a set of wooden toy soldiers. It occurred to me, standing there, that I'd written Jesse into the script without knowing it. After a bit of time setting up the soldiers and giving them marching orders, William rose from the ground, discarded his pajamas to reveal his army uniform, and extracted his cello from the floor. Tabitha had wrapped the instrument expertly to make it appear like one of the toy soldiers. As William played, Roland marched out in his uniform. Then William paused playing and shouted, "Attention!" When he took up his cello once again, Roland began to sing the final song before our patriotic segment, "What I Gave."

"I gave my wonder to the army's cause as we sailed across the sea."
Guy marched out next, standing behind him.
"I gave my tune to the bugler, hummed a song 'neath the reveille."
William stopped playing and directed Sidney with his bow, encouraging him to march out with a series of turns and taps as he sang.

"I gave my lessons to the one at the helm—it wasn't me."

Crowley emerged in uniform, but with his chef's hat still on. He pretended to startle when he realized he had it on and William made a point to reprimand him like an officer would.

"I gave dreams of meals back home while in the trenches we lay."

William lifted his cello from the floor, held it against his chest, and kept playing as he walked to the front of the line of soldiers. He turned his back to the audience, pretended to inspect the men, then set his cello down, faced the crowd, and sang a cappella.

"All my life I've planned for this. All my life I've known it—that someday I'd lead a troop of men toward justice. I'm afraid—who wouldn't be—and yet my veins are quaking. If I was meant to give my life, it'll be in the peacemaking."

They joined together then, their five-part harmony near heavenly.

"We are soldiers, yes, we are. I am and you are too. United we stand for harmony, and yet, when all is through, these jackets withdrawn to a box, I pray I'll return to the man I am, the man war couldn't take from me."

The audience erupted with cheers when the men flung their arms around each other and took their bows.

After the merriment died down just a bit, I stepped out onto the stage and the men gathered up their instruments as the backdrop transformed to the city. Guy, who had dipped behind the stage to change back into his tuxedo, found his place beside me.

"Aren't these Camp Greene men spectacular?" I called out. The audience shouted affirmations. "Mr. Murphy." I signaled to the light man at the back of the theatre. He was going to loathe what I was about to do, and yet I realized it was essential. There were soldiers present, and being a part of Camp Greene had taught me a lot about what a doughboy needed from a show. "If you can hear me, please turn on the houselights. This next bit is a celebration of our country, and we'd like it if the whole place could join us in singing these songs in tribute to our men at the front and our men who will be sent to the front."

The lights came up and I unhooked my outer skirt as they did, flinging the fabric to one of the stagehands to reveal my matching trousers.

"Miss Calla Connolly, the darling of the American Expeditionary Forces!" Guy shouted, gesturing toward me. The crowd yelled and clapped and chanted my name. I laughed and bowed, thinking that just weeks ago, Lenor was reveling in the country calling her the same thing.

"If you'll humor us for a moment," I called out. "Before we get on to your favorites, my friend Guy Werths here and I are going to introduce you to a song that means a great deal to us, a song about our dear Camp Greene. It's called 'Found Myself.'"

Marshall's orchestra began to play, and I watched as Sidney, Crowley, William, and Roland bowed their heads to their instruments as well.

Guy began to sing, and as his gaze met mine, I found my eyes tearing. I recalled that fateful night onstage at Camp Greene's Liberty Theatre, the way I'd mistaken Guy for Caspar. I could still feel the hope and then the crushing heartache in my chest. I could feel the chill of the fever and the hoarse scratch in my throat. I could see Jesse's face in the back of the theatre, the way he'd delivered the horrible news of soldiers lost. That night had changed my life.

I looked over the audience. Goose bumps prickled my skin, though this time from gratitude and not illness. It was a magical scene. Perhaps, on a night like this, a miracle could happen. My eyes drifted over the men in uniform. There were at least three hundred in attendance. I searched each face, suddenly struck with the hope that perhaps he was here, perhaps he was going to surprise me. My gaze swept over every soldier, but Jesse wasn't among them.

I started singing with Guy and a stillness settled on my soul, an otherworldly knowing that made tears fall from my eyes. I hadn't let myself consider it before, but now it was clear—I'd lost them both. I could feel it. And yet not truly, not ever.

Sidney played an interlude, and I found my parents in the audience. They were sitting next to Colonel Pitt, who was moved to tears, dabbing at his eyes with his handkerchief. Others were smiling, the words and music warming their hearts. It had never been clearer to me than in that moment that I'd been destined to stay here, stateside, all along, to sing light into the souls of our men as they began their march toward war. Perhaps my boots would never settle on French soil, but my music, my love, would find its way there anyway. It had found a home in the hearts of the men at Camp Greene and these men before me, and they would carry it with them into battle. It would never leave them. I knew it was so because the memory of their faces would never leave me. And perhaps that would have to be enough.

EPILOGUE

M a'am, Miss Connolly, ma'am." Our poor chauffeur, Mr. Kerwin, an older Yank who'd been assigned to us by the YMCA, nearly screamed the last word as two German planes roared over our heads. "For the last time, won't you consider going back?"

The bright sun struck the silver metal and I waited for the planes to descend, to fly low enough to set a bomb on the tips of our noses, but they didn't this time.

I laughed and Mr. Kerwin glanced back at me as the old Cadillac bumped along the shell-shot road. Mother nudged me, a prompting to sober and respect Mr. Kerwin's terror. Guy cleared his throat and waved his hat as camion after camion rendered nearly white with dust sped past on our right side. Our soldiers were packed inside each truck, their faces shadowed by canvas roofs, singing and waving at us as they went by. I lifted my hands and smiled, and when I realized they were singing "Hail, Hail, the Gang's All Here," I joined in. And then, in a few minutes more, we were alone on the ruined road again, the pops of gunfire in the distance almost completely eclipsed by the sound of the wind.

"It's quite dangerous," our chauffeur attempted again, slowing the engine.

"Yes, I know, Mr. Kerwin. But we've been back and forth to the front these last three months and have seen more bombings and assaults than many of the soldiers. Two little planes won't cause us to shake the shimmy," I shouted.

We'd arrived in London three weeks after the Allies, including the Third Division, held the Germans off the Marne River at Château-Thierry. As planned, the 543rd had been sent to the Surmelin Valley sector before the offensive began. When the Germans attacked, our men had been situated along the front lines—at the aqueduct, at the woods, and at the Paris-Metz railroad. In the midst of the onslaught, as the regiment held the river and the rail line, several enemy battalions attacked from the east, an area exposed after France's 125th Division withdrew. At that point, the regiment was not only holding the original front sector but also holding a line five-thousand-yards long to the east. It had been as dangerous a mission as they'd always assumed, but the assumption hadn't taken into account the might of our Camp Greene men. Though we'd had casualties, it was the Huns who'd truly been vanquished, and by the end of the day, the German army's advance toward Paris was halted in great part by the valor of the 543rd Regiment of the Third Division.

Despite their victory, I'd retreated to my room at the Casino Theatre when I heard the news. I'd read the names of the 437 men of the 543rd who'd lived beside me for over a month and had given their lives for our country and cried for them. Jesse was not among the names. In fact, ever since our parting, I'd poured over the papers, but news of his whereabouts or his demise were never published. I'd settled on the idea that I'd simply missed the announcement of his death. Emma hadn't received word of him or from him at all—I'd written her once inquiring—so his loss was hardly a fact, and yet, when I thought of him, the same weighty, hollow feeling struck my spirit that did when I thought of Caspar. My heart knew.

I'd received word that I'd been cleared to go to the front the week after the Allies' victory on the Marne, after I no longer knew of any forthcoming army operations. The next day Mr. Shubert promised my cast roles in any show they chose at the war's conclusion, and then Guy, Sidney, Crowley, Roland, and William were ordered back to Camp Greene for the duration of the conflict, assigned to a labor battalion that would remain at camp and wouldn't see combat. Colonel Tucker, who'd assumed command of Camp Greene after Jesse, didn't offer an explanation for the assignment, but I had a feeling he found the men to be ill-suited for war after they'd abandoned.

Guy, who'd been struggling with guilt over avoiding deployment with the 543rd, asked Colonel Tucker if he could be sent over instead. Goldie and I had been stunned by his request, and Goldie had begged him to change his mind. Goldie and Guy had just been married the day after they arrived in New York, but Guy wouldn't be moved. His request was granted, and he was sent over with a regiment from Camp Upton. Goldie promised she'd follow him as soon as she was assigned a hospital post. But when he broke his leg so severely it wouldn't heal correctly, they discharged him before he saw the front, before Goldie's paperwork had gone through. Rather than returning home right away, he asked if he could accompany me. He said he could play when a piano was available and that cheering the troops at the front was the least he could do. I'd wired Goldie to ask if I should send him home, but she said no, that he'd never get over leaving the other men of the 543rd otherwise, so I agreed to take him with me.

Mother was along because prior to my stint in London, she'd always accompanied me, and this time, despite my insistence otherwise, she was worried about my spirits. I would go to the front. I would see mutilation and death of both body and mind. Mother, though a small child at the time, had seen some horrors of the War Between the States. She'd grown up on her grandmother's farm near Buffington Island on the Ohio River and had witnessed her grandmother and parents rushing out to the fields where many enemy soldiers lay dying and wounded. Some of the men had been brought into the house, their limbs torn off, and she'd never forgotten it. She knew I'd never forget what I'd see on the front and was keen to be alongside me.

"What of the rumors of peace?" Mr. Kerwin screeched as the wind shifted and the shattering boom of shells rang in our ears. He turned down a makeshift road around a bridge that had been blasted.

"It could be propaganda," Guy shouted. "Our men have cleared the Argonne Forest of Huns and have taken Sedan's rail station and are now poised to move onto German soil in an offensive there. If they all believe peace is imminent, wouldn't they tread more lightly?"

"It's not in our blood to tread lightly," I said, feeling pride burble up in my chest. Every single Allied soldier I'd encountered on this tour had been the finest, strongest sort of stock, willing to fight until the strike of the pen on the armistice papers.

Mr. Kerwin's Cadillac jerked as it struck a shell hole and kept on toward the edge of the Argonne Forest in the distance. I could see a large group of soldiers, at least four hundred in number, gathered in the center of a field and directed Mr. Kerwin to drive off the road and toward them as the road proper had ended.

"Calla, this is a battlefield," Guy said, turning around from the passenger seat. His eyes widened. We'd performed on the periphery of many battlefields in the months we'd been here, but never in the center of one. The ground we were driving across was strewn with spent rifles, helmets, detonated grenades, and aerial torpedoes.

"Stop here," I told Mr. Kerwin. "Suppose you run over a grenade? I don't think that would be the sort of show the men were expecting. If you'd like to wait in the auto with Mother, Guy and I will find our way."

Already the soldiers spied us and some walked toward our auto, their dust-covered bodies and soiled uniforms a different picture entirely than their faces, which appeared like vibrant rays of sunshine. A mangled German lorry, its cab dented and smashed, its bed still solid, seemed to be at the epicenter of the soldiers. I supposed that was to be my stage. I'd performed on about every sort of surface, from dressing tables to scaffolding to atop a horse. I'd laughed my way through that show, knowing that Jesse would find my circus-like performance hilarious.

Guy got out of the Cadillac and stepped gingerly toward my door and opened it. I smiled. To every other soldier, Guy would look like he'd spent the last months in a trench, same as them. He was still a part of it after all, just in a different capacity, like a bugler or a trumpeter, and wore his uniform every day. But the way he walked, limping a bit around the spent grenades, gave him away.

"They've already canvased the field for live bombs and hauled most of them off when they took away the fallen," I said. I shivered in the near-winter chill and smoothed my dress, made of the same olive drab the men wore. General Pershing had seen to it that I looked the part, a veritable member of the AEF.

"Then why did you stop Mr. Kerwin from driving across the field?" Guy asked. He grinned and offered his arm. We started toward the few men advancing our direction and the crush of them beyond who had started cheering and shouting my name.

"I said they took away *most* of them. I have no doubt they'll be finding live grenades and bombs for years to come. It's much easier to spy a whole bomb right in front of your feet than it is to see it from the seat of an auto."

The moment we reached the soldiers, they swallowed us up. I grasped their bloodstained hands and kissed their dusty cheeks as they reached for me, and then a group of them hoisted me onto the old dented lorry while Guy was left to scramble up the wreckage. Standing on the platform, I realized my previous judgment of the auto's stability was off. Every time we moved at all, the wooden bed moaned and squeaked. The last time I'd performed on something so unstable, I'd been standing on a half-rotten door stacked on top of produce crates with Basil. When he'd found out from the papers that I was in France, he'd written to me and apologized for the awful way he'd treated me, and assured me the photograph remained in his possession. I accepted his apology, knowing the toll fear and grief could take on a person's sensibilities. When I'd reached the front at Amiens, I was able to find out where he was stationed and asked him to come and perform with me. I did it to honor Caspar. After giving me back my photograph and Caspar's tags, he'd performed a few numbers with me on that rickety door. It only took a few notes to realize Caspar had been right—the man couldn't carry a tune. Regardless, he hopped down from our makeshift stage, smiling after the finale, sure that he'd eventually find himself on the stage. I didn't correct him. It didn't matter. What mattered was that he was going back to fighting with hope in his heart.

"Good morning, gents!" I shouted when Guy made it onto the lorry and the cheering died down a bit. In the distance, a symphony of rifle fire popped, and I waited for the wind to shift and clear it before I went on. "You've stolen the Huns morale to such a degree that even this lorry is shuddering in fear."

The men laughed.

"This here is my dear friend and your comrade in arms, Guy Werths. He's going to make sure I don't tumble off this platform and he'll sing with me too, as I hope you will," I said. "But before we officially start the show, I heard a story I thought you all might enjoy."

I looked out at the crowd in front of me. Most of the men, like the soldiers at Camp Greene, were in their early twenties, but here, at the precipice of the front, mere days aged men. Despite the light in their eyes at seeing me, the evidence of the trauma they carried was marked in the gray of their skin. In a matter of hours, these men would march five miles south, toward the enemies' rifles once again, in an effort to defend the newly captured rail stronghold at Sedan, a mission the Allies had been pressing toward since July.

When I'd first reached the front, I'd sobbed for hours after each show, knowing that many of the men I'd just performed for would be gone the next day. Even now, the knowledge of death awaiting some of these brave men made my heart ache, but when melancholy threatened, I thought of Caspar and remembered that I wasn't here to save the men from death. I couldn't. I was here to save them from despair.

"I had occasion to speak with a lovely sergeant when I first arrived who had served early in the Battle of the Somme," I started. I paced when I spoke and turned this way and that to ensure I was interacting with as many soldiers as I could. "He told me a story about how he was on his way to the front when he and his troop came to a very deep shell hole. He said he waded in first and that the water was up to his armpits. As he was getting out the other side, he heard laughter and a lot of splashing behind him. He looked back and saw a tin hat floating along the surface of the water. One of the other soldiers proclaimed that this was their first casualty—not shot but drowned. To their surprise, however, a head and then a muddy body emerged from the water, and he realized it was a private in their troop, Joe Smith. Joe was only five feet, one inch and he had sunk into the deepest part of the hole."

The soldiers laughed and I did too.

"What sort of tune shall we start with, Guy? A sad song?" I asked.

"No!" Guy shouted, encouraging the soldiers to do the same.

"A song about sweethearts?"

"No!" they shouted again.

I laughed.

"Well, Guy and I have just come from Broadway about three months ago and this one is dear to our hearts—and I know yours too."

I looked at Guy and we began "Goodbye Broadway, Hello France!" together. The men joined in quickly, in a deep swell that always made my eyes fill. To keep the spirits light, I danced and attempted a cartwheel, though I nearly fell into Guy when I landed as a result of the bed's tilt. He caught me and righted my balance and we laughed. When the song was over, we launched into "Over There," followed by "I Have It All."

At the final line, when Guy and I typically went into harmony and concluded the song, a crash of cannon fire so loud it popped my ears, stopped us. And then there was a symphony of buglers playing reveille.

I glanced at the soldiers and then back at Guy, not sure what this meant or what to do, but then a colonel on a white horse came bursting through the line of trees from the forest.

"It's over!" he shouted.

The men stared at him, at each other, at us, unable to figure out what was happening, if he was speaking the truth or mistaken. It seemed terribly unlikely that after all these years, the fighting, the dying, was over just like that.

"Did you hear me?" the colonel said, riding closer. "The Huns have surrendered! It's over!"

At once the men cheered, but it was a sound I'd never heard— equal parts wailing and joyful, guttural and elated. It was the sort of sound you felt, the sort of noise that came from the very marrow of your being. I fell to my knees on the bed of the truck and wept. Guy stood, his expression one of shock, and then, when a soldier reached up to shake his hand, he began to cheer along with them. I stood and the words of "The Star-Spangled Banner" came quickly to my lips.

The soldiers' voices joined mine, this time the quivering lips and hopeful eyes replaced by the elated realization of their futures— they would live past this war; they would go home to their families.

We stood there singing "The Stars and Stripes Forever," "Yankee Doodle," "Battle Hymn of the Republic," "America the Beautiful." Some men had tears in their eyes while others could hardly contain their relief and bounced on the balls of their feet as we celebrated.

I paused for a moment to take in the scene, and a hush fell over the abandoned battlefield. I turned in time to see soldiers emerging from the forest, from the front. They were bloody, covered in mud, and wore a deep sadness on their faces despite the joy of the moment. Some carried men draped in sheets on stretchers, men who'd fallen in the very last moments of the war. My body had warmed throughout the show, but now goose bumps prickled my skin as scores of soldiers poured from the woods, carrying the many lost men with them.

Guy began to sing "Found Myself (The Song of Camp Greene)," but I barely heard him at first. It had been a favorite on our tour, but I hadn't realized until this moment how beloved it was. The soldiers sang along to it as though it were in the American canon. My voice melded with the rest as the surviving men carried the lost along the edge of the crowd.

"Found the news alarming, the trouble everywhere. Found myself out marching, wondering if the world would care. Found my answer in a letter, found that I was, in fact, held dear. Found myself a world away, but my heart still living here."

A deep, tone-deaf voice pushed away from the beautiful chorus of the other men and I glanced toward its source walking behind a line of stretchers. At first I was sure I was mistaken. His whole body was covered in dust and a great gash bloodied his leg, but he glanced up at me and I froze. A cry lodged in my throat, and I leapt from the lorry without thinking. I stumbled over my skirt and pushed past a few soldiers, and his hands captured my forearms and pulled me to him. His lips met mine with a fervor that matched my own, and I threaded my arms against his back, holding him close, as though if I lost my grip, I'd lose him again.

"I thought you were gone," I said when we finally parted. "I was certain you'd left me forever."

My heart was beating fast, skipping against his chest, and tears blurred my eyes. I could feel his heart, too, proof he was alive and whole, that I'd been wrong, and I placed my palm atop it. He ran his thumb across my cheek, drying the tears, and then he leaned down and kissed me again.

"I'm sorry I didn't believe you. Our last moments have haunted me. I was desperate to write you, but I wasn't allowed to. They sent me over ahead of the 543rd and I led them into battle as planned. I haven't been back to a base since," he said. "But whether I lived or died, I would have been with you always. I told you before."

Guy was still singing, a smile in his voice, and all around us were shouts of "Peace at last!"

"Found myself wondering, would I make it back alive? Found myself considering that my mind was full of lies. Found myself remembering Camp Greene, the others too. Found myself in knowing that my truest self was found in you."

I let my cheek drop to his chest and closed my eyes as his arms, his warmth enveloped me.

"Pershing had your show playing on the radio in the camp when the rest of the men from Greene arrived. I've had this song in my mind ever since and the memory of your face always with me, yet I've wondered what you meant by that last line, or rather who you were speaking of. Did you find what you were looking for over here?" he asked, his fingers threading the hair at my nape.

I lifted my head and met his gaze. The deep ache, the inexplicable yearning I'd felt, was replaced by a joy so full I could hardly contain it.

"I have now," I said. "I found peace with Caspar's memory the moment my feet touched French soil, but from the moment we parted, I've only been looking for you."

He smiled. "Now here we are, together. Our life is just beginning. That is, if you'll still be my wife."

I nodded and he took my head in his hands and kissed me again. I realized then, as shouts of elation continued around us and as my heart echoed their refrain, that I'd been mistaken. The men hadn't needed me nearly as much as I'd needed them. I was the one who'd needed cheering. I was the one who'd needed to be made whole again.

THE END

AUTHOR'S NOTE

Hi, dear readers! First of all, thank you so much for spending time in Calla's world and for reading my work. It means the world to me that you picked up *The Star of Camp Greene*. Second, if you flipped here before you've finished the story, you might want to wait and come back when you've finished reading. This note has a lot of spoilers, and I'd hate for it to ruin the fun!

As is the process with all of my novels, I've been mulling over and researching this story for years. Although I've lived in Charlotte most of my life and I'm sure I had heard about Camp Greene somewhere along the way at Myers Park Traditional Elementary or Sedgefield Middle or South Meck High, I didn't remember it. Back in 2017, I did a panel discussion with fellow Charlotte authors Tommy Tomlinson and Sarah Crosland—who had just released a book called *Secret Charlotte*—and was drawn to the idea that there were many things about the city even us native Charlotteans didn't know. I went home and immediately started reading. The book covered tons of interesting landmarks—Lakewood Park was one!—but when I came across Camp Greene, the World War I army training camp that gave the neighborhood its name, doubled the size of Charlotte back in 1917, and encompassed over six thousand acres, stretching from near downtown Charlotte into Gaston County, I knew I'd write a book about it someday. I was hooked.

When the United States entered the war in April 1917, the army was not what it is today. It was a small organization made up of only 133,000 soldiers, and the army's operations were mainly focused on keeping peace in the Philippines. At the declaration of war, the army was suddenly tasked with drafting, training, and organizing three million new soldiers. To teach the men the skills needed to join the Allied troops in Europe, the War Department decided to build thirty-two training facilities across the country. When Charlotte's chamber of commerce heard about these camps, their ears perked up. They'd been eager to find a way to grow the town since the early 1900s, and leaders knew that securing an army training camp could be just the boost the economy needed. Charlotte threw its name in the ring and was ultimately competing with Athens, Georgia; Wilmington, North Carolina; and Fayetteville, North Carolina, for the camp. Though the fight for the camp was hotly contended, the Charlotte location between Sloan's Ferry Road and Tuckaseegee Road was ultimately selected because of good soil conditions, two rail lines parallelling the border roads, two highly elevated farmhouses—the Sid Alexander house and the James Dowd house—that could be used as possible headquarters, along with plentiful timber, streams, and large fields.

From July to September 1917, a workforce of 7,856 employees built an entire city. The swiftness with which it was put together was miraculous. Camp Greene consisted of a sizable hospital, brigade and division headquarters, a YWCA Hostess House for women relatives of the soldiers, a post office, a library, a YMCA, a bakery, rifle and artillery ranges, 190 regimental areas each requiring sleeping tents, mess halls, shower and bath buildings, and roads to connect everything.

Troops arrived at Camp Greene beginning in September 1917, mainly hailing from New England. At the beginning of the war, the army thought it best to distance troops a bit from home. The second group of soldiers to arrive were from the West—and two brought their mascots—bears—with them to camp.

By 1918 Camp Greene was housing and training sixty thousand men and served as the headquarters for both the Third and Fourth Divisions. In the two years of Camp Greene's existence, seventeen different men served as commander of camp alongside their other duties. The role was nearly like that of a town mayor. General Joseph Dickman, commander of the Third Division, and General George Cameron, commander of the Fourth Division, served in the capacity the longest, though many commanders served in between. Jesse's duties are inspired by the fifteen other camp commanders who either served in an ad interim basis or for a short time.

As I mentioned, the Third and Fourth Divisions' headquarters were stationed at Camp Greene as well as the Third Division's Fifth and Sixth Infantry Brigades. When I began to read newspaper archives, diary entries, and historical accounts detailing the impact these men had on the war, many of whose training had originated at Camp Greene, I was blown away. I found myself particularly struck by the diary of a soldier who served with the Thirty-Eighth Regiment of the Sixth Brigade in the Third Division during the Second Battle of the Marne. The soldier described in detail the harrowing and heroic stand his regiment took against the Germans in the Surmelin Valley—the complete and sudden abandonment of the French troops on one entire side, the vicious hand-to-hand combat, the orders to remain and fight no matter the cost. The Thirty-Eighth Regiment's resilience that day helped turn the tide of the war toward the Allies, and it earned the Third Division the nickname "the Rock of the Marne."

I couldn't stop thinking about the account of that battle and knew I wanted to incorporate it into my story. You might find the details of the battle familiar, as they match the storyline of the 543rd regiment in the novel. In early drafts, the 543rd was the 38th, but as I pondered the alterations I made to history to strengthen the plot of my story, I decided to change it to a nonexistent regimental number. In real life, the commanders didn't know—at least not according to public knowledge—that the 38th would be assigned to such a perilous mission. The soldiers who made up the regiment also weren't chosen because of various attributes that would make them better suited to such a fight.

However, it *is* true that army policy dictated that every enlisted soldier and officer below major take eight aptitude tests upon arrival at camp. These tested concentration, judgment, intelligence, and morality. The results were intended to help assign each soldier to the role best suited to him in order to achieve the safest possible outcome for the army as a whole. Regardless, the assessments could be harsh. Some soldiers were flagged for hysteria and the fact that they wet the bed. Some were blatantly written up as dumb, moronic, "a boob."

I thought about these judgments as I read over diary entries and letters from all sorts of men who fought in the Great War. Some were clearly glad to serve, prepared in both mind and skill. I read about men, primarily dual citizens, who had even fought in Europe before America entered the war and whose experience followed them into battle alongside their countrymen like a ghost. Those accounts also added to Jesse's character.

Some soldiers, however, were not as eager to fight. Some were terrified, and rightfully so. One of the most impactful series of letters I read were from a soldier who was a trumpet player. He hadn't been sent overseas yet, but his hints at fear were palpable and his words were almost lyrical. His only bit of joy seemed to be that he thought he might start playing with the army band—a part of camp life I didn't detail in my story in order to emphasize the soldiers' desperation to play with Calla. I could tell he wanted to say more than he could in his letters, that he didn't belong there, training for war, but couldn't because of the censors. His account inspired Guy, Crowley, Sidney, Roland, and William.

War wasn't the only threat to life at Camp Greene, however. Like the rest of the world, Charlotte and Camp Greene had severe Spanish flu outbreaks in 1918, and the epidemic claimed officers, soldiers, and civilians quickly and equally. The prevention methods included masking, citywide shutdowns, seven-day quarantines, and keeping a distance of six feet. Sound familiar?

As I learned more and more about Camp Greene, I knew my story would be primarily set there. Though I appreciate all history, I'm always drawn to the American experience, and I wanted to feel what it would have been like to live in an American army camp an ocean away from the front lines, as the army grew into what it is today. The problem was, I was having trouble with my main character. I couldn't seem to see her.

I'd read extensively about Elsie Janis, the Sweetheart of the American Expeditionary Forces, a vaudeville star who'd financed her own six-month tour at the front lines during the war and whose efforts greatly influenced the start of the USO in World War II. I had always found her inspiring and unbelievably strong, but as I researched another book set in New York, I happened upon a mention of her in the *New York Times*, and suddenly everything clicked into place. The article stated that prior to Elsie's tour at the front, General Pershing had asked her to visit the American army camps first. At once I could see her at Camp Greene, a Broadway darling, reeling from the death of her fiancé, Basil Hallam—a British actor and singer who was serving with the Kite Balloon Section of the Royal Flying Corps in France at the Somme when his balloon tether snapped and drifted into enemy territory, forcing him to jump out to avoid capture. The two had planned to tour the front together when his service was through.

At first I found my new research on Elsie's life so compelling that I thought maybe I'd change course to focus more on Elsie and that the novel could be biographical. But every time I started writing, the storyline had Elsie becoming suddenly ill with Spanish flu and overhearing a secret told by a desperate colonel that would lead to her being forced to stay at Camp Greene.

I've been writing and publishing novels for almost a decade now, and I've learned to follow inspiration rather than strongarm a story into what I think it should be. Something truly magical takes place when you let your characters lead. From that imagined hospital room, Calla and Jesse were born. Although Calla and Elsie share a similar backstory and goal, Elsie did not have the same experiences at Camp Greene that Calla went on to have, so I thought it best to let my character be inspired by Elsie rather than be her.

Jesse's character came to me almost fully formed. That's rare. Normally I get to know my characters as I write, but I felt that I already knew Jesse, probably because I'd read so many personal words from men like him.

Though Calla and Jesse were at odds at first, I knew from the start that they actually had so much in common—their hearts in two places, yearning to go overseas—and that when they found that out, they'd be each other's confidants and advocates.

My friend Kristy Woodson Harvey likes to ask authors what their books are *really* about. I love that question. On the surface, this book is about the bravery of women and men who served our country in a variety of ways and stood up for what was right— whether they were terrified or confident facing the war. It's also about Camp Greene, about shining a light on an important place history often forgets, a place I wish I could see, a place that shaped the city I call home.

But what's this book really about? From the beginning of time, we've needed each other more than we realize. We need encouragement, hope, a shoulder to rest our head on, and we should offer the same to our neighbors. We are our best selves when we consider the needs of others and press toward the greater good for all. We are stronger together.

RECOMMENDED FURTHER READING

Borch, Fred L III. *Judge Advocates in the Great War.* The Judge Advocates General's Corps, 2021.

Crosland, Sarah. *Secret Charlotte: A Guide to the Weird, Wonderful, and Obscure.* Reedy Press, 2017.

Graham, R. W. *The Operation of the 38th U.S. Infantry in the Champagne-Marne Defensive.* 1918.

Janis, Elsie. *The Big Show: My Six Months with the American Expeditionary Forces.* Cosmopolitan Book Corporation, 1919.

Mitchell, Miriam Grace, and Edward Spaulding Perzel. *The Echo of the Bugle Call, Charlotte's Role in World War 1.* Heritage Printers, 1979.

Wooldridge, J. W. *The Rock of the Marne, a Chronological Story of the 38th Regiment, U.S. Infantry.* The University Press, 1920.

ACKNOWLEDGMENTS

First, foremost, and always, thank you, Jesus, for the gift of stories and for imagination. When I write, I get a little tiny glimpse of how you might write each of our stories, and I'm grateful.

Writing about the army during World War I felt like putting together a million-piece puzzle. I couldn't have done it without the insights of Karey Marren, John Brunetti, and Fred L. Borch III. Thank you for answering all of my questions and follow-up questions and follow-up questions!

Thank you to Sheila Bumgarner with the Robinson-Spangler Carolina Room of the Charlotte Mecklenburg Library, who pulled countless photographs and files and maps for me.

Thank you to my fantastic agent, Kate McKean, for the encouragement, the listening, the cheering on. You're the best!

I'm the luckiest author in the world because somehow I get to work with the most amazing team at Harper Muse! Kimberly Carlton—thank you for your razor-sharp eye and your constant belief in me and my stories. Thank you to Kerri Potts, Margaret Kercher, and Taylor Ward for shouting the news of my stories from the rooftops! Thanks to Julie Breihan for shaping this novel into something I'm truly proud of. Thanks to Nekasha Pratt, Colleen Lacey, and Amanda Bostic for your excitement and support.

Forever thankful to my author buddies who understand this beautiful, weird writing life. Couldn't do it without you, Kimberly Brock, Marybeth Whalen, Kim Wright, Erika Montgomery, Cheyenne Campbell, Kristy Woodson Harvey, Jenni L. Walsh, Meagan

Church, Adele Myers, Vanessa Miller, Sarah McCoy, Leslie Hooten, Sarah Henning, Erika Robuck, Melissa Ferguson, Brooke Lea Foster, Annabel Monaghan, Michelle Gable, Rachel McMillan, Meredith Jaeger, Aimie Runyan, Wade Rouse, Yvette Corporon, Heather Webb, Eliza Knight, Lauren Edmondson, Camille Di Maio, Mary Kay Andrews, Madeline Martin, Heather Bell Adams, Amy Jo Burns, Lauren Denton, Kimmery Martin, Sarah Loudin Thomas, Kristy Cambron, and Taylor Brown.

Thanks to my best friends who don't look at me like I'm crazy when they see me at the bus stop looking like a cave dweller because I've been writing all day, are always there for me, and served as perfect inspiration for Goldie! Love you, Maggie Tardy, Mindy Ferguson, Christine Scott, Carolyn Lux, Jessica Shanks, Julie Cribb, Julie Barfield, Katie Gignac, Kristin Conway, Michelle Cowan, Arden McLaughlin, Ronni Bishop, Courtney Joyce, Jodie Bolowitz, Katie Burgess, Kasey Fisher, Krisha Chachra, Jamie Harrington, Joy Haser, Hollie Hogan, Laura McKnight, Sanghee Ku, Megan Fair, Kizzie Kincer, Gracemarie Bartle, Liz Moore Powell, Katie Pesta, Megan Maloney, Angie Quigley, Jen Price, Amelia McGirt, Amanda Shanks, Britt Stiling, Thuvan Cordero, Megan McCarthy, Elaine Ulery, Sarah Ward, Rudy Saunders, Stacy McLaughlin, Merriweather Franklin, Kitty Hurdle, Becky Chavaree, Janet Zylstra, Kay Houser, Loraine Tolliver, and Pat Brooks.

Authors and booksellers have a special bond. We wouldn't be able to exist without each other, and I'm thankful to have found bookseller friends who are like family! Thank you to Olivia Meletes-Morris and Wendy Meletes of Litchfield Books; Sally Brewster, Sherri Smith, Halli Gomez, and Jamie Brewster of Park Road Books; Alison Sheridan of Cleary's Bookstore; Kimberly Daniels Taws of the Country Bookshop; Gary Parkes and Karen Schwettman of FoxTale Book Shoppe; Sharon Davis of Book Bound; Maggie Robe of Flyleaf Books; Lisa Lee Swope of Bookmarks; Jen Sherman of Bookish Cedar Creek; Stephanie Crowe of Page & Palette; Sue Lucey of Page 158 Books; Shaye Gadomski of New Chapter Books; Ashley Warlick, Alyssa Fikse, and Beth Johnson of M. Judson Booksellers;

Tina Greene-Bevington of Bay Books; Lady Vowell Smith of The Snail on the Wall; Andrea Jasmin and Adah Fitzgerald of Main Street Books; Keebee Fitch of McIntyre's Books; Jill Hendrix of Fiction Addiction; Justin Souther of Malaprop's Boosktore; Dawn Miller of Pelican Bookstore; Dawn Nolan and Dawn Hylbert of Cicada Books; Dan Carlisle of Taylor Books; Anne-Marie Johnson of Books-A-Million Beckley; Matt Browning and Brian Mann of Plot Twist Books; Ashley Skeen and Mandee Cunningham of Booktenders; Sedley Abercrombie of Pig City Books; Leslie Logeman of Highland Books; Marlene England of WordPlay; and Stephanie VanAlmen of So Much More to the Story.

I am absolutely, positively indebted to the editors, writers, book clubs, bookstagrammers, reviewers, and book lovers who read, champion, and love my stories! Thank you, Adam Rathe, Annissa Armstrong, Bubba Wilson, Laura Beth Vietor, Linda Burrell, Dawn Fowler, Cassie Bustamante, Ashley Hasty, Ron Block, Ashley Kaufman, Martha Yesowitch, JJ Holshouser, Caroline Sanders Clements, Isabelle Eyman, Francene Katzen, Ashley Blank, Molly Neville, Lisa Harrison, Brenda Gardner, Lysette House, Cristina Reely, Krista Hall, Valerie Souders, Nicole Fincher, Reca Porter, Christine Mott, Tammi Tremblay, Andrea Lowry, Anna Kate, Melanie Highsmith, Nancy Betler, Samantha Gross, Laura Murray, Amanda Anson, Cindy Jones, Ashley Curran, Sarah Floyd, Alex Dudich, Renee Blankenship, Tamara Welch, Terilynn Knezek, Ana Raquel, Jayda Justus, Noelle Dunn, Nina Sumner, Dallas Strawn, Harris Murray, Phyllis Mahoney, Julie Chan, Besty Asplund, Mary Hudome, Debby Cooperman Stone, Barbara Luffman, Lanie Wood, Angel Cinco, Barbara Khan, Beyond the Pages Book Club, Bookbonders Book Club, Friends & Fiction Book Club, the Queens University Friends of the Library, and many, many more I'm accidentally leaving out here.

Thank you to my family, who has always encouraged me to live my dreams—Lynn and Fred Wilkerson; Jed, Hannah, Reece, and Davis Wilkerson; Gran Lee Ballard; Momma Sandra Wilkerson; Diannah, Johnny, and Jeremy Callaway; Josh, Bethany, Elise, and

Mady Callaway; Cindy Hanna; Bill Sothern; Samantha Hanna; Jamie, Jancis, Porter, and Maeve Hanna; Jim Wilkerson; John Auge; Bill Ballard; Janine Hopkins; Blair and Zach Markell; Davis Ballard; Maggie, Drew, Ava, and Claire Tardy; Sarah and Richard Gotlieb; Lori and Randy Musil; Keith, Brittany, and Rhett Musil; Jeremy Musil; Ryan Musil; Becky Callaway; and Alice Jean Gauldin.

Finally, words can't express how thankful I am for my little family, John, Alevia, and John. You are my best story come true. Thanks for always cheering me on.

DISCUSSION QUESTIONS

1. Nothing was going to stop Calla Connolly from making it to the front lines to perform for the soldiers—and then she comes down with the Spanish flu. Have you ever had your plans derailed by something out of your control? How did you navigate your frustrations and disappointments?

2. Being kept at Camp Greene after overhearing a sensitive conversation is yet another setback for Calla, and yet she finds purpose during her time there. Have you managed to make the most of a situation in the midst of disappointment? If so, what tools helped you to be resilient?

3. Still reeling from the loss of her fiancé, Calla believes that performing for the soldiers is the only thing preventing sorrow from swallowing her whole. Have you ever held on so tightly to an idea or a purpose to protect yourself from a deeper hurt? What shifts for Calla to allow her to sit with her sadness?

4. What unexpected friendships develop at Camp Greene? Which ones stood out to you most and why?

5. Describe Calla's relationship with Jesse. Which one do you identify with more and why?

6. Jesse and his sister, Emma, love each other deeply, but disagree on many things. Describe someone in your life you love but disagree with. How have you been able to maintain your relationship and navigate conflict with them?

7. What does Calla learn about herself during her time at Camp Greene? What does she learn about letting herself love again?

8. If you could tell Calla one thing about her relationship with Lenor, what would it be? Have you ever known someone like Lenor? If so, how did you react to their behavior?

9. After being wrongfully accused of treason, Calla's name is eventually cleared. Have you ever been accused of something you didn't do? How did you feel when it first happened? How did you feel when the truth finally came out?

10. Before Camp Greene, Calla's sole focus was performing for the soldiers on the front lines. As the book ends she realizes she needed Camp Greene just as much as the soldiers needed her encouragement. Describe the importance of camaraderie at Camp Greene. Have you ever been somewhere like Camp Greene?

11. If you were given the choice to support the war effort from home or go fight on the front lines, which would you choose and why?

12. Throughout the novel, Calla keeps fun center stage. How important do you think joy is in life? Do you tend to place more emphasis on having fun or being pragmatic?

ABOUT THE AUTHOR

Photo by Bethany Callaway Photography

JOY CALLAWAY is the author of *What the Mountains Remember, All the Pretty Places, The Grand Design, The Fifth Avenue Artists Society,* and *Secret Sisters.* She holds a BA in journalism and public relations from Marshall University and an MMC from the University of South Carolina. She resides in Charlotte, North Carolina, with her husband, John, and her children, Alevia and John.

✳ ✳ ✳

Connect with her online at joycallaway.com
Instagram: @joywcal
Facebook: @JoyCallawayAuthor

FOR MORE FROM JOY CALLAWAY

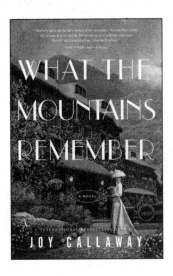

"Joy Callaway never fails to bring the past to life in brilliant color. This book has it all: the lush mystery of the mountains, the dauntless resolve of a woman at work, and the breathtaking art of building something that will last for generations. I absolutely loved it."

**—AMY JO BURNS, AUTHOR OF *MERCURY*,
FOR *WHAT THE MOUNTAINS REMEMBER***

**AVAILABLE IN PRINT, E-BOOK,
AND DOWNLOADABLE AUDIO**

LOOKING FOR MORE GREAT READS? LOOK NO FURTHER!

HARPER MUSE

*Illuminating minds
and captivating hearts
through story.*

Visit us online to learn more:
harpermuse.com

Or scan the below code and sign up to receive
email updates on new releases, giveaways,
book deals, and more:

@harpermusebooks